CHRISTMAS *with* MISS READD

* * * * * * * * * * * * *

Comprising

CHRISTMAS AT FAIRACRE

A COUNTRY CHRISTMAS

Miss Read

This omnibus first published in Great Britain in 2011 by Orion Books,
an imprint of The Orion Publishing Group Ltd,
Orion House, 5 Upper St Martin's Lane,
London WC2H 9EA

An Hachette UK Company

1 3 5 7 9 10 8 6 4 2

For further copyright details see pg 509

A CIP catalogue record for this book is
available from the British Library.

ISBN 978 1 4091 2396 5

Typeset at The Spartan Press Ltd,
Lymington, Hants

Printed in Great Britain by Clays Ltd, St Ives plc

The Orion Publishing Group's policy is to use papers that
are natural, renewable and recyclable products and made
from wood grown in sustainable forests. The logging and
manufacturing processes are expected to conform to the
environn

Contents

*

Foreword by Miss Read

I am delighted to see this winter collection from my writings about the imaginary village of Fairacre and its surroundings.

Winter may not be everyone's favourite season, but of all the year's festivals Christmas takes pride of place, and has lost none of its magic. This, no doubt, is partly because we hark back to the excitements of childhood Christmases but also because we look forward to renewing friendships and to taking part in the foremost of the church's festivals.

But the fact that Christmas Day falls in the dreariest time of the year also highlights its impact. We are usually in the grip of winter's cold, early darkness, frost and snow, and all the ills that they bring. Doubly precious, therefore, are our domestic comforts – a blazing fire, sustaining food, the comfort of friends and, at the end of the day, a warm bed.

In this collection of my writings about winter you will find many of these things. The celebrations and adventures mostly take place in the imaginary village of Fairacre, especially the school, the nearby market town of Caxley, or in that neighbourhood. Outside, the winter landscape has a beauty of its own: bare branches against a clear sky, brilliant stars on a frosty night and perhaps a swathe of untouched snow. But these beauties are best when seen from the comfort of one's home, with a good fire crackling and the smell of crumpets toasting for tea.

Although more than just the season of Christmas is covered in *The White Robin*, I am very pleased that this story has been included since it rather stood on its own.

That is the charm of the winter season, the contrast between the cold and the warmth, the light and the dark. I hope you will enjoy Christmas and the wintertime in the book before you.

Miss Read 1991

CHRISTMAS AT FAIRACRE

*

Comprising

NO HOLLY FOR MISS QUINN

CHRISTMAS AT FAIRACRE SCHOOL

THE CHRISTMAS MOUSE

*

NO HOLLY FOR MISS QUINN

Illustrated by J. S. Goodall

For Betty and Alan with love

CHAPTER ONE

If you take the road from the downland village of Fairacre to Beech Green, you will notice three things.

First, it is extremely pretty, with flower-studded banks or wide grass verges, clumps of trees, and a goodly amount of hawthorn hedging.

Second, it runs steadily downhill, which is not surprising as the valley of the river Cax lies about six miles southward.

Third, it loops and curls upon itself in the most snakelike manner, so that, if you are driving, it is necessary to negotiate the bends prudently, in third gear, and with all senses alert.

Because of the nature of the road then, a certain

attractive house, set back behind a high holly hedge, escapes the attention of the passer-by. Holly Lodge began modestly enough as a small cottage belonging to a farming family at Beech Green. No one knows the name of the builder, but it would have been some local man who used the materials to hand, the flints from the earth, the oak from the woods and the straw from the harvest fields, to fashion walls, beams and thatched roof. When the work was done, he chipped the date 1773 on the king beam, collected his dues, and went on to the next job.

It is interesting to note that the first occupant of the cottage when preparing for Christmas in that year would be unaware of the exciting events happening on the other side of the Atlantic, which would have such influence upon the lives of his children, and those who would follow them, as tenants of the farmer. The Boston Tea Party would mean nothing to him, as he brought in his Christmas logs for the hearth. But a hundred and seventy years later, Americans would live under that thatched roof, in time of war, and be welcomed by the villagers of Fairacre.

By that time, the modest two-up-and-two-down cottage had been enlarged so that there were three bedrooms and a bathroom upstairs, and a large kitchen below. The lean-to, of its earlier days, which had housed the wash tub, the strings of onions and the dried bunches of herbs for winter seasoning, had vanished. Despite war-time stringencies, the house was cared for and the garden trim, and the owner John Phipps, serving with his regiment, longed for the day of his return.

It never came. He was killed in the Normandy landings on D-Day, and the house was sold. It changed hands several times, and partly because of this, and partly because of its retired position, about a mile from the centre of Fairacre, Holly Lodge always seemed secret and aloof. The people who took it were always 'outsiders', retired worthies from Caxley in the main, with grown-up families and a desire for a quiet life in a house small enough to be manageable without domestic help.

The last couple to arrive, some two hundred years after the builder had carved his date on the king beam, were named Benson. Ambrose Benson was a retired bank manager from Caxley and his wife Joan, once a school mistress, was a bustling sixty-year-old. Their only son was up at Cambridge, their only daughter married with three children.

Fairacre, as always, was interested to see the preparations being made before the couple moved in. The holly hedge, unfortunately, screened much activity, and the fact that Holly Lodge was some distance from the village itself dampened the usual ardour of the gossip hunters. Nevertheless, it was soon learned that an annexe was being built at one end of the house, comprising a sitting-room, bedroom, bathroom and kitchen which would be occupied by Mrs Benson's elderly mother.

Mr Willet, caretaker of Fairacre School, sexton of St Patrick's and general handyman to the whole village, was the main source of such snippets of news about Holly Lodge as were available. The builder of the annexe, although a Caxley man, was a distant cousin of Mrs Willet's, and asked if her husband could give a hand laying a brick path round the new addition.

It was a job after Mr Willet's heart. He enjoyed handling the old rosy bricks, matching them for colour, aligning them squarely, and making a lasting object of beauty and use. All his spare time, in the month before the Bensons were due to take over, he spent in their garden at his task, humming to himself as he worked.

His happiness was marred only by his impatience with the dilatory and slapdash ways of the builders.

'To see them sittin' on their haunches suppin' tea,' said Mr Willet to his friend Mr Lamb, the postmaster at Fairacre, 'fair makes my blood boil. And that fathead of a plumber has left the new bath standing in the middle of the lawn so that there's a great yellow mark where the grass has been killed.'

'Marvellous, ennit!' agreed Mr Lamb. 'D'you reckon they'll get in on time?'

'Not the way those chaps are carrying on,' snorted Mr Willet. 'Be lucky to get in by Christmas, if you ask me.'

Mr Willet's contribution to the amenities of Holly Lodge was finished before the end of August. The Bensons had hoped to be in residence by then but, as Mr Willet had forecast, they had to await the departure of the plasterer, the painters and the plumber.

At last, on a mercifully fine October day, the removal vans rolled up, and Fairacre had the pleasure of knowing that the newcomers had really arrived.

Joan Benson was soon studied, discussed and finally approved by the village. She was a plump, bird-like little woman, quick in speech and movement, given to wearing pastel colours and rather more jewellery than Fairacre was used to. Nevertheless, she was outstandingly friendly. She joined the Women's Institute and made a good impression by offering to help with the washing-up, a task which the local gentry tended to ignore.

Even Mrs Pringle, the village's arch-moaner, had to admit that 'she'd settled in quite nice for a town woman,' but could not resist adding that 'Time-Alone-Would-Tell'. Ambrose Benson was not much seen in the village, but it was observed that the garden at Holly Lodge was being put into good shape after the ravages of the builders' sojourn, and that he seemed to be enjoying his retirement in the new home.

Mr Partridge, the vicar of Fairacre, had called upon his new parishioners and had high hopes of persuading

Ambrose Benson to take part in the numerous village activities which needed just such a person as a retired bank manager to see to them. How had Fairacre managed to muddle along before the arrival, Ambrose began to wonder, as he listened to the good vicar's account of the pressing needs of various committees, but naturally, he kept this thought to himself.

'A charming fellow,' Gerald Partridge told his wife. 'I'm sure he will be a great asset to Fairacre.'

The third member of the household was rarely seen. Joan's mother was eighty-seven, smitten with arthritis, and had difficulty in getting about. But the villagers agreed that she did the most beautiful knitting, despite her swollen fingers, and smiled very sweetly from the car when her daughter took her for a drive.

When the Bensons' first Christmas at Holly Lodge arrived, it was generally agreed in Fairacre that the vicar might be right.

Ambrose Benson, his wife and mother-in-law could well prove to be an asset to the village.

The winter was long and hard. It was not surprising that little was seen of the newcomers. Holly Lodge, snug behind the high hedge which gave it its name, seemed to be in a state of hibernation. Joan Benson was seen occasionally in the Post Office, or village shop, but Ambrose, it seemed, tended to have bronchial trouble and did not venture far in icy weather. As for old Mrs Penwood, her arthritis made it difficult to get from one room to the other, and she spent more and more time in the relative comfort of a warm bed.

'I shall be extra glad to see the Spring,' admitted Joan to Mr Lamb, as she posted a parcel to her daughter. 'My husband and mother are virtually housebound in this bitter weather. I long to get into the garden, and I know they do too.'

'Won't be long now,' comforted Mr Lamb, looking at the bleak village street through the window.

But Mr Lamb was wrong. Bob Willet, weather prophet among his many other roles, was stern in his predictions.

'We won't get no warmth till gone Easter,' he told those who asked his opinion. 'Then we'll be lucky. Might well be Whitsun afore it picks up.'

'Ain't you a Job's comforter, eh?' chaffed one listener. But he secretly respected Bob Willet's forecasts. Too often he was right.

On one of the darkest days of January, when a grey lowering sky gave the feeling of being in a tent, and Fairacre folk were glad to draw the blinds at four o'clock against such an inhospitable world, news went round the village grapevine that poor Ambrose Benson had been taken by ambulance to Caxley Hospital.

'Couldn't hardly draw breath,' announced Mrs Pringle, who had received the news via Minnie Pringle, her niece, who had had it from the milkman. 'Choking his life out, he was. I've always said that anything attacking the bronichals is proper cruel. It was congested bronichals that carried off my Uncle Albert, and him only fifty-two.'

The next day, the Bensons' daughter arrived, and the following day their son.

Gerald Partridge, the vicar, calling to offer sympathy and help, found the two ladies at Holly Lodge, red-eyed but calm.

'He is putting up a marvellous fight, they tell me,' said Joan Benson, 'and he has always been very fit, apart from this chest weakness. We are full of hope.'

'If there is anything I or my wife can do, please call upon us,' begged the vicar. 'You are all very much in our thoughts, and we shall pray for your husband's recovery on Sunday morning.'

'You are so kind. We've been quite overwhelmed with sympathetic enquiries. Really, Fairacre is the friendliest place, particularly when trouble has struck.'

True to his word, Mr Partridge and his congregation prayed earnestly for Ambrose's restoration to health. But, even as they prayed, the sick man's life was ebbing, and by the time the good people emerged into St Patrick's wintry churchyard, Ambrose Benson had drawn his last painful breath.

This tragic blow, coming at the end of a long spell of anxiety, hit Joan cruelly. For years she and Ambrose had looked forward to his retirement. They had planned trips abroad, holidays in London where they could satisfy their love for the theatre, and, of course, the shared joys of the new home and its garden. Now all was shattered.

In a daze, she dealt with the dismal arrangements for the funeral, thankful to have her son and daughter with her over the first dreadful week of widowhood.

Luckily, Ambrose's affairs had been left in apple-pie

order, as was to be expected from a methodical bank manager, but it was plain that Joan would need to be careful with money in the years ahead.

When her son and daughter departed, after the funeral, Joan was thankful to have the company of her mother in the house. The old lady seemed frailer than ever, and Joan took to sleeping in the spare bed put in her mother's room.

The annexe had been planned on one floor, and during those nights when Joan lay awake, listening to the shallow breathing of her mother, and the queer little whimpers which she sometimes made unconsciously, as the arthritis troubled her dreams, she began to appreciate the charm of the new addition to Holly Lodge.

Sometimes she wondered if she might let it, and install her mother on the ground floor of the main house. Many a night was passed in planning rooms and arranging furniture, and this helped a little in mitigating the dreadful waves of grief which still engulfed her.

It was during this sad time that Joan found several true friends in Fairacre. Mrs Partridge and Mrs Mawne were particularly understanding, visiting frequently, and taking it in turns to sit with Mrs Penwood so that Joan could have a brief shopping expedition in Caxley, or a visit to old friends in the town.

She was met with sympathy and kindness wherever she went in the village, and became more and more determined to remain at Holly Lodge as, she felt sure, Ambrose would have wished her to do.

Spring was late in arriving, as Bob Willet had forecast, and it was late in April that the first really warm day came.

'I shall sit out,' said Mrs Penwood decidedly. 'Put my chair in the shelter of the porch, Joan, and I will enjoy the fresh air after all these months of being a prisoner.'

'It is still quite chilly,' said Joan. 'Do you think it is wise?'

'Of course it's wise!' responded her mother. 'It will do me more good than all the doctor's pills put together.'

With difficulty, Joan settled her mother in the sunshine. She was swathed in a warm cloak, and had a mohair rug over her legs, but Joan was alarmed to find

how cold her hands were when she took her some coffee.

Mrs Penwood brushed aside her daughter's protestations.

'I haven't been so happy since Ambrose—' she began, and hastily changed this to, 'for months. The air is wonderful. Just what I need.'

She insisted on having her light lunch outside, and Joan watched her struggling to hold a spoon with numbed fingers.

'Do come inside after lunch, mother,' she begged. 'You've really had the best of the day, you know.'

But the old lady was adamant. In some ways, thought Joan as she washed up, it was far simpler to cope with half a dozen children. At least they recognized authority, even if they did not always obey it. Old ladies, however sweet-natured, did not see why they should take orders from those younger than themselves.

She returned to find her mother sleeping, and decided to let her have another half an hour before she insisted on moving her indoors. Carefully, she spread another rug over the sleeping form, tucking the cold hands beneath it. Already the air was beginning to cool, and Joan went in to light the fire, ready for a cheerful tea-time.

A few minutes later, she heard cries and groans from her mother, and hurried outside. The old lady appeared to be having a spasm, and made incoherent noises. The only word which Joan could understand was the anguished cry of 'Pain, pain!'

Fear gave her strength to wrest the old lady, coverings and all, from the chair and to stumble with her to the bedroom in the annexe. Swiftly she managed to put her, still fully clothed, into bed, and ran to the telephone.

Their old family doctor from Caxley arrived within the hour, examined his patient minutely, and shook his head.

'I shall give her an injection now,' he told Joan. 'Just see that she remains warm and quiet. I will look in again after this evening's surgery.'

Joan nodded, too stricken to speak.

'Got a good neighbour handy to keep you company?' asked the doctor, knowing how recently she had been widowed.

'I will telephone the vicar's wife,' whispered Joan.

'I'll do it for you,' said the doctor.

Within five minutes, Mrs Partridge arrived, and the doctor went to his car.

'I'm afraid Mrs Penwood is in a pretty poor way,' he confided to the vicar's wife as she saw him off. 'It's a sad task to leave you with, but I will be back soon after seven.'

He was as good as his word. But when Mrs Partridge opened the door of Holly Lodge to him, he saw at once that his patient had gone.

Joan Benson spent that night, and the next one, at the vicarage, and the bonds formed then between the two women were to remain strong throughout their lives.

After this second blow, Joan went to stay for a time with her daughter. The children's chatter, and their need of her, gave her comfort, and she had time to try to put her plans in order.

She decided to stay. Holly Lodge might seem rather large for one widowed lady, but her children and grandchildren would need bedrooms when they visited, and she did not want to part with much-loved possessions.

But the annexe, she decided, must be let. It was quite self-contained, and would make a charming home for some quiet woman in circumstances such as her own, or for that matter, for a mature woman with a job.

The Caxley Chronicle carried an advertisement in early June. Several people came to see Joan Benson but nobody seemed really suitable.

It was Henry Mawne, the vicar's friend and a distinguished ornithologist, who first mentioned Miss Quinn.

'She's secretary to my old friend Barney Hatch in Caxley,' he told Joan. 'I know she needs somewhere. Her present digs are noisy, and she likes a quiet life. Nice woman, thirtyish, keeps old Barney straight, and that takes some doing. Like me to mention it?'

'Yes, please. I would be grateful.'

And thus it came about that Miriam Quinn, personal private secretary to Sir Barnabas Hatch, the financier, came to look at Holly Lodge's annexe one warm June evening, breathed in the mingled scent of roses and pinks, and surveyed the high hedge which ensured privacy, with the greatest satisfaction.

'I should like to come very much,' she said gravely to Joan Benson.

'And I,' said that lady joyfully, 'should like you to. Shall we go inside and settle things?'

CHAPTER TWO

Miss Quinn moved in on a still, cloudless day in July. Fairacre was looking its best, as all downland country does, in summer heat.

Wild roses and honeysuckle embroidered the hedges. The cattle stood in the shade of the trees, swishing away the flies with their tails, and chewing the cud languorously. Dragonflies skimmed the surface of the diminishing river Cax, and a field of beans in flower wafted great waves of scent through the car's open window as Miss Quinn trundled happily towards her new home.

Before her the road shimmered waterily in the heat. It was almost a relief to enter the shady tunnel of trees at Beech Green, before regaining the open fields which led to Fairacre at the foot of the downs.

Her spirits rose as she left Caxley behind. Miriam Quinn had been brought up in a vicarage in a lonely stretch of the Fen country. Space and solitude were the two things which that windswept area had made essential to her happiness. Sometimes, when the canyons of some city streets drove her near to claustrophobic panic, she longed for the great Cambridge sky; and even the pleasant tree-lined road in Caxley, where she had lived since taking up the post with Sir Barnabas, she found stuffy and oppressive.

Now she would live in open country again. The encircling holly hedge, which gave her new abode its

name, would not worry her. The windows of the annexe, she had noticed swiftly, looked mainly upon the flank of the downs. She reckoned that she could see seven or eight miles to the distant woods to the south of Caxley from her sitting-room window.

She reached the signpost saying FAIRACRE 1, and began to look out for the hidden drive on her left which ran beside the high holly hedge to the main gate of Holly Lodge. It was propped open ready for her, she was grateful to see, and her own garage had its door hospitably open.

Miriam Quinn shut the car door and stood for a moment savouring the peace and the blessed coolness of the downland air. Bees hummed among the lime flowers above her, and a tabby cat rolled luxuriously in a fine clump of cat-mint in the sunny border.

Some distance away, Miriam discerned the figure of her new landlady. She was asleep in a deckchair, her head in the shade of a cherry tree, her feet propped up on a footstool in the sunshine.

Intense happiness flooded Miriam's being. The atmosphere of country tranquillity enveloped her like some comforting cloak in bitter weather. Here was home! Here was the peace she sought; the perfect antidote to the hectic atmosphere and pace of the office!

Very quietly, she picked up her case and made her way to the annexe door.

Joan Benson woke with a start and looked at her wrist watch. Almost four o'clock. Good heavens, she must have slept for nearly two hours! Since her mother's death she had found herself taking cat-naps like this, and friends told her that it was nature's way of restoring her after the stress of tending the invalids of the family for so long.

She became conscious of faint noises from the

annexe. Of course, Miss Quinn would have arrived! How shameful not to be awake to greet her!

She struggled from the deck chair, and hastened towards the house to make amends. Miriam Quinn received her apologies with a smile.

'I am going to make tea,' said her new landlady. 'Do join me in the garden. You know that I want you to look upon it as your own. Please feel free to use it whenever you like. I have put up a little washing line for you, behind the syringa bushes. But I will show you everything after tea.'

She was as good as her word. Tea had obviously been prepared with some care. There were homemade scones, and tomato sandwiches, and some delicious shortbread. Miss Quinn could see that Joan Benson was glad to have company, and was equally anxious to be hospitable. She chattered happily as she took her lodger round the garden, pointing out new improvements which Ambrose had made, and the herb patch which she herself had laid out.

'Take what you need,' she urged. 'There is plenty here for us both.'

'You are very kind, Mrs Benson.'

'Oh, do please call me "Joan",' she cried. 'We surely know each other well enough for Christian names.'

'Then you must call me "Miriam",' she responded.

'That's so much more friendly,' agreed her landlady, leading the way back to the house. 'You'll come in for a sherry later on, I hope.'

Miriam chose to treat this as a question rather than a statement.

'I think I ought to get on with my unpacking, if you

don't mind,' she replied. 'And I have one or two telephone calls to make.'

'Of course, of course,' agreed Joan warmly. 'I think you'll find the extension telephone convenient in your sitting-room. I very rarely use the one in my hall.'

She bustled off to collect the tea tray and Miriam returned to the peace of her own small domain. She sat looking at the distant view from the window, marshalling her thoughts.

She could be happy here, and Joan Benson was extremely kind and welcoming. Nevertheless, a small doubt disturbed her peace of mind.

Here they were, within one hour of her moving in, on Christian name terms, and her head already throbbing with the pleasant but interminable chatter of her hostess. She was experienced enough to realise that a recently bereaved woman must be lonely and more than usually grateful for company. The thing was – was she willing to give the time and sympathy which Joan so obviously needed at the moment?

She recognized her own limitations. She liked her own company. She liked the tranquillity of her natural surroundings. She had more than enough people around her during office hours, and Holly Lodge would be, she hoped, her refuge from them. It would be sad if her contented solitude were shattered by the well-meaning overtures of her landlady.

She stood up abruptly, and began to sort out her books. She was going too fast! Of course, Joan would be extra forthcoming at their first meeting. She would be anxious to put her lodger at ease. She must respond as well as her more reserved nature would permit.

Joan deserved much sympathy, and was tackling her difficulties with considerable bravery, she told herself as she tried to come to terms with her new situation.

She lay in bed that night feeling the light breeze blowing across the miles of downland and cooling her cheeks. Somewhere a screech owl gave its eerie cry. A moth pattered up and down the window pane, and the fragrance from Joan's stocks scented the bedroom.

Miriam sighed happily. How quiet it was, after the noise of Caxley! What bliss to live here! She had not felt so free and relaxed since her far-off days in the Cambridgeshire vicarage.

It was all going to be perfect, she told herself sleepily. Quite perfect! Quite perfect – unless Joan became too—

She drifted into sleep.

She woke early and went to the window to savour the unbelievable freshness of the morning. Nothing stirred, except a pair of blackbirds busy among the rose bushes. A blue spiral of smoke rose in the distance. An early bonfire, she wondered? Or, more probably, the smoke from the chimney of a cottage hidden from view in a fold of the downs?

She bathed and dressed, relishing the privacy of her little house, and sat down to her toast and coffee soon after seven. There was no sound from next door, and she chided herself for feeling so relieved. Her need for solitude was even greater than usual first thing in the morning, and she sipped her coffee in contentment, looking around the kitchen and making a note of things yet to be done.

A rattling at the front door disturbed her train of thought. A letter lay on the mat, and as she picked it up she heard the postman pushing the mail through Joan's letter-box.

Her own missive was from Eileen, her sister-in-law, and consisted of two pages of good wishes for Miriam's future happiness in the new house, and news of the three children and Lovell, her husband and Miriam's only brother, two years her senior.

It was good of her to trouble to write, thought Miriam, but really, what an appalling hand she had, and why so many underlinings and exclamation marks? She poured out her second cup of coffee, and pondered on her sister-in-law's inability to buy envelopes which matched the writing paper, and to use a pen which wrote without dropping blots of ink. Such untidiness must irk Lovell as much as it did herself, for they were both neat and methodical, and had been so since childhood.

They had always been devoted to each other, and she remembered her grief when he had gone away to school. He had written regularly, in his neat small handwriting, so different from the untidy scrawl now before her.

From Cambridge he had followed his father into the Church, and was now vicar in a large parish, not far from Norwich, in the East Anglian countryside they both knew so well. Here he had met Eileen, soon after his arrival, and ever since then a certain bleakness had entered Miriam's life.

The old warm comradeship had gone, although no

word was ever uttered. Miriam could understand her brother's love for the girl who so soon became his wife, but she could not help resenting her presence, try as she would.

Eileen was small and pretty, with an appealing air of fragility. Her fluffy fair hair was bound with ribbon. Her tiny shoes were bedecked with bows. She liked light historical novels, chocolate mints, deckle-edged writing paper and pale blue furnishings. She chattered incessantly and laughed a great deal. There was an air of teasing frivolity about her which would have earned her the title of 'minx' in earlier days. She was a complete contrast to the sober and dark-haired Miriam and Lovell, and their earnest parents. It was hardly surprising that Lovell was captivated. He had never met anyone quite so adorable.

On the whole, the marriage had turned out well, despite the Quinns' private misgivings. Eileen had produced three attractive children, the youngest now almost two years old, and although they were allowed far too much licence by their grandparents' standards, Miriam recognized that Eileen was a natural mother, quick to notice ailments and danger, although slapdash in her methods of upbringing. Her innate playfulness made her a good companion to the young things, and if discipline was needed – and often it was, for they were high-spirited children – then Lovell reproved them with due solemnity.

Yes, things could have been much worse, Miriam told herself, stacking the breakfast things neatly. Lovell seemed happy enough, although one could not help wishing that he had found someone with a depth of character and outlook to match his own. But would she have liked such a woman any more than she liked Eileen?

She washed up thoughtfully, and was honest enough to admit that any woman whom Lovell married would have caused the same secret unhappiness. She had been supplanted, and it rankled. It was the outcome of unusual devotion between brother and sister, and she had now learned to live with this unpalatable fact.

She took a last look at herself in the long looking-glass in her bedroom. Her thick dark hair was knotted on her neck. Her navy blue linen frock suited her slim build perfectly, and the plain but expensive shoes matched it exactly. She looked what she was – an attractive efficient business woman in her thirties.

'I wonder why she never married?' she had heard people say.

She wondered herself sometimes. There had been young men in her life, friends of Lovell's, for instance, when he was at Cambridge. Young and friendly, some of them ardent, they had been glad to visit the austere vicarage in the Fens, to enjoy the homely hospitality offered there and the company of Lovell's quiet younger sister.

But, cool and far-seeing, Miriam found none of them as attractive as the prospect of a life free of domestic responsibilities, free of children and free of a life-long partnership which she doubted if she could sustain. With her upbringing, marriage would be for life, and sometimes, watching her hard-working mother, she wondered if she would ever be as selfless.

Single life had its compensation. If she had to stay late at the office, or decided to go straight from there to see a play in London, or to visit friends, then there was no one to inform or to consider. Her decisions needed no discussion with another. Everything was under control.

No one stirred next door as she drove her car towards the gate. The road was empty. The horizon was as clear as her own mind. The day was mapped out. She knew exactly what would be happening at any given time. It was good to know where one was going.

Miriam Quinn was very sure of herself.

Within the next few weeks, news of the efficient paragon who lived in Mrs Benson's annexe had flashed round the village bush telegraph. Henry Mawne was largely to blame.

Gerald Partridge, the vicar, was in sore need of someone to look after the books of the Church Fabric Fund. Henry Mawne, honorary secretary and treasurer to a score or more village concerns, stated flatly that he could not take on any more.

'But what about that nice Miriam Quinn?' he asked of his friend. 'We met her the other night at Joan Benson's.'

'But she must be very busy with her job,' protested the vicar.

'She's home by about six. Why not ask her if she would like the job? She might be glad to meet people.'

The same kindly thought had occurred to other

people in Fairacre, particularly those on committees needing secretaries, treasurers and the vague amorphous quality called 'new blood'. Here was a clever woman, obligingly free of family ties, in good health and possibly lonely, who could prove a godsend to the various organizations in need of help.

Henry Mawne was the first to approach Miriam on behalf of the short-staffed Church Fabric committee. She welcomed him to her shining home, gave him sherry, sparkled at his jokes, and declined the invitation in the most charming manner. Henry retired, hardly realizing that he had been defeated.

The Brownies needed a Brown Owl, the Cubs an Akela. The Women's Institute needed a book-keeper as the last one still worked in shillings and pence, and in any case had lost the account book. The Over Sixties' Club could do with a speaker on any subject, at any time suitable to Miss Quinn.

The Naturalists' Association, the Youth Club, the Play Group, the Welfare Clinic, St Patrick's Choir and the Sunday School were anxious to have Miss Quinn's presence and support, and Miriam soon realized, with amusement and resignation, that much more hummed beneath Fairacre's serene face than she had imagined.

Her tact, her charm and her intelligence, backed by her formidable resolve to keep her life exactly as she wanted it, enabled her to stay clear of any of these entanglements.

Baffled, and slightly hurt, the villagers retired worsted.

Mrs Pringle summed up the general feeling about the newcomer.

'No flies on Miss Quinn! She knows her value, that one, but she ain't for sale!'

CHAPTER THREE

As the weeks passed, Miriam's pleasure grew. Holly Lodge was all that she had hoped for – peaceful, convenient and set among the great windswept countryside for which she had craved.

She took to strolling for an hour each evening before her supper. The air blew away the little tensions and annoyances of the office, and she always returned refreshed.

Sometimes she explored the village of Fairacre, stopping to talk politely to all who accosted her, but as Mr Lamb at the Post Office said: 'She don't make the running. It's you who has to start the conversation, though she's as nice as pie once you get going.'

Henry Mawne and his wife she knew through her employer, and had been invited to their Queen Anne house at the end of the village, on several occasions. The Hales at Tyler's Row, the Partridges at the vicarage, Mr Willet and Mrs Pringle, all were known to her, and she was on nodding terms with the majority of Fairacre's inhabitants.

But, on the whole, she preferred to ramble in the immediate vicinity of Holly Lodge. There she was unlikely to meet well-meaning folk who engaged her in conversation. She revelled in these solitary walks, noting the nuts and berries in the hedges, the flight of the downland birds, and the small fragrant flowers which flourished on the chalky soil.

She skirted the field of barley behind the house when she set off for the downs. Since her coming, the crop had turned from green to gold, fine and upstanding, with heavy ears. She watched it being harvested in August, and listened to the regular thumping of the baler as she ate her simple evening meal in the sitting-room or carried her tray to some quiet corner of the garden.

Joan Benson had quickly realized that the girl preferred to be alone, and she sympathized with her feelings. After all, she told herself, Miriam arrived home tired, having dealt with people and their problems all day.

She had met Sir Barnabas Hatch at the Mawnes and had summed him up astutely as the sort of man who, endowed with twice the average amount of energy and intelligence, expects other people to be equally dynamic. Miriam could well hold her own, and her cool disposition would enable her to cope with any outbursts from her employer. Nevertheless, he must be a demanding person with whom to deal and it was no wonder that the girl needed the peace of her little home at the end of the day.

But although she respected Miriam's desire for privacy, she could not help feeling a little disappointed. She had hoped for company, and although the mere presence of someone next door was a great comfort, she sorely missed the conversation and company of her husband and mother. She found herself switching on the radio, simply to hear another voice during the day, or making some excuse to walk to the village to enjoy a few words with anyone she met.

The days grew shorter. Joan tidied her garden, strung up her onions, planted bulbs and had a massive autumn bonfire which wreathed blue smoke around Holly Lodge for two whole days. She was stirring the last of its embers one Saturday afternoon when Miriam waved to her from the other end of the garden.

'I'm off blackberrying,' she called. 'Shall I pick some for you?'

Joan dropped the hoe she had been using as an outsize poker, and hurried across.

'I'll join you, if I may,' she said. 'I've been meaning to go all the week. Wait half a minute while I fetch a basket.'

Miriam rather welcomed company on this golden afternoon. She had finished the usual weekend chores of washing and shopping. The tradesmen had been paid their weekly dues, the house was clean. The mending awaited her, but otherwise her affairs were in as much apple-pie order here as they were at the office. It would be good to hear Joan's news. She felt slightly guilty about seeing so little of her lately. This afternoon she would make amends.

The two women strode across the stubble of the field to a tall hedge. The sharp straw caught their legs, but it was wonderfully exhilarating to feel the crunch of it beneath their feet. At the farther edge of the field Miriam caught sight of something moving.

'Look!' she said, grasping Joan's arm. 'A covey of partridges! There must be at least ten young ones running along there. I haven't seen that for a long time.'

Joan was struck, for the first time, with the excitement in her companion's face.

'You really are a country girl!' she exclaimed. 'Somehow I hadn't realized it.'

Miriam smiled at her.

'It's why I love Holly Lodge so much,' she told her.

The blackberries were thick and the two women picked steadily. Jet-black, ruby-eyed and pale green, the berries cascaded down the hedge. United in their task, relaxed by the sunshine and sweet air, they talked of this and that, Miriam more forthcoming than ever before, and Joan relishing the chance to chatter again.

An onlooker might have learnt a great deal about the two women's natures, simply by watching their methods of picking. Miriam chose her bush with a shrewd eye to size and ripeness, and then picked swiftly and systematically, from the fat terminal berry, along the sides of the branch until all were gathered. Her movements were rapid but controlled, and not one berry was dropped.

Joan ambled happily between bushes, picking only the large ones. She lacked the concentration of the younger woman, but obviously enjoyed her haphazard forays and was quite content to have only half a basket of fruit, compared with Miriam's brimming one, when the time came to return home.

'I'm going to make tea,' said Miriam. 'Come and join me.'

Joan was delighted to accept, and after depositing her basket in her own kitchen and washing her battle-scarred hands, she returned to the annexe bearing some bronze chrysanthemums.

'I love them,' said Joan, watching her neighbour arrange them, 'but I always feel rather sad. They mean the summer's over. Still, they are very beautiful, and have such a marvellous scent. Rather like very expensive furniture polish, I always think.'

Miriam let her chatter happily, wondering how to broach a subject which had been in her mind for some time.

'Would you mind if I redecorated these rooms, Joan?'

'Not at all,' she said, looking a little surprised. 'But they were done, you know, very recently.'

'That's why I haven't liked to mention it. But, to tell you the truth, I'm not a lover of cream walls, and with this old mahogany I thought a very pale green would look well.'

Joan nodded approvingly.

'It would indeed. Would you get somebody in to do

it? I'm sure Mr Willet could recommend someone reliable. Shall I ask him?'

'No, there's no need. I shall enjoy tackling it myself. I'm quite experienced.'

'What a lot of talents you have! When would you want to start? Can I help at all?'

Miriam began to feel the familiar qualms of apprehension returning.

'I may take a few days off,' she said guardedly. 'I have some time owing to me, and Barnabas has to make a trip overseas soon. I may be able to arrange something then. If not, I could probably do some of it at Christmas time.'

This chance remark sent Joan along a new path.

'I'm writing to my two children this week to see if they can join me for Christmas. I thought if they had plenty of notice, I should have more chance of their company. It would be lovely to have the house full and you could meet them all. Barbara's babies are such fun.'

Miriam's heart sank.

'You're very kind,' she murmured. 'More tea?'

'I simply adore Christmas,' continued Joan, stirring her second cup. 'And Fairacre is the perfect place to spend it. Lots of little parties, and carol singers coming to the door and having a drink and mince pies when they've finished; and always such lovely services at St Patrick's with the church decked beautifully with holly and ivy. Christmas really is *Christmas* at Fairacre!'

Miriam's polite smile masked her inner misgivings. Christmas at the vicarage had always meant a particularly busy day for her father, and a considerable number of elderly relatives who had been invited by her kindly mother because as she said: 'They had nowhere else to go, poor things, and one can't think of them alone at Christmas.'

Miriam had long ago given up feeling guilty about her dislike of Christmas festivities, and latterly had taken pains to keep her own Christmases as quiet as possible. This year she was determined to spend it alone in her new abode, with no turkey, no pudding, no mince pies and – definitely – no holly.

She might have a glass of the excellent port which Barnabas usually gave her with her customary light lunch, and she intended to read some Trollope, earmarked for the winter months. But too much food, too much noise and, above all, too much convivial company she would avoid.

But would she be able to?

She looked at dear kind Joan, rosy with fresh air and relaxed with warmth and company. How she blossomed, thought Miriam, with other people about!

No wonder she loved Christmas. Visiting, and being visited, was the breath of life to the good soul, and the joy of the festival would far outweigh any extra work which it entailed.

'I must be off,' said Joan, struggling to her feet. 'There's bramble jelly to be made next door and I must leave you to tackle your own.'

Miriam closed the door behind her, and returned to the sitting-room deep in thought. It looked as though evading action might well be needed as Christmas approached.

She looked out upon the golden evening. The trees

were beginning to turn tawny with the first cool winds of autumn.

Ah well, she told herself, time enough yet to postpone such troubles!

But the autumn slipped by at incredible speed. It was dark now when Miriam left the office. She was glad to nose her car into the garage and hurry into the annexe to light the fire, which she prudently set in readiness in the morning.

The force of the equinoctial gales surprised her. Now she began to realize how open to the elements was this high downland country, and to appreciate the sagacity of the past owner of Holly Lodge who had had the foresight to plant the thick hedge which gave the house not only its name, but considerable protection from the blasts of winter.

Her own little home gave her increasing satisfaction. She had painted the kitchen white. It took three weekends of hard work to do the job, but Miriam was a perfectionists, and she rubbed down the old paint until not one scrap remained, before she began to apply the undercoat with a steady hand. She enjoyed the work, she exulted in the finished result and, above all, she relished the perfect quiet as she got on with the job.

She was even more determined now to tackle the sitting-room at Christmas. Barney, as she thought of him, was making a business trip to Boston and New York, leaving on December 16 and not returning until after New Year's Day. Miriam had already made the flight bookings for him and for Adèle, his wife. They were meeting their only daughter, who was married to an American, and proposed to spend Christmas at her home and to see their grandchildren. Miriam had been requested to find some toys suitable for children aged six and eight.

'The sort of thing they won't get over there, you know,' said Barney vaguely. 'Adèle's got the main things, but I'd like to take something myself. I'll leave it to you. Not too weighty, of course, because of flying.'

'I won't get an old English rocking-horse,' promised Miriam.

'Oh no! Nothing like that!' exclaimed Sir Barnabas, looking alarmed. Humour, even as obvious as this, did not touch him. 'And no more than five pounds apiece,' he added. He was not a businessman for nothing.

Miriam promised to do her best.

As Christmas approached, the whirl of village activities quickened. Posters went up on barn doors, on the trunks of trees, and on the bus shelter near the church, drawing attention to the usual Mammoth Jumble Sale, the Fur and Feather Whist Drive and the Social and Dance, all to be held – on different dates, of course – under the roof of the Village Hall.

As well as these advertised delights, there were more private junketings, such as the Women's Institute Christmas party, Fairacre School's concert and a wine and cheese party for the Over-Sixties' Club.

An innovation was Mrs Partridge's Open Day at the vicarage, which was her own idea, and to which the village gave considerable attention.

'You can just pop in there,' said Mrs Willet, in the Post Office, 'any time between ten o'clock and seven at night. You pays ten pence to go in, and you pays for your cup of coffee, or your dinner midday, or tea, say, at four o'clock.'

'And what, pray,' said Mrs Pringle, who was buying stamps, 'do you get for dinner? And how much will it be?'

'I think it's just soup and bread and cheese,' said Mrs Willet timidly.

Mrs Pringle snorted, and two stamps fluttered to the ground.

'I don't call that DINNER,' boomed the lady, preparing to bend to retrieve the stamps.

'Here, let me,' said Mr Lamb, the postmaster, hurrying to rescue Mrs Pringle's property. More than likely to have a heart attack, trying to bend over in those corsets, was his ungallant private comment, as he proffered the stamps with a smile.

'Ta,' said Mrs Pringle perfunctorily. She turned again upon little Mrs Willet.

'And *how much* for this 'ere rubbishy snack?'

'I'm not sure,' faltered Mrs Willet. 'It's for charity, you see. Half to the Church Fabric Fund and half to some mission in London that the vicar takes an interest in. Poor people, you know.'

'*Poor people?*' thundered Mrs Pringle. 'In London? Why, we've got plenty of poor in Fairacre as could do with a bit of help at Christmas, without giving it away to foreigners up London. Look at them Coggses! They could do with a bit of extra. That youngest looks half-starved to me.'

'Well, whose fault's that?' asked Mr Lamb, entering the fray. 'We all know Arthur drinks his pay packet – always has done, and always will. If he was given more, he'd drink that too.'

'Who said give Arthur the money?' demanded Mrs Pringle, her four chins wobbling with indignation. 'Give it to that poor wife of his, I say, to get a decent meal for the kids.'

'They do get something from the Great Coal Charity,' said Mrs Willet diffidently.

Mrs Pringle brushed this aside. 'And in my mother's time there wasn't no Great Coal Charity to rely on,' she boomed on.

'She didn't have anything from the Great Coal Charity,' responded Mr Lamb, 'because there wasn't one then.'

'I'll have you know,' said Mrs Pringle with devastating dignity, 'that that there Charity was started in seventeen fifty because the vicar told us himself at a talk he gave the W.I.'

'Maybe,' replied Mr Lamb, 'but it was started as a *Greatcoat* Charity, and six deserving old men and six deserving old women got a woollen greatcoat apiece to keep out the winter cold.'

Mrs Pringle looked disbelieving, her mouth down-turned like a disgruntled turtle's.

'And what happened,' said Mr Lamb, warming to his theme, 'was this. Someone left the crossing off the "t" in "coat" when they was writing up the minutes about George the Fourth's time, and so it went on being called the Great Coal Charity, and instead of a coat you get coal.'

'Well, I never,' exclaimed Mrs Willet. 'I never heard that before!'

'Nor did I,' said Mrs Pringle, with heavy sarcasm. She picked up her stamps and made for the door.

'Which doesn't alter my feelings about bread and cheese dinners. What's dinner without a bit of meat on your plate?'

She banged the door behind her. Mrs Willet sighed.

'That woman,' said Mr Lamb, 'makes me come over prostrate with dismal when she shows that face of hers in here. Now, love, what was it you wanted?'

CHAPTER FOUR

Miriam was wise enough to realize that she could not opt out of Christmas activities completely. Nor did she wish to. She willingly provided boxes of chocolates for raffle prizes at various Fairacre functions, accompanied Joan to a carol service at St Patrick's and drank a glass of sherry at the vicarage Open Day.

There was no doubt about it, this new venture was extremely popular with Fairacre folk. Mrs Partridge and her helpers had decked the downstairs rooms with scarlet and silver ribbons, and all the traditional trappings of Christmas. Holly and ivy, mistletoe and glittering baubles added their beauty, and an enormous Christmas tree dominated the entrance hall.

In each room was a table bearing goods suitable for Christmas presents, and a brisk trade ensured that the Church Fabric Fund and Mr Partridge's pet mission would profit. Miriam recognized the planning which must have gone into this enterprise, and admired the efficiency with which it was run. It was an idea she intended to pass on to Lovell, when she saw him, for future use in his own parish.

These little jaunts she thoroughly enjoyed, and she was grateful for the genuine welcome she was given by her village neighbours. Joan's growing excitement, as the festival approached, was a source of mingled pleasure and apprehension, however.

'Isn't it wonderful?' Joan had said, on the morning of the Open Day. 'Roger is coming for Christmas, after all, and then going with a party of other young people to Switzerland for the winter sports.'

'Marvellous,' agreed Miriam. Barbara, the daughter, her husband and three children had already accepted Joan's invitation and would be in the house for a week. Miriam had listened patiently to Joan's ecstatic arrangements of sleeping, feeding and entertaining the family party for the last week or two. The plans were remarkably fluid, and Miriam had long since given up trying to keep track of who slept where, or when would be best to eat the turkey.

It was quite apparent that she must meet Joan's family at some time, and she had accepted an invitation to have a drink on Christmas Eve. So far she had managed to evade the pressing invitations to every meal which her kind-hearted landlady issued daily. That sitting-room would be painted, come hell or high water, she told herself grimly!

She had arranged with Barney to take some time off during his absence in America. This would give her a few days before Christmas to get on with her decorating, having left the office in apple-pie order after his departure. Tins of paint and three new brushes waited on the top shelf in the kitchen, and she felt a little surge of happiness every time she saw them. She could see the sitting-room, in her mind's eye, a bower of green and white, all ready for the New Year, and the new curtains and cushions she had promised herself.

Almost all her Christmas presents were wrapped and ready to post. Christmas cards began to arrive thick and fast. Usually, she had some plan of display – a white-washed branch to hold them, or scarlet ribbons placed across the walls. But this year she read each with interest and then slipped it into a folder brought from the office, so that all were stacked away, leaving the sitting-room ready for her ministrations.

She was glad when the time came to leave the office for her extended Christmas break. Four days after Barney's departure, with everything left tidy, she distributed her presents to the office staff, and thankfully set off for Fairacre and the decorating.

Lights were strung across the streets of Caxley, and entwined the lamp standards. Christmas trees jostled pyramids of oranges in the greengrocers' shops. Turkeys hung in rows in the butchers', presenting their pink plump breasts for inspection. Children flattened their noses against the windows of the toy shops, while exhausted mothers struggled with laden shopping baskets and wondered what they had forgotten.

Queues formed at the Post Offices, buying stamps for stacks of Christmas cards, weighing parcels bedizened with Christmas stickers, or simply enquiring, with some agitation, the last date for posting to New Zealand and getting the answer they had feared. Yet again, Aunt Flo in Wellington would receive a New Year's card sent by air mail.

The surging crowds, the garish lights, the sheer unappetizing commercialism of the festival disgusted Miriam as she threaded her way slowly along the busy streets. It was good to gain the country road to Fairacre, climbing steadily towards the downs, to smell the frosty air and to know that peace lay ahead, behind the holly hedge.

She spent most of the evening by the fire, relishing her solitude and making plans for the attack on the painting. She reviewed the situation and found it highly satisfactory. Her posting was done. A box containing Christmas presents, to be given by hand to Joan and other local friends, was on a shelf in the kitchen cupboard. The milkman was going to deliver a small chicken in two days' time, ready for her modest Christmas dinner. Christmas boxes for the tradesmen waited on the hall window-sill for distribution as they called.

Nothing – but *nothing* – she told herself with satisfaction, could keep her from her decorating now!

Fired by the thought, she began to gather together the ornaments about the room, stacking them in a large cardboard box. It would save time in the morning, when she would roll up the carpet, take down the curtains and push the large pieces of furniture into the centre of the room. Already she had found two dust sheets to cover the mound, and had planned the best method of building the assorted shapes of sofa, chairs and table into a compact pile. Her methodical mind revelled in such practical arrangements. The job was going to be as efficiently tackled as any at the office, and would give her far more satisfaction.

She prepared the room next morning, and by midday was down to the exacting job of washing down the old paint, and rubbing down any uneven patches on the surface. Joan came in once or twice to see if there was anything she could do to help. Miriam greeted her with a smile, but was obviously so content to work alone that Joan retired after expressing admiration for Miriam's zeal.

'It's going to look marvellous,' she cried. 'Will you have lunch with me? It will save you cooking.'

'I've made a sandwich,' replied Miriam, 'and shall have it with some coffee to save time, if you don't mind.'

Joan was secretly rather relieved. Her whole attention now was on the arrival of Barbara and family in two days' time. After the loneliness of the past months, it was pure joy for her to be preparing food, and decking the house, in readiness for the company which would bring Holly Lodge to life again.

Christmas Day fell on a Thursday. Miriam had high hopes of finishing the painting by then, although she faced the fact that the windows – always a tricky and tedious job – might have to be left for later. As Barney would not be back from America until January 3rd, she had planned to take another few days after Christmas if all were well at the office. There should be ample time to get the sitting-room into perfect order.

By Monday evening the first coat of emulsion paint was on the wall. She stood back, brush in hand, to admire its delicate shade. Yes, it was perfect!

Tomorrow she would put on the second and final coat, she told herself happily, going to the sink to rinse the paint brush. She could hear Joan talking to someone on the telephone. No doubt Barbara was ringing about the travelling plans.

But a moment later, Joan called to her. 'Your brother, Miriam, from Norfolk.'

'Right!' called the girl, drying her hands.

Lovell sounded agitated.

'I've trouble here,' said the deep voice. 'Eileen's just gone to hospital.'

'An accident?'

'No, nothing like that. But most acute stomach pains. Awful sickness. Probably something to do with the gall bladder. She's had this sort of thing off and on for some time, but this morning she had this really terrible attack.'

'Poor Eileen! Where is she? Far away?'

'No. In the local hospital. The thing is, can you possibly come and hold the fort for the next few days? I know it's asking a lot, but over Christmas I shall be extra busy in the parish, and I don't know which way to look for help with the children.'

'I can come,' said Miriam promptly. It was good to know that Lovell turned at once to her when he needed help. The old strong bond between them was re-established in those few words uttered so many miles apart.

'You're a trump, Miriam,' cried Lovell. The relief in his voice warmed her heart. 'I can't tell you how glad I am. And so will the children be, and Eileen, when I tell them.'

'I'll set off first thing,' said Miriam, 'and be with you tomorrow afternoon. Have you got provisions in, or shall I bring something?'

'Oh, I expect everything's here,' said Lovell, but he sounded somewhat vague.

There was a sound of an infant screaming in the background.

'Don't worry,' called Miriam hastily. 'I'll see to things when I arrive.'

'Marvellous!' sighed her brother.

The screaming became louder. Miss Quinn replaced the receiver and went sadly back to the half-painted sitting-room.

'Well,' she said glumly. 'That's that!'

Joan heard the news with distress. Anything to do with illness touched her sympathetic heart, and re-awakened memories of her own two recent bereavements. On this occasion there were further causes for dismay.

'And at Christmas too! And with children in the

home! Dear, oh dear, it couldn't be more unfortunate, especially with the extra services your brother will have to take. If only I could help!'

'I know you would if you could, but you will have enough to do at Holly Lodge. I will telephone as soon as I get there tomorrow.'

There was nothing more to do to the painting until the first coat was thoroughly dry. It should certainly be just that by the time she returned, she thought grimly. Understandable irritation began to flood her as she packed away the brushes and tins. How like Eileen to manage to mess up so many people's affairs!

Immediately she chided herself, but the resentment remained to rankle as she found her case and began to pack. And yet, in a distorted way, she almost felt grateful to Lovell's wife for giving her the chance to have his company for a few days of uninterrupted pleasure. It was years since they had been able to talk without the presence of her flibbertigibbet sister-in-law.

It took her longer to pack than usual. Clearing the sitting-room had meant stacking things in unaccustomed places, and she was hard put to it to find a map showing the route. At last, it turned up, packed among cookery books. Yes, skirt Oxford, make for Bicester, Buckingham, Bedford, Cambridge, Newmarket and then on into Norfolk. It was going to be a longish trip. She must start at first light, and pray for a fine day. There was no knowing what she would find to do when she arrived, and she only hoped that the bitter winter weather, for which East Anglia was noted, would hold off and enable her to return in good time. Oh, that poor sitting-room, she grieved!

She climbed into bed, turned out the light, and determined to put aside tomorrow's worries and get to sleep. The vision of a raddled old housemaid called, unbelievably, Euphrosyne, who had helped at her parents' vicarage, came into her mind.

'What can't be cured must be endured,' was one of her favourite sayings.

Maybe Euphrosyne had the last word there, thought Miriam, settling to sleep.

There was frost on the grass when Miriam looked out first thing in the morning. It was grey and still, overcast, but bitterly cold. In the fold of the downs, scarves of mist floated. No breeze stirred the bare branches, and the birds sat huddled in silence, awaiting any largesse thrown from the kitchen window.

It was a dispiriting sort of day, thought Miss Quinn, brewing her coffee. She only hoped that the mists of Fairacre were not an indication of fog in the flat fields of Bedfordshire and the Fen lands beyond.

She remembered the chill of Lovell's draughty vicarage, and went to look out two extra thick sweaters to throw into the back of the car with her wellington boots. Brought up in that bleak area of England, she prudently went prepared for the worst that the weather could do in December.

Joan called in soon after nine, bearing fruit, biscuits and a flask of coffee.

'I hope I'm in time. Have you made some sandwiches?'

'Well, no,' admitted Miriam, after thanking her. 'I thought I would stop on the way and have a proper

lunch. I shall be ready for it, no doubt, and heaven alone knows if there will be anything prepared at Lovell's. I'm taking eggs for us all to be on the safe side.'

'Good. Do ring as soon as you arrive. I shall be anxious.'

'I will. And do use my bedroom while the family is here if it's any help. I have stripped the bed.'

Joan's face lit up.

'That would be marvellous, if you're sure. Roger could go there, or I could perhaps. How nice of you! I will work it out while I'm making the mince pies this morning.'

It was plain that this new turn would add agreeably to her multifarious plans, and Miriam was glad to see her so occupied.

By half past nine she was on her way, having said

farewell to Joan and left her Christmas presents. The hedges were hoary with rime, and in each dip of the downs the mist still swirled. Thin ice crackled beneath the car wheels, and the whole world looked cold and unwelcoming. She thought with longing of the snug cottage she had left behind, and the work half done.

> *But duty, duty must be done,*
> *The rule applies to everyone,*
> *And painful though that duty be*
> *To shirk the task were fiddle-de-dee*

she sang aloud, cheering herself with the thumping rhythm, as the car sped onward.

To her relief, a watery sun, pallid as the moon, became visible through the clouds as she rattled along the road which by-passed Oxford. On each side lay water meadows, and the leaden sheen of the winding river, its course marked by willows stark in their winter nakedness.

As the sun's strength increased, so did Miss Quinn's spirits rise. It was good to see something different. Good to be visiting Lovell, even in such worrying circumstances. Good, even, to feel unaccustomed sympathy for the tiresome Eileen who had precipitated this journey. Looking after the three children Miriam viewed with some trepidation. They were healthy, high-spirited youngsters, and would no doubt be missing their mother. Miriam knew her limitations. She might be Barney's right hand. She might be the dragon that frightened the typing pool. Whether she would be as efficient as aunt-cum-housekeeper remained to be seen.

Bicester and Buckingham were passed. Strange, alien Wolverton, an industrial surprise among the flat fields, lay behind her. After Newport Pagnell, she told herself, she would find a likely-looking lane to enjoy Joan's coffee and fruit. Hunger began to assail her, but the sun now shone warmly, and the Midlands, which Hilaire Belloc had found 'sodden and unkind', lay ahead bathed in gentle light.

She turned into a by-lane where the hedge maple gleamed like gold. A robin flew on to a nearby twig, watching her closely. Crumbs had been known to come from car windows.

Miriam crushed one of Joan's biscuits and scattered it for her companion, who darted down to enjoy this unexpected feast.

Watching his sharp beak at work, Miriam sipped her steaming coffee. In amicable silence, the two strangers enjoyed their meal together.

CHAPTER FIVE

She broke her journey at Cambridge, partly because the place was full of happy memories of her own and Lovell's youth and, more practically, because she knew exactly where to go shopping.

She was lucky to find a parking space outside Queen's. Here, at a May Week ball long ago, she had met Martin Farrar, a friend of Lovell's, and had enjoyed a few weeks' mild flirtation with the handsome boy. Where was he now, she wondered? Farming somewhere in a nearby county, she seemed to remember Lovell saying one day – and happily married.

It was bitingly cold, despite the sunshine. The slow-moving Cam was dappled with the last yellow leaves of autumn, and a vicious little wind stirred the dust along Silver Street.

She bought fruit, bacon and sausages, enough to provide a supper and a breakfast to give her time to check the provisions in Eileen's store cupboard.

She also bought a bottle of sherry for Lovell and flowers for the invalid; and, at the last minute, dived into a shabby toy shop for crayons and balloons. Thus armed she returned to the car, and having deposited her purchases, decided to treat herself to a splendid lunch at the Garden House Hotel nearby.

She was on her way again, much fortified, within the hour.

As always, the miles seemed longer than ever after

Newmarket, as the wide heathlands stretched away into the distance, and the well-known East Anglian wind scoured the countryside.

It was almost dark by the time she arrived at the vicarage.

No one answered the bell which she pressed hopefully at the front door, so she pushed it open, to be greeted by the pungent smell of burning.

The wide hall ran from front door to a glass one at the back. Through it Miriam could see the shabby overgrown garden backed by a lowering sky.

Light spilled from a side door into the hall, and she could hear children laughing. Obviously, all activity was centred in the kitchen.

'Anyone home?' she called advancing, her heels clicking on the black and white marble tiles. Not even a rush mat, thought Miss Quinn, to mitigate the piercing cold to one's feet!

There were screams of excitement as two little girls tumbled through the door, and rushed upon her.

'Auntie Miriam! You've come! We thought you'd be here when we'd gone to bed!'

Two pairs of sticky hands caressed her new Welsh tweed suit lovingly. She bent to kiss the children. The extraordinary smell seemed to envelop them.

'We're making toffee,' said Hazel importantly.

'Only it's a bit caught,' added Jenny. 'Come and see.'

She followed them into the kitchen. Hazel, the nine-year-old, led her to the electric stove. Jenny, two years younger, indicated the saucepan, and Miriam's heart plummeted.

A tar-like substance coated one of the open element electric plates, and made rivulets down the once white front of the stove.

The residue gleamed malevolently from the bottom of the buckled saucepan. That was one utensil, thought Miriam, which would have to be replaced.

'Where is the toffee?' she enquired.

'It's here, you see, but we just ran out into the garden to tell Daddy the telephone was ringing, and it all went sort of fizzy and buzzled all over the stove.'

'That's right,' corroborated Jenny, licking a sticky finger. 'It tastes funny, but it's set, hasn't it?'

'It certainly has,' said Miriam with distaste. 'Put it in the sink to soak.'

'But it's *toffee*,' wailed Jenny, sensing adult disapproval. 'We can *eat* it! There's a pound of sugar in it.'

'There's a pound of sugar,' agreed Miriam, 'but it's mostly over the stove. Cheer up, I'll make you some fudge instead. But where's Daddy?'

'He went to find Robin. He's in the garden somewhere. We'll show you.'

She followed their prancing figures into the dusky garden. Both children were dark-haired, like their father, but she could not believe that she and Lovell had ever been quite so thin.

Did Eileen feed them properly, or were they allowed to leave food if they were too impatient to eat it? Time would tell.

In any case, they were not lacking in energy. They hopped and skipped ahead of her, leaping over brambles and tussocks of grass that must once have been a lawn in more spacious days.

'She's come! Daddy, she's come!' screamed the little girls, and out from behind a hedge came Lovell holding his youngest in his arms.

'You dear girl!' he cried, depositing Robin at his feet. He put his arms round Miriam in a bear hug. They had never been demonstrative, and this welcoming embrace made all the irritations of the journey drop away. His face was cold, his hair rough, and smelling of all outdoors: a wintry, bruised-grass, autumn-bonfire smell, as different from the acrid scent of burning which had greeted her as sea-mist is from Midland fog.

In that instant, she was transported back to their shared childhood when together they climbed trees, or rolled, screaming with delight, down a grassy slope in

the vicarage garden. Sudden tears pricked her eyes, and Lovell, holding her now at arm's length, said, 'You look cold. Come inside.'

The two little girls bounced ahead, but Robin held up his arms to be carried. Miriam watched Lovell hoist him aloft again, and thought how like his mother the young boy looked. He had the same fair hair and blue eyes, the wide brow and pointed chin which gave Eileen her childlike air.

She held out a hand to him, but he turned away from her, burying his face in his father's neck.

'That's no way to welcome an aunt,' chided Lovell. 'Why, she's going to be the angel in the house, if only you knew it!'

'Wait and see!' laughed Miriam, following her brother indoors.

*

It seemed to Miriam, as she surveyed the sitting-room where most of the family activities went on, that a strong charwoman, rather than an angel, was needed in the place.

Toys littered the table, the chairs and the carpet. Copper, the ageing cocker spaniel, was curled up on the rumpled cover of the couch in front of the fire. A log had rolled off, and lay mouldering in the hearth, filling the room with pungent smoke. A glass vase, containing six dead chrysanthemums and an inch of dark green slime, decorated the mantelpiece, with a half-eaten banana beside it.

Lovell, dropping Robin beside the spaniel, caught sight of his sister's face, and laughed.

'Ghastly, isn't it? We had a sort of scratch lunch, and that banana is Robin's contribution.'

'Well,' said Miriam, trying to sound briskly cheerful, 'that can soon be put right. What's happened to Annie?'

Annie was a young girl from the village who came for a couple of hours or so in the late afternoon each day to help Eileen with the children's tea and bathtime.

'She's off over Christmas,' explained Lovell. 'The family has gone to Ely to stay with the grandmother, but she will be back on Monday, I hope.'

Miriam hoped so too. She bent to remove a grubby handkerchief from Robin's grasp. He was busy wiping Copper's nose, and the dog resented it. The child set up an ear-splitting wail, and the two little girls rushed to comfort him.

Miriam hastily returned the handkerchief, and the wailing ceased as though a siren had been switched off.

'Perhaps I'd better take up my case,' she said to Lovell, 'and then I will cook a meal for us all.'

'Goody-goody!' shouted Hazel.

'Gum-drops!' yelled Jenny. 'That's what we say: "Goody-goody-gum-drops!" Do you say that? Do you say: "Goody-goody-gum-drops!" when you're pleased? We do, don't we, Hazel? We *always* say: "Goody-goody—" '

'Not now you don't,' said Lovell firmly. 'Let Aunt Miriam have a few minutes' peace. Shall I take you up?'

'No, no,' replied Miriam hastily. 'I expect I'm in the usual room, aren't I?'

'I'll come with you,' said Jenny.

'No, let me!' said Hazel.

'*Only one!*' bellowed Lovell, above the din. 'You show Aunt Miriam to her room, Hazel, and then come down again. We'll set the table in the kitchen.'

Miriam deposited her basket of groceries on the kitchen dresser, averting her eyes from the appalling state of the cooker. Hazel was swinging on the newel post at the foot of the stairs, her dark hair flying behind her.

'Daddy's going to see Mummy this evening,' she announced, prancing up the stairs in front of Miriam. 'Can I go too?'

With a shock, Miriam realized that she had forgotten to ask after the mistress of the house in the turmoil of her arrival.

'We must ask Daddy,' said she diplomatically. 'The

hospital staff may not want too many visitors all at once.'

'But why not? I bet my mummy would like to see me, and I could tell her about the toffee we made, and having bread and peanut butter for lunch today.'

By now they had traversed the long passage over the hall and Hazel flung open the door of the spare room. The light switch failed to work.

Miriam set down her heavy case and groped her way to a bedside table where she remembered that a reading lamp stood. Mercifully, it worked. Obviously, the main light needed a new bulb. She must see about that later on.

The room was cold and musty, and it was apparent that neither of the twin beds was made up. Lumpy rectangles composed of folded blankets showed through the candlewick bedspreads. She must face that job as soon as the children were in bed, and put in a hot bottle if she were to escape pneumonia in this chilly Norfolk climate. She had a strong suspicion that this room had not been used since her last visit in the early summer.

'Shall I help you unpack?' enquired Hazel, eyeing the case hopefully.

'No. I'll do it later. You run downstairs and help Daddy. I'm just coming.'

She hung up her coat on a peg on the back of the door. There was no coat-hanger to be seen in the clothes cupboard. What a house, thought Miriam! A vision of her own neat domain floated before her, and she had to wrench her mind to other matters to overcome the sudden flood of depression which engulfed her.

The bathroom was next door, chillier even than her room. The bath was grimy. The wash basin was worse, and had what looked like a used medical plaster, recently stripped from someone's damaged finger, stuck to a cracked piece of soap. Miriam gingerly picked up this revolting amalgam and dropped it into an ancient enamel slop pail which seemed to do service as a wastepaper basket. Luckily, the bath rack provided her with a large tablet of Lifebuoy soap, and she was grateful for its disinfectant properties.

She unpacked a clean overall which she had prudently brought with her, and descended the stairs.

Lovell was slicing bread at the dresser, and Robin was sitting on the floor at his feet eating the crumbs that fell.

'Is it tea or supper?' asked Jenny.

Miriam looked at Lovell. 'As they had so light a lunch,' she said, 'what about my cooking eggs and bacon for you? And sausages if you like. Do they have a meal like that before bedtime?'

'Oh yes! Yes! We *always* have something like that, don't we?'

Their faces were rapturous. It was quite plain that they were hungry.

Lovell found her the frying pan, which was surprisingly clean, and she set about unpacking and cooking the provisions she had brought with her. Lovell, unasked, opened an enormous tin of baked beans and within twenty minutes Miriam's first meal was on the table.

There had been little culinary art in providing it and still less finesse in presenting it, straight from the pan to the waiting plates, but the children's evident relish as they demolished the meal gave her infinite satisfaction.

Now she found time to make amends and enquire after the patient.

'I'll know more when I've seen her this evening,' said Lovell. 'I'll help you to put this mob to bed and drive over to the hospital. You won't mind being left?'

'Of course not. I'll go tomorrow to see her.'

'At the moment she is under observation, I gather. She's on a pretty strict diet, and having tests. If that doesn't have any result, then they'll think of surgery.'

'What's surgery?' asked Hazel.

'It's cutting people up,' explained Jenny kindly. 'Like making chops at the butcher's.'

At this point, Robin turned his mug upside down on the tablecloth and watched the milk creep towards the edge.

'He always does that when he's finished,' said Jenny indulgently. 'Isn't he a funny boy?'

Miriam rose to fetch a dish cloth, and began to mop up the mess. Only Lovell's presence restrained her from giving a sharp reprimand to the drowsy Robin, who now leant back sucking his thumb.

The little girls watched her efforts with interest.

'We bathed Copper with that cloth this afternoon. He was smelly, so we *squeezed* it out in soapy water, and gave him a *lovely* wash.'

Miriam stopped her labours abruptly, and transferred the cloth to a battered tidy-bin beneath the sink. At this rate, she thought, a packet of 'J' cloths must take priority on tomorrow's shopping list.

'We'll wash up,' said Lovell, rising to his feet, 'and I think Robin's ready for bed if you could cope with him.'

At this, the comatose boy became instantly alert and shook his head violently.

'No! Dadda do! Dadda do!' he yelled, scarlet in the face.

'I think you'd better tonight,' said Miriam swiftly. 'He'll be more obliging when he knows me. We'll clear up here.'

The two males vanished, and Miriam and the girls set about making order out of chaos. There seemed to be a dearth of tea cloths and a decidedly vague idea of where they were kept.

'They just hang about,' said Hazel. 'On the back of that chair usually.'

'I mean the *clean* ones,' said Miriam, her voice sharp with exasperation.

'I think they're in this drawer,' said Jenny, struggling with an over-full dresser drawer stuffed with jam pot covers, pieces of string, two soup ladles and what looked like half a colander. A few pieces of tattered cloth were intermingled with debris and, after close inspection, proved to be extremely ancient tea cloths.

'Aren't you getting excited about Christmas?' enquired Jenny, patting a spoon with one of the tattered rags, as her contribution to wiping the cutlery. 'I am. I've asked Father Christmas for a painting set. Lots of different pots and brushes.'

'I hope you'll get them,' said Miriam civilly.

'Oh, she'll get them,' announced Hazel, in a meaningful way, 'but whether *Father Christmas* will bring them, I don't know.'

Jenny's face became suffused with angry colour.

'Of course he'll bring them! My letter to him went *straight* up the chimney! Yours fell back and got burnt up, and serve you right.'

'Now, now,' said Miriam warningly. Really, she thought, I sound just like my mother! How stupid 'Now, now!' sounded! Almost as idiotic as 'Now then', a phrase which could bring on partial madness if considered for too long.

It was quite apparent that Hazel was wise to the

myth of Santa Claus, whilst her sister was still touchingly a believer in the Christmas fairy. She must try and get a quiet word with the older child before too much damage was done.

Lovell reappeared as they were finishing. He looked exhausted and Miriam's heart was smitten.

'Go and sit by the fire, and I'll bring you some coffee,' she said. 'You don't need to set off immediately, do you?'

'Visiting hours are seven until eight-thirty,' he said. 'Goodness, it looks clean in here! I didn't bath Robin, just washed his face and hands. He's asleep already.'

Scandalized, the little girls spoke together.

'But Robin *always* has a bath!'

'Annie *always* does him all over! He needs a bath.'

'Mummy says we *must* have a bath before bed. Robin won't like it when he wakes up and finds he's all dirty still.'

'He won't wake up,' said their father shortly.

'We'll give him an extra long one tomorrow,' promised Miriam, setting the kettle to boil, 'as it's Christmas Eve!'

When Lovell had drunk his coffee and departed, carrying Miriam's bouquet and some magazines for Eileen, she took the girls up to the bathroom and bribed them into the steaming bath with one of her precious bath cubes.

'I'll come back in ten minutes to see if you are really clean,' she told them, and left them to their own devices while she unpacked her case.

Later, scrubbed and sweet-smelling in their flowered

night gowns, they held up their arms for a goodnight kiss, and Miriam admitted to herself that just now and again – for very brief periods – children could be very winning.

She descended the long staircase feeling a hundred years old. Fairacre and Holly Lodge seemed light years away. This reminded her that she had promised to ring Joan.

But not before she had revived herself with coffee, she told herself, making for the kitchen. Peremptory barking greeted her. Copper stood pointedly by his empty plate.

'Amazingly enough,' Miriam told him, 'I know where your supper is!'

She tipped out the remains of a tin of dog food she had noticed in the larder, and Copper wolfed it down with relish.

He accompanied her to the fireside when she sank into her armchair with the cup of coffee and attempted to climb on her lap.

'Some other time, Copper, old boy,' said Miriam faintly, fending him off. 'It's as much as I can do to support myself.'

She lay back and listened to the little domestic sounds of the old house. The fire whispered, a log shifted at its heart, the dog snored gently after his meal. Outside the wind stirred the trees, and somewhere a distant door banged as the breeze caught it.

Gradually, the peace that surrounded her took effect. It had been a long day, and tomorrow would be an even harder one. But meanwhile, the children slept as soundly as the dog on the rug at her feet, and the night enfolded the quiet house.

When Lovell returned, he found his sister fast asleep in the armchair.

CHAPTER SIX

Miss Quinn woke with a start, and sat bolt upright in bed.

Close at hand a church clock was striking midnight, and its pulsing rhythm filled the room.

Bewilderment and panic ebbed away, as she lay down again. Of course, she was safe in her brother Lovell's vicarage! This spare room, she remembered now, was close to the church tower.

It must be frosty tonight to be able to hear so clearly. Morning light would show rimy grass, no doubt, and ice-covered puddles, the little birds huddled patiently on sparkling twigs awaiting any bounty flung from the kitchen.

The last stroke died away, and the old house sank back into silence. Sleep enveloped Lovell and the three children whom she had come to look after, over Christmas, whilst their mother was in hospital.

Poor Eileen, she thought! Was she asleep too, or lying awake, as she was herself? She envisaged the shadowy ward, a night nurse sitting in the one small pool of light, alert for any sound from a restless patient. How much luckier she was, to be here alone and free from pain!

With a sudden shock, she realized that it was now Christmas Eve. There would be wild excitement from her two nieces in the next few hours. Robin would be too young to understand, though no doubt he would be infected by the general fever of anticipation. Did the children hang up stockings here, she wondered, or pillow cases, as she and Lovell had done, in just such a draughty vicarage years ago?

One Christmas in particular she recalled vividly in that old Cambridgeshire house. She must have been about the same age as young Jenny asleep next door. Her milk teeth were beginning to wobble, and one in the front, she remembered, had been tipped back and forth so often by her questing tongue that her mother had begged her to 'pull it out and have done with it'. But fear had held her back, and even Lovell's pleas to 'give it a good jerk' were in vain.

Lovell, two years older, was young Miriam's hero. He could climb to the top of their yew tree, while she stuck, trembling, half-way. He could make a whistle with his pen-knife and a hollow reed. He had bloodied Billy Boston's nose when he swore about their father, and he learnt geometry at the new day school in Cambridge.

Whatever Lovell did, Miriam tried to do. Whatever Lovell told her, she believed implicitly. Whatever Lovell said was right was so, and whatever Lovell found wrong was, of course, quite wrong.

That particular Christmas Miriam was much exercised in her mind. Ruby, her six-year-old friend at school, had stated categorically that there was no Father Christmas. Miriam was horrified at such an infamous statement.

'Of course there is! You get presents, don't you?'

Ruby, skipping busily at the time, was offhand.

'Your mum or dad puts 'em there,' she puffed, twirling the rope.

'I don't believe it,' said Miriam stoutly, but a cold hand seemed to clutch at her stomach. Could it be true? Could her father and mother have told her lies? Could Lovell?

Never, she told herself! Lovell always told her the truth. If there were no Father Christmases, Lovell would have said so. It was Ruby who told lies.

'You don't know what you're talking about,' she told the skipper robustly. 'I just *know* there's a Father Christmas, so there!'

'Better stay awake and find out,' shouted Ruby to Miriam who was walking away.

And maybe I will, thought Miriam, stubbornly, just to prove she's wrong.

In the few days left before Christmas she often asked her mother about this problem. But, as always, the vicarage was fast filling up with elderly relatives who were coming to spend Christmas with the family, and Mrs Quinn was busy with preparations.

Nevertheless, both parents replied kindly to Miriam's tentative enquiries about the authenticity of Father Christmas, but were vague and preoccupied. On the whole though, she felt slightly reassured.

Among the Christmas guests was a recently-widowed young aunt with her four-year-old son, Sidney. The child was delicate, and made even more so by his mother's molly-coddling.

'Naturally she fusses over him,' Miriam heard her mother say to one of the elderly second cousins. 'He's all she has now, and he is a dear little boy.'

Lovell and Miriam did not think so. They thought him spoilt, a cry-baby and a tale-teller. The fact that the poor child lisped, only made him more ridiculous in their eyes. With childish heartlessness they teased the little boy, without mercy, whenever they had him alone.

It so happened that this particular Christmas Eve brought snow to bleak East Anglia, and the three children were wrapped up warmly and sent to play, with injunctions to make a snowman. Lovell and Miriam, strong and boisterous, threw themselves into the task joyfully, but Sidney, half-afraid of the bigger children and disliking the cold, did little.

'Come on, Thid,' shouted Lovell, 'lend a hand!'

'Thid, Thid, Thilly-Thid-Thid!' mocked Miriam, following Lovell's lead as usual.

The child shook his head unhappily, near to tears.

Irritated by his apathy, the two young savages began to chase him round and round the half-built snowman. Within two minutes the little boy was sobbing, and struggling to escape from his tormentors. They pursued him ruthlessly, until at last he fell wailing into the snowman and the bigger children, incensed at the damage, rolled the child back and forth in the snow.

'Now look what you've done!'

'All our work spoilt! We'll pay you out for this!'

They began stuffing snow down the neck of the child's jersey, giggling now, but still enjoying the feeling of power over this weakling.

Sidney's cries attracted his mother. The three children were driven into the kitchen and the young Quinns were accused by Sidney's hysterical mother of gross cruelty. Mrs Quinn banished her two to their bedrooms for an hour, after apologies all round, and Miriam spent the time wobbling the front tooth and thinking about the existence, or otherwise, of Father Christmas.

Called down to tea after their penance, Miriam spoke urgently to Lovell as they went into the dining-room.

'Ruby Adair at school said there wasn't a Father Christmas. Is it true?'

An extraordinary look came over Lovell's face. It was as though Miriam had hit him. He stuttered when he replied, a thing he only did when very upset.

'You don't want to believe everything Ruby says,' he managed to say. 'I've never told you that, have I?'

The tension, which had screwed Miriam's inside into a painful knot, lessened at once, and the feeling of relief carried her through the hours until bedtime. She even managed to speak kindly to the loathsome Sidney who insisted on sitting close to his mother.

Bedtime came. The three children prepared the traditional snack for Father Christmas, a mince pie from each one, and a glass of orange squash which Sidney chose as the best drink available.

Miriam watched Lovell closely as they placed the food in the hearth. His face was solemn, and he was being uncommonly gentle with young Sidney. He would not take such trouble, thought Miriam with relief, if he did not truly expect Father Christmas to arrive.

The children went to bed. Over each bed rail hung an empty pillow case. Miriam looked at hers as she lay awake. If, as silly Ruby said, one's parents filled it, then she would be bound to hear them.

Despite her intention to stay alert, she was asleep in ten minutes. The sound of the door opening woke her, hours later.

'All right?' she heard her mother whisper.

Her father answered: 'Fast asleep!'

Cold with horror, she lay motionless.

She saw the empty pillow case twitched from the bed rail, and felt the bump of a full one as it was lodged at the foot of the bed. So *that* was how it was done!

The door closed noiselessly. She lay there, numbed with shock. A painful lump swelled in her throat, and hot tears began to trickle. Ruby was right.

To think that all this time her parents had lied! And

Lovell too! It was cruel. All these years she had loved Father Christmas, and now it was spoilt.

She crept from her bed, and squatting on the floor, she felt the various shapes in the pillow case. There was the doll she had asked for, and this box must be the tea-set or a jigsaw puzzle. She could smell the fragrance of the tangerine tucked in a corner, and could hear the rattle of the nuts in the other.

Tears continued to course down her cheeks. She would not unpack things until morning light. And would she enjoy them then, she wondered, knowing that Lovell had betrayed her? Would things ever be the same again?

Her feet were cold as stones, and she clambered back into bed. As she did so, her restless tongue finally broke the loose tooth from its precarious moorings. Still weeping, she felt the edge of the new tooth thrusting through. She pulled the clothes about her, and fell into an uneasy sleep.

Leaden-eyed and leaden-hearted next morning, she did her best to share in the general excitement.

At the breakfast table she thanked all her relatives for their gifts. She could hardly bear to look at Lovell, so happy and unconcerned.

Sidney was flushed with joy and excitement.

'All gone!' he said, showing her Father Christmas's empty plate. 'Did you thee him?'

He pressed against Miriam anxiously.

'Did you thee him?' he persisted.

Conscious of the eyes of all upon her, her heart raging with bitterness, Miriam took a deep breath. She turned her blazing gaze upon the traitor Lovell.

'No, I *didn't*,' she burst forth. 'I *didn't* see Father Christmas, Sidney. But I'll tell you what I *did* see!'

The child looked up at her, smiling and trusting.

Lovell's gaze was steady. Across the breakfast table, brother and sister were locked in a look.

Very slowly Lovell shook his head. Briefly, and with a wealth of meaning, he glanced at Sidney, and then looked back at Miriam. It was a conspiratorial look, and it filled Miriam's quivering body with warmth and comfort. Now, in a flash, she understood. Suddenly, she was grown up. Hadn't she felt the first of her adult teeth this very morning?

A little child, as she had been until now, had the right to believe in this magic. She felt suddenly protective towards the young boy beside her. She, and Lovell, and all the other people present, knew, and faced the responsibilities of knowing, this precious secret. Now, she too was one of the elect.

'What did you thee?' asked Sidney.

'I saw the door closing,' said Miriam. 'That's all.'

Across the table, Lovell smiled at her with approval. Her heart leapt, and Christmas Day became again the joyful festival she had always known.

How sharply it came back, thought Miss Quinn, that memory of thirty years ago! The shock of her enlightenment was some measure of the joy she had formerly felt in the myth of Father Christmas. She was glad that Jenny and Robin were still ardent believers, and she must try and make sure that Hazel, on the brink of knowledge, did not suffer as she had done as a child, and did not tarnish the glitter for the younger ones.

Somewhere, in some distant copse, a fox gave an eerie cry.

The scudding clouds parted briefly, and a shaft of moonlight fell across the bed.

The night was made for sleeping, said Miriam to herself, and tomorrow there was much to be done. There were children to be tended, Eileen to visit, provisions to organize, and all to be accomplished amidst the joyous frenzy of Christmas Eve.

Resolutely, she applied herself to sleep.

CHAPTER SEVEN

She awoke, much refreshed, still with the memories of past Christmas times about her, and determined to make the present one happy for the children.

It was still dark, but she could hear children's voices. Perhaps they were already up? She put her warm feet upon the chilly linoleum and went to the door. The house felt icy.

Sure enough, the two little girls were scampering about the long passage half-dressed. They greeted her with cries of joy, and bounced into her room unbidden. Wails from Robin could be heard in the distance.

'Oh, he's all right,' said Hazel casually. 'Daddy's put him on his potty, and he doesn't want to go. That's all.'

Jenny was fingering Miriam's hair brush.

'I've asked Father Christmas for one like this,' she said.

Hazel's lip began to curl in a derisory manner, and Miriam, recalling her night-time memory, put a hand on her arm. There was no mistaking the alert glance that the child flashed at her. She knew all right!

Remembering Lovell's meaningful shake of the head so long ago, she repeated the small gesture to his daughter. The child half-smiled in return, squeezed the restraining hand upon her arm, and remained silent.

That, thought Miriam, thankfully, was one hurdle surmounted!

'What do you have for breakfast?' she enquired, tactfully changing the subject.

'Cornflakes, or shredded wheat,' said Hazel.

'Sometimes toast, if there's time,' said Jenny.

'What does Daddy have?' asked Miriam, secretly thinking that Eileen should surely cook a breakfast, if not for the children, then for a man off to his parish duties in the coldest part of England.

'The same,' they chorused.

'Go and get dressed,' said Miriam, 'and I'll make toast for us all, and perhaps a boiled egg.'

'Oh, lovely!' squealed the children. 'Let's go and tell Robin!'

They fled, leaving Miriam to have the bathroom in peace.

At breakfast, Miriam broached the practical problem of catering for the household for four days. The basic things seemed to be in the house, and she knew that there were Brussels sprouts, cabbages and carrots in the vegetable garden.

A Christmas pudding stood on the pantry shelf, but she would have to make mince pies and other sweets and where was the turkey – or was it to be a round of beef?

Lovell was vague. He rather thought a friend of theirs was supplying the turkey, but he would have imagined it would have been delivered by now.

'Will it be dressed?' asked Miriam, with considerable anxiety. She might be Sir Barnabas's right hand, but she knew her limits. Drawing a fowl was not among her talents.

'Dressed?' queried Hazel, egg-spoon arrested half-way to her mouth. 'What in?'

Gales of giggles greeted this sally.

'A bonnet,' gasped Jenny, 'and shawl! Like Jemima Puddleduck. That's what turkeys dress in!'

The two little girls rolled about in paroxysms of mirth. Lovell cast his eyes heavenward, in mock disdain.

'Dressed means ready to put in the oven,' explained Miriam, laughing.

'I know a boy at school who can pull out the tubes and smelly bits,' said Hazel, recovering slightly. 'Is that what you mean?'

'Exactly,' said Miriam.

At that moment the telephone rang, and Lovell vanished.

'It might still have its feathers on,' remarked Jenny.

'And it's head,' added Hazel.

Miriam's qualms intensified.

'How do you get its head off?' enquired Jenny conversationally, scraping the last of her egg from the shell.

Miriam was spared replying as Lovell returned.

'The chairman of Eileen's bench. Just enquiring.'

Eileen, she remembered now, had recently been made a magistrate. Frankly she wondered if she were capable of the task, but simply said politely: 'Does she worry much about her duties?'

'What she really worries about,' replied Lovell, 'is whether she should wear a hat or not.'

Then, sensing that this might smack of disloyalty, he enlarged on the many compliments he had heard from her fellows on the bench, on Eileen's good sense and fair-mindedness.

His discourse was cut short by a ring at the back door. Hazel skipped off to answer it and came back, much excited.

'It's the turkey man, Aunt Miriam, and it's all right! He's bare!'

Construing this correctly, Miriam felt a wave of relief, and hurried to fetch the bird, Lovell following close behind to pay the bill.

A little later, she sallied forth with several baskets, and the three children in tow. Lovell had to conduct a funeral service and visit two desperately sick parishioners. He would be back to late lunch, and then stay at the vicarage while Miriam visited the hospital.

'Can you possibly get back by about four, do you think?' he enquired, consulting a list anxiously. 'I'm supposed to call at the village hall to have tea with the Over-Sixty Club, and be at a Brownies' Carol Service in the next parish at the same time. Then I must have a word with the flower ladies, and get ready for the midnight service.'

Miriam assured him that she could manage easily.

'Can we come and see Mummy?'

'Yes, can we?' clamoured the girls. Miriam looked at Lovell.

'Sister made no objection last time, as long as they behave, of course, and aren't there too long. But how do you feel?'

'I'd like their company,' said Miriam, and they fell upon her with shrieks of joy.

The grocer's shop was one of three in the village. Across the road was the butcher's, and next door was the Post Office which sold sweets and tobacco.

The proprietor of the village stores bore a strong resemblance to Mrs Pringle of Fairacre. She had the same square frame, the identical short cropped hair and an expression of malevolent resignation.

Fortunately, the similarity ended there, and she turned out to be unusually helpful about the needs of the vicarage household.

'Did you want the piece of gammon Mrs Quinn asked about? I've put it by, in case.'

'Yes, please,' said Miriam. At least it would make a change from turkey in the days to come.

'And you'll want potatoes,' Mrs Bates informed her. 'That half-hundred-weight was nearly finished last week, Annie told me.'

Miriam, slightly dazed, remembered that Eileen's mother's help was a local girl.

'I'm her auntie,' vouchsafed Mrs Bates, scrabbling in a box of potatoes hidden behind the counter. Fair-acre all over again, thought Miriam!

'Take five pounds now, and my Bert'll bring up ten pounds later if that suits you. You don't want to hump all that lot, and Robin's push-chair's not that strong.'

Miriam agreed meekly. It was quite a change to be managed. Was this how Barney felt when she mapped out his routine?

With a shock she remembered there had been no preparations made for lunch at home. For the first time

in her life, she bought fish fingers, and a ready made blackcurrant tart. How often she had watched scornfully the feckless mothers buying expensive 'convenience' foods. Now, with three children distracting her, and the clock ticking on inexorably, she sympathized with them. Catering for one, she began to realize, was quite a different matter from trying to please the varying tastes of five people, and hungry ones at that.

'Where's Robin?' she enquired suddenly. The child had vanished.

Hazel and Jenny were talking to a boy in the doorway.

'Probably in the road,' said Mrs Bates. 'And the traffic's something awful this morning.'

There was a hint of mournful satisfaction in this

remark that reminded Miriam yet again of the distant Mrs Pringle.

She rushed to the door, heart thudding, calling his name. The road was clear, except for a scrawny dog carrying a large bone.

'It's all right!' shouted Mrs Bates behind her. 'He's here.'

The child was sitting on the floor, hidden behind the end of the counter, beside a rolled-down sack containing dog biscuits which he was eating with the voracity of one just released from a concentration camp.

'Robin, *really*!' exclaimed his aunt. Like Tabitha Twitchit, she thought suddenly, I am affronted.

'Don't worry, miss. He's partial to dog biscuits. And these are extra pure,' she added virtuously.

'You must let me pay you,' said Miriam, hauling the child to his feet and brushing yellow sulphur biscuit crumbs from his coat.

'Oh, he's welcome,' said Mrs Bates indulgently. 'I'll just add up the other.'

By the time she had visited the butcher, to buy steak and kidney for a casserole for the evening meal, and then the Post Office for stamps and sweets, Miriam seemed to have accumulated three heavy baskets.

The wind was now boisterous, and carrying rain bordering on sleet. The children did not seem to notice the cold, but Miriam, struggling with the erratic push-chair and the shopping, felt frozen through.

Ah! Dear Holly Lodge, she thought with longing! Tucked into the shelter of the downs, screened by that stout hedge, when would she see it again?

*

'What a lovely, lovely lunch,' sighed Jenny, leaning back replete.

'Excellent!' agreed her father.

Miriam was secretly amused. If her friends could have seen the meal she had assembled, fish fingers, instant potatoes, tinned beans and bottled tomato sauce, followed by the bought fruit pie, her standing as a first-class cook would have taken a jolt.

And yet it had been relished. Perhaps there was a moral here, but there was certainly no time to pursue the thought, with the washing-up to be done, the girls to get ready, and Robin to be put down for his afternoon nap. She must put the steak and kidney in a slow oven too, so that it would cook gently while they were at the hospital. How on earth did mothers manage? She was more exhausted now, at midday, than she was at the end of a hard week at the office.

At half past two she set out, with the girls in a state of wild excitement in the back of the car. They were carrying their Christmas presents for Eileen, and keeping an eye on Miriam's. Tomorrow Lovell would be the only visitor at the hospital, while Miriam took charge at home.

Eileen looked prettier and younger than ever, propped against her pillows in a frilly pale blue nightgown. It so happened that Miriam's present was also a nightgown, but a black chiffon one threaded with narrow black satin ribbon. It would make a splendid contrast, she thought, to the one she was now wearing.

Eileen greeted them all with hugs and kisses.

'You are a perfect angel to come to our rescue,' she

said when the little girls had been settled, in comparative peace, with some magazines. 'Have you had a terrible time coping?'

Miriam reassured her.

'I think all the shopping's done. No doubt I've forgotten something quite vital like bread, but I've remembered stuffing for the bird and even salted peanuts in case people come in for drinks.'

'That's more than I should have done,' said Eileen cheerfully, and Miriam began to feel more drawn to her sister-in-law than ever before. There was something engaging about such candour.

'Is that lady dying?' asked Jenny, in a high carrying voice, her finger pointing to a grey-faced woman dozing in the next bed. Miriam went cold with shock.

Eileen laughed merrily.

'Good heavens, no! Mrs White is getting better faster than any of us. Be very quiet, darling, so that she doesn't wake up.'

At this point, Sister arrived, and asked Eileen if the children would like to see the Christmas tree in the children's ward. They departed happily.

'By the way,' said Miriam, 'did you know that Hazel has tumbled to Father Christmas?'

'Yes. I hope she won't tell Jenny yet.'

Miriam explained what had happened.

'Always problems,' said Eileen. 'And with some you will be wrong whatever you do. I thought this when Lovell and I were invited out together, the other evening. He was suddenly taken ill. Of course I rang our hostess, and she said; "Will you feel like coming?" What do you do? Say "Yes" and be branded as callous to one's husband's sufferings, and probably greedy to boot, or say "No" and let down the hostess?'

'Insoluble,' agreed Miriam. 'Or, worse still, wondering whether to pull the lavatory chain, in the dead of night, in someone else's house. If you do, you can imagine the startled hostess saying: "You'd think she would have more sense than to rouse the whole household!" On the other hand, one is liable to be branded a perfect slut if the hostess visits the loo first in the morning!'

They laughed together, and Miriam, for the first time, felt completely at ease in Eileen's presence.

'But tell me about yourself,' she said. 'Are they getting things right?'

'I think so. They couldn't be kinder, and once the results of the tests are through I may be able to come home. Strict diet, and all that, and weekly check-ups, but I've a strong suspicion it won't come to surgery.'

'Thank God for that!' said Miriam.

'You must be longing to get back to Fairacre,' said Eileen. 'The vicarage is such a barn of a place. But Lovell is terribly grateful to you for coming up so quickly, and so am I, as you know. We should have foundered without you. Ah, here comes Sister.'

The children had been given a chocolate toy from the tree, and were starry-eyed with pleasure.

'Shall I unwrap your presents while you're here?' asked Eileen.

'Yes, yes. Do it now!' they clamoured.

With great care, she undid the wrappings, read the lop-sided cards covered in kiss-crosses, and finally displayed a canvas book mark embroidered in lazy-daisy-stitch by Hazel, and a thimble in a walnut-shell case from Jenny.

'Perfect!' smiled Eileen, putting the thimble on her finger, and the bookmark in the novel by her bed. 'Now Christmas has really begun!'

Miriam looked at her watch.

'I must take them back. Lovell has to be off again by four. He'll be in tomorrow, and I'll come again after that.'

'Dear Miriam,' murmured Eileen, as they kissed. 'No wonder Lovell adores you. You are an absolute tower of strength.'

Miriam called into Sister's room, as they went out, to thank her for the children's presents, and to enquire after Eileen's progress.

'She's doing very well. We couldn't have a better patient, and a real help to the others in the ward.'

'She says you are all very good to her.'

'That's nothing to Mr Quinn's kindness to my old

mother,' said Sister, with energy. 'You don't forget help like that when you're in trouble. He lives by his beliefs, that brother of yours.'

'He tries to, I know,' replied Miriam, much moved.

'Come on, Aunt Miriam, we've got to get our things ready for Father Christmas,' urged the girls.

'First things first,' called Sister, as they left the hospital.

The wind had become a vicious howling gale by the time they reached home. The sleet slanted across the headlights, and a wicked draught blew from the east under the vicarage doors. Water was blowing out to the landing, from a window which took the brunt of the weather, and Miriam searched for something to staunch the flow.

'Mummy just leaves it,' said Jenny, faintly surprised at so much fuss over some intruding rain. 'It always dries up after a bit.'

Exhausted as she was, Miriam began to sympathize with this *laissez-faire* attitude, although it was against all her principles. She rammed a shabby towel against the crack, and hoped for the best.

Lovell had departed into the waste of wind and water, and Robin's bathtime arrived. Hazel and Jenny accompanied her to the bathroom, anxious to help and to explain to the boy the importance of hanging up his stocking.

Less hostile than the previous evening, nevertheless the child still resented Miriam's attention.

'Dadda do!' he muttered sulkily. 'Go away!'

'You're a bad boy,' scolded Hazel, 'to say that to

Aunt Miriam when she's come all this way to look after you!'

Robin responded by blowing a mouthful of soapy water over his sister. Most of it went on Miriam's skirt.

Jenny improved the shining hour by telling the child about Father Christmas.

'And he'll creep in to your room, in a red coat,' she began, but was interrupted by a fearful screeching from her brother.

'No want! No want!' he screamed, shaking his head violently.

Jenny looked resignedly at Miriam who was doing her best to soap his thrashing legs.

'You know, he's frightened, that's what! He's just *frightened* of Father Christmas. What'll we do?'

Hazel came to the rescue.

'Put his stocking on the banisters, then he'll be all right, won't he?'

She looked at Miriam with a conspiratorial glance.

'Good idea,' she said hastily, praying that the secret would still be kept.

She hauled the boy out of the water, amidst more shricking, and muffled his cries in a warm towel. The bathroom, steamy and damp, was the warmest place in the house, and she was loath to leave it to put the child into his cot in the chilly bedroom. What this place needs, she told herself, and will never get, is a thoroughly efficient central-heating system.

The two little girls had climbed into the bath together, lured into an early bedtime by the promise of supper by the fire downstairs, and the happy prospect of hanging up stockings.

Miriam left them there while she warmed their milk in the kitchen. Outside, the rain lashed at the window, and the branches of the apple tree creaked and groaned. A particularly fierce draught under the larder door made a noise like a banshee wailing. This was Norfolk at its worst, thought Miriam, but at least the stove was warm, and the comforting smell of the steak casserole counteracted the bleakness outside.

The sitting-room was snug with the curtains drawn and the fire blazing. The two little girls nursed their bowls of cornflakes liberally topped with brown sugar and raisins, and asked Miriam to tell them about Christmas when she was small.

'Well,' began Miriam, 'we used to hang up pillow cases, your daddy and I.'

'So do we. And stockings.'

'And we left a mince-pie and some milk for Father Christmas, in the hearth.'

'So do we,' they chorused.

'And after he'd been,' said Miriam, looking squarely at Hazel, whose face remained rapt, 'we took our pillow cases into grandma and grandpa's bed and undid all our parcels.'

'And what did you have?'

Miriam suddenly remembered the agonizing night when she felt her parcels as the tears rolled down her cheeks. She could taste them now, salty and bitter, and feel the lump in her aching throat.

'Are you all right?' asked Hazel.

'Yes, just thinking,' said Miriam. 'Oh, a doll, and a tea set with little flowers on it, and, of course, a tangerine and nuts and sweets. Lots of lovely things.' And heartbreak, she added silently. God, that heartbreak! Nothing in her adult life had ever hurt quite so piercingly.

'Can we bring our things into your bedroom?' asked Jenny, spooning up the last drop.

'Of course you can!' cried Miriam. 'On Christmas Day you can do anything you like! Within reason,' she added prudently.

They skipped upstairs before her, and accompanied her to the linen cupboard for two pillowcases. A pair of Eileen's stockings already hung over their bed rail.

'Do you think they'll be full?' asked Jenny.

'Positively brimming over,' Miriam promised her, tucking them in, and praying that sleep would soon engulf them.

Later that evening, she and Lovell drowsed before the fire, before he went over to the church for his late service. In her lap billowed the great black mass of Lovell's cassock.

'Must have caught my heel in the hem,' he said apologetically, as he handed it over. 'Do you mind?'

She now stitched languidly, thinking yet again how many varied tasks fell to the lot of a married woman.

'I wish I could have found someone else to do it – and to help you in the house,' said Lovell. 'But everyone's so busy at Christmas time. Looking back, I realize how lucky we were at home to have dear old Euphrosyne and her like, coping in the kitchen. It meant Mother had the energy needed to cope with parish affairs.'

'From what I hear,' said Miriam, snipping black cotton, 'Eileen does very well.'

'She has to do far too much,' sighed Lovell. 'How did she look today?'

'Ravishing as ever,' said Miriam, and told him about her visit, and Sister's kindness, and her remark about his own.

Lovell looked surprised.

'Really? I did nothing you know. Just called now and again.'

'And she also said that Eileen was a marvellous patient and a great help in the ward.'

His face softened.

'She's the bravest person I know. She's been so sweet with that poor woman in the next bed. A terminal case, they call it. She wasn't expected to live through the night.'

Miriam remembered her niece's query, her own horror, and Eileen's courageous laughter. There was certainly more to this sister-in-law of hers than she had ever imagined.

'Well, there you are,' she said, shaking out the cassock. 'I shall wait up for you, and we'll have the fun of filling the pillowcases together.'

'You shouldn't. You look whacked, so don't stay up just for me.'

He shrugged into the cassock, threw his coat over his shoulders and made for the door.

'I shall be back soon after one, I expect,' he shouted above the wind, waved, and was gone.

Miriam was about to return to the fireside when she

remembered that she had intended to stuff the turkey and prepare some of the vegetables for the morrow.

Should she go into the kitchen and tackle these chores? Or should she give way to temptation and collapse into the armchair?

Bravely, she made her way towards the larder, followed by Copper, ever-anxious for a meal.

'And to think,' she told the dog, 'that I'm known as a working woman. I wonder what Eileen is?'

CHAPTER EIGHT

The day began, in pitch darkness, at five-thirty. Miriam's door opened, and Hazel and Jenny entered dragging their spoils behind them.

'You said we could come,' beamed Hazel.

'And you said we could do anything we liked on Christmas Day, so here we are!'

Miriam sat up and switched on the bedside lamp. Her head was heavy with sleep, her eyes felt as though they were full of biscuit crumbs. But this was Christmas morning, and although it had come far too soon for comfort, Christian feelings must predominate.

'Happy Christmas, darlings,' she said, between yawns. 'Switch on the electric fire, Hazel, and both come into bed. You must be frozen.'

They joyously flung their laden pillow cases on to their aunt's stomach, partially winding her. Their bare feet were like four ice-blocks pressed against her own warm legs. Their hands, diving for their treasures were mottled with the cold.

'Where's Robin?' asked Miriam.

'Still asleep. So's Daddy. Shall we go and fetch them?'

'No, no. They'll come along later. Let's see all these gorgeous things.'

She duly admired books, jigsaw puzzles, and a complicated board game which she feared would be beyond her when the time came for it to be played.

There were recorders, played with more enthusiasm than harmony, dolls and their clothes – remarkably sophisticated to Miriam's eye. No doll of hers ever had ski clothes, bathing dresses, or evening cloaks. These beauties even had handbags to match their different outfits. The girls were enchanted.

Miriam had given Hazel a toy sewing machine, and Jenny a little cooking stove. She was relieved to see how ecstatically these were received, and promised to help them when they started to use them.

'I shall make tiny, tiny, dear little chips and fry them in this frying pan,' cried Jenny. 'You can have some for supper.'

Miriam lay back on her pillow and watched them affectionately. Everything enchanted them, even the two plain aprons sent by a distant great-aunt. It was good to see such unspoilt children. Lovell and Eileen had done a good job with these two, thought their aunt proudly.

She looked about the room, which was now beginning to get warm. The children had hung a red paper bell over the door, when they had decorated the house with all the Christmas paper chains, folding fans and other ornaments earlier in the week. It really looked rather pretty, thought Miriam, remembering how she and Lovell had always adored unfolding these showy decorations as children to deck the old Fenland vicarage. What would these children think of her own bare quarters at Holly Lodge if they could see them?

But something indefinable was missing. Was it the smell of tangerines?

Before she could pin it down, Lovell came in carrying Robin with his stocking.

'Merry Christmas!' they all shouted.

'It's marvellously warm in here,' said Lovell. 'Reminds me of Christmas morning at home when we used to have the Valor Perfection stove alight in the bedroom.'

'That's it!' cried Miriam. 'I've been missing the smell of paraffin!'

'And a good thing too, I should think,' said Lovell, helping his youngest to unwrap a furry panda.

'But it was heavenly in the dark,' remembered Miriam, 'making lovely patterns on the ceiling.'

'And lovely smuts when it smoked,' added Lovell.

The little girls were busily opening their brother's presents and urging him to admire them. Robin appeared to be as sleepy as Miriam felt herself, and greeted each discovery with a marked lack of enthusiasm.

'What we need,' said Miriam, when the last parcel was undone, and the bedroom floor was awash with Christmas wrappings, 'is an early breakfast. And then you can play with your new toys before we go to church.'

Lovell had a service at eight, and Miriam proposed to take the children to the eleven o'clock service, bringing them out before the sermon.

'But you can't leave the *turkey*,' protested Hazel, as though it were an invalid aunt in need of constant care.

'I can, you know,' said Miriam. 'You'll see.'

'I could cook something on my stove,' said Jenny. 'Peas, say.'

'There'd only be a mouthful,' said Hazel.

'I could *keep on* cooking peas,' replied Jenny snappily. 'Then there'd be enough. Fish shops *keep on* cooking, don't they, Aunt Miriam? Everyone has enough.'

By mid-morning tempers were beginning to fray. After such an early awakening, and now that the toys had been inspected, the children started to quarrel.

It was the first time that Miriam had seen the two sisters at war, and she was staggered at the ferocity of the battle. She was at a loss too, to know how best to quell this uprising.

Robin, more animated than he had yet appeared, looked on the scene with approval, clapping his hands as Jenny clutched her sister's long hair and attempted to haul it from her scalp.

Hazel retaliated with a resounding smack on

Jenny's cheek. Screams rent the air, and Miriam rushed to part them. This was something entirely new to her. Once, she remembered, she had been called to a couple in the typing room at the office who had reduced each other to tears over some business about a boyfriend. That had been bad enough, but this was real commando stuff.

A sharp scratch from Hazel's finger nail caused her such sudden pain that involuntarily she smacked the child's arm, and Jenny's too. The manoeuvre worked like a charm, both fell apart, open mouthed with astonishment.

'Mummy *never*, *never* hits us!' exclaimed Hazel, much shocked.

'Nor Daddy,' cried Jenny, coming to her late enemy's support.

The words: 'More fool them,' hovered on Miriam's lips, but she forbore to utter them. She was still suffering from pain, shock and some shame at the violence of her reaction.

'You can go upstairs, and get ready for church,' she said instead. 'And no more nonsense!'

They went out quietly, but before they had reached the stairs Miriam heard them giggling together, all conflict over.

An ominous pattering noise, attracted her attention. Robin was inspecting a growing puddle on the kitchen floor.

'Good boy!' he said approvingly. 'Good boy, Robin.'

Sighing, Miriam went in search of a bucket and floor cloth.

*

An hour later, she and her charges sat decorously in church awaiting Lovell's entrance.

The building was plain, with only a few mural tablets bearing testimony to the virtues of the deceased and the grief of those mourning them. A threadbare banner hung from one wall, a reminder of the gallantry of an East Anglian regiment and

Old unhappy far-off things
And battles long ago.

The church was half full, which Miriam rightly construed as a good congregation. She had attended a service here with only three other worshippers, on one occasion.

The organ swelled into a recognizable tune, and the congregation rose as the choir entered, followed by Lovell.

'That's my Daddy!' cried Robin joyously, much to the delight of nearby worshippers. Jenny and Hazel shook their heads with disapproval, but were obviously secretly proud of their brother's intelligence.

The service began, but its measured beauty failed to hold Miriam's attention, distracted as she was by having to find the place for the two little girls, and by restraining Robin who was busy licking the varnished pew shelf, as though it were made of butterscotch, which it somewhat resembled.

This activity was accompanied by loud smacking noises and an appreciative growling such as puppies make when enjoying a bone. Miriam's efforts to divert him were met with vociferous resistance, and a renewed

attack upon the woodwork. A particularly solemn silence, at the end of one of the prayers, was broken by a crunching sound. Robin, raising his head to admire his toothwork, turned, dribbling heavily, to Miriam, and patted the wet shelf encouragingly.

'Auntie bite!' he demanded. 'Auntie bite too!'

'No!' hissed Miriam fiercely. Really, to think that a two-year-old could cause so much embarrassment! She was conscious of considerable merriment in the pews behind her. Should she take the child out, she wondered?

Luckily, at this juncture they all stood for the hymn preceding the sermon.

'Do we put our money in now?' enquired Hazel loudly. 'Because I've lost mine.'

Jenny, with sisterly concern, fell to the floor and began searching busily along a very dusty heating pipe.

'P'raps it's rolled under the seat,' she suggested, pointing with a black hand. Hazel bent down, as though about to join her in the depths.

'Leave it,' begged Miriam helplessly. 'I will give you some more.'

'But we *can't* just leave it!' protested Jenny. By now her face was striped with grime. She looked like a very cross tiger cub.

'It's not now anyway,' responded Jenny. 'It's the next hymn we put the money in. Daddy does his talking, and then we put it in, don't we, Aunt Miriam?'

'Well, we won't be here then,' argued Hazel, 'so what shall we do with our money? Aunt Miriam, we don't want any collection money, so can we keep it?'

Powerless to check this flow of conversation, Miriam saw, with infinite relief, that Lovell was ascending the stairs to the pulpit. This was her cue to remove his lively offspring.

She began to usher the children into the aisle. Fortunately, she had purposely taken a pew near to the door. Robin resisted strongly, and appealed to the distant figure in the pulpit.

'Dadda!' he screamed lustily. 'Dadda do! Dadda do!'

The two little girls contented themselves with waving cheerfully as they made for the door, but Robin sat suddenly in the aisle and refused to budge.

An elderly sidesman, seeing Miriam's dilemma, advanced and picked up the boy, who made himself as stiff as a board, whilst keeping up a barrage of ear-splitting yells.

He was borne towards the door, Miriam following. She gave one apologetic backward glance towards Lovell. His dark face was impassive, but there was a gleam in his eye which told her clearly of his enjoyment of the scene.

'Like a sweet?' said the sidesman to Robin, when they gained the porch. The screams stopped abruptly.

He deposited the boy on the gravel path outside and felt in his waistcoat pocket. Hazel and Jenny watched with attention.

He produced three small fruit drops each wrapped in cellophane, and handed them down.

'Always as well to have sweets on you when there are children around,' he said kindly to Miriam, and departed before she had time to thank him properly.

It was wonderful to be out in the air again. The wind was still strong, but the rain had gone, and now the scudding clouds parted, and the sun lit up the wide Norfolk fields around the flint church.

'I *love* Christmas,' said Jenny, cheek bulging. 'Do you?'

Miriam looked at the three children, so quickly transformed into angels.

'Yes,' she said. 'I do.'

The turkey which had been left to its own devices in the oven, much to the concern of the two little girls, had assumed a luscious golden brown when Miriam returned to baste it.

She put on the vegetables and topped up the water in the steamer holding the Christmas pudding before going to set the table.

She had ransacked the airing cupboard and at last had found a large white damask cloth, old and beautifully starched, with several darns executed, she guessed, by a long-dead hand. No one these days, surely, could be bothered to do such fine work.

Spread upon the dining-room table and decorated with two candlesticks borrowed from the mantelpiece, it began to look more like a festive board, although Miriam cursed herself for forgetting to buy crackers, those instant decorations. As it was, there was no time to search for flowers or ribbons, but she filched a few holly sprigs from above the pictures where the children had put them, and set them round the candlesticks.

'It's *marvellous*!' cried Hazel.

'Can we put some pretty things on too?' queried Jenny.

'Yes, do,' said Miriam, rushing to the kitchen to attend to an ominous hissing noise.

When she returned, she found that Hazel had added a small sleigh holding Father Christmas and bath cubes, an inspired present from an aunt in America, whilst Jenny had purloined the fairy from the top of the Christmas tree to add to the scene.

Robin's contribution was a toy camel with three lead legs and one of plasticine. It added an exotic touch as it leant, in a drunken fashion, against a candlestick.

Lovell admired everything warmly when he returned from church, and the meal was as cheerful as he and Miriam could make it for the children.

Afterwards, the two adults dozed while Robin slept upstairs and the two little girls played with their new toys. A walk was planned for three o'clock, but when the time came Miriam saw that Lovell was still deep in sleep. Now she observed how tired he looked, how the lines had deepened in his face and how his dark hair was showing flecks of grey. His work and Eileen's illness were taking their toll of his energy, and she grieved for him.

Quietly, she slipped from the room and summoned Hazel and Jenny. A look into Robin's room showed the boy as deep in slumber as his father.

'We'll play games at the end of the garden,' said Miriam, 'instead of going for a walk. Then we can be near Robin if he wakes.'

'Goody-goody-gum-drops!' cried Jenny. 'We'll have longer with our toys then.'

The kitchen garden was a vast area with a mellowed brick and flint wall. A hundred years or so earlier it must have been the pride of a head gardener and probably two or three under-gardeners. Now it sheltered only a few rows of Brussels sprouts, carrots and cabbages, but it afforded a playground out of the wind and far enough away from the house for the children's shouts to be unheard.

Miriam showed them how to play two-ball against the wall and was surprised and proud to find that she had not lost her skill over the years. After initial difficulties, the girls soon became quite dextrous, the only snag being that only two balls could be found, and they had to take it in turns.

'As soon as the shops open,' promised Miriam, 'I'll buy you two new ones each.'

'But that's not till Monday,' wailed Hazel. 'It's ages away!'

'*What can't be cured must be endured*,' Miriam said cheerfully, quoting Euphrosyne.

'I don't understand that,' said Jenny flatly.

'It means you have to lump it!' her sister told her, appropriating the balls briskly.

The men folk were much refreshed after their naps, and over tea Lovell spoke of the Boxing Day meet which was always held in the square of the local market town.

'Shall we go?' he asked.

'Yes, yes!' chorused the children. 'All in one car! All squashed up and cosy. And take our presents so we can play while we wait!'

Lovell looked at Miriam. She thought quickly. Certainly lunch would be cold turkey, and that presented no difficulties, but she longed to attack some of the more urgent cleaning that had obviously been neglected since Eileen's departure. She did not want Lovell to see her scrubbing his kitchen floor, but that was what she had planned to do if she could manage it unobserved. Then there was the gammon to cook, and a vast amount of necessary sweeping and dusting to do. To have two hours alone would suit her plans perfectly.

'I think I'll stay here if you don't mind,' she replied. 'There are several things to do, and I really ought to ring Joan. I shall probably catch her in the morning.'

'Of course, of course,' said Lovell. He spoke sympathetically. To his eyes, the girl looked absolutely exhausted and he felt horribly guilty. She worked hard at the office, had undertaken a long journey, and was coping superbly with his family. Obviously, it would do her good to have a brief time on her own.

'I'll take the brood off soon after ten,' he promised.

'The meet is at eleven, and we'll be back before one o'clock.'

'Marvellous!' said Miriam, with relief.

The rest of the day passed quietly. Lovell went to the hospital to see Eileen, and the children, tired after all the excitement, were docile enough to go to bed early.

Miriam put the gammon to boil, averted her eyes from the state of the kitchen floor, and fell, bone-weary, into an armchair.

A vision of Holly Lodge as it would be in the New Year, if she ever returned to her ministrations there, floated before her. Quiet, warm, clean – a haven of solitude and silence – it hung before her mind's eye as beautiful as a jewel.

She sighed, and slept.

CHAPTER NINE

It was overcast when Miriam awoke next morning. From her bedroom window she looked out across the flat countryside towards the sea, some twenty miles away.

Inky-dark clouds were moving in slowly, dwarfing the trees and farmsteads with menacing stature. Already, a boisterous wind was blowing, and Miriam predicted storms before long. She only hoped that the rain would hold off long enough for the family to enjoy the Meet.

They all drove off in high spirits, and Miriam returned from waving goodbye to tackle the worst of the mess.

She tidied the larder, ruthlessly throwing away the flotsam and jetsam of the past week, stale bread, ancient scraps of cheese, decaying and unidentifiable morsels on saucers, withered apples and the like. The birds descended in a flock, sea-gulls among the more usual visitors, and snapped up this bounty.

She scrubbed the sink and draining boards, thankful that, with all its drawbacks, the vicarage was blessed with plenty of hot water.

There was something rather satisfying, she found, in scrubbing the tiles of the kitchen floor. The clean sweet-smelling wetness, which grew as she retreated backwards from it on her knees, delighted her, and although she doubted if anyone would ever notice the result of her labours, she was content with her small reward of a job well done.

That finished, she mounted the steep stairs, manhandling the vacuum sweeper and dusters, and set about the bedrooms. The chaos of the girls' room was daunting, and the fact that the dirty linen basket was overflowing was another reminder of work ahead. Really, thought Miriam, dusting vigorously, I should never have made a wife and mother! Looking after Barney from nine till five is more than enough for me!

By twelve-thirty the house looked reasonably tidy, and she skinned the gammon, gave up a fruitless search for bread crumbs with which to adorn it, and set the table. It was while she was doing this that she heard the car return, and voices in the hall.

She emerged from the kitchen to find that Lovell was accompanied by another man.

Who could this stranger be? She looked again, and hurried forward smiling.

'Why, Martin, how lovely to see you again!'

'Brought him back from the Meet for a drink,' said Lovell beaming. 'It must be nearly a year since we met.'

'And more like ten since I saw Miriam,' said Martin. 'And as elegant as ever.'

They moved into the sitting-room, the children following.

'You run and play in the garden for a few minutes,' directed Lovell.

'But we're hungry!'

'When is lunch ready?'

'Can't we have a drink too?'

The protests came thick and fast.

'Have an apple each,' suggested Miriam diplomatically, 'and go and practise two-ball.'

This solution pleased all, and the adults were left to sip their sherry in peace.

It appeared that Martin Farrar's farm lay some twelve miles on the other side of the market town.

'Corn mainly, and sugar beet,' he told Miriam, 'though I keep a few head of cattle. I'm hoping to have pigs some day too. But tell me your news. Where do you live now?'

Miriam told him about the job in Caxley, and her new home at Holly Lodge. She found herself rattling away – Martin had always been a good listener, she remembered – and was about to enlarge on her interrupted decorating of the sitting-room when she remembered Lovell's feelings, and checked herself.

'I stopped in Cambridge, on the journey up,' she said instead, and that opened the way to a flood of happy reminiscences.

'You'll stay to lunch, won't you?' said Lovell. He turned to Miriam anxiously. 'Is it all right? It's cold turkey, I believe?'

'Quite right. And gammon too. And it will be lovely if you can stop.'

'I'd love to,' said Martin.

Miriam retired to the kitchen to finish her preparations. She was slightly puzzled. What about Martin's wife? Would she be waiting lunch for him? No mention had been made of her. Perhaps she was away. But, at Christmas time? Had they parted?

Perplexed, she assembled pickles and an un-opened giant-size packet of potato crisps. She put in the oven the batch of mince pies she had made earlier, and hoped that the cheese board would provide for any empty corners left by the lunch she had prepared.

The children ate hungrily, their appetites whetted by the fresh air. As they ate, the first of the raindrops spattered against the window, and the wind began to roar more loudly.

'We're in for it, I'm afraid,' said Martin. 'The glass was going back this morning. As long as we don't get snow, I don't mind.'

'Do you remember the winter of 1962 and 1963?' asked Lovell. 'My parents were marooned in the vicarage for four weeks, with eight-foot drifts cutting them off. Thank God, my mother always did a lot of bottling and preserving. Father said he hoped never to face another bottled gooseberry in his life-time!'

'We were just married,' said Martin, 'and had misjudged the fuel amounts. Binnie walked about clutching a hot-water bottle all day. It taught us to stock up properly another time.'

'I was in London,' said Miriam, 'a bitter waste of brown slush everywhere. Town snow is so much worse than country snow.'

After lunch, the little girls elected to paint at the kitchen table and Miriam left them to enjoy the new paints and painting books while she put Robin to bed, and Lovell made coffee.

The rain now lashed the house, and Miriam stuffed the towel again into the vulnerable landing window before going downstairs to the fireside.

Martin was helping himself to Lovell's brew and surveying the weather.

'I ought to be getting back pretty soon. I'm the cattle man this afternoon, and it's going to get dark early today.'

They sat at peace, enjoying the warmth of the fire and their coffee.

Miriam looked at Martin as he gazed somnolently at the blazing logs. He had worn well. His hair was thick, his face tanned with his outdoor life, and he was as lean as he had always been. And yet, there was an air of unhappiness about him. Perhaps he felt the same about herself. Perhaps it was simply the passing of the years, the change from the effervescence of youth to the sobriety of middle-age.

Middle-age! It was a shock to realize that she was

half-way to her three-score years and ten. Martin must be nearing forty.

He put his cup down in the hearth with a clatter, and stretched luxuriously.

'Oh, if I could only stay by this fire! Instead, I must go back and bash swedes.'

'Do you really bash swedes?' asked Miriam.

'Not today,' said Martin, with a laugh. 'Just feed the cattle with something less demanding.'

He held out his hand.

'Thank you for giving me lunch, and for your company. I come your way about twice a year. Perhaps I may call in, now I know where you live?'

'I shall look forward to it.'

'Well, it may be in a few weeks' time. There's a cattle dealer in Wales I want to see.'

He made his farewells, and they watched him race through the rain to his Land-Rover. The rain was now torrential, and the branches clashed overhead in the force of the gale, but Martin's grin was cheerful as he waved goodbye.

'Nice to see him again,' said Lovell as they shut the door against the weather. 'We live so near really, and were such close friends in the old days, it seems absurd to lose touch as we have done.'

The fireside was doubly snug after their brush with the weather outside. Peace reigned in the kitchen, and Robin slept aloft. Miriam and Lovell resumed their seats with relief.

She lay back, musing about the encounter. It was good to see Martin again. Their early flirtation had

been a happy one, and it was comforting to see, once again, the unfeigned affection and admiration in his looks. She hoped she would see him again when he travelled to Wales next.

'What is Martin's wife like?' she asked.

'Martin's wife?' Lovell looked startled.

'Binnie, he called her,' said Miriam.

Lovell shook his head sadly.

'Poor Binnie! I should have remembered that you knew nothing about it. She died two years ago – quite that, longer perhaps. I can't quite remember.'

'How ghastly for Martin! What was it?'

'One of those incredibly stupid accidents that strain one's religious beliefs sorely. She was bathing within a few yards of the shore, when a freak wave carried her out to sea, and a sort of whirlpool sucked her under.

There were treacherous currents there always, we heard later.'

'Was Martin there?'

'He had gone to fetch towels from the car, and returned to find the rescue operation going on. The ghastly thing was that the body wasn't washed up until the next tide.'

'Poor Martin! And no children?'

'There was one on the way, which made it worse, of course. I heard Martin was in an appalling state of shock for months. His old mother was a tower of strength, and went to live at the farm with him.'

'I remember her,' replied Miriam, recalling the ramrod figure of Mrs Farrar, her white hair and her deep voice. 'Dreadful for her too.'

'Anyway,' said Lovell, 'he seems to have recovered, and let's hope he may find someone else one day.'

'That's Robin,' exclaimed Miriam, at the sound of a distant wailing.

And she went to resume her duties.

She travelled alone to see Eileen that evening, Lovell volunteering to see his family into bed.

As she drove through the roaring night, buffeted by a fierce north-easter, she suddenly remembered that she had still forgotten to telephone Joan. Martin's arrival had put it out of her head.

Lovell's account of Martin's tragedy had moved her deeply. Why did these things have to happen? Lovell's comment about the strain on one's religious beliefs, in the face of such senseless horror, was understandable. If he, so secure and ardent in his faith, could feel thus, how easy it was to forgive weaker souls who turned against their religion in such circumstances. Martin appeared to have weathered his own storm remarkably well. Possibly, the fact that his work must go on in rain or shine had helped him through the worst. She was glad she knew about it, if she were to see him in the future. When she had said that she would look forward to seeing him again, she had spoken from her heart.

Eileen was wearing the new black nightgown, and looked prettier than ever. She was in good spirits.

'I ought to know very soon if I'm coming home next week,' she told Miriam. 'How I long for it! Tell me, how are you managing?'

Miriam told her the scraps of news, how helpful the children had been, how she had introduced them to two-ball, how beautiful the church had looked decked for Christmas and, finally, how Lovell had brought Martin to lunch.

Eileen's face lit up.

'I'm so glad! We feel so terribly sorry for him, and we wish we saw more of him. He ought to marry again. He's such a dear.'

She looked at Miriam with such an openly speculative eye that it was impossible not to laugh. Eileen laughed too, with such infectious gaiety that the woman in the next bed said: 'She's as good as a tonic is Mrs Quinn!'

And it was then that Miriam suddenly realized that here was a new neighbour. Mrs White, of the grey sad countenance, had gone, it seemed, to a colder bed under the Norfolk sky.

'I'm not really match-making,' said Eileen lightly.

'I should hope not,' replied Miriam. 'Tell me, how did Christmas Day go in here?'

Eileen was willing to be deflected from the subject of Martin, much to Miriam's relief, and launched into a spirited account of the chief surgeon's prowess in turkey-carving, the morning carols, and the visit of the Mayor and his retinue.

Miriam stayed later than she intended, revelling in Eileen's racy descriptions, and the undoubted fact that she seemed stronger and more relaxed after her few days in hospital.

'You'll have Annie back on Monday,' said Eileen, as they said goodbye. 'And with any luck, I'll be home very soon after.'

'We'll have a grand celebration,' promised Miriam, fastening her coat, before leaving the warmth of the ward to face the gales outside.

CHAPTER TEN

The weekend passed remarkably peacefully. Miriam felt more confident now that she was becoming accustomed to the routine of the household. One great blessing was that all the family seemed to eat most of the things she put before them, although turkey in a mild cheese sauce was greeted by Jenny with the remark that she 'didn't like white gravy'. However, her helping vanished, assisted, no doubt, by Hazel's offer to eat her share.

The craze for two-ball persisted, and the two little girls spent any rain-free periods – which were few – bouncing and catching the balls against the wall of the kitchen garden, twirling and clapping as Miriam had shown them.

It seemed a good idea to drive into the market town on Saturday morning, in the hope that a toy shop would be open. They were lucky enough to find a sports shop doing a brisk trade with two girls buying ski-ing equipment and a scoutmaster buying camping stoves. A basket of rubber balls, red, blue, yellow and green, drew Hazel and Jenny like a magnet, and they ended by selecting two red and two green.

'I think you should have three each,' said Miriam. 'You ought to have a spare in case one gets lost.'

'But can you afford it?' asked Hazel anxiously. 'After Christmas too?'

'I think so,' said Miriam.

'But you haven't got a husband to give you any money like Mummy,' protested Jenny. 'Are you sure?'

'I go to work, you know, so I earn some money.'

'A lot? A pound a week?'

'A little more than that,' admitted Miriam.

The girls sighed with relief.

'Then you're quite rich, aren't you?' smiled Hazel.

'Well then, thank you very much,' said Jenny, choosing a yellow one for her spare ball. 'You are kind, as well as rich.'

The baker's shop was open next door, and Miriam bought fresh currant buns for tea, and a veal and ham pie as a change from the turkey.

'You must be *really* rich,' observed Hazel, as they climbed into the car with their purchases, 'if you can buy a great big pie like that. Mummy always makes ours, because she says they are so dear in the shops.'

'Well, this is a treat,' explained Miriam. And a time and energy saver for a struggling aunt, she added to herself.

She found time to ring Joan, who sounded busy and happy.

'Roger goes tomorrow. A friend is picking him up and they are flying to Switzerland at six o'clock. Plenty of snow there, they say.'

'None at Fairacre, I hope?'

'Not yet, but it's cold enough.'

They exchanged news. Barbara and the family were off on the Monday. And when could Joan hope to see Miriam?

'With luck, during next week,' said Miriam. 'It

depends if Eileen is allowed home, and how strong she feels.'

'Well, Holly Lodge is waiting for you,' said Joan. 'So come as soon as you can.'

'I can promise that,' Miriam assured her.

The gales continued, rising to their height on Sunday night. There were tales of fishing-boats smashed at their moorings, and of large ships riding out the storm within sight of the Norfolk coast. At places the sea had flooded the marshland, and great damage was reported from the seaside towns on the Norfolk and Suffolk coasts. Men spent the weekend filling sandbags to block the gaps in the sea wall where the violence of the high tide had breached it.

At the vicarage, some tiles were blown from the roof and an ancient apple tree was toppled, its roots exposed to the children's horrified gaze, and its branches enmeshing a chicken house which was mercifully empty.

For the first time, Miriam saw the children frightened that night. The house shuddered in the onslaught, and the banshee wailings, which Miriam had thought belonged to the kitchen only, were increased to envelop the upstairs corridors.

Miriam left a night-light burning in a saucer of water to comfort the little girls. The tall shadows, made by the brave little light, took her back in an instant to her own childhood in just such a bleak vicarage, and she kissed the little girls with extra warmth and sympathy.

The nine o'clock news was devoted largely to the

havoc caused by the storm, related with the usual zest with which the imparting of bad news is passed on. Shades of Mrs Pringle, thought Miriam, watching a woman smugly explaining how she had found her neighbour pinned beneath her own coal-shed and describing, with relish, the extent of her injuries.

'That's enough of that!' said Lovell, switching it off. 'If I know anything about it, it will have blown itself out within twenty-four hours.'

It was at twelve the next day that the telephone rang, and it was Eileen on the line, sounding highly jubilant.

'It looks as though I can come home tomorrow. Isn't it wonderful? Can Lovell fetch me in the afternoon? The doctor wants to see me in the morning, and it's really simpler if I have lunch here.'

'Marvellous!' cried Miriam. 'Let me call Lovell. He's in the garden, sawing the apple tree into logs.'

'Any damage?'

'Very little,' Miriam told her, 'and the wind is dying down nicely.'

'Look out for floods by the river,' warned Eileen. 'The papers haven't arrived yet, and they say a lot of people have had to leave their houses in the low-lying part of the town. Poor things! Can you imagine anything worse than finding your carpets floating downstairs?'

'Yes. Floating upstairs. Here's Lovell now,' called Miriam, handing over the telephone to her windblown brother.

She could hear the excitement in his voice as she returned to the mound of washing which she was tackling. With any luck, she thought, it would be dry and ironed before the mistress of the house returned. And tomorrow morning, she must go foraging for food again.

That afternoon, when she and the children returned from a windy walk, they found Annie on the doorstep. The children rushed to greet her. Robin put his arms up round her waist and kissed the fourth button of her raincoat rapturously.

'How lovely to see you,' cried Miriam. 'Come in, and tell me what you usually do.'

'Well,' said Annie, 'I help to get tea, and then I bath Robin, and then I do anything Mrs Quinn wants – ironing usually, or a bit of mending, and then I help put Jenny and Hazel to bed and then I go home.'

She was a thick-set cheerful girl with long straight hair tied in a pony-tail and the brightest dark eyes which Miriam had ever seen.

'That sounds wonderful,' said Miriam. 'Let's get tea together now, and I'll start the ironing while you put Robin to bed later on.'

'And my mum said, as it's school holidays and Mrs Quinn's been took bad, I can come most of the day, just when it helps. I could do shopping at that, and take the children out for their walk. Just what's best.'

'You are an angel,' said Miriam fervently. 'I'll speak to Mr Quinn when he comes in, and we'll arrange something.'

Tea was taken at the kitchen table, and Miriam could see how competent and calm the young girl was with her charges, and how much they adored her. It was a noisy meal, with constant interruptions to fetch new toys to be admired. No doubt about it, thought Miriam, Annie was a treasure.

Miriam heard Lovell come in, and hurried into the sitting-room to tell him the good news.

'God bless Annie!' he said sincerely. 'For this week anyway, it would seem perfect if she came, say, at eleven and had coffee with us, and stayed the rest of the day, up till the children's bedtime, if her mother is agreeable.'

'Go and have a word with her,' suggested Miriam.

And so, to everyone's relief and joy, matters were arranged.

Annie's addition to the household was certainly a blessing, as Miriam soon discovered. By the time she arrived on Tuesday morning, Miriam had put Eileen and Lovell's bedroom to rights, had changed sheets, put out fresh soap and towels, and even found a few sprigs of yellow winter jasmine to put in a little vase by Eileen's bed.

Annie departed towards the village, after her coffee, with a long shopping list, three baskets and the children. Copper decided to accompany them too, and for the first time Miriam found herself the only living thing in the house; Lovell was out visiting sick parishioners.

It was bliss to have the kitchen to herself, and to be able to follow a train of thought without urgent infant demands for attention. She prepared lunch, and even made a large batch of shortbread which, with any luck, could be stored in a tin for future use when she herself had gone back to Fairacre.

She had purposely made no firm plans for her return. It all depended on Eileen, but secretly she longed to get back within the next few days to finish her sitting-room and to be ready for the office on the following Monday.

Her meditations were soon interrupted by the return of Annie and her charges, and the necessity of storing away shopping and setting the table for lunch.

'Why can't we go with Daddy to fetch Mummy?' complained Hazel.

'Because it will be much nicer to get things ready for her here,' said Miriam firmly. 'You can put a hot bottle in her bed in case she feels tired, and Jenny can get the tea-tray ready.'

They looked doubtful about these arrangements but fell in with the plans without argument. On such a joyous occasion, fighting seemed out of place.

As if to add to the general air of festivity, the sun had come out, and the wind was less violent, although strong enough to send great galleons of white cloud scudding across the blue sky. On the wide Norfolk fields below, the clouds chased each other across hedges and ditches, so that the countryside was alternately lit with golden sunshine and deepest shadow. The change in the weather brought a refreshment of spirit, and when at last Lovell's car drew up at the front door, and Eileen emerged with arms outstretched, the family burst from the front door with cries of excitement.

'Do you want to go to bed?' demanded Hazel, when their mother was at last sitting by the fire.

'Heavens, no!' cried Eileen. 'Why?'

'Because I've put in a bottle for you.'

'That's very kind, but it will do beautifully for later on.'

'Have some tea,' urged Jenny, anxious to display her preparations.

'Not at three, darling,' said her mother. 'Just let me sit and look at you all and the house. It's so marvellous to be back. And how *clean* everything looks!'

Miriam was amused to find herself as gratified with this last compliment as she was when Barney gave her a rare pat on the back for some meticulously arranged conference, or for some particularly diplomatic handling of a difficult client.

It was good to see the family united again, and to see too how much Annie was included in the general reunion. Eileen was genuinely touched at the girl's offer of help while she was on holiday, and when at last the young people went off in her charge, Eileen spoke of her to Miriam.

'She's absolutely splendid with children. We hope she'll be able to take up nursery training. It's what she wants to do, and Lovell and I are going to do all we can to persuade her mother to let her. She's about the most unselfish person I ever met – next to you, I should say.'

'Not me!' protested Miriam. 'I am *horribly* selfish. All I think about is my own affairs.'

'Then the virtue is all the greater when you put them aside so readily to come to our aid,' said Eileen firmly.

Later that evening when the children were abed and Annie had departed, the three sat by the fire in amicable drowsiness.

'Are you sure you wouldn't sooner be in bed?' asked Miriam.

'No, it's bliss to be here, and honestly I feel better, if anything, than when I went in. The diet's helped a lot, and all I need now is a little exercise to get my legs less wobbly.'

'You look more relaxed,' agreed Lovell, 'but I shouldn't venture out for a day or two. After that hot-house of a hospital you'll find the vicarage garden pretty chilly.'

'Pottering round the house will suit me,' said Eileen. 'And I hope Miriam will stay on now for a holiday instead of being a hard-working housekeeper, and let me look after her, for a change.'

'I shall stay as long as I'm needed,' said Miriam, 'but let's see how you feel tomorrow morning before we make plans. I've thoroughly enjoyed myself here. It's been a break—'

'*But*,' broke in Eileen, 'you have your own affairs to see to, and we've trespassed on your precious free time already. Honestly, my darling Miriam, I am perfectly recovered, and I think next week's check-up will be the last that's needed, so if you want to go ahead with your own plans, *please* feel free.'

'Well,' said Miriam, weakening in the face of this reasoning, 'let's decide tomorrow morning. If all is well, perhaps I could go on Thursday. Now that Annie's here—'

'Even if Annie weren't here, we could manage, I feel sure. Lovell can be here pretty well non-stop until Sunday, and the girls are quite big enough to help now.'

At that moment the telephone rang and Lovell went to answer it. He returned to say:

'It's for you, Miriam. It's Martin on the telephone.'

'Look, Miriam,' said Martin, 'this Welsh trip has cropped up sooner than I thought. The dealer has some good cattle at the moment, and I propose going down on Saturday and coming back on Sunday. Can we meet?'

Miriam thought quickly.

'What about Sunday lunch with me? Something pretty simple, as I'm in the throes of decorating and the paint may still be wet, but—'

'No, no. I insist on taking you out to lunch. But Sunday will be fine for me. Do you know somewhere?'

'I'll book a table in Caxley,' said Miriam. 'Shall we

say twelve-thirty at "The Bull"? It's just off the Market Square.'

'Lovely!' said Martin. 'Now we've found each other again, it will be good to catch up with old times.'

'Yes, indeed,' said Miriam politely. But she wished he had said: 'Now we've *met* each other again' instead of '*found each other*' which sounded uncomfortably intimate to one of her temperament.

'Martin's coming my way next weekend,' she said, returning to the fireside. 'And taking me out to lunch.'

'Well, he hasn't lost much time,' said Lovell, with a satisfaction which his sister found distasteful in the circumstances. But she forbore to retort.

Next morning, to her surprise, she found that Eileen was in the kitchen before her, and was busy frying bacon and eggs for the family.

She smiled at Miriam's astonishment.

'This is just to show you how fit I am. I feel a positive fraud being treated as an invalid.'

'How did you sleep?'

'Like a top. Woke up an hour ago feeling I could mow the lawn, walk to Norwich, and eat a couple of horses.'

'Wonderful! You've certainly recovered.'

She began to cut bread ready to toast. It was good to see Eileen in command again.

'So, Miriam dear, don't linger here on our behalf if you really want to get back. I couldn't help overhearing your remark to Martin that you were in the midst of decorating. You are an absolute marvel to have dropped everything – paint brushes included – to come all this way.'

She put down the fork with which she was turning the bacon and came to put her arms around Miriam.

'This isn't speeding the parting guest. I'd like you to stay, you know, but if you can't now, then come very soon for a real holiday. But if you'd feel happier about getting back, please believe me when I say we can really manage now, and will *never* forget your kindness when we were in trouble.'

Miriam hugged her affectionately.

'If you're quite sure, then I might even push off later this morning. The weather seems more settled, and if Annie turns up as usual, I'd feel quite happy about leaving you with that stout support.'

And so it fell out that at half past eleven, with her case in the car, sandwiches cut by Eileen, a flask filled by Annie, and a posy of mixed winter flowers collected by the children, Miriam was ready to start on her long journey.

All the family, including Annie, were on the doorstep to wave goodbye. Their embraces had been unusually warm and loving, and Miriam was astonished to realize how sad she felt at parting. To think that just over a week ago she had arrived in a mood of stern duty! Now it was as much as she could do to keep back the tears as she drove away.

'Don't forget you're coming at Easter!' shouted Hazel.

'Before if you can!' added Eileen.

'A thousand thanks!' called Lovell. 'I shall be writing.'

She hooted all the way down the drive in reply to their valedictions, and had to fumble for a handkerchief when she was safely out of their sight.

The floods were out between St Neots and Bedford, and traffic was diverted round narrow lanes bordering water-logged fields. At Newport Pagnell there were more floods, but the sky was clear and the wind had dropped to a gentle breeze, and Miriam pushed on steadily.

There was plenty of time now for uninterrupted thought. A lot of good had come from this week's visit. She had learnt to know Eileen better and to appreciate the strength of character that lay behind the babyish good looks. She remembered her gaiety and courage in the face of death at the hospital, her honest gratitude for help given. Now she began to see why Lovell loved her so much. It made her own feelings towards her brother much more comfortable. If Lovell were happy, then she too was happy. It was as simple as that.

And how much greater now was her bond with the children! They were all of them – Lovell, Eileen and she herself – much closer because of this adversity. She felt better for having gone. It had jolted her out of her own selfish rut, and a good thing too, she told herself.

'*Cast your bread upon the waters!*' she remembered. Well, she had certainly received a bountiful return.

It was dark when she arrived at Holly Lodge, and Joan was out. Probably having a New Year's Eve drink

with friends in Fairacre, thought Miriam, suddenly remembering the date.

She put away the car, and carried her things indoors. The pleasant smell of new paint greeted her. She breathed it in with rapture.

Here she was at last! At home, and alone, ready for all that might befall in the New Year.

What would it hold for her? She remembered Martin, and was warmed by the thought of his friendship which might grow – who knew? – into something dearer.

Well, it was nice to be wanted, Lovell and his family had proved that. But not for always, thought Miriam, looking for a vase for her Norfolk nosegay. She was glad to have met Martin again, glad to know she would see him soon, and glad to know that the bond with her family was more closely knit.

But this was where she was happiest. For her, spinsterhood was truly blessed. She walked into her empty sitting-room and closed the door behind her, the better to relish that sweet solitude which to her was the breath of life.

A vision of the vicarage rose before her – the paper chains, the expanding fans and bells, the tinsel, the mistletoe, the holly.

Here there was no holly for Miss Quinn, but she felt a glow as warm as its red berries at the joy of being home, a joy which, she knew, would remain ever green in the years which lay ahead.

CHRISTMAS AT FAIRACRE SCHOOL

Illustrated by J. S. Goodall

Miss Read is the head teacher at the small school in the downland village of Fairacre, and she is the narrator in the many books about Fairacre. Here she describes the scene at the end of term as the school prepares to break up for the Christmas holidays.

Preparations for Christmas are now in full swing. For weeks past, the shops in Caxley have been a blaze of coloured lights and decorated with Father Christmases, decked trees, silver balls and all the other paraphernalia. Even our grocer's shop in Fairacre has cotton-wool snow, hanging on threads, down the window, and this, together with the crib already set up in the church, all add to the children's enchantment.

It has turned bitterly cold, with a cruel east wind which has scattered the last of the leaves and ruffles the feathers of the birds who sit among the bare branches. The tortoise stoves are kept roaring away, but nothing can cure the fiendish draught from the skylight above my desk, and the one from the door, where generations of feet have worn the lintel into a hollow.

Yesterday afternoon the whole school was busy making Christmas decorations and Christmas cards. There is nothing that children like more than making brightly-coloured paper chains, and their tongues wagged happily as the paste brushes were plied, and yet another glowing link was added to the festoons that lay heaped on the floor. All this glory grows so deliciously quickly and the knowledge that, very soon, it will be swinging aloft above their heads among the pitch-pine rafters – an enchanting token of all the joys that Christmas holds in store – makes them work with more than usual energy.

In Miss Jackson's room the din was terrific, so excited were the chain-makers. The only quiet group here was the one which was composed of about eight small children who had elected to crayon Christmas cards instead. Among them was the little Pratt boy. I stopped to admire his effort. His picture was of a large and dropsical robin, with the fiercest of red breasts and very small and inadequate legs, as there was only a quarter of an inch of space left at the bottom for these highly necessary appendages. His face was solemn with the absorption of the true artist.

'It's for Miss Bunce,' he told me. 'You knows – the one at Barrisford what took me to the hostipple to have my eye done. She writes to me ever so often, and sometimes sends me sweets. D'you reckon she'll like it?'

He held up his masterpiece and surveyed it anxiously at arm's length.

I told him truthfully that I was sure she would like it very much, and that all sensible people liked robins on Christmas cards. With a sigh of infinite satisfaction he replaced it on the desk, and prepared to face the horrid intricacies of writing 'HAPPY CHRISTMAS' inside.

By right and ancient custom at Fairacre School the last afternoon of the Christmas term is given up to a tea-party.

The partition had been pushed back so that the two classrooms were thrown into one, but even so the school was crowded – with children, parents and friends. Mrs Finch-Edwards was there, showing her baby daughter Althea to Miss Clare. Miss Jackson, who had dressed the Christmas tree alone, was receiving congratulations upon its glittering beauty from Miss Partridge. Mr Robert's hearty laugh rustled the paper-chains so near his head, and the vicar beamed upon us all, until Mrs Pringle gave him the school cutting-out scissors and reminded him of his responsibilities. For it was he who would cut the dangling presents from the tree before the party ended.

Mrs Coggs and Mrs Waites had walked up together from Tyler's Row, and now sat, side by side, watching their sons engulf sardine sandwiches, iced biscuits, sponge cake, jam tarts and sausage rolls, all washed down with frequent draughts of fizzy lemonade through a gurgling straw. Mr Willet, at one end of the

room, had the job of taking the metal tops off the bottles, and with bent back, and purple, sweating face, had been hard put to it to keep pace with the demand.

It was a cheerful scene. The paper-chains and lanterns swung from the rafters, the tortoise stoves, especially brilliant today from Mrs Pringle's ministrations, roared merrily, and the glittering tree dominated the room.

The children, flushed with food, heat and excitement, chattered like starlings, and around them the warm, country voices of their elders exchanged news and gossip.

After tea, the old well-loved games were played, 'Oranges and Lemons' with Miss Clare at the piano, and Mr and Mrs Partridge making the arch, 'Poor

Jenny sits a-weeping', 'The Farmer's in his Den', 'Nuts and May' and 'Hunt the Thimble'. We always have this one last of all so that we can regain our breath. The children nearly burst with suppressed excitement as the seeker wandered bewildered about the room, and on this occasion the roars of 'Cold, cold!' or 'Warmer, warmer!' and the wild yielding of 'Hot, hot! You're *real* hot!' nearly raised the pitch-pine roof.

The presents were cut from the tree, and the afternoon finished with carols, old and young singing together lustily and with sincerity. Within those familiar walls, feuds and old hurts forgotten, for an hour or two at least, Fairacre had been united in joy and true goodwill.

It was dark when the party ended. Farewells and Christmas greetings had been exchanged under the night sky, and the schoolroom was dishevelled but quiet. The Christmas tree, denuded of its parcels and awaiting the removal of its bright baubles on the morrow, still had place of honour in the centre of the floor.

Joseph Coggs' dark eyes had been fixed so longingly on the star at its summit that Miss Clare had unfastened it and given it into his keeping when the rest of the children had been safely out of the way.

The voices and footsteps had died away long ago by the time I was ready to lock up and go across to my peaceful house. Some of the bigger children were coming in the morning to help me clear up the aftermath of our Christmas revels, before Mrs Pringle started her holiday scrubbing.

The great Gothic door swung to with a clang, and I turned the key. The night was still and frosty. From the distant downs came the faint bleating of Mr Roberts' sheep, and the lowing of the bull in a nearby field. Suddenly a cascade of sound showered from St Patrick's spire. The bell-ringers were practising their Christmas peal. After that first mad jangle the bells fell sweetly into place, steadily, rhythmically, joyfully calling their message across the clustered roofs and the plumes of smoke from Fairacre's hearths, to the grey, bare glory of the downs that shelter us.

I turned to go home, and to my amazement, noticed a child standing by the school gate.

It was Joseph Coggs. High above his head he held his tinsel star, squinting at it lovingly as he compared it with those which winked in their thousands from above St Patrick's spire.

We stood looking at it together, and it was some time before he spoke, raising his voice against the clamour of the bells.

'Good, ain't it?' he said, with the utmost satisfaction.

'Very good!' I agreed.

THE CHRISTMAS MOUSE

Illustrated by J. S. Goodall

To Elizabeth Ann Green
who started this story

CHAPTER ONE

The rain began at noon.

At first it fell lightly, making little noise. Only the darkening of the thatched roofs, and the sheen on the damp flagstones made people aware of the rain. It was dismissed as 'only a mizzle'. Certainly it did not warrant bringing in the tea towels from the line. Midday meals were taken in the confident belief that the shower would soon blow over. Why, the weathermen had predicted a calm spell, hadn't they, only that morning?

But by two o'clock it was apparent that something was radically wrong with the weather forecast. The wind had swung round to the northwest, and the drizzle had turned to a downpour. It hissed among the dripping trees, pattered upon the cabbages in cottage gardens and drummed the bare soil with pock marks.

Mrs Berry, at her kitchen window, watched the clouds of rain drifting across the fields, obscuring the distant wood and veiling the whole countryside. A vicious gust of wind flung a spatter of raindrops against the pane with so much force that it might have been a handful of gravel hurled in the old lady's face. She did not flinch, but instead raised her voice against the mounting fury of the storm.

'What a day,' said Mrs Berry, 'for Christmas Eve!'

Behind her, kneeling on the rush matting, her daughter Mary was busy buttoning her two little girls into their mackintoshes.

'Hold still,' she said impatiently, 'hold still, do! We'll never catch the bus at this rate.'

They were fidgeting with excitement. Their cheeks were flushed, their eyes sparkling. It was as much as they could do to lift their chins for their mother to fasten the stiff top buttons of their new red mackintoshes. But the reminder that the bus might go without them checked their excitement. Only two afternoon buses a week ran past the cottage, one on market day, and one on Saturday. To miss it meant missing the last-minute shopping expedition for the really important Christmas presents – those for their mother and grandmother. The idea of being deprived of this joy brought the little girls to partial submission.

Mary, her fingers busy with the buttons, was thinking of more mundane shopping – Brussels sprouts, some salad, a little pot of cranberry jelly for the turkey, a few more oranges if they were not too expensive, a lemon or two. And a potted plant for Mum. A cyclamen perhaps? Or a heather, if the cyclamen proved to be beyond her purse. It was mean the way these florists put up the prices so cruelly at Christmas. But there, she told herself, scrambling to her feet, the poor souls had to live the same as she did, she supposed, and with everything costing so much they would have to look after themselves like anyone else.

'You wait here quietly with Gran for a minute,' she adjured the pair, 'while I run and get my coat on, and fetch the baskets. Got your money and your hankies? Don't want no sniffing on the bus now!'

She whisked upstairs and the children could hear her hurrying to and fro above the beamed ceiling of the kitchen.

Old Mrs Berry was opening her brown leather purse. There were not many coins in it, and no notes, but she took out two silver fivepenny pieces.

'To go towards your shopping,' said the old lady. 'Hold out your hands.'

Two small hands, encased in woollen gloves knitted by Mrs Berry herself, were eagerly outstretched.

'Jane first,' said Mrs Berry, putting the coin into the older girl's hand. 'And now Frances.'

'Thank you, Gran, thank you,' they chorused, throwing their arms round her comfortable bulk, pressing wet kisses upon her.

'No need to tell your mum,' said Mrs Berry. 'It's a little secret between us three. Here she comes.'

The three hurried to the cottage door. The rain was coming down in sheets, and Mary struggled with an umbrella on the threshold.

'Dratted thing' – she puffed – 'but can't do without it today. I'll wager I forget it in some shop, but there it is. Come on now, you girls. Keep close to me, and run for it!'

Mrs Berry watched them vanish into the swirling rain. Then she shut the door upon the weather, and returned to the peaceful kitchen.

She put her wrinkled hand upon the teapot. Good, it was still hot. She would have another cup before she washed up.

Sitting in the wooden armchair that had been her husband's, Mrs Berry surveyed the kitchen with pleasure. It had been decorated a few years before and young Bertie, Mary's husband, had made a good job of it. The walls were white, the curtains cherry-red cotton, and the tiles round the sink were blue and white. Bertie, who had set them so neatly, said they came from a fireplace over in Oxfordshire and were from Holland originally. The builder, a friend of his, was about to throw them out but Bertie had rescued them.

A clever boy with his hands, thought Mrs Berry, stirring her tea, though she could never understand what poor Mary saw in him, with that sandy hair and those white eyelashes. Still, it did no good to think ill of the dead, and he had made a good husband and father for the few short years he and Mary had been married. This would be the third Christmas without him – a sad time for Mary, poor soul.

Mrs Berry had once wondered if this youngest daughter of hers would ever marry. The two older girls were barely twenty when they wed. One was a farmer's wife near Taunton. The other had married an American, and Mrs Berry had only seen her twice since.

Mary, the prettiest of the three girls, had never been one for the boys. After she left school, she worked in the village post office at Springbourne, cycling to work in all weather and seeming content to read and knit or tend the garden when she returned at night.

Mrs Berry was glad of her daughter's company. She had been widowed in 1953, after over thirty years of tranquil marriage to dear Stanley. He had been a stonemason, attached to an old-established firm in Caxley, and he too cycled daily to work, his tools strapped securely on the carrier with his midday sandwiches. On a day as wild and wet as this Christmas Eve, he had arrived home soaked through. That night he tossed in a fever, muttering in delirium, and within a week he was dead – the victim of a particularly virulent form of influenza.

In the weeks of shock and mourning that followed, Mary was a tower of strength to her mother. Once the funeral was over, and replies had been sent to all the friends and relatives who had written in sympathy, the two women took stock of their situation. Thank God, the cottage was her own, Mrs Berry said. It had taken the savings of a lifetime to buy when it came on the market, but now they had a roof over their heads and no weekly rent to find. There was a tiny pension from Stanley's firm, a few pounds in the post office savings bank, and Mary's weekly wage. Two mornings of housework every week at the Manor Farm brought in a few more shillings for Mrs Berry. And the farmer's wife, knowing her circumstances, offered her more work, which she gladly accepted. It was a happy household, and Mrs Berry was as grateful for the cheerful company she found there as for the extra money.

Mother and daughter fell into a comfortable routine during the next few years. They breakfasted together before the younger woman set off on her bicycle, and Mrs Berry tidied up before going off to her morning's work at the farmhouse. In the afternoon, she did her own housework, washed and ironed, gardened, or knitted and sewed. She frugally made jams and jellies, chutneys and pickles for the store cupboard, and it was generally acknowledged by her neighbours that Mrs Berry could stretch a shilling twice as far as most. The house was bright and attractive, and the door stood open for visitors. No one left Mrs Berry without feeling all the better for her company. Her good sense, her kindness and her courage brought many people to her door.

Mary had been almost thirty when she met Bertie Fuller. He was the nephew of the old lady who kept the Springbourne post office and had come to lodge with her when he took a job at the Caxley printing works.

Even those romantically inclined had to admit that nothing as fantastic as love at first sight engulfed Mary and Bertie. She had never been one to show her feelings and now, at her age, was unlikely to be swept off her feet. Bertie was five years her senior and had been married before. There were no children of this first marriage, and his wife had married again.

The two were attracted to each other and were engaged within three months of their first meeting.

'Well, my dear, you're old enough to know your own mind,' said Mrs Berry, 'and he seems a decent, kindly sort of man, with a steady job. If you'd like to have two rooms here while you look for a house you're both welcome.'

No, the villagers agreed, as they gossiped among themselves, Mary Berry hadn't exactly caught 'a regular heart-throb', but what could you expect at thirty? She was lucky really to have found anyone, and they did say this Bertie fellow was safe at the printing works, and no doubt was of an age to have sown all the wild oats he wanted.

The wedding was as modest as befitted the circumstances, and the pair were married at Caxley registry office, spent their brief honeymoon at Torquay, and returned to share the cottage with old Mrs Berry. It was October 1963 and the autumn was one of the most golden and serene that anyone could recall.

Their first child was due to arrive the following September. Mary gave up her job at the post office in June.

The summer was full of promise. The cottage garden flowered as never before, and Mary, resting in a deck chair, gazed dreamily at the madonna lilies and golden roses, and dwelt on the happy lot of the future baby. They had all set their hearts on a boy, and Mary was convinced that it would be a son. Blue predominated in the layette that she and Mrs Berry so lovingly prepared.

When her time came she was taken to the maternity wing of the local cottage hospital, and gave birth to a boy, fair and blue eyed like his father. She held him in her arms for a moment before returning him to the nurse's care. In her joy she did not notice the anxious looks the doctor and nurse exchanged. Nor did she realize that her child had been taken from her bed straight to an oxygen tent.

In the morning, they broke the news to her that the boy had died. Mary never forgot the utter desolation that gripped her for weeks after this terrible loss. Her husband and mother together nursed her back to health, but always, throughout her whole life, Mary remembered that longed-for boy with the blue gaze, and mourned in secret.

A daughter, Jane, was born in the spring of 1966, and another, Frances, in 1968. The two little girls were a lively pair, and when the younger one was beginning to toddle, Bertie and Mary set about finding a cottage of their own. Until that time, Mrs Berry had been glad to have them with her. Mary's illness, then her second pregnancy, made her husband and mother particularly anxious. Now, it seemed, the time had come for the young family to look for their own home. Mrs Berry's cottage was becoming overcrowded.

The search was difficult. They wanted to rent a house to begin with, but this proved to be almost impossible. The search was still on when the annual printing-house outing, called the wayzgoose, took place. Two buses set off for Weymouth carrying the workers and their wives. Mary decided not to go on the day's outing. Frances had a summer cold and was restless, and her mother had promised to go to a Women's Institute meeting in the afternoon. So Bertie went alone.

It was a cloudless July day, warm from the sun's rising until its setting. Mary, pushing the pram along a leafy lane, thought enviously of Bertie and his companions sitting on a beach or swimming in the freshness of the sea. She knew Weymouth from earlier outings and loved its great curved bay. Today it would be looking its finest.

The evening dragged after the children had gone to bed. Usually, the adults retired at ten, for all rose early. On this evening, however, Mrs Berry went upstairs alone, leaving Mary to await Bertie's coming. Eleven o'clock struck, then twelve. Yawning, bemused with the long day's heat, Mary began to lock up.

She was about to lock the front door when she heard a car draw up. Someone rapped upon the door, and when Mary opened it, to her surprise she saw Mr

Partridge, the vicar, standing there. His kind old face was drawn with anxiety.

'I'm sorry to appear so late, my dear Mrs Fuller, but a telephone message has just come to the vicarage.'

'Yes?' questioned Mary.

The vicar looked about him in agitation. 'Do you think we might sit down for a moment?'

Mary remembered her manners. 'Of course; I'm so sorry. Come in.'

She led the way into the sitting room, still bewildered.

'It's about Bertie,' began the vicar. 'There's been an accident, I fear. Somewhere south of Caxley. When things were sorted out, someone asked me to let you know that Bertie wouldn't be home tonight.'

'What's happened? Is he badly hurt? Is he dead? Where is he?'

Mary sprang to her feet, her eyes wild.

The vicar spoke soothingly. 'He's in Caxley hospital, and being cared for. I know no more, my dear, but I thought you would like to go there straight away and see him.'

Without a word Mary lifted an old coat from the back of the kitchen door.

The vicar eyed her anxiously. 'Would it not be best to tell Mrs Berry?' he suggested.

She shook her head. 'I'll leave a note.'

He waited while she scribbled briefly upon a piece of paper, and watched her put it in the middle of the kitchen table.

'No point in waking her,' she said, closing the front door softly behind her.

The two set off in silence, too worried to make conversation. The air was heavy with the scent of honeysuckle. Moths glimmered in the beams of the headlights, and fell to their death.

How easily, Mary thought – fear clutching her heart – death comes to living things. The memory of her little son filled her mind as they drove through the night to meet what might be another tragedy.

At the hospital they were taken to a small waiting room. Within a minute, a doctor came to them. There was no need for him to speak. His face told Mary all. Bertie had gone.

The wayzgoose, begun so gaily, had ended in tragedy. The two buses had drawn up a few miles from Caxley to allow the passengers to have a last drink before closing time. They had to cross a busy road to enter the old coaching inn, famed for its hospitality. Returning to the bus, Bertie and a friend waited some time for a lull in the traffic. It was a busy road, leading to the coast, and despite the late hour the traffic was heavy. At last they made a dash for it, not realizing that a second car was overtaking the one they could see. The latter slowed down to let the two men cross, but the second car could not stop in time. Both men were hurled to the ground, Bertie being dragged some yards before the car stopped.

Despite appalling injuries, he was alive when admitted to hospital, but died within the hour. The organizer of the outing, knowing that Mary was not on the telephone, decided to let the local vicar break the news of the accident.

Mr Partridge and poor Mary returned along the dark lanes to the darker cottage, where he aroused Mrs Berry, told her the terrible story and left her trying to comfort the young widow.

If anyone can succeed, Mr Partridge thought as he drove sadly to his vicarage, she can. But oh, the waste of it all! The wicked waste!

CHAPTER TWO

Old Mrs Berry, remembering that dreadful night, shook her head sadly as she washed up her cup and saucer at the sink. The rain still fell in torrents, and a wild wind buffeted the bushes in the garden, sending the leaves tumbling across the grass.

In Caxley it would not be so rough, she hoped. Most of the time her family would be under cover in the shops, but out here, at Shepherds Cross, they always caught the full violence of the weather.

Mrs Berry's cottage was the third one spaced along the road that led to Springbourne. All three cottages were roomy, with large gardens containing gnarled old apple and plum trees. Each cottage possessed ancient hawthorn hedges, supplying sanctuary to dozens of little birds.

An old drovers' path ran at right angles to the cottages, crossing the road by Mrs Berry's house. This gave the hamlet its name, although it was many years since sheep had been driven along that green lane to the great sheep fair at the downland village ten miles distant.

Some thought it a lonely spot, and declared that they 'would go melancholy mad, that they would!' But Mrs Berry, used to remote houses since childhood, was not affected.

She had been brought up in a gamekeeper's cottage in a woodland ride. As a small child she rarely saw anyone strange, except on Sundays, when she attended church with her parents.

She had loved that church, relishing its loftiness, its glowing stained-glass windows and the flowers on the altar. She paid attention to the exhortations of the vicar too, a holy man who truly ministered to his neighbours. From him, as much as from the example of her parents, she learned early to appreciate modesty, courage, and generosity.

When she was old enough to read she deciphered a plaque upon the chancel floor extolling the virtues of a local benefactor, a man of modest means who nevertheless '*was hospitable and charitable for all his Days*' and who, at his end, left '*the interest of Forty Pounds to the Poor of the parish forever.*'

It was the next line or two which the girl never forgot, and which influenced her own life. They read:

Such were the good effects of
Virtue and Oeconomy
Read, Grandeur, and Blush

Certainly, goodness and thrift, combined with a horror of ostentation and boasting, were qualities which Mrs Berry embodied all the days of her life, and her daughters profited by her example.

Mrs Berry left the kitchen and went to sit by the fire in the living room. It was already growing dark, for the sky was thick with storm clouds, and the rain showed no sign of abating.

Water bubbled in the crack of the window frame, and Mrs Berry sighed. It was at times like this one

needed a man about the place. Unobtrusively, without complaint, Stanley and then Bertie had attended to such things as draughty windows, wobbly door knobs, squeaking floorboards and the like. Now the women had to cope as best they could, and an old house, about two hundred years of age, certainly needed constant attention to keep it in trim.

Nevertheless, it looked pretty and gay. The Christmas tree, dressed the night before by Jane and Frances – with many squeals of delight – stood on the side table, spangled with stars and tinsel, and bearing the Victorian fairy doll, three inches high, which had once adorned the Christmas trees of Mrs Berry's own childhood. The doll's tiny wax face was brown with age but still bore that sweet expression which the child had imagined was an angel's.

Sprigs of holly were tucked behind the picture frames, and a spray of mistletoe hung where the oil lamp had once swung from the central beam over the dining table.

Mrs Berry leaned back in her chair and surveyed it all with satisfaction. It looked splendid and there was very little more to be done to the preparations in the kitchen. The turkey was stuffed, the potatoes peeled. The Christmas pudding had been made in November and stood ready on the shelf to be plunged into the steamer tomorrow morning. Mince pies waited in the tin, and a splendid Christmas cake, iced and decorated with robins and holly by Mrs Berry herself, would grace the tea table tomorrow.

There would also be a small Madeira cake, with a delicious sliver of green angelica tucked into its top. The old lady had made that for those who, like herself, could not tackle Christmas cake until three or four hours after Christmas pudding. It had turned out beautifully light, Mrs Berry remembered.

She closed her eyes contentedly, and before long, drifted into a light sleep.

Mrs Berry awoke as the children burst into the room. A cold breeze set the Christmas tree ornaments tinkling and rustled the paper chain, which swung above the door.

The little girls' faces were pink and wet, their bangs stuck to their foreheads and glistened with dampness. Drops fell from the scarlet mackintoshes and their woolly gloves were soaked. But nothing could damp their spirits on this wonderful day, and Mrs Berry forbore to scold them for the mess they were making on the rug.

Mary, struggling with the shopping, called from the kitchen.

'Come out here, you two, and get off those wet things! What a day, Gran! You've never seen anything like Caxley High Street. Worse than Michaelmas Fair! Traffic jams all up the road, and queues in all the shops. The Caxley traders will have a bumper Christmas, mark my words!'

Mrs Berry stirred herself and followed the children into the kitchen to help them undress. Mary was unloading her baskets and carrier bags, rescuing nuts and Brussels sprouts which burst from wet paper bags on to the floor, and trying to take off her own sodden coat and headscarf all at the same time.

'I seem to have spent a mint of money,' she said apologetically, 'and dear heaven knows where it's all gone. We'll have a reckon-up later on, but we were that pushed and hurried about I'll be hard put to it to remember all the prices.'

'No point in worrying,' said Mrs Berry calmly. 'If 'tis gone, 'tis gone. You won't have wasted it, I know that, my girl. Here, let's put on the kettle and make a cup of tea. You must be exhausted.'

'Ah! It's rough out,' agreed Mary, sounding relieved now that she had confessed to forgetting the cost of some of her purchases. 'But it's the rush that takes it out of you. If only that ol' bus came back half an hour later 'twould help. As it is, you have to keep one eye on the town clock all the time you're shopping.'

The little girls were delving into the bags, searching for their own secret shopping.

'Now mind what you're at,' said Mary sharply. 'Take your treasures and put 'em upstairs, and I'll help you pack 'em up when we've had a cup of tea.'

'Don't tell,' wailed Jane. 'It's a secret!'

'A secret!' echoed Frances.

'It still is,' retorted their mother. 'Up you go then, and take the things up carefully. And put on your slippers,' she shouted after them, as they clambered upstairs clutching several small packets against their chests.

'Mad as hatters, they are,' Mary confided to her mother. 'Barmy as March hares – and all because of Christmas!'

'All children are the same,' replied Mrs Berry, pouring boiling water into the teapot, and peering through the silvery steam to make sure it was not overfull. 'You three were as wild as they are, I well remember.' She carried the tray into the living room. 'Could you eat anything?' she asked.

'Not a thing,' said Mary, flopping down, exhausted, into the armchair by the fire, 'and a biscuit will be enough for the girls. They're so excited they won't sleep if they have too much before bedtime.'

'We'll get them upstairs early tonight,' said her mother. 'There are still some presents to pack.'

'We'll be lucky if they go to sleep before nine,' prophesied Mary. 'I heard Jane say she was going to stay awake to see if Father Christmas really does come. She doesn't believe it anymore, you know. I'm positive about that, but she don't let on in case he doesn't come!'

'She's seven,' observed Mrs Berry. 'Can't expect her to believe fairy tales all her life.'

'They've been telling her at school,' said Mary. 'Once they start school they lose all their pretty ways. Frances has only had six months there, but she's too knowing by half.'

The women sipped their tea, listening to the children moving about above them and relishing a few quiet moments on their own.

'They can have a good long time in the bath tonight,' said Mary, thinking ahead, 'then they'll be in trim to go to church with you tomorrow.'

'But wouldn't you like to go?'

'No, Mum. I'll see to the turkey while you're out. The service means more to you than me. Somehow church doesn't seem the same since Bertie went. Pointless, somehow.'

Mrs Berry was too taken aback to comment on this disclosure, and the entry of the children saved her from further conversation on the matter.

Her thoughts were in turmoil as she poured milk into the children's mugs and opened the biscuit tin for their probing fingers.

That unguarded remark of Mary's had confirmed her suspicions. She had watched Mary's growing casualness to religious matters and her increasing absences at church services with real concern. When Stanley died, she had found her greatest consolation in prayer and the teachings of the Church. 'Thy Will Be Done,' it said on the arch above the chancel steps, and for old Mrs Berry those words had been both succour, support and reason.

But, with the death of Bertie, Mary had grown hard, and had rejected a God who allowed such suffering to occur. Mrs Berry could understand the change of heart, but it did not lessen her grief for this daughter who turned her face from the comfort of religious beliefs. Without submission to a divine will, who could be happy? We were too frail to stand and fight alone, but that's what Mary was doing, and why she secretly was so unhappy.

Mrs Berry thrust these thoughts to the back of her mind. It was Christmas Eve, the time for good will to all men, the time to rejoice in the children's pleasure, and to hope that, somehow, the warmth and love of the festival would thaw the frost in Mary's heart.

'Bags not the tap end!' Mrs Berry heard Jane shout an hour later, as the little girls capered naked about the bathroom.

'Mum, she *always* makes me sit the tap end!' complained Frances. 'And the cold tap drips down my back. It's not fair!'

'No grizzling now on Christmas Eve,' said Mary briskly. 'You start the tap end, Frances, and you can change over at halftime. That's fair. You're going to have a nice long bathtime tonight while I'm helping Gran. Plenty of soap, don't forget, and I'll look at your ears when I come back.'

Mrs Berry heard the bath door close, and then open again.

'And stop sucking your facecloth, Frances,' scolded

her mother. 'Anyone'd think you're a little baby, instead of a great girl of five.'

The door closed again, and Mary reappeared, smiling.

'They'll be happy for twenty minutes. Just listen to them!'

Two young treble voices, wildly flat, were bellowing 'Away in a manger, no crib for a bed,' to a background of splashes and squeals.

'Did you manage to find some slippers for them?' asked Mrs Berry.

'Yes, Tom's Christine had put them by for me, and I had a quick look while the girls were watching someone try on shoes. There's a lot to be said for knowing people in the shops. They help you out on occasions like this.'

She was rummaging in a deep oilcloth bag as she spoke, and now drew out two boxes. Inside were the slippers. Both were designed to look like rabbits, with shiny black beads for eyes, and silky white whiskers. Jane's pair were blue, and Frances' red. They were Mrs Berry's present to her grandchildren, and she nodded her approval at Mary's choice.

'Very nice, dear, very nice. I'll just tuck a little chocolate bar into each one—'

'There's no need, Mum. This is plenty. You spoil them,' broke in Mary.

'Maybe, but they're going to have the chocolate. Something to wear is a pretty dull Christmas present for a child. I well remember my Aunt Maud – God rest her, poor soul. What a dance she led my Uncle Hubert! She used to give us girls a starched white pinafore every Christmas, and very miserable we thought them.' She shook her head. 'Ungrateful, weren't we? Now I can see it was a very generous present, as well as being useful; but my old grandad gave us two sugar mice, one pink and one white with long string tails, and they were much more welcome, believe me.'

'Like the tangerine and toffees you and Dad used to tuck in the toe of our stockings.' Mary smiled. 'We always rushed for those first before unpacking the rest. Funny how hungry you are at five in the morning when you're a child!'

'Get me some wrapping paper,' said Mrs Berry briskly, 'and I'll tie them up while those two rascals are safe for ten minutes. They've eyes in the backs of their heads at Christmastime.'

Mary left her mother making two neat parcels. Her wrinkled hands, dappled with brown age spots, were as deft as ever. Spectacles on the end of her nose, the old lady folded the paper this way and that, and tied everything firmly with bright red string.

Mary took the opportunity to smuggle a beautiful pink cyclamen into her own bedroom and hide it behind the curtain on the windowsill. It had cost more than she could really afford, but she had decided to forego a new pair of winter gloves. The old ones could be mended, and who was to notice the much sewn seams in a little place like Shepherds Cross?

She drew the curtains across to hide the plant and to keep out the draught, which was whistling through the cracks of the ancient lattice-paned window. Outside, the wind roared in the branches; a flurry of dead wet leaves flew this way and that as the eddies caught them. The rain slanted down pitilessly, and as a car drove past, the beams of its headlights lit up the shining road where the raindrops spun like silver coins.

She took out from a drawer her own presents for the children. There were two small boxes and two larger ones, and she opened them to have one last look before they were wrapped. In each of the smaller boxes a string of little imitation pearls nestled against a red mock-velvet background. How pretty they would look on the girls' best frocks! Simple, but good, Mary told herself, with satisfaction. As Mum had said, children wanted something more than everyday presents at Christmas, and the two larger boxes *were* rather dull perhaps.

They held seven handkerchiefs, one for each day of the week, with the appropriate name embroidered in the corner. Sensible, and would teach them how to spell too, thought Mary, putting back the lids.

She was just in time, for at that moment the door burst open and she only had a second in which to thrust the boxes back into the drawer, when two naked cherubs skipped in, still wet with bath water.

'What d'you think—' she began, but was cut short by two vociferous voices in unison.

'The water's all gone. Frances pushed out the plug—'

'I never then!'

'Yes, you did! You know you did! Mum, she wriggled it out with her bottom—'

'Well, she never changed ends, like you said. I only

wriggled 'cos the cold tap dripped down my back. I couldn't help it!'

'She done it a-purpose.'

'I never. I told you—'

Mary cut short their protestations.

'You'll catch your deaths. Get on back to the bathroom and start to rub dry. Look at your wet foot marks on the floor! What'll Gran say?'

They began to giggle, eyeing each other.

'Let's go down and frighten her, all bare,' cried Jane.

'Don't you dare now!' said their mother, her voice sharpened by the thought of the slippers being wrapped below.

A little chastened by her tone, the two romped out of the room, jostling together like puppies. Mary heard their squeals of laughter from behind the bathroom door, and smiled at her reflection in the glass.

'"Christmas comes but once a year,"' she quoted aloud. 'Perhaps it's as well!'

She followed her rowdy offspring into the bathroom.

Twenty minutes later the two girls sat barefoot on their wooden stools, one at each side of the fire. On their laps they held steaming bowls of bread and milk, plentifully sprinkled with brown sugar.

'You said we could hang up pillow slips tonight,' remarked Jane, 'instead of stockings.'

'I haven't forgotten. There are two waiting on the banisters for you to put at the end of your bed.'

'Will Father Christmas know?' asked Frances anxiously, her eyes wide with apprehension.

'Of course he will,' said their grandmother robustly. 'He's got plenty of sense. Been doing the job long enough to know what's what.'

Mary glanced at the clock.

'Finish up now. Don't hang it out, you girls. Gran and I've got a lot to do this evening, so you get off to sleep as quick as you can.'

'I'm staying awake till he comes,' said Jane firmly.

'Me too,' echoed Frances, scooping the last drop of milk from the bowl.

They went to kiss their grandmother. She held their soft faces against hers, relishing the sweet smell of soap and milk. How dear these two small mortals were!

'The sooner you get to sleep, the sooner the morning will come,' she told them.

She watched them as, followed by Mary, they tumbled up the staircase that opened from the room.

'I *shall* stay awake!' protested Jane. 'I shan't close my eyes, not for *one minute*! I promise you!'

Mrs Berry smiled to herself as she put another log on the fire. She had heard that tale many times before. If she were a betting woman she would lay a wager that those two would be fast asleep within the hour!

But, for once, Mrs Berry was wrong.

CHAPTER THREE

Upstairs, in the double bed, the two little girls pulled the clothes to their chins and continued their day-long conversation.

A nightlight, secure in a saucer on the dressing table, sent great shadows bowing and bending across the sloping ceiling, for the room was crisscrossed with draughts on this wild night from the ill-fitting window and door. Sometimes the brave little flame bent in a sudden blow from the cold air, as a crocus does in a gust of wind, but always it righted itself, continuing to give out its comforting light to the young children.

'Shall I tell you why I'm going to stay awake all night?' asked Jane.

'Yes.'

'Promise to do what I tell you?'

'Yes.'

'Promise *faithfully*? See my finger wet and dry? Cross your heart? *Everything?*'

'Everything,' agreed Frances equably. Her eyelids were beginning to droop already. Left alone, free from the vehemence of her sister, she would have fallen asleep within a minute.

'Then eat your pillow,' demanded Jane.

Frances was hauled back roughly from the rocking sea of sleep.

'You know I can't!' she protested.

'You promised,' said Jane.

'Well, I unpromise,' declared Frances. 'I can't eat a pillow, and anyway what would Mum say?'

'Then I shan't tell you what I was going to.'

'I don't care,' replied Frances untruthfully.

Jane, enraged by such lack of response and such wanton breaking of solemn vows, bounced over on to her side, her back to Frances.

'It was about Father Christmas,' she said hotly, 'but I'm not telling you now.'

'He'll come,' said Frances drowsily.

This confidence annoyed Jane still further.

'Maybe he won't then! Tom Williams says there isn't a Father Christmas. That's why I'm going to stay awake. To see. So there!'

Through the veils of sleep which were fast enmeshing her, Frances pondered upon this new problem. Tom Williams was a big boy, ten years old at least. What's more, he was a sort of cousin. He should know what he was talking about. Nevertheless . . .

'Tom Williams don't always speak the truth,' answered Frances. In some ways, she was a wiser child than her sister.

Jane gave an impatient snort.

'Besides,' said Frances, following up her point, 'our teacher said he'd come. She don't tell lies. Nor Mum, nor Gran.'

These were powerful allies, and Jane was conscious that Frances had some support.

'Grownups hang together,' said Jane darkly. 'Don't forget we saw *two* Father Christmases this afternoon in Caxley. What about that then?'

'They was men dressed up,' replied Frances stolidly. 'Only *pretend* Father Christmases. It don't mean there isn't a real one as 'll come tonight.'

A huge yawn caught her unawares.

'You stay awake if you want to,' she murmured, turning her head into the delicious warmth of the uneaten pillow. 'I'm going to sleep.'

Secure in her faith, she was asleep in five minutes, but Jane, full of doubts and resentful of her sister's serenity, threw her arms above her head, and, gripping the rails of the brass bedstead, grimly began her vigil. Tonight she would learn the truth!

Downstairs, the two women assembled the last few presents that needed wrapping on the big table.

They made a motley collection. There were three or four pieces of basketwork made by Mary, who was neat with her fingers, and these she eyed doubtfully.

'Can't see myself ever making a tidy parcel of these

flower holders,' she remarked. 'D'you think just a Christmas tag tied on would be all right?'

Mrs Berry surveyed the hanging baskets thoughtfully.

'Well, it always looks a bit slapdash, I feel, to hand over something unwrapped. Looks as though you can't be bothered—'

'I can't,' said Mary laconically.

'But I see your point. We'd make a proper pig's ear of the wrapping paper trying to cover those. You're right, my girl. Just a tag.'

Mary sat down thankfully and drew the packet of tags towards her. The presents were destined for neighbours, and the tags seemed remarkably juvenile for the elderly couples who were going to receive the baskets. Father Christmas waved from a chimney pot, a golliwog danced a jig, two pixies bore a Christmas tree, and a cat carried a Christmas pudding. Only two tags measured up to Mary's requirements, a row of bells on one and a red candle on the other. Ah well, she told herself, someone must make do with the pixies or the cat, and when you came to think of it the tags would be on the back of the fire this time tomorrow, so why worry? She wrote diligently.

Outside the wind still screamed, rattling the window, and making the back door thump in its frame. The curtains stirred in the onslaught, and now and again a little puff of smoke came into the room from the log fire, as the wind eddied round the chimney pot.

Mrs Berry looked up from the jar of honey she was wrapping.

'I'll go and see if the rain's blowing in under that door at the back.'

She went out, causing a draught that rustled the wrapping paper and blew two of Mary's tags to the floor. Mrs Berry was gone for some minutes, and returned red-faced from stooping.

'A puddle a good yard wide,' she puffed. 'I've left that old towel stuffed up against the crack. We'll have to get a new sill put on that threshold, Mary. It's times like this we miss our menfolk.'

Mary nodded, not trusting herself to speak. Hot tears pricked her eyes, but she bent lower to her task, so that her mother should not see them. How was it, she wondered, that she could keep calm and talk about her loss, quite in control of her feelings, for nine tenths of the time, and yet a chance remark, like this one, pierced her armour so cruelly? Poor Gran! If only she knew! Better, of course, that she did not. She would never forgive herself if she thought she had caused pain.

Unaware of the turmoil in her daughter's mind, Mrs Berry turned her attention to a round tin of shortbread.

' 'Pon my word,' she remarked. 'I never learn! After all these years, you'd think I'd know better than to pick a round tin instead of a square 'un. I'll let you tackle this, Mary. It's for Margaret and Mary Waters. They're good to us all through the year, taking messages and traipsing round with the parish magazine in all weathers.'

Mary reached across for the tin, then checked. The

eyes of the two women met questioningly. Above the sound of the gale outside they had heard the metallic clink of their letter box.

'I'll go,' said Mary.

An envelope lay on the damp mat. She opened the door, letting in a rush of wind and rain and a few sodden leaves. There was no one to be seen, but in the distance Mary thought she could see the bobbing light of a flashlight. To shout would have been useless. To follow, in her slippers, idiotic. She pushed the door

shut against the onslaught, and returned to the light with the envelope.

'For you, Mum,' she said, handing over the glistening packet.

Mrs Berry withdrew a Christmas card, bright with robins and frosted leaves, and two embroidered white handkerchiefs.

'From Mrs Burton,' said Mrs Berry wonderingly. 'Now, who'd have thought it? Never exchanged presents before, have we? What makes her do a thing like this, I wonder? And turning out too, on such a night. Dear soul, she shouldn't have done it. She's little enough to spare as it is.'

'You did feed her cat and chickens for her while she was away last summer,' said Mary. 'Perhaps that's why.'

'That's only acting neighbourly,' protested Mrs Berry. 'No call for her to spend money on us.'

'Given her pleasure, I don't doubt,' answered Mary. 'The thing is, do we give her something back? And, if so, what?'

It was a knotty problem. Their eyes ranged over the presents before them, already allotted.

'We'll have to find *something*,' said Mrs Berry firmly. 'What about the box of soap upstairs?'

'People are funny about soap,' said Mary. 'Might think it's a hint, you know. She's none too fond of washing, nice old thing though she is.'

They racked their brains in silence.

'Half a pound of tea?' suggested Mrs Berry at last.

'Looks like charity,' replied Mary.

'Well, I wouldn't say no to a nice packet of tea,' said Mrs Berry with spirit. 'What about one of our new tea towels then?'

'Cost too much,' said Mary. 'She'd mind about that.'

'I give up then,' said Mrs Berry. 'You think of something. I must say these last-minute surprises are all very fine, but they do put you to some thinking.'

She tied a final knot round the honey pot and rose to her feet again.

'Talking of tea, what about a cup?'

'Lovely,' said Mary.

'Shall I cut us a sandwich?'

'Not for me. Just a cup of tea.'

The old lady went out, and Mary could hear the clattering of cups and saucers, and the welcome tinkle of teaspoons. Suddenly, she felt inexpressibly tired. She longed to put her head down among the litter on the table and fall asleep. Sometimes she thought Christmas was more trouble than it was worth. All the fuss and flurry, then an empty purse just as the January bills came in. If only she had her mother's outlook! She still truly loved Christmas. She truly celebrated the birth of that God who walked beside her every hour of the day. She truly loved her neighbour – even that dratted Mrs Burton, who was innocently putting them to such trouble.

Mrs Berry returned with the round tin tray bearing the cups and saucers and the homely brown teapot clad in a knitted tea cosy. Her face had a triumphant smile.

'I've thought of something. A bottle of my blackcurrant wine. How's that? She can use it for her cough, if she don't like it for anything better. What say?'

'Perfect!' said Mary. In agreement at last, they sipped their tea thankfully.

Still awake upstairs, Jane heard the chinking of china and the voices of her mother and grandmother. Beside her, Frances snored lightly, her pink mouth slightly ajar, her lashes making dark crescents against her rosy cheeks.

Jane's vigil seemed lonelier and bleaker every minute. What's more, she was hungry, she discovered. The thought of the blue biscuit tin, no doubt standing by the teacups below, caused her stomach to rumble. Cautiously, she slid her skinny legs out of bed, took a swift glance at the two empty pillowcases draped expectantly one each end of the brass bed rail, and crept to the door.

The wind was making so much noise that no one heard the latch click, or the footsteps on the stairs. The child opened the bottom door, which led directly into the living room, and stood blinking in the light like a little owl caught in the sunshine.

'Mercy me!' gasped Mrs Berry, putting down her cup with a clatter. 'What a start you gave me, child!'

'Jane!' cried her mother. 'What on earth are you doing down here?' Her voice was unusually sharp. Surprised and startled, she could have shaken the child in her exasperation.

'I'm hungry,' whispered Jane, conscious of her unpopularity.

'You had a good supper,' said Mary shortly. 'Time you was asleep.'

'Let her come by the fire for a minute,' pleaded Mrs Berry. 'Shut that door, my dear. The draught fairly cuts through us. Want a cup of tea, and a biscuit?'

The child's face lit up. 'Shall I fetch a cup?'

'Not with those bare feet,' said Mary. 'I'll get your mug, and then you go straight back to bed as soon as you're finished. Your gran's too good to you.'

She hurried kitchenwards, and the child sat on the rag rug smiling at the flames licking the log. It was snug down here. It was always snug with Gran.

She put a hand on the old lady's knee. 'Mum's cross,' she whispered.

'She's tired. Done a lot today, and you know you should really be abed, giving her a break.'

They always hang together, these grownups, thought Jane rebelliously; but she took the mug of weak tea gratefully, and the top biscuit from the tin when it was offered, even though it was a Rich Tea and she knew there were Ginger Nuts further down.

'Is Frances asleep?' asked Mary.

'Yes. I couldn't get off.'

'You told me you didn't intend to,' replied her mother. 'Trying to see Father Christmas, silly girl. As though he'll come if you're awake! The sooner you're asleep the sooner he'll come!'

Torn with doubts, the child looked swiftly up into her grandmother's face. It told her nothing. The familiar kind smile played around the lips. The eyes looked down at her as comfortingly as ever.

'Your mother's right. Drink up your tea, and then snuggle back into bed. I'll come and tuck you up this time.'

Jane tilted her mug, put the last fragment of biscuit into her mouth, and scrambled to her feet.

'Whose presents are those?' she said, suddenly aware of the parcels on the table.

'Not yours,' said Mary.

'Neighbours',' said her grandmother in the same breath. 'You shall take some round for us tomorrow. And I want you to carry a bottle of wine very carefully to Mrs Burton. Can you do it, do you think?'

The child nodded, hesitated before her mother, then kissed her warmly on the cheek.

'You hussy!' said Mary, but her voice was soft, and the child saw that she was forgiven. Content at last, she followed her grandmother's bulk up the narrow stairs.

The flame of the night light was burning low in the little hollow of its wax. The shadows wavered about the room as the old woman and the child moved towards the bed.

'Now, no staying awake, mind,' whispered Gran, in a voice that brooked no argument. 'I don't know who's been stuffing your head with nonsense, but you can forget it. Get off to sleep, like Frances there. You'll see Father Christmas has been, as soon as you wake up.'

She kissed the child, and tucked in the bedclothes tightly.

Jane listened to her grandmother's footsteps descending the creaking stairs, sighed for her lost intentions, and fell, almost instantly, into a deep sleep.

CHAPTER FOUR

'My! That was a lucky escape,' said Mrs Berry. 'Good thing we hadn't got out those pillowcases!'

Two pillowcases, identical to those hanging limply upstairs, had been hidden behind the couch in the cottage parlour for the last two days. Most of the presents were already in them. A doll for each, beautifully dressed in handsewn clothes, joint presents from Mary and her mother; a game of Ludo for Frances and Snakes and Ladders for Jane; and a jigsaw puzzle apiece. All should provide plenty of future pleasure.

The American aunt had sent two little cardigans, pale pink and edged with silver trimming – far more glamorous than anything to be found in the Caxley shops. The less well-off aunt at Taunton had sent bath salts for both, which, Mary knew, would enchant the little girls. There were also gifts from kind neighbours – a box of beads, a toy shop (complete with tiny metal scales), and several tins of sweets, mint humbugs and homemade toffee among them.

A stocking, waiting to be filled with small knick-knacks, lay across each pillowcase. As soon as the children were safely asleep, the plan had been to substitute the full pillowcases for the empty ones.

'I thought she might reappear,' admitted Mary. 'She's twigged, you know, about Father Christmas. Some of the children at school have let it out.'

'She won't come down again, I'm certain,' replied Mrs Berry comfortingly. 'Let's fill up the stockings, shall we? We can put the last-minute odds and ends in when we carry up the pillowcases.'

Mary nodded agreement and went to the parlour, returning with the limp stockings. They were a pair of red and white striped woollen ones, once the property of the vicar's aunt, and reputedly kept for skating and skiing in her young days. Mary had bought them at a jumble sale, and each Christmas since they had appeared to delight the little girls.

From the dresser drawer, Mrs Berry collected the store of small treasures that had been hidden there for the last week or so. A few wrapped sweets, a curly stick of barley sugar, a comb, a tiny pencil and pad, a brooch and a handkerchief followed the tangerines that stuffed the toe of each stocking. Then, almost guiltily, Mrs Berry produced the final touch – two small wooden Dutch dolls.

'Saw them in the market at Caxley,' she said, 'and couldn't resist them, Mary. They reminded me of a family of Dutch dolls I had at their age. They can amuse themselves dressing them up.'

The dolls were tucked at the top, their shiny black heads and stiff wooden arms sticking out attractively. The two women gazed at their handiwork with satisfaction.

'Well, that's that!' said Mrs Berry. 'I'm just going to clear away this tray and tidy up in the kitchen, and I shan't be long out of bed.'

'I'll wait till I'm sure those two scallywags are really asleep,' answered Mary. 'I wouldn't put it past our

Jane to pretend, you know. She's stubborn when she wants to be, and she's real set on finding out who brings the presents.'

The hands of the clock on the mantelpiece stood at ten o'clock. How the evening had flown! Mary tidied the table, listening to the gale outside, and the sound of her mother singing in the kitchen.

She suddenly remembered her own small presents upstairs still unwrapped and crept aloft to fetch them. The door of the girls' room was ajar. She tiptoed in and looked down upon the sleeping pair. It seemed impossible that either of them could be feigning sleep, so rhythmically were they breathing. What angels they looked!

She made her way downstairs and swiftly wrapped up the necklaces and handkerchiefs. The very last, she thought thankfully! Just a tag for Mum's cyclamen, and I can write that and tie it on when I go to bed.

She selected the prettiest tag she could find, and slipped it into her skirt pocket to take upstairs.

Mrs Berry reappeared, carrying the glass of water that she took to her bedroom every night.

'I'll be off then, my dear. Don't stay up too long. You must be tired.'

She bent to kiss her daughter.

'The girls have gone off, I think, but I'll give them another ten minutes to make sure.'

'See you in the morning, then, Mary,' said the old lady, mounting the stairs.

Mary raked the hot ashes from the fire and swept up the hearth. She fetched the two bulging pillowcases and put the stockings on top of them. Then she sat in the old armchair and let exhaustion flood through her. Bone-tired, she confessed to herself. Bone-tired!

Above her she could hear the creaking of the floor-boards as her mother moved about, then a cry and hasty footsteps coming down the stairs.

The door flew open and Mrs Berry, clad in her flannel nightgown, stood, wild eyed, on the threshold.

'Mum, what's the matter?' cried Mary, starting to her feet.

'A mouse!' gasped Mrs Berry, shuddering uncontrol-lably. 'There's a mouse in my bedroom!'

The two women gazed at each other, horror struck. Mary's heart sank rapidly, but she spoke decisively.

'Here, you come by the fire, and let's shut that door. The girls will be waking up.'

She pushed up the armchair she had just vacated and Mrs Berry, still shuddering, sat down thankfully.

'You'll catch your death,' said Mary, raking a few bright embers together and dropping one or two shreds of dry bark from the hearth on to the dying fire. 'You ought to have put on your dressing gown.'

'I'm not going up there to fetch it!' stated Mrs Berry flatly. 'I know I'm a fool, but I just can't abide mice.'

'I'll fetch it,' said Mary, 'and I'll set the mousetrap too while I'm there. Where did it go?'

Mrs Berry shivered afresh.

'It ran under the bed, horrible little thing! You should've seen its tail, Mary! A good three inches long! It made me cry out, seeing it skedaddle like that.'

'I heard you,' said Mary, making for the kitchen to get the mousetrap.

Mrs Berry drew nearer to the fire, tucking her voluminous nightgown round her bare legs. A cruel draught whistled in from the passage, but nothing would draw her from the safety of the armchair. Who knows how many more mice might be at large on a night like this?

Mary, her mouth set in a determined line, reappeared with the mousetrap and went quietly upstairs. She returned in a moment, carrying her mother's dressing gown and slippers.

'Now you wrap up,' she said coaxingly, as if she were addressing one of her little daughters. 'We'll soon catch that old mouse for you.'

'I'm ashamed to be so afeared of a little creature,'

confessed Mrs Berry, 'but there it is. They give me the horrors, mice do, and rats even worse. Don't ask me why!'

Mary knew from experience this terror of her mother's. She confronted other hazards of country life with calm courage. Spiders, caterpillars, bulls in fields, adders on the heath, any animals in pain or fury found old Mrs Berry completely undaunted. Mary could clearly remember her mother dealing with a dog that had been run over and writhed, demented with pain, not far from their cottage door. It had savaged two would-be helpers, and a few distressed onlookers were wondering what to do next when Mrs Berry approached and calmed the animal in a way that had seemed miraculous. But a mouse sent her flying, and Mary knew, as she found some wood to replenish the fire, that nothing would persuade her mother back to the bedroom until the intruder had been dispatched.

She settled herself in the other armchair, resigned to another twenty minutes or more of waiting. She longed desperately for her bed, but could not relax until her mother was comfortably settled. She listened for sounds from above – the click of the mousetrap that would release her from her vigil, or the noise of the children waking and rummaging for the pillowcases, wailing at the nonappearance of Father Christmas.

But above the noise of the storm outside, it was difficult to hear anything clearly upstairs. She pushed the two telltale pillowcases under the table, so that they were hidden from the eyes of any child who might enter unannounced, and leaned back with her eyes closed.

Invariably, Bertie's dear face drifted before her when she closed her eyes, but now, to her surprise and shame, another man's face smiled at her. It was the face of one of Bertie's workmates. He too had been one of the party on that tragic wayzgoose, and had written to Mary and her mother soon after the accident. She had known him from childhood. Rather a milksop, most people said of Ray Bullen, but Mary liked his gentle ways and thought none the less of him because he had remained a bachelor.

'Some are the marrying sort, and some aren't,' she had replied once to the village gossip who had been speculating upon Ray's future. Mary was all too conscious of the desire of busybodies to find her a husband in the months after Bertie's death. They got short shrift from Mary, and interest waned before long.

'Too sharp tongued by half,' said those who had been lashed by it. 'No man in his senses would take her on, and them two girls too.'

Here they were wrong. One or two men had paid attention to Mary, and would have welcomed some advances on her side. But none were forthcoming. Truth to tell, Mary was in such a state of numbed shock for so long that very little affected her.

But Ray's letter of condolence had been kept. There was something unusually warm and comforting in the simple words. Here was true sympathy. It was the only letter that had caused Mary to weep and, weeping, to find relief.

She saw Ray very seldom, for their ways did not cross. But that afternoon in Caxley he had been at the bus stop when she arrived laden with baskets and anxious about the little girls amidst the Christmas traffic. He had taken charge of them all so easily and naturally – seeing them on to the bus, disposing of the parcels, smiling at the children and wishing them all well at Christmas – that it was not until she was halfway to Shepherds Cross that Mary realized that he had somehow contrived to give the little girls a shilling each. Also, she realized with a pang, he must have missed his own bus, which went out about the same time as theirs.

She supposed, leaning back now in the armchair, that her extreme tiredness had brought his face before her tonight. It was not a handsome face, to be sure, but it was kind and gentle, and, from all she heard, Ray Bullen had both those qualities as well as strong principles. He was a Quaker, she knew, and she remembered a little passage about Quakers from the library book she was reading. Something about them 'making the best chocolate and being very thoughtful and wealthy and good.' It had amused her at the time, and though Ray Bullen could never be said to be wealthy, he was certainly thoughtful and good.

She became conscious of her mother's voice, garrulous in her nervousness.

'It's funny how you can sense them when you're frightened of them. Not that I had any premonition tonight, I was too busy thinking about getting those pillowcases safely upstairs. But I well remember helping my aunt clear out her scullery when I was a child. No older than Frances, I was then, and she asked me to lift a little old keg she kept her flour in. And, do you know, I began to tremble, and I told her I just couldn't do it. "There's a mouse in there!" I told her.

'She was so wild. "Rubbish!" she stormed. She was a quick-tempered woman, red haired and plump, and couldn't bear to be crossed. "Pick it up at once!"

'And so I did. And when I looked inside, there *was* a mouse, dead as a doornail and smelling to high heaven! I dropped that double quick, you can be sure, and it rolled against a bottle of cider and smashed it to smithereens. Not that I waited to see it happen. I was down at the end of the garden, in the privy with the door bolted. She couldn't get at me there!'

Mary had heard the tale many times, but would not have dreamed of reminding her mother of the fact. It was her mother's way, she realized, of apologizing for the trouble she was causing.

Mrs Berry hated to be a nuisance, and now, with Mary so near to complete exhaustion, she was being the biggest nuisance possible, the old lady told herself guiltily. Why must that dratted mouse arrive in her bedroom on Christmas Eve?

In the silence that had fallen there was the unmistakeable click of a mousetrap. Mary leaped to her feet.

'Thank God!' said Mrs Berry in all seriousness. Panic seized her once more. 'Don't let me see it, Mary, will you? I can't bear to see their tails hanging down.'

'I'll bring the whole thing down in the wastepaper basket,' promised Mary.

But when she returned to the apprehensive old lady waiting below, she had nothing in her hand.

'He took a nibble and then got away,' she said. 'We'll have to wait a bit longer. I've set it a mite finer this time.'

'I wish you had a braver mother,' said Mrs Berry forlornly. Mary smiled at her, and her mother's heart turned over. The girl looked ten years younger when she smiled. She didn't smile enough, that was the trouble. Time she got over Bertie's loss. There was a time for grieving, and a time to stop grieving. After all, she was still young and, smiling as she was now, very pretty too.

Conversation lapsed, and the two tired women listened to the little intimate domestic noises of the house, the whispering of the flames, the hiss of a damp log, the rattle of the loose-fitting window. Outside, the rain fell down pitilessly. Mrs Berry wondered if the rolled-up towel was stemming the flood at the back door but was too tired to go and see.

She must have dozed, for when she looked at the clock it was almost eleven. Mary was sitting forward in her chair, eyes fixed dreamily on the fire, miles away from Shepherds Cross.

She stirred as her mother sat up.

'I'll go and see if we've had any luck.'

Up the stairs she tiptoed once more, and returned almost immediately. She looked deathly pale with tiredness, and Mrs Berry's heart was moved.

'Still empty. He's a fly one, that mouse. What shall we do?'

Mrs Berry took charge with a flash of her old energy and spirit.

'You're going to bed, my girl. You're about done in,

I can see. I'll stay down here for the night, for go up to that bedroom I simply cannot do!'

'But, Mum, it's such a beast of a night! You'd be better off in bed. Just wake me if the trap springs and I'll come and see to it. It's no bother, honest.'

'No, Mary, you've done more than enough, and tomorrow's a busy day. I'll be all right here in the armchair. 'Tisn't the first time I've slept downstairs, and the storm don't trouble me.'

Mary looked doubtfully at the old lady but could see that her mind was made up.

'All right then, Mum. I'll go and fetch your eider-down and pillow, and see you've got enough firing handy.'

Yet again she mounted the stairs, while Mrs Berry made up the fire and bravely went to have a quick look

at the towel by the back door. No more water had seeped in, so presumably the defenses were doing their work satisfactorily. She returned to the snug living room to find Mary plumping up the pillow.

'Now, you're sure you're all right?' she asked anxiously. 'If I hear that trap go off before I get to sleep, shall I call you?'

'No, my dear. You'll be asleep as soon as your head hits the pillow tonight. I can see that. I shall settle here and be perfectly happy.'

Mary retrieved the pillowcases, kissed her mother's forehead, and went to the staircase for the last time that night.

'Sleep well,' she said, smiling at her mother, who by now was wrapped in the eiderdown. 'You look as snug as a bug in a rug, as the children say.'

'Good night, Mary. You're a good girl,' said her mother, watching the door close behind her daughter.

Nearly half-past eleven, thought Mrs Berry. What a time to go to bed! Ten o'clock was considered quite late enough for the early risers of Shepherds Cross.

She struggled from her wrappings to turn off the light and to put a little small coal on the back of the fire. The room was very pretty and cosy by the flickering firelight. There was no sound from upstairs. All three of them, thought Mrs Berry, would be asleep by now, and that wretched mouse still making free in her own bedroom, no doubt.

Ah well, she was safe enough down here, and there was something very companionable about a fire in the room when you were settling down for the night.

She turned her head into the feather-filled pillow. Outside the storm still raged and she could hear the rain drumming relentlessly upon the roof and the road. It made her own comfort doubly satisfying.

God pity all poor travellers on a night like this, thought Mrs Berry, pulling up the eiderdown. 'There's one thing: I shan't be awake long, storm or no storm.'

She sighed contentedly and composed herself for slumber.

CHAPTER FIVE

But tired though she was, Mrs Berry could not get to sleep. Perhaps it was the horrid shock of the mouse, or the unusual bustle of Christmas that had overtired her. Whatever the reason, the old lady found herself gazing at the rosy reflection of the fire on the ceiling, her mind drifting from one inconsequential subject to the next.

The bubbling of rain forcing its way through the crack of the window reminded her of the more ominous threat at the back door. Well, she told herself, that towel was standing up to the onslaught when she looked a short while ago. It must just take its chance. In weather like this, usual precautions were not enough. Stanley would have known what to do. A rolled-up towel wouldn't have been good enough for him! Some sturdy carpentry would have made sure that the back door was completely weather-proof.

Mrs Berry sighed and thought wistfully of their manless state. Two good husbands gone, and no sons growing up to take their place in the household! It seemed hard, but the ways of God were inscrutable and who was to say why He had taken them first?

She thought of her first meeting with Stanley, when she was nineteen and he two years older. She had been in service then at the vicarage. Her employer was a predecessor of Mr Partridge's, a bachelor who held the living of Fairacre for many years. He was a vague, saintly man, a great Hebrew scholar who had written a number of learned commentaries on the minor prophets of the Old Testament. His parishioners were proud of his scholarship but, between themselves, admitted that he was 'only ninepence in the shilling' when it came to practical affairs.

Nevertheless, the vicarage was well run by a motherly old body who had once been nurse to a large family living in a castle in the next county. This training stood her in good stead when she took over the post of housekeeper to the vicar of Fairacre. She was methodical, energetic and abundantly kind. When a vacancy occurred for a young maid at the vicarage, Mrs Berry's parents thought she would be extremely lucky to start work in such pleasant surroundings. They applied for the post for their daughter, then aged thirteen.

Despite her lonely upbringing in the gamekeeper's cottage, Amelia Scott, as she was then, was a friendly child, anxious to help and blessed with plenty of common sense. The housekeeper realized her worth, and trained her well, letting her help in the kitchen as well as learning the secrets of keeping the rest of the establishment sweet and clean.

She thrived under the old lady's tuition, and learned by her example to respect the sterling qualities of her employer. He was always ready to help his neighbours, putting aside his papers to assist anyone in trouble, and welcoming all – even the malodorous vagrants who 'took advantage of him', according to the housekeeper – into his study to give them refreshment of body and spirit.

One bright June morning, when the dew sparkled on the roses, Amelia heard the chinking of metal on stone, and leaned out of the bedroom window to see two men at work on one of the buttresses of St Patrick's church. The noise continued all the morning, and as the sun rose in the blue arc of a cloudless sky, she wondered if the master would send her across with a jug of cider to wash down the men's dinners, as he often did. Then she remembered that he was out visiting at the other end of the parish. The housekeeper too was out on an errand. She was choosing the two plumpest young fowls, now running about in a neighbour's chicken run, for the Sunday meal.

Amelia was helping Bertha, the senior housemaid, to clean out the attics when they heard the ringing of the back-door bell.

'You run and see to that,' said Bertha, her arms full of derelict pillows. 'I'll carry on here.'

Amelia sped downstairs through the shadows and sunlight that streaked the faded blue carpet, and opened the back door.

A young man, with thick brown hair and very bright dark eyes, smiled at her apologetically.

He held his left hand, which was heavily swathed in a red spotted handkerchief, in his right one, and dark stains showed that he was bleeding profusely.

'Been a bit clumsy,' he said. 'My tool slipped.'

'Come in,' said Amelia, very conscious that she was alone to cope with this emergency. She led the way to the scullery and directed the young man to the shallow slate sink.

'Put your hand in that bowl,' she told him, 'and I'll

pump some water. It's very pure. We've got one of the deepest wells in the parish.'

It was certainly a nasty gash, and the pure water, so warmly recommended by Amelia, was soon cloudy with blood.

'Keep swilling it around,' directed Amelia, quite enjoying her command of the situation, 'while I get a bit of rag to bandage it.'

'There's no need miss,' protested the young man. 'It's stopping. Look!'

He held out the finger, but even as he did so, the blood began to well again. Amelia took one look and went to the bandage drawer in the kitchen dresser. Here, old pieces of linen sheeting were kept for just such an emergency, and the housekeeper's pot of homemade salve stood permanently on the shelf above.

No one quite knew what the ingredients of this cure-all were, for the recipe's secret was jealously guarded, but goose grease played a large part in it, along with certain herbs that the old lady gathered from the hedgerows. During the few years of Amelia's residence at the vicarage she had seen this salve used for a variety of ailments, from chilblains to the vicar's shaving rash, and always with good results.

She returned now with the linen and the pot of ointment. The young man still smiled, and Amelia smiled back.

'Let me wrap it up,' she said. 'Let's put some of this stuff on first.'

'What's in it?'

'Nothin' to hurt you.' Amelia assured him. 'It's good for everything. Cured some spots I had on my chin quicker 'n lightning.'

'I don't believe you ever had spots,' said the young man gallantly. He held out the wounded finger, and Amelia twisted the strip round and round deftly, cutting the end in two to make a neat bow.

'There,' she said with pride, 'now you'll be more comfortable.'

'Thank you, miss. You've been very kind.'

He picked up the bloodied handkerchief.

'Leave that there,' said Amelia, 'and I'll wash it for you.'

'No call to trouble you with that,' said the young man. 'My ma will wash it when I get back.'

'Blood stains need soaking in cold water,' Amelia

told him, 'and the sooner the better. I'll put it to soak now, then wash it out.'

'Well, thank you. We're working on the church for the rest of the week. Can I call in tomorrow to get it?'

Amelia felt a glow of pleasure at the thought of seeing him again, so soon. She liked his thick hair, his quick eyes, and his well-tanned skin – a proper nut-brown man, and polite too. Amelia looked at him with approval.

'I'll be here,' she promised.

'My name's Berry,' said the young man. 'Stanley Berry. What's yours?'

'Amelia Scott.'

'Well, thank you, Amelia, for a real good job. I must be getting back to work or I'll get sacked.'

She watched him cross the garden in the shimmering heat, the white bandage vivid against the brown background of his skin and clothes. He paused in the gateway leading to the churchyard, waving to her.

Delighted, she waved back.

'You've taken your time,' grumbled Bertha, when she returned to the attic. She looked at Amelia's radiant face shrewdly. 'Who'd you see down there? Prince Charming?'

Amelia forbore to answer, but thought that Bertha seemed to have guessed correctly.

The next morning the young man called to collect his handkerchief. Amelia had washed and ironed it with extreme care, and had put it carefully on the corner of the dresser to await its owner.

He carried a bunch of pink roses, and at the sight of them Amelia felt suddenly shy.

'You shouldn't have bothered,' she began, but the young man hastily put her at ease.

'My ma sent them, to thank you for what you did, and for washing the handkerchief. She said you're quite right. She'd have had the devil's own job to get out the stain if I'd left it till evening.'

Amelia took the bunch and smelled them rapturously.

'Please do thank her for them. They're lovely. I'll put them in my room.'

Stanley gave her a devastating smile again.

'I picked them,' he said gently.

'Then, thank you too,' said Amelia, handing over the handkerchief.

They stood in silence for a moment, gazing at each other, loath to break the spell of this magic moment.

'Best be going,' said Stanley, at length. He gave a gusty sigh, which raised Amelia's spirits considerably, and set off, stuffing the handkerchief in his pocket. He had not gone more than a few steps when he halted and turned.

'Can I come again, Amelia?'

'*Please*,' said Amelia, with rather more fervour than a well-bred young lady should have shown. But then Amelia always spoke her mind.

There was no looking back, no hesitation, no lovers' quarrels. From that first meeting they trod a smooth, blissfully happy path of courtship. They were both even-tempered, considerate people, having much the same background and, most important of all, the same sense of fun. There were no family difficulties, and the wedding took place on a spring day as sunny as that on which they had first met.

They lived for the first few years at Beech Green, in a small cottage thatched by Dolly Clare's father, who was one of their neighbours. The first two girls were born there, and then the house at Shepherds Cross was advertised to let. It was considerably bigger than their first house, and although it meant a longer cycle ride for Stanley, this did not deter him.

Here Mary was born. They had hoped for a boy this time, but the baby was so pretty and good that the accident of her sex was speedily forgotten.

Amelia and Stanley were true homemakers. Amelia's early training at the vicarage had given her many skills. She could make frocks for the children, curtains, bed-spreads, and rag rugs as competently as she could make a cottage pie or a round of shortbread. The house always looked as bright as a new pin, and Stanley saw to it that any stonework or woodwork was in good repair. They shared the gardening and it was Mrs Berry's pride that they never needed to buy a vegetable.

The longing for a son never left Amelia. She liked a man about the place, and it was doubly grievous when Stanley died so suddenly. She lost not only her lover and husband, but the comfort of all that a shared life meant.

Mary's Bertie brought back to the cottage the feeling of comfort and reliability. The birth of her grandson had meant more to Mrs Berry than she cared to admit. It was the continuance of male protection that subconsciously she needed. The baby's early death was something she mourned as deeply as Mary and Bertie had.

A piece of wood fell from the fire, and Mrs Berry stirred herself to reach for the tongs and replace it. Not yet midnight! She seemed to have been lying there for hours, dreaming of times passed.

Poor Stanley, poor Bertie, poor baby! But what a blessing the two little girls were! Mary knew how to bring up children. Plenty of fun, but no nonsense when it came to doing as they were told. Say what you will, thought old Mrs Berry, it didn't do people any harm to have a little discipline. You could cosset them too much, and give in to their every whim, and what happiness did that bring?

She remembered neighbours in the early days of her marriage at Beech Green. They were an elderly pair when their first child arrived, a pale sickly little fellow called, much to the ribaldry of some of the Beech Green folk, Clarence.

The baby was only put out into the garden on the warmest days, and then he was so swaddled in clothes that his normally waxen complexion was beaded with perspiration. The doctor harangued the doting mother; friends and neighbours, genuinely concerned for the child's health, proffered advice. Nothing was of any avail. Clarence continued to be smothered with love.

Not surprisingly, he was late in walking and talking. When he was at the toddling stage, his mother knitted him a long pair of reins in scarlet wool, and these were used in all his walks abroad. Mrs Berry herself had seen the child tethered by these same red reins to the fence near the back door, so that his mother could keep an eye on him as she worked.

He was a docile child, too languid to protest against his restrictions and, never having known freedom, he accepted his lot with a sweet meekness that the other mothers found pathetic.

Clarence reached the age of six, still cosseted, still adored, still forbidden the company of rough playmates who might harm him. But one bleak December day he fell ill with some childish infection that a normal boy would have thrown off in a day or two. Clarence drooped and died within the week, and the grief of the parents was terrible to see.

Poor Clarence and his red reins! thought Mrs Berry, looking back over the years. She thought of him as 'the sweet dove' that died, in Keats' poem. Long, long ago she had learned it, chanting with the other children at the village school, and still, seventy years on, she could remember it.

I had a dove, and the sweet dove died;
And I have thought it died of grieving:
Oh, what could it grieve for? Its feet were tied
With a silken thread of my own hand's weaving;
Sweet little red feet! Why should you die—
Why should you leave me, sweet bird, why?
You lived alone in the forest tree,
Why, pretty thing, would you not live with me?
I kissed you oft and gave you white peas;
Why not live sweetly, as in the green trees?

Yes, that was Clarence! 'Tied with a silken thread' of his poor mother's weaving. The stricken parents had moved away soon after the tragedy, and very little was heard of them, although someone once said that the mother had been taken to the madhouse, years later, and was never fit to be released.

Thank God, thought Mrs Berry, turning her pillow, that children were brought up more sensibly these days. She thought of Mary's two vivacious daughters, their glossy hair and round pink cheeks, their exuberance, their inexhaustible energy. Well, they were quiet enough at the moment, though no doubt they would wake early and fill the house with their excitement.

Mrs Berry rearranged the eiderdown, turned her cheek into the pillow, and, thanking God for the blessing of a family, fell asleep at last.

CHAPTER SIX

An unaccustomed sound woke the old lady within an hour. She slept lightly these days, and the stirring of one of her granddaughters or the mewing of a cat was enough to make her instantly alert.

She lay listening for the sound again. The wind still moaned and roared outside, the rain pattered fitfully against the windowpane, and the fire whispered as the wood ash fell through the bars of the grate.

It was a metallic noise that had roused her. What could it be? It might possibly be caused by part of the metal trellis which she and Mary had erected against the front porch to aid the growth of a new rose. Could it have blown loose?

But she could have sworn that the sound was nearer at hand, somewhere inside the house. It was not the welcome click of the mousetrap at its work. Something downstairs . . .

She sat upright in the chair. The fire had burned very low, and she leaned forward to put a little more wood on it, taking care to make no noise. Her ears strained for a repetition of the sound.

Now she thought she could hear a slight scuffling noise. A bird? Another mouse? Her heart began to beat quickly. And then the tinny sound again, as though a lid were being lifted from a light saucepan, or a cake tin. Without doubt, someone was in the kitchen!

Mrs Berry sat very still for a minute. She felt no fear,

but she was cautious. She certainly did not intend to rouse the sleeping family above. Whoever it was, Mrs Berry felt quite capable of coping with him. Some rough old tramp probably, seeking a dry billet from the storm and, if left alone, on his way before the house stirred at daybreak. Mrs Berry began to feel justifiable annoyance at the thought of some wastrel making free with her accommodation, and, what was more to the point, rifling the larder.

She bent to pick up the poker from the hearth. There was only one chance in ten that she would need to use it, but it was as well to be armed. It gave her extra confidence, and should the man be so silly as to show fight, then she would lay about him with energy and leave him marked.

Tightening her dressing-gown cord round her ample waist, Mrs Berry, poker in hand, moved silently to the door of the living room. This door, then a short passage, and then the kitchen door needed to be negotiated before she came face to face with her adversary. Mrs Berry determined to take the obstacles at a rush, catching the intruder before he had a chance to make his escape.

For one brief moment, before she turned the doorknob, the battered face of an old woman swam into Mrs Berry's mind. The photograph had been given pride of place in the local paper only that week, and showed the victim of some young hooligans who had broken into her pathetic home to take what they could. Well, Mrs Berry told herself sturdily, such things might happen in a town. It wouldn't occur in a little homely place like Shepherds Cross! She had dealt with plenty of scoundrels in her day, and knew that a stout heart was the best defence against bullies. Right would always triumph in the end, and no good ever came of showing fear!

She took a deep breath, a firmer grip on the poker, and flung open the door. Four quick determined steps took her to the kitchen door. She twisted the knob, and pushed the door open with her foot.

There was a stifled sound, something between a sob and a scream, a scuffle, and an unholy clattering as a large tin fell upon the tiles of the kitchen floor.

Mrs Berry switched on the light with her left hand, raised the poker menacingly in her right, and advanced upon her adversary.

Upstairs, Jane stirred. She lay still for a minute or two, relishing the warmth of her sister's back against hers, and the delicious warm hollow in which her cheek rested.

Then she remembered, and sat up. It was just light enough to see that the two empty pillowcases had vanished. She crept carefully out of bed, and went to the foot. There on the floor stood two beautifully knobbly pillowcases, and across each lay an equally beautiful striped stocking.

He had been! Father Christmas had been! Wild excitement was followed by a wave of shame. And she had not seen him! She had fallen asleep, after all her resolutions! It would be a whole year now before she could put Tom Williams' assertion to the test again. She shivered in the cold draught that blew under the door.

Her hands stroked the bulging stocking lovingly. There was the tangerine, there were the sweets, and this must be a dear little doll at the top. If only morning would come! She did not intend to undo the presents now. She would wait until Frances woke.

She crept back to bed, shivering with cold and excitement. She thrust her head into the hollow of her pillow again, leaned back comfortably against her sister, sighed rapturously at the thought of joys to come, and fell asleep again within a minute.

*

Mrs Berry's stern gaze, which had been directed to a point about six feet from the ground, at a height where her enemy's head should reasonably have been, now fell almost two feet to rest upon a pale, wretched urchin dressed in a streaming wet raincoat.

At his feet lay Mrs Berry's cake tin, luckily right way up, with her cherished Madeira cake exposed to the night air. The lid of the cake tin lay two yards away, where it had crashed in the turmoil.

'*Pick that up!*' said Mrs Berry in a terrible voice, pointing imperiously with the poker.

Snivelling, the child did as he was told, and put it on the table.

'*Now the lid!*' said Mrs Berry with awful emphasis. The boy sidled nervously towards it, his eyes fixed fearfully upon the menacing poker. He retrieved it and replaced it fumblingly, Mrs Berry watching the while.

The floor was wet with footmarks. The sodden towel had been pushed aside by the opening door. Mrs Berry remembered with a guilty pang that she had forgotten to lock the door amidst the general excitement of Christmas Eve.

She looked disapprovingly at the child's feet, which had played such havoc upon the kitchen tiles. They were small, not much bigger than Jane's, and clad in a pair of sneakers that squelched with water every time the boy moved. He had no socks, and his legs were mauve with cold and covered with goose pimples.

Mrs Berry's motherly heart was smitten, but no sign of softening showed in her stern face. This boy was nothing more than a common housebreaker and thief. A minute more and her beautiful Madeira cake, with

its artistic swirl of angelica across the top, would have been demolished – gulped down by this filthy raga-muffin.

Nevertheless, one's Christian duty must be done.

'Take off those shoes and your coat,' commanded Mrs Berry, 'and bring them in by the fire. I want to know more about you, my boy.'

He struggled out of them, and picked them up in a bundle in his arms. His head hung down and little droplets of water ran from his bangs down his cheeks.

Mrs Berry unhooked the substantial striped roller towel from the back of the door and motioned to the boy to precede her to the living room.

'And don't you dare to make a sound,' said Mrs Berry in a fierce whisper. 'I'm not having everyone woken up by a rapscallion like you.'

She prodded him in the back with the poker and followed her reluctant victim to the fireside.

He was obviously completely exhausted and was about to sink into one of the armchairs, but Mrs Berry stopped him.

'Oh, no you don't, my lad! Dripping wet, as you are! You towel yourself dry before you mess up my furniture.'

The boy took the towel and rubbed his soaking hair and wet face. Mrs Berry studied him closely. Now that she had time to look at him, she saw that the child was soaked to the skin. He was dressed in a T-shirt and grey flannel shorts, both dark with rainwater.

'Here, strip off,' commanded Mrs Berry.

'Eh?' said the boy, alarmed.

'You heard what I said. Take off those wet clothes. Everything you've got on.'

The child's face began to pucker. He was near to tears.

'Lord, boy,' said Mrs Berry testily, 'I shan't look at you. In any case, I've seen plenty of bare boys in my time. Do as you're told, and I'll get you an old coat to put on while your things dry.'

She stood a chair near the fire and hung the child's sodden coat across the back of it. His small sneakers were placed on the hearth, on their sides, to dry.

The boy slowly divested himself of his wet clothing, modestly turning his back towards the old lady.

She thrust more wood upon the fire, looking at the blaze with satisfaction.

'Don't you dare move till I get back,' warned Mrs Berry, making for the kitchen again. An old duffel coat of Jane's hung there. It should fit this skinny shrimp well enough. Somewhere too, she remembered, a pair of shabby slippers, destined for the next jumble sale, were tucked away.

She found them in the bottom of the shoe cupboard and returned to the boy with her arms full. He was standing shivering by the fire, naked but for the damp towel round his loins.

He was pathetically thin. His shoulder blades stuck out like little wings, and every rib showed. His arms were like sticks, his legs no sturdier, and they were still, Mrs Berry noticed, glistening with water.

'Sit down, child,' she said, more gently, 'and give me that towel. Seems you don't know how to look after yourself.'

He sat down gingerly on the very edge of the armchair, and Mrs Berry knelt before him rubbing energetically at the skinny legs. Apart from superficial mud, Mrs Berry could see that the boy was basically well cared for. His toe nails were trimmed, and his scarred knees were no worse than most little boys'.

She looked up into the child's face. He was pale with fatigue and fright, his features sharp, the nose prominent; his small mouth, weakly open, disclosed two slightly projecting front teeth. Mouselike, thought Mrs Berry, with an inward shudder, and those great ears each side of the narrow pointed face added to the effect.

'There!' said Mrs Berry. 'Now you're dry. Put your feet in these slippers and get this coat on you.'

The child did as he was told in silence, fumbling

awkwardly with the wooden toggle fastenings of the coat.

'Here, let me,' said Mrs Berry, with some exasperation. Deft herself, she could not abide awkwardness in others. The boy submitted to her ministrations, holding up his head meekly, and gazing at her from great dark eyes as she swiftly fastened the top toggles.

'Now pull that chair up close to the fire, and stop shivering,' said Mrs Berry briskly. 'We've got a lot to talk about.'

The boy did as he was bidden, and sat with his hands held out to the blaze. By the light of the fire, Mrs Berry observed the dark rings under the child's eyes and the open drooping mouth.

'Close your mouth and breathe through your nose,' Mrs Berry told him. 'Don't want to get adenoids, do you?'

He closed his mouth, swallowed noisily, and gave the most appallingly wet sniff. Mrs Berry made a sound of disgust, and struggled from her chair to the dresser.

'Blow your nose, for pity's sake,' she said, offering him several paper handkerchiefs. He blew noisily, and then sat, seemingly exhausted by the effort, clutching the damp tissue in his skinny claw.

'Throw it on the back of the fire, child,' begged Mrs Berry. 'Where on earth have you been brought up?'

He looked at her dumbly and, after a minute, tossed the handkerchief towards the fire. He missed and it rolled into the hearth by the steaming sneakers.

Mrs Berry suddenly realized that she was bone tired, it would soon be one o'clock, and that she wished the wretched child had chosen some other house to visit at such an hour. Nevertheless, duty beckoned, and she girded herself to the task.

'You know what you are, don't you?' she began. The boy shook his head uncomprehendingly.

'You are a burglar and a thief,' Mrs Berry told him. 'If I handed you over to the police, you'd get what you deserve.'

At this the child's dark eyes widened in horror.

'Yes, you may well look frightened,' said Mrs Berry, pressing home the attack. 'People who break into other people's homes and take their things are nothing more than common criminals and have to be punished.'

'I never took nothin',' whispered the boy. With a shock, Mrs Berry realized that these were the first words that she had heard him utter.

'If I hadn't caught you when I did,' replied Mrs Berry severely, 'you would have eaten that cake of mine double quick! Now wouldn't you? Admit it. Tell the truth.'

'I was hungry,' said the child. He put his two hands on his bare knees and bent his head. A tear splashed down upon the back of one hand, glittering in the firelight.

'And I suppose you are still hungry?' observed Mrs Berry, her eyes upon the tear that was now joined by another.

'It's no good piping your eye,' she said bracingly, 'though I'm glad to see you're sorry. But whether 'tis for what you've done, or simply being sorry for yourself, I just don't know.'

She leaned forward and patted the tear-wet hand.

'Here,' she said, more gently, 'blow your nose again and cheer up. I'll go and get you something to eat, although you know full well you don't deserve it.' She struggled from her chair again.

'It won't be cake, I can tell you that,' she told him flatly. 'That's for tea tomorrow – today, I suppose I should say. Do you realize, young man, that it's Christmas Day?'

The boy, snuffling into his handkerchief, looked bewildered but made no comment.

'Well, what about bread and milk?'

A vision of her two little granddaughters spooning up their supper – days ago, it seemed, although it was only a few hours – rose before her eyes. Simple and nourishing, and warming for this poor, silly, frightened child!

'Thank you,' said the boy. 'I like bread and milk.'

She left him, still sniffing, but with the second paper handkerchief deposited on the back of the fire as instructed.

'Not a sound now,' warned Mrs Berry, as she departed. 'There's two little girls asleep up there. And their ma. All tired out and need their sleep. Same as I do, for that matter.'

She cut a thick slice of bread in the cold kitchen. The wind had not abated, although the rain seemed less violent, Mrs Berry thought, as she waited for the milk to heat. She tidied the cake tin away, wondering whether she would fancy the cake at tea time after all its vicissitudes. Had those grubby paws touched it, she wondered?

She poured the steaming milk over the bread cubes, sprinkled it well with brown sugar and carried the bowl to the child.

He was lying back in the chair with his eyes shut, and for a moment Mrs Berry thought he was asleep. He looked so defenceless, so young, and so meekly mouselike, lying there with his pink-tipped pointed nose in the air, that Mrs Berry's first instinct was to tuck him up in her dressing gown and be thankful that he was at rest.

But the child struggled upright, and held out his skinny hands for the bowl and spoon. For the first time he smiled, and although it was a poor, wan thing as smiles go, it lit up the boy's face and made him seem fleetingly attractive.

Mrs Berry sat down and watched him attack the meal. It was obvious he was ravenously hungry.

'I never had no tea,' said the child, conscious of Mrs Berry's eyes upon him.

'Why not?'

The boy shrugged his shoulders.

'Dunno.'

'Been naughty?'

'No.'

'Had too much dinner then?'

The child gave a short laugh.

'Never get too much dinner.'

'Was your mother out then?'

'No.'

The boy fell silent, intent upon spooning the last delicious morsels from the bottom of the bowl.

'I don't live with my mother,' he said at last.

'With your gran?'

'No. A foster mother.'

Mrs Berry nodded, her eyes never moving from the child's face. What was behind this escapade?

'Where have you come from?' she asked.

The boy put the empty bowl carefully in the corner of the hearth.

'Tupps Hill,' he answered.

Tupps Hill! A good two or three miles away! What a journey the child must have made, and in such a storm!

'Why d'you want to know?' said the boy, in a sudden panic. 'You going to send the police there? They don't know nothin' about me runnin' off. Honest! Don't let on, madam, please, madam!'

The 'madam' amused and touched Mrs Berry. Was this how he had been told to address someone in charge of an institution, or perhaps a lady magistrate at some court proceedings? This child had an unhappy background, that seemed certain. But why was he so scared of the police?

'If you behave yourself and show some sense,' said Mrs Berry, 'the police will not be told anything at all. But I want to know more about you, young man.'

She picked up the bowl.

'Would you like some more?'

'Can I?' said the child eagerly.

'Of course,' said Mrs Berry, resting the bowl on one hip and looking down at the boy.

'What's your name?'

'Stephen.'

'Stephen what?'

'It's not my foster mother's name,' said the boy evasively.

'So I imagine. What is it, though?'

'It's Amonetti. Stephen Amonetti.'

Mrs Berry nodded slowly, as things began to fall into place.

'So you're Stephen Amonetti, are you? I think I knew your dad some years ago.'

She walked slowly from the room, sorting out a rag bag of memories, as she made her way thoughtfully towards the kitchen.

CHAPTER SEVEN

Amonetti!

Pepe Amonetti! She could see him now, as he had first appeared in Beech Green during the final months of the last war. He was a very young Italian prisoner of war, barely twenty, and his dark curls and sweeping black eyelashes soon had all the village girls talking.

He was the youngest of a band of Italian prisoners allotted to Jesse Miller, who then farmed a large area at Beech Green. He was quite irrepressible, bubbling over with the joy of living – doubly relishing life, perhaps, because of his short time on active service.

As he drove the tractor, or cleared a ditch, or slashed back a hedge, he sang at the top of his voice, or chattered in his pidgin English to any passer-by.

The girls, of course, did not pass by. The string of compliments, the flashing glances, the expressive hands, slowed their steps. Pepe, with his foreign beauty, stood out from the local village boys like some exotic orchid among a bunch of cottage flowers. In theory, he had little spare time for such dalliance. In practice, he managed very well, with a dozen or more willing partners.

The young lady most in demand at Beech Green at that time was a blonde beauty called Gloria Jarvis.

The Jarvises were a respectable couple with a string of flighty daughters. Gloria was one of the youngest, and had learned a great deal from her older sisters. The fact that the air base nearby housed several hundred eager young Americans generous with candy, cigarettes and nylon stockings had hastened Gloria's progress in the art of making herself charming.

As was to be expected, 'them Jarvis girls' were considered by the upright members of the community to be 'a fair scandal, and a disgrace to honest parents.' Any man, however ill-favoured or decrepit, was reckoned to be in danger from their wiles, and as soon as Pepe arrived at Beech Green it was a foregone conclusion that he would fall prey to one of the Jarvis harpies.

'Not that he'll put up much of a fight,' observed one middle-aged lady to her neighbour. 'Got a roving eye himself, that lad.'

'Well,' replied her companion indulgently, 'you knows what these foreigners are! Hot blooded. It's all that everlasting sun!'

'My Albert was down with bronchitis and chilblains all through the Italian campaign,' retorted the first lady. 'No, you can't blame the climate for their goings-on. It's just that they're made that way, and them Jarvis girls won't cool their blood, that's for sure.'

It was not long before Pepe's exploits, much magnified in conversations among scandalized matrons, were common knowledge in the neighbourhood, and it was Gloria Jarvis who was named as being the chief object of his attentions.

Gloria may have lost her heart to Pepe's Latin charms, but she did not lose her head. An Italian prisoner of war had little money to spend on a girl, and Gloria continued to see a great deal of her American admirers who spent more freely. Those of them who knew about Pepe dismissed the affair good-naturedly. Gloria was a good-time girl, wasn't she? So what?

Pepe, on the other hand, resented the other men's attentions, and became more and more possessive as time went by. He certainly had more hold over the wayward Gloria than his rivals, and though she tossed her blonde Edwardian coiffure and pretended indifference, Gloria was secretly a little afraid of Pepe's passion.

The war ended in 1945, a few months after their first meeting, and Pepe elected to stay on in England as a farm worker. By this time, a child was on the way, and Gloria and Pepe were married at the registry office in Caxley.

The child, a girl, had Pepe's dark good looks. A blond boy, the image of his mother, appeared a year later, and the family began to be accepted in Beech Green. Pepe continued to work for Jesse Miller and to occupy one of his cottages.

For a few years all went well, and then Pepe vanished. Gloria and the two children had a hard time of it, although Jesse Miller kindheartedly allowed them to continue to live in the cottage. It was during these difficult days that Mrs Berry had got to know Gloria better.

She was vain, stupid and a slattern, but she was also abandoned and in despair. Mrs Berry helped her to find some work at a local big house, and now and again looked after the children to enable Gloria to go shopping or to visit the doctor. The old Jarvises were dead, by now, and the older sisters were little help.

Mrs Berry showed Gloria how to make simple garments for the children, taught her how to knit and, more useful still, how to choose the cheap cuts of meat and cook them so that a shilling would stretch to its farthest limit.

Happily married herself, Mrs Berry urged Gloria to find Pepe and make it up, if only for the sake of the family. But it was two years before the errant husband was traced, and another fifteen months before he could be persuaded to return.

He had found work in Nottingham, and came back to Beech Green just long enough to collect Gloria and the children, their few poor sticks of furniture and their clothes. They left for Nottingham one grey December day, but Pepe had found time to call at Mrs Berry's and to thank her for all she had done.

Handsomer than ever, Pepe had stood on her doorstep, refusing to come in, his eyes shy, his smile completely disarming. No one, least of all Mrs Berry, could have remained hostile to this winning charmer with his foreign good manners.

'I did nothing – no more than any other neighbour,' Mrs Berry told him. 'But now it's your concern, Pepe. You see you treat her right and make a fresh start.'

'Indeed, yes. I do mean to do that,' said Pepe earnestly. He thrust his hand down inside his greatcoat and produced a ruffled black kitten, which he held out to Mrs Berry with a courtly bow.

'Would you please to accept? A thank you from the Amonettis?'

Mrs Berry was taken aback but rallied bravely. She knew quite well that the kitten was their own, and that they could not be bothered to take it with them to their new home. But who could resist such a gesture? And who would look after the poor little waif if she did not adopt it?

She took the warm furry scrap and held it against her face.

'Thank you, Pepe. I shall treasure it as a reminder of you all. Good luck now, and mind my words.'

For some time after this Mrs Berry heard nothing of the Amonettis. The kitten, named Pepe after its donor, grew up to be a formidable mouser and was much loved by the Berry family. Years later, someone in Caxley told Mrs Berry that Pepe had vanished yet again, and that Gloria had returned to live with a sister in the county town twenty miles away. Whilst there, she had had one last brief reconciliation with Pepe, but within a week there had been recriminations, violence and police action. After this, Pepe had vanished for good, and it was generally believed that this time he had returned to Italy.

The outcome of that short reunion must be Stephen, Mrs Berry thought to herself, as she stood in her draughty kitchen preparing the boy's meal. Gloria's present circumstances she knew from hearsay. She continued to live in one room of her sister's house and was what Mrs Berry still thought of as 'a woman of the streets.' No wonder that the boy had been taken into the care of the local authority. His mother, though to be pitied in some ways, Mrs Berry told herself charitably, was no fit person to bring up the boy, and heaven above knows what the conditions of the sister's house might be! Those Jarvis girls had all been first-class sluts, and no mistake!

Mrs Berry picked up the tray and carried it back to the fireside.

The child's smile was stronger this time.

'You are very kind,' he said, with a touch of his father's grace, reaching hungrily for the food.

She sat back in the armchair and watched the boy. Now that he had eaten and was getting warm, the pinched look, which sharpened his mouselike features, had lessened. His cheeks glowed pink and his lustrous dark eyes glanced about the room as he became more relaxed. Given time, thought Mrs Berry, this boy could become as bewitching as his father. But, at the moment, he was unhappy. What could have sent the child out into such a night as this? And furthermore, what was to be done about it?

Mrs Berry bided her time until the second bowlful had vanished, then took up the poker. The boy looked apprehensive, but Mrs Berry, ignoring him, set the poker about its legitimate business of stirring the fire into a blaze, and then replaced it quietly.

'Now,' she said, in a businesslike tone, 'you can just explain what brings you into my house at this time of night, my boy.'

There was a long pause. In the silence, the clock on the mantel shelf struck two and a cinder clinked into the hearth. The wind seemed to have shifted its quarter slightly, for now it had found a crevice by the window and moaned there as if craving for admittance.

'I'm waiting,' said Mrs Berry ominously.

The boy's thin fingers fidgeted nervously with the toggle fastenings. His eyes were downcast.

'Not much to tell,' he said at last, in a husky whisper.

'There must be plenty,' replied Mrs Berry, 'to bring you out from a warm bed on Christmas Eve.'

The child shook his head unhappily. Tears welled up again in the dark eyes.

'Now, that's enough of that!' said the old lady. 'We've had enough waterworks for one night. If you won't tell me yourself, you can just answer a few questions. And I want the truth, mind!'

The boy nodded, and wiped his nose on the back of his hand. Mrs Berry pointed in silence to the paper hankies beside him. Meekly, he took one and dried his eyes.

'You say you live at Tupps Hill?'

The child nodded.

'Who with?'

A look of fear crept over the mouselike face.

'You tellin' the police?'

'Not if you tell me the truth.'

'I live at Number Three. With Mrs Rose.'

'Betty Rose? And her husband's Dick Rose, the roadman?'

'That's right.'

Mrs Berry digested this information, whilst the child took advantage of the lull in the interrogation to turn his shoes in the hearth. They were drying nicely.

Mrs Berry tried to remember all she knew about the Roses. They had been married some time before her own girls, she seemed to recall, and Betty's mother had been in good service at Caxley. Other than that, she knew little about them, except that they were known to be a respectable honest pair and regular churchgoers. Dick Rose was a slow methodical fellow, who would never rise above his present job of road sweeper in Caxley, from what Mrs Berry had heard.

'Any children?' she asked.

'Two!' replied the boy. He looked sulky. Was this the clue? Was the child jealous for some reason?

'How old?'

'Jim's eleven, two years older 'n me. Patsy's eight, nearly nine. A bit younger 'n me.'

That would be about right, thought Mrs Berry,

trying to piece the past together from her haphazard memories, and the child's reluctant disclosures.

'You're lucky to live with the Roses,' observed the old lady, 'and to have the two children for company.'

The boy gave a sniff, but whether in disgust or from natural causes it was impossible to say.

'You get on all right?'

'Sometimes. Patsy tags on too much. Girls is soppy.'

'They've usually got more sense than boys,' retorted Mrs Berry, standing up for her own sex. 'You notice it isn't Patsy who's run out into a storm and got into trouble.'

The child stuck out his lower lip mutinously but said nothing. The drenched raincoat was now steaming steadily, and Mrs Berry turned it on the back of the chair. The boy's thin T-shirt, which had been hanging over the fire screen, was now dry, and Mrs Berry smoothed it neatly into shape on her knee before folding it.

'Patsy's got a watch,' said the boy suddenly.

'Has she now?'

'So's Jim. They both got watches. Patsy and Jim.'

'For Christmas, do you mean?'

'No, no!' said the child impatiently. 'Patsy had hers in the summer, for her birthday. Jim had his on his birthday. Last month it was.'

'They were lucky.'

She waited for further comment, but silence fell again. The boy was clearly upset about something, some injustice connected with the watches, some grievance that still rankled. His fingers plucked nervously at a piece of loose cotton on the hem of the duffel coat.

His face was thunderous. Pepe's Latin blood was apparent as his son sat there brooding by the fire.

'They're their own kids, see?' said the boy, at length. 'So they give 'em watches. I reckon my real mum'd give me one – just like that, if I asked her.'

Light began to break through the dark puzzle in Mrs Berry's mind.

'Do you know where she is?'

The child looked up, wide eyed with amazement.

'Course I do! She's with me auntie. I sees her once a month. She says she'll have me back, soon as she's got a place of her own. Ain't no room at Auntie's, see?'

Mrs Berry did see.

'I want to know more about these watches. When is your birthday?'

'Second of February.'

'Well, you might be lucky too, and get a watch then.'

'That's what *they* say!' said the boy with infinite scorn in his voice. His head was up now, his eyes flashing. The mouse had become a lion.

'If they means it,' he went on fiercely, 'why don't they let me have it for Christmas? That's what I asked 'em.'

'And what did they say?'

'Said as there was too much to buy anyway at Christmas. Couldn't expect a big present like a watch. I'd 'ave to wait and see.'

'Fair enough,' commented Mrs Berry. The Roses had obviously done their best to explain matters to the disappointed child.

'No, it ain't fair enough!' the child burst out. 'Dad

Rose, 'e gets extra money Christmastime – a bonus they calls it. *And* all his usual pay. They could easy afford one little watch. The other two've got theirs. Why should I have to wait? I'll tell you why!'

He leaned forward menacingly. Mrs Berry could see why Pepe had had such a hold over poor stupid Gloria Jarvis. Those dark eyes could be very intimidating when they flashed fire.

'Because I'm only the foster kid, that's why! They gets paid for havin' me with 'em, but they won't give me a watch, same as their own kids 've got. They don't care about me, that's the truth of it!'

The tears began to flow again, and Mrs Berry handed him a paper hanky in silence. It was coming out now – the whole, sad, silly, simple little story. Soon she would know it all.

'I thought about it when I got to bed,' sniffed Stephen Amonetti, mopping his eyes. 'Soon as Jim was asleep, I crept out. They never heard me go. They was watching the telly. Never heard nothing. I knows the way.'

'Where to?'

'Me mum, of course. She'd understand. I bet she'd give me a watch for Christmas, *and* let me stay with her too, if she knowed how I was feeling. Anyway, you wants your own folk at Christmastime. I fair hates the Roses just now.'

He blew his nose violently, threw the hanky to the back of the fire as instructed, and flopped back in the chair, with a colossal shuddering sigh. The duffel coat fell apart, displaying his skinny bare legs. His hands drooped from the arms of the chair.

Mrs Berry stooped to put another log on the fire, before beginning her lecture. That done, she settled back in the armchair.

'As far as I can see,' she began severely, 'you are a thoroughly silly, spoiled little boy.'

She glanced across at her visitor and saw that she was wasting her breath.

Utterly exhausted, his pink mouse nose pointing towards the ceiling and pink mouse mouth ajar, Mrs Berry's captive was deep in slumber.

CHAPTER EIGHT

Upstairs in her draughty bedroom Mary stirred. Some faint noise had penetrated the thick folds of sleep that wrapped her closely. Too tired to open her eyes or to sit up, she tried bemusedly to collect her thoughts.

Could she have heard voices? She remembered that her mother was below. Perhaps she had turned on the little radio set for company, she told herself vaguely.

Should she go and inspect the mousetrap? The bed was seductively warm, her limbs heavy with sleep. To stir outside was impossible. Besides, she might wake the children as well as her mother.

Exhausted, she turned over, relishing the comfort of her surroundings after the bustle of the day. She began to slip back into unconsciousness, and her last remembrance of Christmas Eve was the sight of Ray Bullen's smile as he hoisted young Frances on to the bus.

With a feeling of warm contentment, Mary drifted back to sleep.

Old Mrs Berry rearranged the eiderdown and put her tired head against the back of the chair. Through half-closed eyes she surveyed her visitor.

He was snoring slightly, and Mrs Berry's maternal instinct made her want to approach the boy and quietly close his mouth. It was shameful the way some people let their children grow up to be mouth breathers – leading the way to all sorts of infections in later life, besides encouraging snoring, an unnecessary complication to a shared bedroom. Why, Mrs Berry could recall, from when she was in service, many a shocking case among the gentry of couples agreeing to separate bedrooms simply on account of snoring!

However, on this present occasion, Mrs Berry proposed to let sleeping dogs lie. The child was not her permanent responsibility. But Betty Rose ought to look into the matter herself, and quickly, before the habit grew worse.

Her thoughts hovered round the events that had led to the boy's presence under her roof. As far as she could judge, the boy was sensibly cared for by the Roses, who seemed to have tackled the child's grievance sympathetically.

There was no doubt in Mrs Berry's mind that the child was far better off where he was than with that fly-by-night mother of his. As for thinking that she would have him back permanently to live with her – well, that was just wishful thinking on the child's part. The local authority would not allow that, especially in the sordid circumstances in which Gloria now appeared to live and work.

Stephen Amonetti! Mrs Berry mused, her eyes still on her visitor. He would not be an easy child to bring up, with Pepe and Gloria as parents. She pitied the Roses, and commended them for having the pluck to take on this pathetic outcome of a mixed marriage. He would need a firm hand, and plenty of affection too, to right the wrongs the world had done him. It could not be easy for the Roses, trying to be fair to their own two and to fit this changeling into their family.

She remembered Pepe's quick jealousy of Gloria's earlier rivals. Plainly, this child was as quick to resentment as his father had been. She remembered the fury in those dark eyes as the boy spoke of the watches. That smouldering jealousy was a legacy from his Latin father. The thoughtlessness, culminating in the flight from home, careless of the feelings of others, was a legacy from his casual mother.

This boy was going to be a handful, unless someone pulled him to his senses, thought Mrs Berry. The Roses, respectable people though they were, might well be too gentle with the child, too ineffectual, although they apparently were doing their best to cope with this cuckoo in their nest. After all, Dick Rose left home early in the morning and was late back at night. It would fall upon Betty's shoulders, this responsibility, and with two children of her own to look after the task might be too great for her.

The child had been thinking on the wrong lines for too long, Mrs Berry told herself. He had harboured grievances, resented authority, and indulged in self-pity. The old lady, with the strong principles instilled by her Victorian upbringing, condemned such wrong-headedness roundly. That the child was the victim, to a certain extent, of his circumstances, she was ready to concede, but the matter did not end there. She was heartily sick of the modern theories that condoned wrongdoing on the grounds that the wrongdoers were to be pitied and not blamed.

Every individual, she firmly believed, had the freedom

of choice between good and evil. If one were so wicked, or thoughtless, or plain stupid enough to choose to do evil, then one must be prepared to take the consequences. Children, naturally, had to be trained and helped to resist temptation and to choose the right path, but to consider them as always in the right, as so many people nowadays seemed to do, was to do them a disservice, thought old Mrs Berry.

Her own children had been brought up with clear standards. Little Amelia Scott had learned the virtues early, from the plaque in the church extolling modesty and economy, from her upright parents, and from the strict but kindly teachings of the village schoolteachers, the Scriptures and the vicar of the parish. These stood her in good stead when she became a mother.

She had also been told of the things which were evil: lying, boasting, stealing, cruelty and loose living and thinking. It seemed to Mrs Berry that in these days evil was ignored. Did modern parents and teachers think that by burying their heads in the sand, evil would vanish? It had to be faced today, as bravely as it always had been in the past. It was there, plain for all to see, in the deplorable accounts of murder, bloodshed, violence and exploitation appearing in newspapers and shown on every television screen. The trouble was, thought Mrs Berry, that too often it was shrugged off as 'an aspect of modern living', when it should have been fought with the sword of righteousness, as she and her generation had been taught to do.

It was a great pity that the seven deadly sins were not explained to the young these days. There, asleep in the chair, was the victim of one of them – Envy. Had he been brought up to recognize his enemies in time, young Stephen might have been safely asleep in his own bed, instead of lying there caught in a web of his own weaving.

For, one had to face it, Mrs Berry told herself, this self-indulgence in envy and self-pity had led the boy to positive wrongdoing. He was, in the eyes of the law and all right-thinking people, a burglar and a would-be thief.

He was also guilty of disloyalty to the Roses, who were doing their best to bring him up. And he had completely disregarded the unhappiness this flight might cause them.

All this she intended to make clear to the child as soon as he awoke. But there was a further problem – a practical one. How could she get the child home again without involving her own family or the Roses?

Would they have missed him yet? Would they have rung the police? As soon as the child woke, she would try and find out the usual practice at night in the Roses' house. Would they on Christmas Eve have put the children's presents on their beds, as she and Mary had done? If so, would they have noticed that the boy was missing from their son's side?

All this must be discovered. Meanwhile, it was enough that the boy was resting. She too would close her eyes for a catnap. They both needed strength to face what was before them.

She dropped, thankfully, into a light doze.

The boy woke first. Bending to feel his drying shoes, he knocked the poker into the hearth. This small clatter roused the old lady.

She was alert at once, as she always was when she woke up, despite her age.

The clock stood at twenty minutes past three, and although the wind still moaned at the window, there seemed to be no sound of rain pattering on the pane. The worst of the storm appeared to be over.

Mrs Berry felt the raincoat. It was practically dry. She carefully turned the sleeves inside out and re-arranged the garment so that it had the full benefit of the fire's heat.

It was very cosy in the room. Refreshed by her nap, the old lady looked with approval at the two red candles on the mantelpiece waiting to be lit at teatime – today, Christmas Day, the day they had prepared for, for so long.

The Christmas tree sparkled on the side table. The paper chains, made by the little girls' nimble fingers, swayed overhead and the holly berries glimmered as brightly as the fire itself.

'Merry Christmas!' said Mrs Berry to the boy.

'Thank you. Merry Christmas,' he responded. 'It don't seem like Christmas, somehow.'

'I'm not surprised. You haven't made a very good start with it, have you?'

Stephen shook his head dismally.

'What's more,' continued the old lady, 'you've put your poor foster parents, and me, to a mint of worry and trouble, by being such a wicked, thoughtless boy.'

'I'm sorry,' said the child. There was something perfunctory about the apology which roused Mrs Berry's ire.

'You *say* it,' she said explosively, 'but do you *mean*

it? Do you realize that all this trouble stems from your selfishness? You've been given a good home, food, warmth, clothes, comfort, taken into a decent family, and how do you repay the Roses? You ask for something you know full well is too expensive for them to give you, and then you sulk because it's not forthcoming!'

The boy opened his mouth as though to protest against this harangue, but Mrs Berry swept on.

'You're a thoroughly nasty, mean-spirited little boy, eaten up with envy and jealousy, and if you don't fight against those things you're going to turn into a real criminal. You understand what I say?'

'Yes, but I never—'

'No excuses,' continued Mrs Berry briskly. 'You see what your sulking and envy led you to – breaking into my house and helping yourself to my Madeira cake. Those are crimes in themselves. If you were a few years older, you could be sent to prison for doing that.'

The child suddenly bent forward and put his head in his hands. She could see that he was fighting tears, and remained silent, watching him closely, and hoping that some of her words of wisdom had hit their mark.

'Have you ever had a spanking?' she asked suddenly.

'Only from me real mum. She gave me a clout now and again. The Roses don't hit none of us.'

'They're good people, better than you deserve, I suspect. I warrant if you'd been my little boy, you'd have had a few smacks by now, to show you the difference between right and wrong.'

There was a sniffing from the hidden face, but no comment. Mrs Berry's tone softened.

'What you've got to do, my child, is to start afresh. You've seen tonight where wickedness and self-pity lead you. For all we know, Mr and Mrs Rose are distracted – their Christmas spoiled – just because you must have your own way. And if they've told the police, then that's more people upset by your thoughtlessness.

'No, it's time you thought about other people instead of yourself. Time you counted your blessings, instead of making yourself miserable about things you covet. No selfish person is ever happy. Remember that.'

The boy nodded, and lifted his head from his hands. His cheeks were wet, and his expression was genuinely penitent.

'What we've got to do now,' said Mrs Berry, 'is to put things right as quickly and quietly as we can. Tell me, do you think the Roses will have missed you?'

The child looked bewildered.

'They don't never look in once they've tucked us up. They calls out, softlike, "Good night," when they goes to bed but don't open the door.'

'Not even on Christmas Eve?' asked Mrs Berry, broaching the subject delicately. Did the child still believe in Father Christmas? He had had enough to put up with this night, without any further painful disclosures.

'We has our presents on the breakfast table,' said Stephen, catching her meaning at once. 'And our stockings at teatime, when we light the candles on the Christmas tree.'

'So they may not know you left home?'

'I don't see how they can know till morning.'

'I see.'

Mrs Berry fell silent, turning over this fact in her mind. There seemed to be every hope that the child was right. If so, the sooner he returned, and crept back to bed, the better. It seemed proper in her straightforward mind, that having done wrong the boy himself should put it right. She discounted the wrong done against herself and her own property, although she sincerely hoped that the child had learned his lesson. It was his attitude to his foster parents, and to all others with whom he must work and live, that must be altered.

'Do you go to church?' asked Mrs Berry.

'To Sunday school. Sometimes we go to Evensong.'

'Then you've heard about loving your neighbour.'

The child looked perplexed.

'Is it a commandment? We had to learn ten of those once, off of the church wall, at Sunday school.'

'It's another commandment: "Love thy neighbour as thyself." Do you understand what it means?'

The child shook his head dumbly.

'Well, it sums up what I've been telling you. Think about other people and their feelings. Consider them as much as you consider yourself. Put yourself in your foster parents' place, for instance. How would you feel if the boy you looked after was so discontented that he ran away, making you feel that you had let him down, when all the time you had been doing your level best to make him happy?'

The boy looked at his hands, and said nothing.

'You're going to go back, Stephen, and get into that

house as quietly as you can, and get into bed. Can you do it?'

'Of course. The larder window's never shut. I've been in and out dozens of times.'

'And you say nothing at all about what has happened tonight. It's a secret between you and me. Understand?'

'Yes,' he whispered.

'There's no need for anyone to be upset by this, except you. I hope you'll have learned your lesson well enough to be cheerful and grateful for all that you are given, and all that's done for you, on Christmas Day. Do you promise that?'

The boy nodded. Then his eyes grew round, as he looked at Mrs Berry in alarm.

'But s'pose they've found out?'

'I was coming to that,' said the old lady calmly. 'You tell them the truth, make a clean breast of it, and say you'll never do it again – and mean it, what's more!'

The child's eyes grew terrified. 'Tell them about coming in here?'

'Of course. And tell them I should like to see them, to explain matters.'

'And the police?'

'If the police have been troubled, then you apologize to them too. You know what I told you. You must face the consequences whatever they are. This night should make you think in future, my boy, and a very good thing too.'

She stood up, and moved to the window. Outside, the rain had stopped, but a stiff wind blew the ragged clouds swiftly across a watery moon, and ruffled the surface of the puddles.

It was a good step to Tupps Hill, but Stephen must be on his way shortly. Mrs Berry was not blind to the dangers of the night for a young child walking the lanes alone, but it was a risk that had to be taken. At least the weather was kinder, the child's clothing was dry, and he had eaten and slept. He had got himself into this situation, and it would do him no harm, thought Mrs Berry sturdily, to get himself out of it. In any case, the chance of meeting anyone abroad at half-past three on Christmas morning was remote.

'Put your clothes on,' directed the old lady, 'while I make us both a cup of coffee.'

She left him struggling with the toggle fastenings as she went into the kitchen. When she returned with the steaming cups of coffee, the boy was lacing his shoes. He looked up, smiling. He was so like Pepe, in that fleeting moment, that the years vanished for old Mrs Berry.

'Lovely and warm,' Stephen said approvingly, holding up his feet.

Mrs Berry handed him his cup, and offered the biscuit tin. As he nibbled his Ginger Nut with his prominent front teeth, Stephen's resemblance to a mouse was more marked than ever.

The old lady shuddered. Was her own little horror, the mouse, still at large above? Mrs Berry craved for her bed. She was suddenly stiff and bone-tired, and longed for oblivion. What a night it had been! Would the boy ever remember anything that she had tried to teach him? She had her doubts, but one could only try.

Who knows? Something might stick in that scatter-brained head.

She motioned to the child to fetch his coat, turned the sleeves the right way out, and helped to button it to the neck. His chin was smooth and warm against her wrinkled hand, and reminded her with sudden poignancy of her own sleeping grandchildren.

She held him by the lapels of his raincoat, and looked searchingly into his dark eyes.

'You remember the promise? Say nothing, if they know nothing. Speak the truth if they do. And in future, do what's right and not what's wrong.'

The child nodded solemnly.

She kissed him on the cheek, gently and without smiling. They went to the front door together, Mrs Berry lifting a bar of chocolate from the Christmas tree as she passed.

'Put it in your pocket. You've a long way to go and may get hungry. Straight home, mind, and into bed. Promise?'

'Promise.'

She opened the door quietly. It was fairly light, the moon partially visible through fast-scudding clouds. The wind lifted her hair and rustled dead leaves in the road.

'Goodbye then, Stephen. Don't forget what I've told you,' she whispered.

'Goodbye,' he whispered back.

He stood motionless for a second, as if wondering how to make his farewell, then turned suddenly and began the long trudge home.

Mrs Berry watched him go, waiting for him to turn, perhaps, and wave. But the child did not look back, and she watched him walking steadily – left, right, left, right – until the bend in the lane hid him from her sight.

CHAPTER NINE

Back in the warm living room Mrs Berry found herself swaying on her feet with exhaustion. She steadied herself by holding on to the back of the armchair that had been her refuge for the night.

It was years since she had felt such utter tiredness. It reminded her of the days when, as a young girl, she had helped with the mounds of washing at the vicarage. She had spent an hour or more at a time turning the heavy mangle – a monster of cast iron and solid wood – in the steamy atmosphere of the washhouse.

She looked now at her downy nest of feather pillow and eiderdown, and knew that if she sat down sleep would engulf her. She would be stiff when she awoke for every nerve and sinew in her old body craved for the comfort of her bed, with room to stretch her heavy limbs.

She would brave that dratted mouse! Ten chances to one it had made its way home again, and, in any case, she was so tired she would see and hear nothing once she was abed.

She glanced round the room. The fire must be raked through, and the two telltale coffee cups washed and put away. Mrs Berry had no intention of telling Mary and the little girls about her visitor.

She put all to rights, moving slowly, her limbs leaden, her eyes half-closed with fatigue. She drew back the curtains, ready for the daylight, and scanned the stormy sky.

The moon was high now. Ragged clouds skimmed across its face, so that the glimpses of the wet trees and shining road were intermittent. The boy should be well on his way by now. She hoped that he had avoided the great puddles that silvered his path. Those shoes would be useless in this weather.

The old lady sighed, and turned back to the armchair, folding the eiderdown neatly and putting the plump pillow across it. Gathering up her bundle, she took one last look at the scene of her encounter with young Stephen. Then, shouldering her burden, she opened the door to the staircase and went, very slowly, to her bedroom.

Exhaustion dulled the terror that stirred her at the thought of the mouse still at large. Nevertheless, the old lady's heart beat faster as she quietly opened the bedroom door. The great double bed was as welcome a sight as a snug harbour to a storm-battered boat.

Mary had turned down the bedclothes. They gleamed, smooth and white as a snowdrift, in the faint light of the moon.

The room was still and cool after the living room. Mrs Berry stood motionless, listening for any scuffle or scratching that might betray her enemy. But all was silent.

She switched on the bedside lamp, which had been Mary's last year's Christmas present. It had a deep-pink shade that sent a rosy glow into the room. The old lady replaced her pillow and spread out the eiderdown, then, nerving herself, she bent down stiffly to look under the bed and see if the intruder was still there.

All was as it should be. She scanned the rest of the floor, and saw the mousetrap. It was empty, and the second piece of cheese was still untouched.

Mrs Berry's spirits rose a little. Surely, this might mean that the mouse had returned to his own home? He would either have been caught, or the cheese would have been eaten, as before. But the trap must not be left there, a danger to the grandchildren, who would come running in barefoot, all too soon, to show their tired grandmother the things that Father Christmas had brought.

Mrs Berry took a shoe from the floor and tapped the trap smartly. The crack of the spring snapping made her jump but now all was safe. She could not bring herself to touch the horrid thing with her bare fingers, but prodded it to safety, under the dressing table, with her shoe.

Sighing with relief, the old lady climbed into bed, drew up the bedclothes and stretched luxuriously.

How soon, she wondered, before Stephen Amonetti would be enjoying his bed, as she did now?

At the rate he was stepping out, thought Mrs Berry drowsily, he must be descending the long slope that led to the fold in the downs at the foot of Tupps Hill.

She knew that road well. The meadows on that southern slope had been full of cowslips when little Amelia Scott and her friends were children. She could smell them now, warm and sweet in the May sunshine. She loved the way the pale green stalks grew from the flat rosettes of leaves, so like living pen wipers, soft and fleshy, half hidden in the springy grass of the downland.

The children made cowslip balls as well as bunches to carry home. Some of the mothers made cowslip wine, and secretly young Amelia grieved to see the beautiful flowers torn from their stalks and tossed hugger-mugger into a basket. They were too precious for such rough treatment, the child felt, though she relished a sip of the wine when it was made, and now tasted it again on her tongue, the very essence of a sunny May day.

On those same slopes, in wintertime, she had tobogganed with those same friends. She remembered a childhood sweetheart, a black-haired charmer called

Ned, who always led the way on his homemade sled and feared nothing. He scorned gloves, hats, and all the other winter comforts in which loving mothers wrapped their offspring, but rushed bareheaded down the slope, his eyes sparkling, cheeks red, and the breath blowing behind him in streamers.

Poor Ned, so full of life and courage! He had gone to a water-filled grave in Flanders' mud before he was twenty years old. But the memory of that vivacious child remained with old Mrs Berry as freshly as if it were yesterday that they had swept down the snowy slope together.

In those days a tumbledown shack had stood by a small rivulet at the bottom of the slope. It was inhabited by a poor, silly, old man, called locally Dirty Dick. He did not seem to have any steady occupation, although he sometimes did a little field work in the summer months, singling turnips, picking the wild oats from the farmers' standing corn, or making himself useful when the time came round for picking apples or plums in the local orchards.

The children were warned not to speak to him. Years before, it seemed, he had been taken to court in Caxley for some indecent conduct, and this was never forgotten. The rougher children shouted names after him and threw stones. The more gently nurtured, such as little Amelia, simply hurried by.

'You're not to take any notice of him,' her mother had said warningly.

'Why not?'

A look of the utmost primness swept over her mother's countenance.

'He is sometimes a very *rude* old man,' she said, in a shocked voice.

Amelia enquired no further.

His end had been tragic, she remembered. He had been found, face downwards, in the little brook, a saucepan in his clenched hand as he had dipped for water to boil for his morning tea. The doctor had said his heart must have failed suddenly. The old man had toppled into the stream and drowned in less than eight inches of spring flood water.

Young Amelia had heard of his death with mingled horror and relief. Now she need never fear to pass that hut, dreading the meeting with 'a very *rude* old man', whose death, nevertheless, seemed unnecessarily cruel to the soft-hearted child.

Well, Stephen Amonetti would have no Dirty Dick to fear on his homeward way, but he would have the avenue to traverse, a frightening tunnel of dark trees lining the road for a matter of a hundred yards across the valley. Even on the hottest day, the air blew chill in those deep shadows. On a night like this, Mrs Berry knew well, the wind would clatter the branches and whistle eerily. Stephen would need to keep a stout heart to hold the bogies at bay as he ran the gauntlet to those age-old trees.

But by then he would be within half a mile of his home, up the steep short hill that overlooked the valley. A small estate of council houses had been built at Tupps Hill, some thirty years ago, and though the architecture was grimly functional and the concrete paths gave an institutional look to the area, yet most of the tenants – countrymen all – had softened the bleakness with climbing wall plants and plenty of bright annuals in the borders.

The hillside position, too, was enviable. The houses commanded wide views over agricultural land, the gardens were large and, with unusual forethought, the council had provided a row of garages for their tenants, so that unsightly, old shabby cars were screened from view. Those lucky enough to get a Tupps Hill house were envied by their brethren.

If only Stephen could get in unobserved! Mrs Berry stirred restlessly, considering her visitor's chances of escaping detection. Poor little mouse! Poor little Christmas mouse! Dear God, please let him creep into his home safely!

And then she froze. Somewhere, in the darkness close at hand, something rustled.

Her first instinct was to snatch the eiderdown from the bed, and bolt. She would fly downstairs again to the safety of the armchair, and there await the dawn and Mary's coming to her rescue.

But several things kept her quaking in the warm bed. Extreme tiredness was one. Her fear that she would rouse the sleeping household was another. The day ahead would be a busy one, and Mary needed all the rest she could get. This was something she must face alone.

Mrs Berry tried to pinpoint the position of the rustling. A faint squeaking noise made her flesh prickle. What could it be? It did not sound like the squeak of a mouse. The noise came from the right, by the window. Could the wretched creature be on the windowsill? Could it be scrabbling, with its tiny claws, on the glass of the windowpane, in its efforts to escape?

Mrs Berry shuddered at the very thought of confronting it, of seeing its dreadful stringy tail, its beady eyes, and its more than likely darting to cover into some inaccessible spot in the bedroom.

All her old terrors came flying back, like a flock of evil black birds, to harass her. There was that ghastly dead mouse in her aunt's flour keg, the next one with all those pink hairless babies in her father's toolbox, the one that the boys killed in the school lobby, the pair that set up home once under the kitchen sink, and all those numberless little horrors that Pepe the cat used to bring in, alive and dead, to scare her out of her wits.

But somehow, there had always been someone to cope with them. Dear Stanley, or Bertie, or brave Mary, or some good neighbour would come to her aid. Now, in the darkness, she must manage alone.

She took a deep breath and cautiously edged her tired old legs out of the bed. She must switch on the bedside lamp again, and risk the fact that it might stampede the mouse into flight.

Her fingers shook as she groped for the switch. Once more, rosy light bathed the room. Sitting on the side of the bed, Mrs Berry turned round to face the direction of the rustling, fear drying her throat.

There was no sound now. Even the wind seemed to have dropped. Silence engulfed the room. Could she have been mistaken? Could the squeaking noise have been caused by the thorns of the rosebush growing against the wall? Hope rose. Immediately it fell again.

For there, crouched in a corner of the windowsill, was a tiny furry ball.

Old Mrs Berry put a shaking hand over her mouth to quell any scream that might escape her unawares. Motionless, she gazed at the mouse. Motionless, the mouse gazed back. Thus transfixed, they remained. Only the old lady's heavy breathing broke the silence that engulfed them.

After some minutes, the mouse lifted its head and snuffed the air. Mrs Berry caught her breath. It was so like Stephen Amonetti, as he had sprawled in the armchair, head back, with his pointed pink nose in the air. She watched the mouse, fascinated. It seemed oblivious of danger and sat up on its haunches to wash its face.

Its bright eyes, as dark and lustrous as Stephen's, moved restlessly as it went about its toilet. Its minute pink paws reminded Mrs Berry of the tiny pink shells she had treasured as a child after a Sunday-school outing to the sea. It was incredible to think that something so small could lead such a full busy life, foraging, making a home, keeping itself and its family fed and cleaned.

And that was the life it must return to, thought Mrs Berry firmly. It must go back, as surely as Stephen had, to resume its proper existence. Strange that two creatures, so alike in looks, should flee their homes and take refuge on the same night, uninvited, under her roof!

The best way to send this little scrap on its

homeward journey would be to open the window and hope that it would negotiate the frail stairway of the rosebush trained against the wall, and so return to earth. But the thought of reaching over the mouse to struggle with the window catch needed all the courage that the old lady could muster, and she sat on the bed summoning her strength.

The longer she watched, the less frightened she became. It was almost like watching Stephen Amonetti all over again – a fugitive, defenceless, young, and infinitely pathetic. They both needed help and guidance to get them home.

She took a deep breath and stood up. The bed springs squeaked, but the mouse did not take flight. It stopped washing its whiskers and gazed warily about it. Mrs Berry, gritting her teeth, approached slowly.

The mouse shrank down into a little furry ball, reminding Mrs Berry of a fur button on a jacket of her mother's. Quietly, she leaned over the sill and lifted the window catch. The mouse remained motionless.

The cold air blew in, stirring the curtain and bringing a breath of rain-washed leaves and damp earth.

Mrs Berry retreated to the bed again to watch developments. She sat there for a full minute before her captive made a move.

It raised its quivering pink nose and then, in one bound, darted over the window frame, dragging its pink tail behind it. As it vanished, Mrs Berry hurried to the window to watch its departure.

It was light enough to see its tiny shape undulating down the crisscross of thorny rose stems. But when it finally reached the bare earth, it was invisible to the old lady's eyes.

She closed the window carefully, sighed with relief and exhaustion, and clambered, once more, into bed.

Her two unbidden visitors – her Christmas mice – had gone! Now, at long last, she could rest.

Behind the row of wallflower plants, close to the bricks of the cottage, scurried the mouse, nose twitching. It ran across the garden path, dived under the cotoneaster bush, scrambled up the mossy step by the disused well, turned sharp right through the jungle of dried grass beside the garden shed, and streaked, unerringly, to the third hawthorn bush in the hedge.

There, at the foot, screened by ground ivy, was its hole. It dived down into the loose sandy earth, snuffling the dear frowsty smell of mouse family and mouse food.

Home at last!

At much the same time, Stephen Amonetti lowered himself carefully through the pantry window.

The house was as silent as the grave, and dark inside, after the pallid glimmer of the moon's rays.

With infinite caution he undid the pantry door, and closed it behind him. For greater quietness, he removed his wet shoes and, carrying them in one hand, he ascended the staircase.

The smells of home were all about him. There was a faint whiff of the mince pies Mrs Rose had made on Christmas Eve mingled, from the open door of the bathroom, with the sharp clean smell of Lifebuoy soap.

Noiselessly, he turned the handle of the bedroom door. Now there was a stronger scent – of the liniment that Jim used after football, boasting, as he rubbed, of his swelling muscles. The older boy lay curled on his side of the bed, dead to the world. It would take more than Stephen's entry into the room to wake him.

Peeling off his clothes, Stephen longed for bed, for sleep, for forgetfulness. Within three minutes, he was lying beside the sleeping boy, his head a jumble of cake tins, fierce old ladies, stormy weather, sore feet.

And somewhere, beyond the muddle, a hazy remembrance of a promise to keep.

CHAPTER TEN

It was light when Mrs Berry awoke. She lay inert in the warm bed, relishing its comfort, as her bemused mind struggled with memories of the night.

The mouse and Stephen! What a double visitation, to be sure! No wonder she was tired this morning and had slept late. It must be almost eight o'clock – Christmas morning too! Where were the children? Where was Mary? The house was uncommonly quiet. She must get up and investigate.

At that moment, she heard footsteps outside in the road, and the sound of people greeting each other. Simultaneously, the church bell began to ring. Yes, it must be nearly eight o'clock, and those good parishioners were off to early service!

Well, thought Mrs Berry philosophically, she would not be among the congregation. She rarely missed the eight o'clock service, but after such a night she would be thankful to go later, at eleven, taking the two little girls with her.

She struggled up in bed and gazed at the sky. It was a glory of grey and gold: streamers of ragged clouds, gilded at their edges, filled the world with a luminous radiance, against which the bare twigs of the plum tree spread their black lace.

She opened the window, remembering with a shudder the last time she had done so. Now the air, fresh and cool, lifted her hair. The bells sounded clearly, as the neighbours' footsteps died away into the distance.

'Awake then?' said Mary, opening the door. 'Happy Christmas!'

She bore a cup of tea, the steam blowing towards her in the draught from the window.

'You spoil me,' said Mrs Berry. 'I ought to be up. Proper old sleepyhead I am today. Where are the children?'

'Downstairs, having breakfast. Not that they want much. They've been stuffing sweets and the tangerine from their stockings since six!'

She put the cup on the bedside table and closed the window.

'They wanted to burst in here, but I persuaded them to let you sleep on. What happened to the mouse? Is it still about? I see the trap's sprung.'

'I let it out of the window,' said Mrs Berry. She could not keep a touch of pride from her voice.

'You never! You brave old dear! Where was it then?'

'On the sill. I got so tired by about three, I risked it and came up. I don't mind admitting I fair hated reaching over the little creature to get at the latch, but it made off in no time, so that was all right.'

'That took some pluck,' said Mary, her voice warm with admiration. 'Can I let those rascals come up now, to show you their presents?'

'Yes, please,' said Mrs Berry, reaching for her cup. 'Then I'll get up, and give you a hand.'

Mary called down the staircase, and there was a thumping of feet and squeals and shouts as the two excited children struggled upstairs with their loot.

'Look, Grandma,' shouted Frances, 'I've put on my slippers!'

'Look, Grandma,' shouted Jane, 'Father Christmas brought me a dear little doll!'

They flung themselves upon the bed, Mary watching them with amusement.

'Mind Gran's tea,' she warned.

'Leave them be,' said her mother lovingly. 'This is how Christmas morning should begin!'

Smiling, Mary left the three of them and went downstairs.

On the door mat lay an envelope. Mary's heart sank, as she bent to pick it up. Not another person they'd forgotten to send to? Not another case of Mrs Burton all over again? Anyway, it was too late now to run about returning Christmas cards. Whoever had sent it must just be thanked when they met.

She took it into the living room and stood with her back to the fire, studying the face of the envelope with some bewilderment. Most of the cards were addressed to 'Mrs Berry and Family,' or to 'Mrs Berry and Mrs Fuller,' but this was to 'Mrs Bertie Fuller' alone, and written in a firm hand.

Wonderingly, Mary drew out the card. It was a fine reproduction of 'The Nativity' by G. van Honthorst, and inside, beneath the printed Christmas greetings, was the signature of Ray Bullen. A small piece of writing paper fluttered to the floor, as Mary, flushing with pleasure, studied the card.

She stooped to retrieve it. The message it contained was simple and to the point.

I have two tickets for the New Year's Eve concert at the Corn Exchange. Can you come with me? Do hope so!

RAY

Mary sat down with a thud on the chair recently vacated by young Jane. Automatically, she began stacking the girls' bowls sticky with cornflakes and milk. Her hands were shaking, she noticed, and she felt shame mingling with her happiness.

'Like some stupid girl,' she scolded herself, 'instead of a widow with two girls.'

She left the crockery alone, and took up the note again. It was kind of him – typical of his thoughtfulness. Somehow, he had managed to write the card after seeing her yesterday, and had found someone in the village who would drop it through her letterbox on the way to early service. It must have taken some organizing, thought Mary, much touched. He was a good sort of man. Bertie had always said so, and this proved it.

As for the invitation, that was a wonderful thing to have. She would love to go and knew that her mother would willingly look after the children. But would she approve? Would she think she was being disloyal to Bertie's memory to accept an invitation from another man?

Fiddlesticks! thought Mary robustly, dismissing such mawkish sentiments. Here was an old friend offering to take her to a concert – that was all. It was a kindness that would be churlish to rebuff. Of course she would go, and it would be a rare treat too!

Calmer, she rose and began to take the dishes into the kitchen, her mind fluttering about the age-old problem of what to wear on such a momentous occasion. There was her black, but it was too funereal, too widowlike. Suddenly she wanted to look gay, young, happy – to show that she appreciated the invitation, she told herself hastily.

There was the yellow frock she had bought impulsively one summer day, excusing her extravagance by persuading herself that it was just the thing for the Women's Institute outing to the theatre. But when the evening had arrived she had begun to have doubts. Was it, perhaps, too gay for a widow? Would the tongues wag? Would they say she was 'after' someone? Mutton dressed as lamb?

She had put it back in the cupboard, and dressed herself in the black one. Better be on the safe side, she had told herself dejectedly, and had felt miserable the whole evening.

Yes, the yellow frock should have an airing, and her bronze evening shoes an extra shine. Ray Bullen should have no cause to regret his invitation.

She turned on the tap, as the children came rushing into the room.

'Why, Mummy,' exclaimed Frances, wide eyed with amazement, '*you're singing!*'

Upstairs Mrs Berry put on her grey woollen jumper and straightened the Welsh tweed skirt. This was her working outfit. Later in the morning she would change into more elegant attire, suitable for church-going, but there was housework to be done in the next hour or two. Last of all, she tied a blue and white spotted apron round her waist, and was ready to face the day.

Once more, she opened the window. The small birds chirped and chatted below, awaiting their morning crumbs. A grey and white wagtail teetered back and forth across a puddle, looking for all the world like a miniature curate, with his white collar and dove-grey garments. The yellow winter jasmine starred the wall below, forerunner of the aconites and snowdrops soon to come. There was a hopeful feeling of spring in the air, decided Mrs Berry, gazing at the sky. How different from yesterday's gloom!

The children's happiness was infectious. Their delight in the simple presents warmed the old lady's heart and set her thinking of that other child, less fortunate, who had no real family of his own and who had wept because of it.

How was he faring? Had he, after all, found a watch among his parcels? Mrs Berry doubted it. The Roses had spoken truly when they told the child that a watch was too much to expect at Christmas. No doubt, lesser presents would make him happy, assuaging to some extent that fierce longing to have a watch like Patsy's and Jim's. A passionate child, thought Mrs Berry, shaking her head sadly. Pepe all over again! It made life hard for the boy, and harder still for those who had to look after him. Would he ever remember any of the good advice she had tried to offer? Knowing the ways of children, she suspected that most of her admonitions had gone in one ear and out of the other.

Ah well! One could only hope, she thought, descending the staircase.

*

Mary had set a tray at the end of the table for her mother. Beyond it stood the pink cyclamen and a pile of parcels. The two children, hopping from leg to leg with excitement, hovered on each side of the chair.

'Come on, Gran! Come and see what you've got. Mum gave you the plant!'

'Mary,' exclaimed Mrs Berry, hands in the air with astonishment, 'you shouldn't have spent so much money on me! What a beauty! And so many buds to come out too. Well, I don't know when I've seen a finer cyclamen, and that's a fact.'

She kissed her daughter warmly. Why, the girl seemed aglow! Christmas was a comforting time, for old and young, thought Mrs Berry, reaching out for the parcels.

'Open mine first,' demanded Frances.

'No, mine,' said Jane. 'I'm the oldest.'

'I'll open them together,' said the old lady, taking one in each hand. 'See, I'll tear this bit off this one, then this bit off that one—'

She tugged at the wrappings gently.

'No, no!' cried Jane, unable to bear the delay. 'Do one first – don't matter which – then the other. But read the tags. We wrote 'em ourselves.'

Mrs Berry held the two tags at arm's length. Her spectacles were mislaid amidst the Christmas debris.

'"Darling Grandma, with love from Jane,"' she read aloud. She shook the parcel, then smelled it, then held it to her ear. The children hugged each other in rapture.

'Why do you listen to it?' queried Frances. 'Do you think there's a bird in it?'

'A watch perhaps,' said Mrs Berry, surprised by her own words.

'A *watch*?' screamed the girls. 'But you've got a watch!'

'So I have,' said Mrs Berry calmly. 'Well, let's see what's in here.'

Wrapped in four thicknesses of tissue paper was a little egg-timer.

'Now, *that*,' cried the old lady, 'is *exactly* what I wanted. Clever Jane!'

She kissed the child's soft cheek.

'Now mine!' begged Frances. 'Quick! Undo it *quick*, Gran.'

'I must read the tag. "Dear Gran, Happy Christmas, Frances." Very nice.'

'Undo it!' said the child.

Obediently, the old lady undid the paper. Inside was a box of peppermint creams.

'My favourite sweets!' said Mrs Berry. 'What a kind child you are! Would you like one now?'

'Yes please,' both said in unison.

'I hoped you'd give us one,' said Frances, beaming. 'Isn't it lucky we like them too?'

'Very lucky,' agreed their grandmother, proffering the box.

'Let Gran have her breakfast, do,' Mary said, appearing from the kitchen.

'But she's got lots more parcels to open!'

'I shall have a cup of tea first,' said the old lady, 'and then undo them.'

Sighing at such maddening adult behaviour, the two children retired to the other end of the table where they had set out a tiny metal tea set of willow pattern in blue and white.

'This is my favourite present,' announced Frances, 'and the teapot pours. See?'

Mary and her mother exchanged amused glances. The set had been one of several small toys they had bought together in Caxley to fill up the stockings. The chief present for each girl had been a doll, beautifully dressed in handmade clothes worked on secretly when the girls were in bed. It was typical of children the world over that some trifle of no real value should give them more immediate pleasure than the larger gifts.

At last, all the presents were unwrapped. Bath cubes, stockings, handkerchiefs, sweets, a tin of biscuits, another of tea, and a tablecloth embroidered by Mary – all were displayed and admired. Mary's presents had to be brought from the sideboard and shown to her mother, to please the two children, despite the fact that Mrs Berry had seen most of them before.

'Now, what's to do in the kitchen?' asked Mrs Berry, rising from the table.

'Nothing. The pudding's in, and the bird is ready, and the vegetables.'

'Then I'll dust and tidy up,' declared Mrs Berry. 'Upstairs first. I can guess what the girls' room looks like!'

'At least there are no mice!' laughed Mary.

The children looked up, alert.

'No mice? Was there a mouse? Where is it now?'

Their grandmother told them about the intruder,

and how she had settled by the fire, but at last gone up to bed and had let the mouse out of the window.

What would they have said, she wondered, as she told her tale, if she had told them the whole story? How their eyes would have widened at the thought of a boy – a *big* boy of nine – breaking into their home and trying to steal their grandmother's Madeira cake! As it was, the story of the real mouse stirred their imagination.

'I expect it was hungry,' said Jane with pity. 'I expect it smelled all the nice Christmas food and came in to have a little bit.'

'It had plenty of its own sort of food outdoors,' Mrs Berry retorted tartly.

'Perhaps it just wanted to see inside a house,' suggested Frances reasonably. 'You shouldn't have frightened it away, Gran.'

'It frightened *me* away,' said the old lady.

'Perhaps it will come back,' said Jane hopefully.

'That,' said her grandmother forcefully, 'I sincerely hope it will not do.'

And she went upstairs to her duties.

When the children and her mother had departed to church, the house was blessedly quiet. Mary, basting the turkey and turning potatoes in the baking dish, had time to ponder her invitation. As soon as the children were safely out of the way she would have a word with her mother, then reply.

But where should she send it? There had been no address on the note, and although she knew the part of Caxley in which Ray lived, she could not recall the name of the road, and certainly had no idea of the number. Perhaps the best thing would be to send it to the office of *The Caxley Chronicle*, where he worked. He would be going into work, no doubt, on the day after Boxing Day. Plenty of time to spare before New Year's Eve.

Now that the first initial surprise of the invitation was over, Mary found herself growing more and more delighted at the thought of the evening outing. Caxley had produced a New Year's Eve concert as long as she could remember, and she and Bertie had attended several of them.

The Corn Exchange was always full. It was something of an occasion. The mayor came, all the local gentry sat in the front rows, and everyone knew that the music provided would be good rousing stuff by Handel and Bach and Mozart, with maybe a light sprinkling of Gilbert and Sullivan, or Edward German, or Lionel Monckton, as a garnish.

It was definitely a social affair, when one wore one's best, and hoped to see one's friends and be seen by them. It would be good, thought Mary, to have a personable man as an escort instead of attending a function on her own.

Kind Ray! Good Quaker Ray! How did that passage go in the library book – 'Very thoughtful and wealthy and good'? She could vouch for two of those virtues anyway!

She slammed the oven door shut and laughed aloud.

At one o'clock the Christmas dinner – everything done to a turn – was set upon the table, and the two little girls attacked their plates with enviable appetite. Their elders ate more circumspectly.

Nevertheless, at two o'clock it was the children who played energetically on the floor with their new toys, whilst Mary and her mother lay back in their armchairs and succumbed to that torpor induced by unaccustomed rich food.

'We must take a turn in the fresh air before it gets dark.' Mrs Berry yawned; Mary nodded agreement drowsily.

They woke at three, much refreshed, donned their coats and gloves, and set off. The bright clouds of morning had gone; a gentle grey light veiled the distant scene.

The four of them walked towards the slope where young Stephen had walked scarcely twelve hours earlier. Mrs Berry's mind was full of memories of her Christmas visitor. She strode along, dwelling on the oddity of events that had brought one of the Amonetti family into her life once more.

Ahead of her, holding a child by each hand, Mary was running a few steps, then stopping suddenly to bring the two children face to face in an ecstatic embrace. It was a game they had loved as toddlers, but it was years, thought Mrs Berry, since Mary had played it with them.

Their delighted screams matched the calling of the flight of rooks above, slowly winging homewards against the evening sky.

Now they had reached the top of the slope, and Mary, breathless, stopped to wait for her mother.

They stood together looking across the shallow valley, already filling with the pale mist of winter.

'That's Tupps Hill over there, isn't it?' said Mary.

Her mother nodded. 'D'you remember the Roses?'

'Vaguely,' said Mary. 'Why?'

There was an intensity about her mother's gaze that made Mary curious.

The old lady did not answer for a moment, her eyes remained fixed upon the shadowy hill beyond the rising mist.

'I might call on them one day,' she said, at last. 'Not yet awhile. But some day – some day, perhaps.' She turned suddenly. 'Let's get home, Mary dear. There's no place like it – and it's getting cold.'

CHAPTER ELEVEN

It was hardly surprising at teatime, to find that the family's appetite was small, despite the afternoon walk.

'I'll just bring in the Christmas cake,' said Mary, 'and the tea tray. Though I expect you'd like a slice of your Madeira, wouldn't you?'

'No, thank you,' replied Mrs Berry hastily.

She pondered on the fate of the Madeira cake as Mary clattered china in the kitchen. It certainly seemed a terrible waste of sugar and butter and eggs, not to mention the beautiful curl of angelica that cost dear knows how much these days. But there it was. The thought of those pink paws touching it was enough to put anyone off the food.

Perhaps she could cut off the outside, and slice the rest for a trifle? Waste was something that Mrs Berry abhorred. But at once she dismissed the idea. It was no good. The cake must go. No doubt the birds would relish it, but she must find an opportunity for disposing of it when Mary was absent from the scene. Explanations would be difficult, under the circumstances.

Mary returned with the tray. To the accompaniment of cries of appreciation from the children the candles were lighted on the Christmas tree and at each end of the mantelpiece.

Outside, the early dusk had fallen, and the shadowy room, lit by a score of flickering candle flames and the glow from the fire, had never looked so snug and magical, thought Mrs Berry. If only their menfolk could have been with them . . .

She shook away melancholy as she had done so often. The time for grieving was over. There was much to be thankful for. She looked at Mary, intent upon cutting the snowy cake, and the rosy children, their eyes reflecting the light from the candles, and she was content.

And that child at Tupps Hill? Was he as happy as her own? She had a feeling that he might be – that perhaps he had been able to let the Christmas spirit soothe his anxious heart.

Jane's Christmas cracker had yielded a tiny spinning top that had numbers printed on it. When it came to

rest, after being twirled on the table, the number that was uppermost gave the spinner his score. This simple toy provided part of the evening's play time, and all four played.

Later, Mrs Berry played Ludo with the children – a new game found in Frances' pillow slip – while Mary wrote some thank-you letters. By seven o'clock both children were yawning, although they did their best to hide this weakness from the grown-ups. It would be terrible to miss anything on this finest day of the year.

'Bed,' said Mary firmly, and as the wails greeted her dictum, she relented enough to say: 'You can take your toys upstairs and play with them for a little while.'

Within half an hour, they were safely in bed, and Mary and her mother sat down to enjoy the respite from the children's clamour.

'Why, there's a new Christmas card!' exclaimed Mrs Berry, her eye lighting on Mary's from Ray.

Mary rose to fetch it from the mantelpiece and handed it to her mother.

'Someone dropped it through the letterbox first thing this morning. I bumped into Ray yesterday when we were shopping and he helped us on to the bus with our parcels.'

'Typical of the Bullens,' commented Mrs Berry, studying the card with approval. 'I knew his mother when she was young. A nice girl.'

Mary took a breath. This seemed as propitious a time as any other to mention the invitation.

'There is a note somewhere. He has asked me to go to the New Year's Eve concert. Would you mind? Looking after the girls, I mean?'

'Good heavens, no! I'm glad to think of you getting out a little. You'll enjoy an evening with Ray Bullen,' said her mother easily.

Mrs Berry leaned back in the chair and closed her eyes. It had been a long day, and she was near to sleep. A jumble of impressions, bright fragments of the last twenty-four hours, jostled together in her tired mind like the tiny pieces of coloured glass in a child's kaleidoscope.

Stephen's mousey face, his pink hand spread like a starfish upon his knee, with a shining tear upon it. Her own shadow, poker in hand, monstrously large on the passage wall as she approached the unknown intruder. The furry scrap crouched on the windowsill with the wild weather beyond. Stephen's resolute back, vanishing round the bend of the lane as he marched home. The reflection of the candles in her grandchildren's eyes. The candles in the church – dozens of them today – and the sweet clear voices of the choir boys.

She woke with a jerk. The clock showed that she had slept for ten minutes. Her last impression still filled her mind.

'It was lovely in church this morning,' she said to Mary. 'Flowers and candles, and the boys singing so sweetly. You should have come.'

'I will next Sunday,' Mary promised. 'A New Year's resolution, Mum.'

There was a quiet happiness about Mary that did not escape Mrs Berry's eyes, but in her wisdom she said nothing.

Things, she knew in her bones, were falling, delicately and rightly, into place.

'I'll go and tuck up the girls,' said Mrs Berry, struggling from her chair, 'and switch off their light.'

She mounted the stairs and was surprised to see that both children were in her own room. They were kneeling on her bed, very busy with something on the windowsill.

They turned at her approach.

'We're just putting out a little supper for the Christmas mouse,' explained Jane.

On the ledge was one of the doll's tin willow pattern plates. Upon it were a few crumbs of Christmas cake and one or two holly berries.

'They're apples for him,' said Frances. 'When people call you should always offer them refreshment, Mummy says.'

Mrs Berry remembered the steaming bowl of bread and milk clutched against a duffel coat.

'She's quite right,' she said, smiling at them. 'But somehow I don't think that mouse will come back.'

Stephen's dwindling figure, striding away, came before her eyes. The children looked at her, suddenly forlorn. She offered swift comfort.

'But I'm sure of one thing. That Christmas mouse will remember his visit here for the rest of his life.'

The rising moon silvered the roofs at Shepherds Cross and turned the puddles into mirrors. The sky was cloudless. Soon the frost would come, furring the grass and hedges, glazing the cattle troughs and water butts.

Dick Rose, at Tupps Hill, was glad to get back to the fireside after shutting up the hens for the night.

The table had been pushed back against the wall, and the three children were crawling about the floor, engrossed in a clockwork train that rattled merrily around a maze of lines set all over the floor. Betty sat watching them, as delighted as they were with its bustling manoeuvres.

'It's only fell off once,' said Stephen proudly, looking up at his foster father's entrance.

'Good,' said Dick. He never wasted words.

'Are you sad Father Christmas never brought you a watch?' asked Patsy of Stephen.

Dick's eyes met his wife's. Patsy was still young enough to believe in the myth, and the boys had nobly resisted enlightening her.

Stephen turned dark eyes upon her.

'Never thought about it,' he lied bravely. 'I've got all this, haven't I?'

He picked up the little train, and held it, whirring, close to his face. He turned and smiled – the radiant warm smile of his lost father – upon his foster parents.

'You're a good kid,' said Dick gruffly. 'And your birthday ain't far off.'

For the first time since Stephen's tempestuous arrival, he thought suddenly, the boy seemed part of the family.

There was a stirring beneath the third bush in the hawthorn hedge. A sharp nose pushed aside the ground-ivy leaves, and the mouse emerged into the moonlight.

It paused, sniffing the chill air, then ran through the dry grass by the shed, negotiated the mossy step by the wellhead, and stopped to nibble a dried seed pod.

On it ran again, parting the crisp grass with its sinuous body, diving down ruts, scrambling up slopes, until it gained the wet earth behind the wallflower plants.

Between the plants and the brick wall of the cottage it scampered, until it reached the foot of the rosebush, where it stopped abruptly. Far, far above it, lights glowed from the windows.

A tremor shook its tiny frame. Its nose and whiskers quivered at the sense of danger, and it turned to double back on its tracks, away from the half-remembered terrors of an alien world.

It hurried out into the moonlight and made for the open field beyond the hawthorn hedge. There among the rimy grass and the sweet familiar scents, its panic subsided.

Nibbling busily, safely within darting distance of its hole, the Christmas mouse was at peace with its little world.

A COUNTRY CHRISTMAS

Miss Read

VILLAGE CHRISTMAS

Illustrated by J. S. Goodall

To Jill and John with love

The darkness throbbed with the clamour of church bells. The six sonorous voices of St Patrick's peal chased each other, now in regular rhythm, now in staccato clashes, as the bell-ringers sweated at their Christmas peal practice.

The night was iron-cold. Frost glittered on the hedges and fields of Fairacre although it was not yet eight o'clock. Thatched roofs were furred with white rime beneath a sky brilliant with stars. Smoke rose in unwavering blue wisps from cottage chimneys, for the air was uncannily still.

The sound of the bells carried far in such weather. At Beech Green, three miles away, Miss Clare heard them clearly as she stooped to put her empty milk bottle tidily on her cottage doorstep, and she smiled at the cheerful sound. She knew at least four of those six bell-ringers for she had taught them their lessons long ago at Fairacre School. Arthur Coggs, furtively setting rabbit snares by a copse near Springbourne, heard them as clearly. The shepherd, high on the downs above the village, and the lonely signalman tending his oil-lamps on the branch line which meandered along the Cax valley to the market town, heard them too.

Nearer at hand, in the village of Fairacre, the bells caused more positive reactions. The rooks, roosting in the topmost boughs of the elm trees hard by the reverberating belfry, squawked an occasional protest at this disturbance. A fox, slinking towards Mr Willet's hen run, thought better of it as the bells rang out, and beat a retreat to the woods. Mrs Pringle, the dour cleaner of Fairacre School, picked up a flake of whitewash with disgust from the spotless floor where it had fluttered from the quaking kitchen wall, and a new baby nearby, awakened by the clamour, wailed its alarm.

Miss Margaret Waters and her sister Mary were quietly at work in their cottage in the village street. They sat, one each side of the big round table in the living room, penning their Christmas cards in meticulous copper plate. Music tinkled from the large old-fashioned wireless set on the dresser by the fireplace, vying with the noise of the bells outside. Mary's grey curls began to nod in time to a waltz, and putting her pen between her teeth, she rose to increase the volume of the music. At that moment an excruciating clashing of St Patrick's peal informed the world of Fairacre that at least three of the six bell-ringers were hopelessly awry in their order.

'Switch it off, Mary, do! Them dratted bells drowns anything else. We may as well save the electric!' exclaimed Margaret, looking over the top of her gold-rimmed spectacles.

Mary obeyed, as she always did, and returned to her seat. It would have been very nice, she thought privately, to hear 'The Merry Widow' waltz all the way through, but it was not worth upsetting Margaret – especially with Christmas so near. After all, it was the season of goodwill. She picked up a card from the central pile and surveyed it with affection.

'All right for Cousin Toby?' she queried, her head on one side. 'He's partial to a robin.'

Her sister looked up from her writing and studied the card earnestly. Sending just the right card to the right person was something which both sisters considered with the utmost care. Their Christmas cards had been chosen from the most modestly priced counter at Bell's, the Caxley stationer's, but even so the amount had been a considerable sum from the weekly pension of the two elderly sisters.

'You don't feel it's a mite spangly? That glitter on the icicles don't look exactly *manly* to me. I'd say the coach and horses myself.'

Mary set aside the robin reluctantly, and began to inscribe the card with the coach and horses:

From your affectionate cousins,
Margaret and Mary

The ancient mahogany clock, set four-square in the middle of the mantelpiece, ticked steadily as it had done throughout their parents' married life and their own single one. A log hissed on the small open fire, and the black kettle on the trivet began to hum. By bedtime it would be boiling, ready for the sisters' hot water bottles. It was very peaceful and warm in the cottage and Mary sighed with content as she tucked in the flap of Cousin Toby's envelope. It was the time of day she loved best, when the work was done, the curtains were drawn, and she and Margaret sat snugly and companionably by the fire.

'That seems to be the lot,' she observed, putting the envelopes into a neat stack. Margaret added her last one. Three, including the rejected robin, remained unused.

'There's bound to be someone we've forgot,' said Margaret. 'Put 'em all on the dresser, dear, and we'll post 'em off tomorrow.'

The church bells stopped abruptly and the room seemed very quiet. Ponderously and melodiously the old clock chimed half past eight from the mantelpiece, and Mary began to yawn. At that moment there came a sharp rapping at the door. Mary's mouth closed with a snap.

'Who on earth can that be, at this time of night?' she whispered. Her blue eyes were round with alarm. Margaret, made of sterner stuff, strode to the door and flung it open. There, blinking in the sudden light, stood a little girl.

'Come in, do, out of the cold,' begged Mary, who had followed her sister. 'Why, Vanessa, you haven't got a coat on! You must be starved with the cold! Come by the fire now!'

The child advanced towards the blaze, plump hands outstretched like pink star-fish. She sniffed cheerfully and beamed up at the two sisters who looked down at her with so much concern. The child's two front milk

teeth had recently vanished and the gap gave her wide smile a gamin air. She shook the silky fringe from her sparkling eyes. Clearly, Miss Vanessa Emery was very happy to be inside Flint Cottage.

'And what do you want, my dear, so late in the day?' enquired Margaret, unusually gentle.

'Mummy sent me,' explained the child. 'She said could you lend her some string to tie up Grandpa's parcel. *Thick* string, she said, if you could manage it. It's a box of apples, you see, off our tree, and sticky tape won't be strong enough on its own.'

'Indeed it won't,' agreed Mary opening the dresser drawer and taking out a square tin. She opened it and placed it on the table for the child to inspect. Inside were neat coils of string, the thickest at the left-hand side and the finest – some of it as thin as thread – in a tidy row on the right-hand. The child drew in her breath with delight and put a finger among the coils.

'Where did you buy it?' she asked.

'*Buy* it?' echoed Margaret, flabbergasted. 'Buy

string? We've never bought a bit of string in all our borns! This comes off all the parcels that have come here over the years.'

'Mum cuts ours off and throws it away,' explained the child unabashed. She picked up a fat gingery coil of hairy twine and examined it closely.

'Could you spare this?' she asked politely.

'Of course, of course,' said Mary, hurrying to make amends for the horrified outburst from her sister. She tucked it into the pocket on the front of the child's cotton apron.

'And now I'll see you across the road,' she added, opening the front door. 'It's so late I expect you should be in bed.'

The child left the fire reluctantly. One hand gripped the string inside her pocket. The other she held out to Margaret.

'Good night, Miss Waters,' she said carefully, 'and thank you for the string.'

'You're welcome,' replied Margaret, shaking the cold hand. 'Mind the road now.'

The two sisters watched the child run across to the cottage opposite. It sat well back from the village street in a little hollow surrounded by an overgrown garden. Against the night sky its thatched roof and two chimneys gave it the air of a great cat crouched comfortably on its haunches. They heard the gate bang, and turned again to their fire, slamming the door against the bitter cold.

'Well!' exploded Margaret. 'Fancy sending a child out at this time of night! And for a bit of string! "Cuts it off" indeed! Did you ever hear of such a wicked waste, Mary?'

'Dreadful!' agreed her sister, but with less vehemence. 'And that poor little mite with no coat on!'

'Well, I've always said, there's some people as have no business to be parents and them Emerys belong to 'em. Three under seven and another on the way! It's far too many. I feel downright sorry for that poor unborn. She can't look after the three she's got already!'

Margaret picked up the poker and rapped smartly at a large lump of coal. It split obediently and burst into joyous flame. The kettle purred with increased vigour, and Margaret moved it further back on the trivet.

The two sisters sat down, one at each side of the blaze. From the cupboard under the dresser Mary drew forth a large bundle, unrolled it and gave one end to Margaret. They were making a hearthrug, a gigantic monster of Turkish design, in crimson and deep blue. Each evening the sisters spent some time thrusting their shining hooks in and out of the canvas as they laboriously added strand after strand of bright wool.

Margaret's end was growing much more quickly than Mary's. Her hook moved more briskly, with sharp staccato jabs, and the wool was tugged fiercely into place. Mary moved more slowly, and she fingered each knotted strand as though she loved it. She would be sorry when the work was finished. Margaret would be glad.

'I must say, they seem happy enough,' observed Mary, reverting to the topic of the Emerys. 'And very healthy too. They're dear little girls – and so polite. Did you notice the way Vanessa shook hands?'

'It's not the children I'm criticizing,' replied Margaret. 'It's their parents. There'll be four little mites under that roof soon, and dear knows how many more to come. And they don't seem to have any idea of bringing them up right! Look at their fancy names, for one thing! Vanessa, Francesca, Anna-Louise – I ask you!'

'I rather like them,' said Mary with spirit. Margaret snorted and jabbed the canvas energetically.

'And all dressed up in that frilly little apron with a heart-shaped pocket, and no decent warm coat on the child's back,' continued Margaret, now in full spate. 'It's all on a par with the house. All fancy lampshades, and knick-knacks hanging on the wall, and great holes in the sheets, for all to see, when she hangs 'em on the line. 'Twasn't no surprise to me to hear she cuts up her string and throws it out. We done right, Mary, not to get too familiar with her. She's the sort as would be in here, everlasting borrowing, given half a chance, as I told you at the outset.'

'I dare say you're right, dear,' responded Mary equably. She usually was, thought Mary, pensively. They worked in silence and Mary looked back to the time when the Emerys had first arrived in Fairacre, three months before, and she had watched from a vantage point behind the bedroom curtain their furniture being carried up the brick path.

It was a golden afternoon in late September and Margaret had gone to St Patrick's to help with the decorations for Harvest Festival. A bilious headache had kept Mary from accompanying her, and she had retired to bed with an aspirin and a cup of tea.

She had slept for an hour and the sound of children's voices woke her. At first she thought the schoolchildren must be running home, but it was only three o'clock by the flowered china timepiece on the mantelshelf, and she had gone to the window to investigate.

A dark green pantechnicon almost blocked the village street. The men were staggering to the house opposite with a large and shabby sideboard between them. Two little girls danced excitedly beside them, piping shrilly to each other like demented moorhens. Their mother, cigarette in mouth, watched the proceedings from the side of the doorway.

Mary was a little shocked – not by the cigarette, although she felt that smoking was not only a wicked waste of money but also very unhealthy – but at the young woman's attire. She wore black tights, with a good-sized hole in the left leg, and a short scarlet

jerkin which ended at mid-thigh. Her black hair was long and straight, and her eyes were heavily made up. To Mary she appeared like an actress about to take part in a play set in the Middle Ages. No one – absolutely no one – dressed like that in Fairacre, and Mary only hoped that the young woman would not hear the remarks which must inevitably come from such village stalwarts as Mrs Pringle and her own sister, if she continued to dress in this manner.

Nevertheless, Mary was glad to see that they had neighbours, and gladder still to see that there were children. The thatched cottage had stood empty all the summer, ever since the old couple who had lived there from the time of their marriage in good Queen Victoria's reign, had departed to a daughter's house in Caxley and had moved from thence to Fairacre churchyard. It would be good to see a light winking through the darkness again from the cottage window, and to see the neglected garden put into order once more, thought Mary.

Her headache had gone and she straightened the bed coverlet and made her way down the steep dark staircase. She was pleasantly excited by the activity outside the front door, and tried to hear what the children were saying, but in vain. A thin wailing could be heard and, peeping out from behind the curtain, Mary saw that the woman now had a baby slung over her shoulder and was patting its back vigorously.

'Three!' breathed Mary, with delight. She was devoted to children and thoroughly enjoyed taking her Sunday School class. To be sure, she was often put out when some of the bigger boys were impudent, and was quite incapable of disciplining them, but small children, and particularly little girls of gentle upbringing, delighted her warm old spinster's heart.

When Margaret returned she told her the good news. Her sister received it with some reserve.

'I'll be as pleased as you are,' she assured Mary, 'if they behaves themselves. But let's pray they ain't the squalling sort. You can hear too much in that bedroom of ours when the wind's that way.'

'I wondered,' began Mary timidly, 'if it would be a kindness to ask 'em over for a cup of tea when we makes it.'

'If she was alone,' replied Margaret after a moment's consideration, 'I'd say "Yes" but with three children and the removal men too, I reckons we'd be overdone. Best leave it, Mary – but it does you credit to have thought of it.'

Mary was about to answer, but Margaret went on. Her expression was cautious.

'We don't want to be too welcoming yet awhile, my dear. Let's see how they turn out. Being neighbourly's one thing, but living in each other's pockets is another. Let 'em get settled and then we'll call. Best not to go too fast or we'll find ourselves babysitting every evening.' A thought struck her. 'Seen the man, Mary?'

Mary admitted she had not.

'Funny!' ruminated her sister. 'You'd have thought he'd be on hand.'

'Maybe he's clearing things up the other end,' suggested Mary.

'Maybe,' agreed Margaret. 'I only hope and pray

she's not a widow woman, or worse still one that's *been left*.'

'We'll soon know,' replied Mary comfortably, well versed in village ways. Fairacre had a lively grapevine, and there would be no secrets unhidden in the cottage opposite, the sisters felt quite sure.

Within a week it was common knowledge that the Emerys had moved from a north London suburb – Enfield, according to Mrs Pringle, Southgate, by Mr Willet's reckoning, though the Vicar was positive that it was Barnet. Much to Margaret's relief, Mr Emery had appeared, and her first glimpse of him was as he put out the milk bottles the next morning whilst still clad in dashing crimson pyjamas with yellow frogging.

He worked 'up the Atomic', as did many other Fairacre residents, but drove there in a shabby old Daimler at about nine, instead of going on the bus which collected the other workers at seven-thirty each morning.

'One of the high-ups,' commented Mr Willet. 'Had a bit of book-learning in science and that, I don't doubt. Looks scruffy enough to have a degree, to my mind. Wants a new razor-blade, by the looks of things, and that duffle coat has seen a few meals down it.'

Fairacre was inclined to agree with Mr Willet's somewhat tart summing-up of Mr Emery, though the female residents pointed out that he seemed to take his share of looking after the children and, say what you like, he had very attractive thick black hair. It was Mrs Emery who provided more fodder for gossip.

As Mary had foreseen, her Bohemian garments

scandalized the older generation. And then, she was so breathtakingly friendly! She had introduced herself to Mr Lamb in the Post Office, and to two venerable residents who were collecting their pensions, shaking hands with them warmly and asking such personal questions as where they lived and what were their names.

'Wonder she didn't ask us how old we be,' said one to the other when they escaped into the open air. 'She be a baggage, I'll lay. I'll take good care to steer clear of that 'un.'

She hailed everyone she met with equal heartiness, and struck horror into every conservative Fairacre heart by announcing her decision to join every possible club and society in the village 'to get to know people', and her intention of taking the little girls with her if the times of the meetings proved suitable.

'Terribly important for them to make friends,' she told customers and assistants in the village shop one morning. Her wide warm smile embraced them all. She seemed unaware of a certain frostiness in the air as she made her purchases, and bade them all goodbye, with considerable gusto, when she left.

Margaret and Mary viewed their ebullient neighbour with some alarm. Three days after her arrival, when Margaret was already planning the best time to call, Mrs Emery knocked briefly on the sisters' front door and almost immediately opened it herself.

'Anyone at home?' she chirped blithely. 'Can I come in?'

Before the startled sisters could reply, she was in the room, with two beaming little girls following her.

'I'm your new neighbour, as I expect you know,' she said, smiling disarmingly. 'Diana Emery. This is Vanessa, and this one Francesca. Say "Hello", darlings.'

'Hello!' 'Hello!' piped the two children.

Mary collected her wits with remarkable composure. She found the Emery family attractive, despite their forward ways.

'There now!' she began kindly. 'We were wondering when to call and see you. Won't you take a cup of coffee? Margaret and I usually have some about this time.'

'I'll get it,' said Margaret swiftly, glad to escape for a moment to take stock of the situation. Mary could see from her expression that she was not pleased by the invasion.

'Lovely!' sighed Mrs Emery, flinging off a loose jacket of jade green, and settling in Margaret's armchair. The two little girls collapsed cross-legged on the hearth-rug and gazed about them with squirrel-bright eyes beneath their silky fringes.

'What about the baby?' asked Mary, concerned lest it should have been left outside. The morning was chilly.

'Not due until the New Year,' replied Mrs Emery nonchalantly. 'And jolly glad I shall be when it's arrived.'

There was a gasp from the doorway as Margaret bore in the tray. She was pink, and obviously put out.

Mary hastened to explain. 'I meant the *third* little girl,' she said.

'Oh, Anna-Louise! She's fast asleep in the pram. Quite safe, I can assure you.'

'We want a brother next time,' announced Vanessa, eyeing the plate of biscuits.

'Three girlth ith three too many,' announced Francesca. 'Thatth's what my daddy thayth.'

'That's a joke,' explained Vanessa.

'Sometimes I wonder,' their mother said, but her tone was cheerful.

Margaret poured coffee and tried to avert her eyes from Mrs Emery's striped frock which gaped widely at the waist fastening, displaying an extraordinary undergarment of scarlet silk. Could it *possibly* be a petticoat, Margaret wondered? Were there really petticoats in existence of such a remarkable colour?

Mary did her best to make small talk. It was quite apparent that Margaret was suffering from shock, and was of little help.

'Is there anything you want to know about the village? Perhaps you go to church sometimes? The services are ten-thirty and six-thirty.'

'We're not much good at church-going,' admitted their neighbour. 'Though I must say the Vicar looks a perfect poppet.'

Margaret swallowed a mouthful of coffee too quickly and coughed noisily. This was downright sacrilege.

'Gone down the wrong way,' explained Francesca, coming close to her and gazing up anxiously into Margaret's scarlet face. Speechless, but touched by the child's solicitude, Margaret nodded.

'And if you want to go to Caxley,' continued Mary, 'there is a bus timetable on the wall of The Beetle and Wedge. Is there anything else we can help you with?'

Mrs Emery put her cup carelessly upon its saucer so that the spoon crashed to the floor. Both children pounced upon it and returned it to the table.

'Well, yes, there is something,' said their mother. 'Could you possibly change a cheque for me? I'm absolutely out of money and want to get some cigarettes. Edgar won't be home until eight or after.'

There was a chilly silence. The sisters had no banking account, and the idea of lending money, even to their nearest and dearest, was against their principles. To be asked, by a stranger, to advance money was profoundly shocking. Margaret found her tongue suddenly.

'I'm afraid we can't oblige. We keep very little in the house. I suggest that you ask Mr Lamb. He may be able to help.' Her tone was glacial, but Mrs Emery appeared unperturbed.

'Ah well,' she said cheerfully, struggling from the armchair and gaping even more hugely at the waist band, 'never mind! I'll try Mr Lamb, as you suggest. Must have a cigarette now and again with this brood to look after.'

She picked up the green jacket and smiled warmly upon the sisters.

'Thank you so much for the delicious coffee. Do pop over and see us whenever you like. We'll probably be seeing quite a bit of each other as we're such close neighbours.'

And with these ominous words she made her departure.

Ever since then, thought Mary, busily prodding her hook in the rug, she and Margaret had fought a polite, but quietly desperate, battle against invasion.

'Be friendly to all, but familiar with few,' said an old Victorian sampler hanging on their cottage wall. The sisters found its advice timely. The children, they agreed, were adorable, and although they appeared far too often for 'a-shilling-for-the-electricity-meter' or 'a-box-of-matches-because-the-shop's-shut' and other like errands, the two sisters had not the heart to be annoyed with them. In any case, it was simple to dismiss them when their business was done, with a piece of chocolate to sweeten their departure.

Mrs Emery, growing weekly more bulky, was more difficult to manage, and the two sisters grew adept at making excuses. Once inside, she was apt to stay over an hour, seriously throwing out the working of the sisters' day. She certainly was an embarrassment as a neighbour.

Mary's eyes strayed to the table, and the rejected

Christmas card with the gay robin among his spangles. A thought struck her, and she put down her hook.

'Margaret,' she said suddenly, 'what about sending that robin to the Emery children?'

Margaret began to look doubtful.

'Well, my dear, you know what a mite of trouble we've had with that woman! I just wonder—'

'Oh, do now!' pressed Mary, her face flushed. ''Tis Christmas! No time for hard thoughts, sister, and them children would just love it. I could slip over with it after dark on Christmas Eve and pop it through the letter box.'

Margaret's face relaxed into a smile.

'We'll do it, Mary, that we will!'

She began to roll up the rug briskly, as the church clock struck ten. Mary gave a happy sigh, and lifted the singing kettle from the trivet.

'Time for bed,' she said, taking two hot water bottles from the bottom of the dresser cupboard. 'Think of it, Margaret! Only three more days until Christmas!'

*

The next three days were busy ones for the ladies at Flint Cottage. Red-berried holly, pale mistletoe and glossy ivy were collected, and used to decorate the living room. Two red candles stood one at each end of the mantelpiece, and a holly garland hung from the brass knocker on the front door.

The cake was iced, the pudding fetched down from the top shelf in the pantry, the mincemeat jar stood ready for the pies and a trifle was made. One of Mrs Pringle's chickens arrived ready for the table, and sausage meat came from the butcher.

Margaret crept away privately while Mary was bringing in logs from the woodshed, and wrapped up two pairs of sensible lisle stockings which she had bought in Caxley for her sister's present. Mary took advantage of Margaret's absence at the Post Office and swiftly wrapped up a pair of stout leather gloves and hid them in the second drawer of the bedroom chest.

All Fairacre was abustle. Margaret and Mary helped to set up the Christmas crib in the chancel of St Patrick's church. The figures of Joseph, Mary and the Child, the shepherds and the wise men reappeared every year, standing in the straw provided by Mr Roberts the farmer, and lit with sombre beauty by discreetly placed electric lights. The children came in on their way from school to see this perennial scene, and never tired of looking.

The sisters helped to decorate the church too. There were Christmas roses on the altar, their pearly beauty set off by sprigs of dark yew amidst the gleaming silverware.

On Christmas Eve the carol singers set out on their annual pilgrimage round the village. Mr Annett, the choir master, was in charge of the church choir and any other willing chorister who volunteered to join the party. This year, the newcomer Mr Emery was among them, for word had soon got round that he sang well and Mr Annett had invited him to join the carol singers. Clad in the duffle coat which Mr Willett thought of so poorly, he strode cheerfully along the frosty lanes of Fairacre, swinging a hurricane lamp as though he had lived in the village all his life, and rattling away to his companions with the same friendly foreign loquacity as his wife's.

One of their stopping places was outside The Beetle and Wedge, strategically placed in the village street. Margaret and Mary opened their window and watched the singers at their work. Their breath rose in silver clouds in the light of the lanterns. The white music sheets fluttered in the icy wind which spoke of future snow to the weather-wise of Fairacre. Some of the lamps were hung on tall stout ash-sticks, and these swayed above the ruffled hair of the men and the hooded heads of the women.

Mr Annett conducted vigorously and the singing was controlled as well as robust. As the country voices carolled the eternal story of joyous birth, Mary felt that she had never been so happy. Across the road she could see the upstairs light in the bedroom of the Emery children, and against the glowing pane were silhouetted two dark heads.

How excited they must be, thought Mary! The stockings would be hanging limply over the bed rail,

just as her own and Margaret's used to hang so many years ago. There was nothing to touch the exquisite anticipation of Christmas Eve.

> *'Hark the herald angels sing,*
> *Glory to the new-born King,'*

fluted the choir boys, their eyes on Mr Annett, their mouths like dark Os in the lamplight. And the sound of their singing rose like incense to the thousands of stars above.

On Christmas morning Margaret and Mary were up early and went to eight o'clock service. A feeling of night still hung about the quiet village, although the sun was staining the eastern sky and giving promise of a fine day ahead.

The lighted crib glowed in the shadowy chancel like the star of Bethlehem itself, and the aromatic smell of the evergreens added to the spirit of Christmas. Later, the bells would ring out and the winter sunshine would touch the flowers and silver on the altar with brightness. All would be glory and rejoicing, but there was something particularly lovely and holy about these quiet early morning devotions, and the two sisters preferred to attend then, knowing that the rest of the morning would be taken up with the cheerful ritual of Christmas Day cooking.

They unwrapped their few parcels after breakfast, exclaiming with genuine pleasure at the modest calendars and handkerchiefs, the unaccustomed luxury of richly perfumed soap or chocolates which friends and relatives had sent.

Margaret thanked Mary warmly for the gloves. Mary was equally delighted with her stockings. They exchanged rare kisses and told each other how lucky they were.

'There's not many,' said Margaret, 'as can say they live as contented as we do here. And under our own roof, thank God, and nothing owing to any man!'

'We've a lot to be thankful for,' agreed Mary, folding up the bright wrappings neatly. 'Best of all each other – and next best, our health and strength, sister.'

'Now, I'm off to stuff the bird,' announced Margaret, rising with energy. 'I'll put on the pudding too while I'm in the kitchen. Must have that properly hotted up by midday.'

She bustled off and Mary began to make up the fire, and sweep the hearth. The two red candles looked brave and gay, standing like sentinels each side of the Christmas cards ranged along the mantelpiece. She wondered if the Emery children had liked the fat robin. She could see them now, in imagination, surrounded by new Christmas presents, flushed and excited at the joy of receiving and of giving.

At that moment, a rapping came at the front door and she rose from her sweeping to open it. Vanessa stood there, looking far from flushed and excited. The child's eyes were large with alarm, her face pale with cold and fright.

'What is it, my love? Come in quickly,' cried Mary.

'It's Mummy. She said, "Could you come over, please?" She's ill.'

'Is Daddy with her?' asked Margaret, appearing in the doorway with her fingers pink and sticky with sausage meat.

'No. He's had to go to Grandma's. Grandpa rang up last night after we'd gone to bed. Grandma's being stroked.'

'Had a stroke,' corrected Margaret automatically. 'Dear me, that's bad news! We'll be over as soon as we've put the dinner in.'

The child's eyes grew more enormous than ever. She looked imploringly at Mary.

'But it's the baby coming! You must come this minute. Please, *please*!'

Without a word Margaret began to take off her kitchen apron.

'Go over, Mary,' she said quietly. 'I'll follow you.'

Indescribable chaos greeted Mary's eyes when she stepped into the Emery's kitchen. It was a large square room with a brick floor, and comfortably warmed by an Esse cooker appallingly streaked with grime. Quantities of anthracite dust were plentifully sprinkled on the floor at its base, and had been liberally trodden about the room.

The débris of breakfast littered the table, and coloured paper, tags and string garnished sticky cereal bowls and mugs. A ginger cat lapped up some milk which dripped from an overturned jug, and the confusion was made more acute by Francesca who stood proudly holding a new scarlet scooter, ringing the shiny bell without cessation.

'Give over, do!' begged Mary, peremptory in her flurry. The child obeyed, still beaming. Nothing could quench her Christmas bliss, and Mary was immediately glad to see that this was so. The sound of Anna-Louise's wailing became apparent, and Mary opened the door of the box staircase and began to mount. The two little girls started to follow her.

'You stop here, there's dears,' said Mary, much agitated. Who knows what terrors might be aloft? 'Pick up the paper and make it nice and tidy.'

To her relief they fell upon the muddle joyously, and she creaked her way above. Mrs Emery's voice greeted her. She sounded as boisterous as ever, and Mary's fears grew less. At least she was conscious!

'You are a darling! You really are!' cried Mrs Emery. She was standing by the window, a vast figure in a red satin dressing gown embroidered on the back with a fierce dragon. Mary suddenly realized how very young she looked, and her heart went out to her.

'We were so sorry to hear about your mother in-law,' began Mary, a little primly.

'Poor sweet,' said Mrs Emery. 'It *would* have to happen now. Edgar went off as soon as he came back from carol-singing. And then, this! *Much* too early. I suppose I've got the dates wrong again. Ah well!'

She sighed, and suddenly clutched the front of her dressing gown again. Mary felt panic rising.

'Do get into bed there's a love,' she begged, turning back the rumpled bedclothes invitingly. The bottom sheet had a tear in it six inches long, and a very dirty rag doll with the stuffing coming out. Mary was appalled. She must put something clean on the bed! Suppose the baby was born in that unhygienic spot! She looked for help towards Mrs Emery, who was bowed before the chest of drawers and gasping in an alarming way.

'You must have clean sheets,' announced Mary with

an authoritative ring in her voice which wholly surprised her.

'Cupboard,' gasped Mrs Emery, nodding towards the next room.

An unpleasant smell was the first thing that Mary noticed about the adjoining bedroom. Anna-Louise was standing in a cot. Her nightgown and the bedding were ominously stained, but her cries had ceased and she threw Mary a ravishing smile.

'You pretty thing!' cried Mary, quite entranced. 'Aunt Mary'll see to you in just a minute.'

She swiftly ransacked the cupboard. She found a roll of mackintosh sheeting and two clean linen ones. Bustling back to the bedroom she set about making the bed with vigorous speed. Mrs Emery was upright again, leaning her damp forehead against the cool window-pane. She consented to be led to the bed, unprotesting, and let Mary remove the flamboyant dressing gown.

'There, there!' soothed Mary, tucking her in as though she were a child. 'I'll bring you a drink.'

'I'm all right now,' whispered the girl, and at that moment Margaret appeared.

'Does Nurse know?' was her first remark. Mary felt suddenly guilty. Of course, it was the first thing she should have found out. Trust Margaret to know exactly what to do!

'Yes,' replied Mrs Emery. 'At least, someone at her house does. Nurse was out on another baby case. They were sending word.'

'What about Doctor Martin?' continued Margaret.

'Nurse will get him, if need be,' said the girl. She

sank back on the pillow and suddenly looked deathly tired. 'It won't come for hours,' she told them. 'It's just that I was worried about the children.'

'I know, I know,' said Margaret gently. 'We'll look after them all right. Leave it all to us.'

'Anna-Louise needs a wash,' said Mary, retiring to the next room. She beckoned Margaret to follow her, and closed the door between the two rooms.

'What on earth shall we do?' she implored Margaret. Margaret, for once, looked flummoxed.

'Dear knows, and that's the honest truth,' admitted her sister. 'Let's hope nature knows best and Nurse comes pretty smartly. This is foreign stuff to us, Mary, but we must hold the fort till help comes.'

She turned to survey Anna-Louise who was jumping rhythmically up and down in the cot, with dire results.

'Land's sake, Mary! That child wants dumping in the bath – and the bedding too!'

'I'll do her,' said Mary swiftly. 'And then I can keep an eye on Mrs Emery up here. You see to things downstairs.'

'Won't do no harm to give Nurse another ring,' observed Margaret, turning to the door. She looked back at her sister. 'Who'd a thought we'd a been spending Christmas like this?'

She vanished downstairs and Mary went to turn on the bath for her charge.

Anna-Louise, well-soaped, was absolutely adorable. Fat and pink, with a skin like satin, she made Mary a willing slave. She patted the water vigorously, sending up showers of spray, and drenching Mary kneeling beside the bath. Mary could have stayed there all day, murmuring endearments and righting the celluloid duck time and time again. But the water cooled rapidly, and there was much to do. She gathered the naked child into a grubby bath towel, and dried her on her lap.

'She hasn't had her breakfast yet,' Mrs Emery said drowsily when the child was dressed. She looked at her daughter with amusement. 'That's Francesca's jumper,' she observed, 'but no matter. Tie a bib on the poor lamb. She's a filthy feeder.'

Below stairs, all was amazingly quiet. The table had been cleared and the two little girls were blissfully engaged in filling in their new Christmas drawing books with glossy long crayons as yet unbroken. Margaret was busy sweeping the floor with a broom from which most of the bristles had long vanished.

'Has the baby come yet?' asked Vanessa, without looking up from the mad oscillation of her crayoning.

'Not yet,' replied Mary, threading Anna-Louise's fat legs through her high-chair. She stood back and surveyed the baby anxiously, 'And what does Anna-Louise like for breakfast?'

Francesca put down her crayon and gazed earnestly at her younger sister. 'She liketh bacon rindth betht,' she told Mary.

'Well, we've no time to cook bacon,' said Margaret flatly, still wielding the broom.

'Egg,' said Vanessa briefly. 'All horrible and runny. That's what she likes.'

The sisters exchanged questioning glances.

'Sounds reasonable,' muttered Margaret, 'if you can find the egg saucepan.'

'It's the milk one as well,' volunteered Vanessa, making for a cupboard. 'Here you are.' She produced a battered saucepan with a wobbly handle, and returned to the drawing book.

'Did you get through to Nurse?' asked Mary agitatedly, as she filled the saucepan.

'Still out. Message supposed to have been passed on.

I reckons we ought to get her husband back. It's his business after all.' Margaret spoke with some asperity.

'I'll go and ask Mrs Emery,' said Mary, 'while the egg boils.'

She returned to the bedroom to find Mrs Emery humped under the bedclothes with her head in the pillow. She was groaning with such awful intensity that Mary's first impulse was to fly for Margaret, but she controlled it. She patted the humped back consolingly and waited for the spasm to pass. Somewhere, far away it seemed, the bells of St Patrick's began to peal for morning service. A vivid picture of the peaceful nave, the holly and the Christmas roses, the fragrance of the cypress and yew, came clearly to Mary, standing helplessly there watching her neighbour in labour. How long ago, it seemed, since she and Margaret knelt in the church! Yet only three hours had gone by.

The spasm passed and Diana Emery's face appeared again.

'Better,' she said. 'Can I have that drink now? Coffee, please – no milk. Any sign of that confounded nurse?'

'She's on her way,' said Mary, 'and we thought we ought to phone your husband.'

'His parents aren't on the telephone,' said Mrs Emery.

'We could ring the police,' suggested Mary with sudden inspiration.

Mrs Emery laughed with such unaffected gaiety that Mary could hardly believe that she had so recently been in such pain.

'It's not *that* serious. Nurse will be along any minute now, and think how wonderful it will be to present Edgar with a fine new baby!'

She sounded so matter-of-fact and cheerful that Mary gazed at her open-mouthed. Was childbearing really undertaken so lightly? She remembered Margaret's tart comments on people who had large families with such apparent fecklessness. How many more would there be in this casual household, Mary wondered? Then she remembered the sight of Anna-Louise in the bath and hoped suddenly, and irrationally, that there would be more – lots more – and that she would be able to enjoy them.

'I'll get your coffee, my love,' she said warmly and went below.

Returning with the steaming black brew, she remembered something. 'Shouldn't we put the baby's things ready for Nurse?' she asked.

'There's not a great deal,' confessed the girl, warming her hands round the cup. 'I intended to do most of the shopping after Christmas in Caxley. So many people about, I just couldn't face it.'

'But you must have *some* things,' persisted Mary aghast.

'In the bottom drawer,' said the girl vaguely. 'And there are lots of Anna-Louise's things that will do, in the airing cupboard.'

Mary was shocked at such a slapdash approach to an important event, and her face must have shown it, for Mrs Emery laughed.

'After the first you don't bother quite so much,' she

confessed. 'You can get by with all the odds and ends the others had.'

Mary found six new nappies in the drawer, and a bundle of small vests, some tiny night-gowns yellow with much washing, and a shawl or two, in the airing cupboard.

'And what shall we put the baby in?' she inquired.

'Anna-Louise's carry-cot. It's in her room. It probably wants clean things in it.' The girl had slipped down into the bed again and closed her eyes. She looked desperately tired, thought Mary, with a pang.

The carry-cot held two dolls, a headless teddy-bear and a shoe, all carefully tucked up in a checked tablecloth. Mary took it downstairs to wash it out and dry it ready for the new occupant.

'If that dratted nurse don't come soon,' said Margaret, 'I'll fetch Doctor Martin myself, that I will! I'll just slip over home, Mary, and turn that bird and add a mite of hot water to the pudding.'

'We'll never have a chance to eat dinner, sister,' cried Mary. 'Not as things are!'

'There's them three to think of,' replied Margaret nodding to the children. 'We've got them to feed, don't forget.'

She lifted the latch and hurried across to their cottage. One or two parishioners, in their Sunday best, were making their way to church. Mary saw Mr and Mrs Willet stop to speak to her sister as she stood with one hand on the door knob. There was much headshaking, and Mrs Willet looked across at the Emerys' house with some alarm.

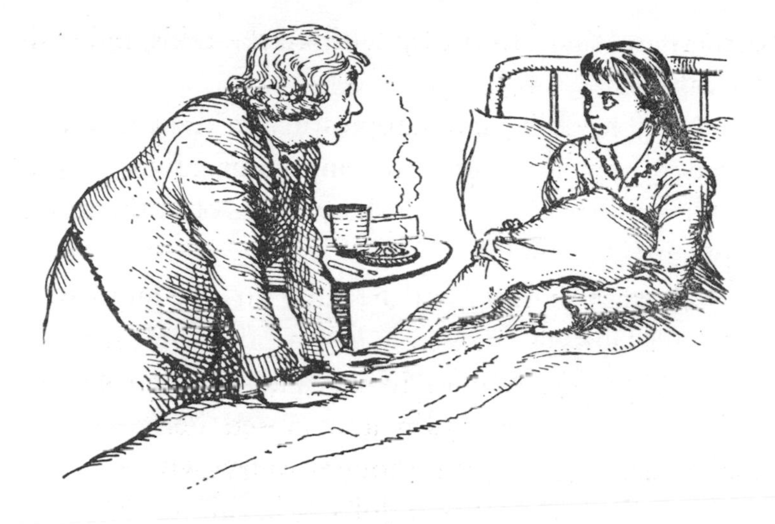

'The news will soon be round Fairacre,' thought Mary, as she dried the carry-cot.

It was clean and peaceful now in the kitchen, and she noticed the paper chains festooned against the ceiling, and the Christmas cards pinned along the rafters. Her own fat robin was there, and she glowed with pleasure. Vanessa and Francesca were still engrossed in their artistic efforts, and Anna-Louise wiped her eggy plate with her fingers and sucked them happily. What dear good children they were, thought Mary!

At that moment she heard their mother calling from overhead. Her voice sounded shrill and desperate. Mary took the stairs at a run. The girl was sitting up in bed, clenching and unclenching her hands on the coverlet.

'You *must* get that nurse – or the doctor, or someone. I can't stick this now. It's coming pretty fast.'

'I'll ring again,' promised Mary, thoroughly frightened by the urgency of the girl's pleas. 'Just lie down again. I'm sure it's better. Can I do anything? Rub your back, say, or bring you a hot bottle?'

She did her best to appear calm, but inwardly terror gripped her. Supposing the baby came this minute? What on earth did you do with a new-born baby? Wasn't there something about cutting a cord? And if so, where did you cut it? And how did you tie it up afterwards? Hadn't she heard once that mothers bled to death if the cord wasn't tied properly? And that wretched carry-cot wouldn't be anywhere near aired, let along made up with clean bedding, if the baby arrived now! Mary found herself shaking with panic, and praying desperately. Don't let it come yet, please, dear Lord! Not until Nurse arrives, please God!

'There, my love—' she began, when she stopped abruptly. The door of the staircase had opened and someone was mounting.

'Margaret!' she cried. 'Quickly, Margaret!'

A sturdy figure appeared in the doorway.

'Nurse! Thank God!' cried Mary, and began to weep.

'You go and make us all a cup of tea,' said Nurse Thomas with gruff kindness. And Mary fled.

An hour later, Margaret and Mary sat at their own table, serving three excited little girls with Christmas dinner. Nurse's car still stood outside the cottage opposite, but Doctor Martin's was not to be seen. Evidently all was going well, and Nurse had everything well in hand.

Mary found herself as excited as the children. What a relief it was to be home again, and to know that Mrs

Emery was being properly nursed! It was impossible to eat amidst such momentous happenings, and she was glad to neglect her own plate and to have the pleasant task of guiding Anna-Louise's teaspoon in the right direction.

St Patrick's clock chimed three, and still no message came from the house across the road.

A few Fairacre folk began to go by, taking an afternoon stroll for the sake of their digestions, between Christmas dinner and the further challenge of iced cake for tea. They noted Nurse's car and the light in the upstairs window, and fell to wondering.

Margaret was reading *The Tale of Two Bad Mice* from a new glossy copy which the children had received that morning, when a tapping came at the door. Mrs Lamb from the Post Office stood outside with a posy of anemones in her hand. She caught sight of the little girls inside and spoke in a whisper.

'For their mother, my dear. Hope all's going well. We heard about it after church. You're going over again, I expect?'

'Yes indeed,' answered Margaret, accepting the bright bunch. 'She'll be pleased with these. Nurse is still there, as you see.' She nodded towards the car.

'Give Mrs Emery our best wishes,' said Mrs Lamb. 'Poor soul, without her husband too! She's got everyone's sympathy, that's a fact.'

She set off homeward, and Margaret returned to the fireside. It began to grow dark, for the afternoon was overcast, and Mary took a taper and lit the bright red candles. The flames stretched and dwindled in the draught and the little girls gazed at them starry-eyed.

'Do you always have candles?' asked Vanessa. 'Or just at Christmas?'

'Just at Christmas,' said Margaret.

She put down the book and gazed at the bright flames with the children. The waiting seemed endless, and suddenly she felt desperately tired. How much longer, she wondered, before they knew?

Just then they heard the sound of a gate shutting and footsteps coming to their door. The two eldest sisters exchanged swift glances. Could it be –?

Mary opened the door and there stood the nurse, smiling.

'Come in,' said Mary.

'I daren't. I'm late now,' said Nurse, 'but all's well.'

Margaret and the children gathered at the door.

'A boy,' Nurse announced proudly. 'Seven pounds and bonny. And Mrs Emery's asleep. Can one of you go over?'

'You go,' said Margaret to Mary. 'I'll bring the children over later.'

'We want to see him,' pleaded Vanessa.

'*Now!*' added Francesca stubbornly.

'Now!' echoed Anna-Louise, not understanding the situation, but glad to try a new word.

'Later on,' responded Nurse firmly. 'Your mummy's tired.'

She turned to go and then looked back. 'Mr Emery rang up. I've told him the news and he'll be back very soon.'

She waved and made her way across the road to the car. 'Tell Mr Emery I'll be in, in the morning,' she called, and drove off in a cloud of smoke.

As if by magic, two heads popped out from the doorway of The Beetle and Wedge. They belonged to the landlord and his wife.

'Couldn't help seeing Nurse go off,' he said to Mary. 'What is it?'

'A boy!' said Mary, smiling.

'Now, ain't that good news?' beamed his wife. 'You tell her we'll be wetting the baby's head in here tonight.'

'Ah, she's a grand little mother, for all her funny ways,' declared her husband. 'Tell her it'll be nice to have another young 'un in the village.'

Mary tiptoed into the silent cottage. Everything seemed to slumber. The cat slept on a chair by the stove. Nothing moved.

She left the door of the staircase ajar so that she could hear the slightest sound from above, and sat down at the table.

In the domestic stillness which enveloped her, after the stress of the day, old and lovely words came into her mind.

'And it came to pass, while they were there, the days were fulfilled that she should be delivered.

'And she brought forth her first-born son; and she wrapped him in swaddling clothes, and laid him in a manger, because there was no room for them in the inn.'

Mary sat motionless, savouring the age-old miracle of the Nativity. And here, in this house, was another Christmas baby! She felt that she could not wait another moment. She must see him.

She slipped off her stout country shoes and tiptoed up the stairs. It was very quiet in the bedroom. Mrs Emery, looking pathetically young and pale, slept deeply. Beside the bed, on two chairs, was the carry-cot.

Mary leant over and gazed in wonder. Swaddled tightly, in the shawl she had found for him in the airing cupboard, was the new-born baby, as oblivious of the world about him as his sleeping mother.

Mary's heart beat with such fervour that she wondered that the sleepers did not wake. Full of joy, she crept below once more, and in her dizzy head beat the words:

'And the angel said unto them, Be not afraid; for behold, I bring you good tidings of great joy which shall be to all people.'

There was a sound outside, and she looked up from lacing her shoes. There stood Mr Emery, his face alight.

'Where is she?' he asked.

'They're both upstairs,' whispered Mary, and opened the staircase door so that he could go aloft and see his son.

Late that night, the two sisters sat each side of the hearth, working at their rug.

'D'you know what Vanessa said when her father fetched her?' asked Margaret. 'She said: "This is the loveliest Christmas we've ever had!" 'Twas good of the child to say it, I thought, after such a muddling old day. It touched me very much.'

'She spoke the truth,' replied Mary slowly. 'Not only for herself, but for all of us here in Fairacre. 'Tis a funny thing, sister, but when I crept up the stairs to take a first look at that new babe, the thought came to me: "Ah! You're a true Fairacre child, just as I was once, born here, and most likely to be bred up here, the Lord willing!" And then another thought came: "You've warmed up us cold old Fairacre folk

quicker'n the sun melts frost." You know, Margaret, them Emerys have put us all to shame, many a time, with their friendly ways, and been snubbed too, often as not. It took a Christmas baby to kindle some proper Christmas goodwill in Fairacre.'

''Tis true,' admitted Margaret, putting down the rug hook, and gazing into the dying fire. Into her tired mind there floated irrelevant memories . . . Mrs Emery's scarlet petticoat, a ginger cat lapping milk, Anna-Louise fumbling with her egg-spoon, while her sisters watched her with squirrel-bright eyes, laughing at her antics . . . all adding up to colour and warmth and gentle loving-kindness.

'Now this has happened,' she said soberly, 'it won't stop at *Christmas* goodwill, sister. The Emerys are part and parcel of this village for good. There's room for all sorts in Fairacre, Mary, but it took a newborn babe to show us.'

She began to roll up the rug briskly.

'Come, sister. Time we was abed.'

THE FAIRACRE GHOST

Illustrated by J. S. Goodall

The Easter holidays are probably more welcome than any other, for they mark the passing of the darkest and most dismal of the three school terms and they herald the arrival of flowers, sunshine and all the pleasures of the summer.

At this time, in Fairacre, we set about our gardens with zeal. Potatoes are put in, on Good Friday if possible, and rows of peas and carrots, and those who have been far-sighted enough to put in their broad beans in the autumn, go carefully along the rows, congratulating themselves, and hoping that the black fly will not devastate the young hopefuls in the next few months.

We admire each other's daffodils, walk down each other's garden paths observing the new growth in herbaceous borders, and gloat over the buds on plum and peach trees. We also observe the strong upthrust of nettles, couch grass and dandelions, among the choicer growth, but are too besotted by the thought of summer ahead to let such things worry us unduly.

It is now that the vicar gets out his garden furniture – a motley collection ranging from Victorian ironwork to pre-war Lloyd-loom – and arranges it hopefully on the vicarage veranda. Now Mr Mawne, our local ornithologist, erects a hide at the end of his lovely garden in order to watch the birds. He weaves a bower of peasticks, ivy-trails and twigs upon the wood and sacking framework, as intricate as the nests of those he watches.

Now the cottage doors are propped open with a chair, or a large stone, and striped cats wash their ears or survey the sunshine blandly through half-closed eyes. Tortoises emerge, shaky and slower than ever, from their hibernation, and sometimes a grass snake can be seen sunning itself in the dry grass.

This is the time for visiting and being visited. For

months we have been confined. Bad weather, dirty roads, dark nights and winter illnesses have kept us all apart. Now we set about refurbishing our friendships, and one of my first pleasures during this Easter holiday was a visit from my godson Malcolm Annett, and his father and mother.

It was a perfect day for a tea party. The table bore a bowl of freshly-picked primroses, some lemon curd made that morning, and a plentiful supply of egg sandwiches. Mr Roberts, the farmer, has a new batch of Rhode Island Red hens who supply me with a dozen dark brown eggs weekly. These are lucky hens, let me say, garrulous and energetic, running at large in the farmyard behind the house, scratching busily in the loose straw at the foot of the ricks, and advancing briskly to the back door whenever anyone emerges holding a plate. No wonder that their eggs are luscious compared with the product of their poor imprisoned sisters.

After tea we ambled through the village, greeting many old friends who were out enjoying the air. Mrs Annett used to teach at Fairacre before she married the headmaster at our neighbouring village Beech Green so that she knows a great many families here. Mr Annett is choirmaster at St Patrick's church at Fairacre, so that he too knows us all well.

We walked by the church and took a fork to the left. It is a lane used little these days, except by young lovers and Mr Roberts' tractors making their way to one of his larger fields. A dilapidated cottage stands alone some hundred yards from the entrance to the lane.

We stopped at its rickety gate and surveyed the outline of its ancient garden. A damson tree, its trunk riven with age, leant towards the remaining patch of roof thatch. Rough grass covered what once had been garden beds and paths, and nettles and brambles grew waist high against the walls of the ruin.

The doors and windows gaped open. Inside, on the ground floor, in what had once been the living room of the cottage, we could see hundredweight paper bags of fertilizer propped against the stained and ragged wall-paper. They belonged to Mr Roberts and were waiting to be spread upon his meadows any day now. Upstairs, the two small bedrooms lay open to the sky. The thatch had retreated before the onslaught of wind and weather, and only the frame of the roof stood, gaunt and rotting, against the evening sky.

'It must have been pretty once,' I said, looking at the triangle of garden and the rose-red of the old bricks.

'The vicar told me it was lived in during the war,' said Mr Annett. 'It housed a family of eight evacuees then. They didn't mind it being haunted, they told Mr Roberts.'

'Haunted?' we cried. I looked at Mr Annett to see if he was joking but his face was unusually thoughtful.

'It is, you know,' he said with conviction. 'I've seen the ghost myself. That's how I came to hear the history of the place from the vicar.'

'Is that why it stays empty?' I asked. It was strange that I had never heard this tale throughout my time at Fairacre.

Mr Annett laughed. 'No, indeed! I told you people lived in it for years. The evacuees said they'd sooner be haunted than bombed and spent all the war years here. I think Roberts found it just wasn't worth doing up after the war, and so it is now in this state.'

We looked again at the crumbling cottage. It was too small and homely to be sinister, despite this tale of a ghost. It had the pathetic look of a wild animal, tired to death, crouching in the familiar shelter of grass and neglected vegetation for whatever Fate might have in store.

'When did you see the ghost?' I asked.

Mr Annett sighed with mock importance. 'Persistent woman! I see I shall have no peace until I have put the whole uncomfortable proceedings before you. It was a very frightening experience indeed, and if you don't mind, I'll tell you the story as we walk. Even now my blood grows a little chilly at the memory. Brisk exercise is the right accompaniment for a ghost story.'

We continued up the lane, with young Malcolm now before and now behind us, scrambling up the banks and shouting with the sheer joy of living. With the scents of spring around us, and the soft wind lifting our hair, we listened to the tale of one strange winter night.

Every Friday night, with the exception of Good Friday, Mr Annett left the school house at Beech Green and travelled the three miles to St Patrick's Church for choir practice.

Some men would have found it irksome to leave the comfort of their homes at seven in the evening and to face the windy darkness of a downland lane. Mr Annett was glad to do so. His love of music was strong enough to make his duty a positive pleasure, and although his impatient spirit chafed at times at the slow progress made by Fairacre's choir, he counted Friday evening as a highlight of the week.

At this time he had much need of comfort. He was a young widower, living alone in the school house, and ministered to by a middle-aged Scotswoman who came in daily. The death of his wife, six months after their marriage, was still too painful for him to dwell upon. She had been killed in an air raid, during the early part of the war, and for Mr Annett life would never be the same again.

One moonlit Friday evening in December, some years after the war had ended, he set out as usual for Fairacre. It was so bright that he could have driven his little car without headlights. The road glimmered palely before him, barred with black shadows where trees lined the road. He was early, for he had arranged to pick up some music from Miss Parr's house and knew that the old lady would want him to stop for a little time.

A maid opened the door. Miss Parr had been invited to her nephew's, but the music had been looked out for him, Mr Annett was told. He drove to St Patrick's, and went inside. It was cold and gloomy. No one had yet arrived, and Mr Annett decided to use his time in taking a stroll in the brilliant moonlight.

There was an unearthly beauty about the night that chimed with the young man's melancholy. He made his way slowly along a little-used lane near the church, and let sad memory carry him on its flood. It was not often that he so indulged himself. After his wife's death, he had moved to Beech Green and thrown himself, almost savagely, into school life. He had filled his time with work and music, so that he fell asleep with exhaustion rather than the numbing despair which had first governed every waking hour.

He passed a broken down cottage on his left, its remnants of thatch silvered with moonlight. Just beyond it a five-barred gate afforded a view of the distant downs. Mr Annett leant upon its topmost bar and surveyed the scene.

Before him lay the freshly ploughed fields, the furrows gleaming in the rays of the moon. Further away, a dusky copse made a black patch on the lower flanks of the downs. Against the clear sky their mighty

bulk looked more majestic than ever. There was something infinitely reassuring and comforting about their solidity, and the young man, gazing at them, let the tranquillity about him do its healing work.

It was very quiet. Far away, he heard a train hoot impatiently as it waited for a signal to allow its passage westward. Nearer, he was dimly conscious of the rustling of dead leaves at the foot of an old crab apple tree which stood hard by the gate. Some small nocturnal animal was foraging stealthily, wary of the silent man nearby.

Sunk in his thoughts, he was oblivious of the passage of time, and was hardly surprised to notice that a strange man had appeared in the lane without any noise of approach.

He came close to Mr Annett, nodded civilly, and leant beside him on the gate. For a moment, the two men rested silently side by side, elbows touching, and gazed at the silvered landscape before them. Despite the stranger's unexpected advent, Mr Annett felt little surprise. There was something gentle and companionable about the newcomer. The schoolmaster had the odd feeling that they were very much akin. Vaguely, he wondered if they had met before somewhere. He shifted along the gate – the stranger seemed excessively cold – and turned slightly to look at him.

He was a loosely-built fellow, of about Mr Annett's age, dressed in dark country clothes which seemed a pretty poor fit.

He wore an open-necked shirt and a spotted neckerchief, tied gipsy fashion, round his throat. He had a small beard, light in colour, which gleamed silver in the moonlight, and his fair hair was thick and wiry.

'Full moon tomorrow,' commented the stranger. For such a big man he had a remarkably small voice, Mr Annett noticed. It was almost falsetto, slightly husky and strained, as though he were suffering from laryngitis.

'So it is,' agreed Mr Annett.

They relapsed again into contemplation of the view. After some time, Mr Annett stirred himself long enough to find some cigarettes. He offered the packet to his companion.

'Thank'ee,' said the man. 'Thank'ee kindly, but I don't smoke these days.'

The schoolmaster lit his cigarette and surveyed the man. 'Haven't I seen you before somewhere?' he asked.

'Most likely. I've lived in Fairacre all my life,' answered the man huskily.

'I'm at Beech Green,' said Mr Annett.

The man drew in his breath sharply, as though in pain. 'My wife came from Beech Green,' he said. He bent his head forward suddenly. By the light of the moon Mr Annett saw that his eyes were closed. The use of the past tense was not lost upon the schoolmaster, himself still smarting with grief, and he led the conversation from the dangerous ground he had unwittingly encountered.

'Whereabouts in Fairacre do you live?' he asked.

The man raised his head and nodded briefly in the direction of the ruined cottage nearby. Mr Annett was puzzled by this, but thought that perhaps he was nodding generally in the direction of the village. Not wishing to distress him any further, and realizing that his choir must be soon arriving at St Patrick's, Mr Annett began to stir himself for departure. It was time he moved, in any case, for he had grown colder and colder since the arrival of the stranger, despite his warm overcoat. The stranger only had on a long jacket, but he seemed oblivious of the frost.

'Well, I must be off,' said Mr Annett. 'I'm due to take choir practice at seven thirty. Are you walking back to the village?'

The man straightened up and turned to face the schoolmaster. The moonlight shone full upon his face. It was a fine face, with high cheekbones and pale blue eyes set very wide apart. There was something Nordic in his aspect, with his great height and wide shoulders.

'I'll stop here a little longer,' he said slowly. 'This is the right place for me. I come most nights, particularly around full moon.'

'I can understand it,' said Mr Annett gently, scanning the sad grave face. 'There is comfort in a lovely place like this.'

A burst of laughter broke from the stranger's lips, all the more uncanny for its cracked wheeziness. His wide-open eyes glittered in the moonlight.

'Comfort?' he echoed. 'There's no comfort for the likes of me – ever!' He began to tear savagely at the neckerchief about his throat. 'You can't expect comfort,' he gasped painfully, 'when you've done this to yourself!'

He pulled the cloth away with a jerk and tore his shirt opening away from the neck with both hands.

By the light of the moon, Mr Annett saw the livid scar which encircled his neck, the mark of a strangling rope which eternity itself could never remove.

He raised his horror-filled eyes to those of the stranger. They were still open, but they glittered no longer. They seemed to be dark gaping holes, full of mist, through which Mr Annett could dimly discern the outline of the crab apple tree behind him.

He tried to speak, but could not. And as he watched, still struggling for speech, the figure slowly dissolved, melting into thin air, until the schoolmaster found himself gazing at nothing at all but the old gnarled tree, and the still beauty of the night around it.

The vicar was alone in the vestry when Mr Annett arrived at St Patrick's.

'Good evening, good evening,' said the vicar boisterously, and then caught sight of his choirmaster's face.

'My dear boy, you look as though you've seen a ghost,' he said.

'You speak more truly than you realize,' Mr Annett answered soberly. He began to walk through to the chancel and his organ, but the vicar barred his way. His kind old face was puckered with concern.

'Was it poor old Job?' he asked gently.

'I don't know who it was,' replied the schoolmaster. He explained briefly what had happened. He was more shaken by this encounter than he cared to admit. Somehow, the affinity between the stranger and himself had seemed so strong. It made the man's dreadful disclosure, and then his withdrawal, even more shocking.

The vicar put both hands on the young man's shoulders. 'Poor Job,' he said, 'is nothing to be frightened of. It is a sad tale, and it happened long ago. After choir practice, I hope you will come back to the vicarage for a drink, and I will do my best to tell you Job's story.'

The younger man managed a wan smile. 'Thank you, Vicar,' he said. 'I should be glad to hear more of him. I had a strange feeling while we were together—' He faltered to a stop.

'What kind of feeling?' asked the vicar gently.

Mr Annett moved restlessly. His brow was furrowed with perplexity. 'As though – it sounds absurd – but as though we were brothers. It was as if we were akin – as if we shared something.'

The vicar nodded slowly, and sighed, dropping his hands from the young man's shoulders. 'You shared sorrow, my son,' he said as he turned away. But his tone was so low that the words were lost in a burst of country voices from the chancel.

Together the two men made their way from the vestry to the duties before them.

The vicarage drawing-room was empty when the vicar and his guest entered an hour or so later. A bright fire blazed on the hearth and Mr Annett gratefully pulled up an armchair. He felt as though he would never be warm again.

He sipped the whisky and water which the vicar gave him and was glad of its comfort. He was deathly tired, and recognized this as a symptom of shock. Part of his mind longed for sleep, but part craved to hear the story which the vicar had promised.

Before long, the older man put aside his glass, lodged three stout logs upon the fire and settled back in his chair to recount his tale.

* * *

Job Carpenter, said the vicar, was a shepherd. He was born in Victoria's reign in the year of the Great Exhibition of 1851, and was the tenth child in a long family.

His parents lived in a small cottage at the Beech Green end of Fairacre, and all their children were born there. They were desperately poor, for Job's father was a farm labourer and times were hard.

At ten years old Job was out at work on the downs, stone-picking, bird-scaring and helping his father to clear ditches and lay hedges; but by the time he was fifteen he had decided that it was sheep he wanted to tend.

The shepherd at that time was a surly old fellow, twisted with rheumatism and foul of tongue. Job served a cruel apprenticeship under him and in the last year or two of the old man's life virtually looked after the flock himself. This fact did not go unnoticed by the farmer.

One morning during lambing time, Job entered the little hut carrying twin lambs which were weakly. There stretched upon the sacks stuffed with straw which made the old man's bed, lay his master, open-eyed and cold.

Within two days Job had been told that he was now shepherd, and he continued in this post for the rest of his life. He grew into a handsome fellow, tall and broad, with blond wiry hair and a curling beard. The girls of Fairacre and Beech Green found him attractive, and made the fact quite plain, but Job was shy and did not respond as readily as his fellows.

One day, however, he met a girl whom he had never seen before. Her family lived in Beech Green but she was in service in London. Job's sister worked with her and the two girls were given a week's holiday at the same time. She walked over to see Job's sister one warm spring evening and the two girls wandered across the downs to see the lambs at play.

Job watched them approach. His sister Jane was tall and fair, as he was. Her companion was a complete contrast. She was little more than five feet in height, with long silky black hair coiled in a thick plait round

her head, like a coronet. She had a small heart-shaped face, sloe-dark eyes which slanted upwards at the corners, and narrow crescents of eyebrows. Job thought her the prettiest thing he had ever seen.

Her name was Mary. To Job, who had a deep religious faith, this seemed wholly fitting. She was a queen among women. Job had no doubts this time and no shyness. Before Mary's week of holiday had ended the two young people came to an understanding.

It was Christmas time before they saw each other again, and only a few letters, written for them by better-schooled friends, passed between Mary and Job during the long months of separation. They planned to get married in the autumn of the following year. Mary would return to London and save every penny possible from her pitiful earnings, and Job would ask for a cottage of his own at Michaelmas.

He was fortunate. The farmer offered him a little thatched house not far from the church at Fairacre. It had two rooms up and two down, and a sizeable triangle of garden where a man could grow plenty of vegetables, keep a pig and a few hens, and so go more than half way towards being self-supporting. A few fruit trees shaded the garden, and a lusty young crab-apple tree grew in the hedge nearby.

The couple married at Michaelmas and were as happy as larks in their new home. Mary took work at the vicarage and found it less arduous than the living-in job in London. She was a quick quiet worker in the house and the vicar's wife approved of her. She was delighted to discover that her new daily was also an excellent needlewoman, and Mary found herself carrying home bundles of shirts whose collars needed turning, sheets that needed sides to middling, and damask table linen in need of fine darning. She was particularly glad of this extra money for by the end of the first year of their married life a child was due, and Mary knew she would have to give up the scrubbing and heavy lifting for a few weeks at least.

The coming of the child was of intense joy to Job. He adored his wife and made no secret of it. The fact that he cleaned her shoes and took her tea in bed in the mornings was known in Fairacre and looked upon as a crying scandal, particularly by the men. What was a woman for but to wait upon her menfolk? Job Carpenter was proper daft to pander to a wife in that namby-pamby way. Only laying up a store of trouble for himself in the future, said the village wiseacres in The Beetle and Wedge. Job, more in love than ever, let such gossip flow by him.

The baby took its time in coming and as soon as Job saw it he realized that it could not possibly survive. His experience with hundreds of lambs gave him a pretty shrewd idea of a 'good do-er' or a weakling. Mary, cradling it in her arms, smiling with happiness, suspected nothing. It was all the more tragic for her when, on the third day, her little son quietly expired.

She lay in a raging fever for a fortnight, and it was months before she was herself again. Throughout the time Job nursed her with loving constancy, comforting her when she wept, encouraging any spark of recovery.

In the two years that followed, two miscarriages occurred and the young couple began to wonder if they would ever have a family. The cottage gave them great joy, and the garden was one of the prettiest in the village, but it was a child that they really wanted. Everyone liked the Carpenters and Job's demonstrative affection for his wife was looked upon with more indulgence by the villagers as time passed.

At last Mary found that she was pregnant yet again. The vicar's wife, for whom she still worked, was determined that this baby should arrive safely, and insisted on Mary being examined regularly by her own doctor. She engaged too a reputable midwife from Caxley to attend the birth, for the local midwife at that time, in Fairacre and Beech Green, was a slatternly creature, reeking of gin and unwashed garments, whose very presence caused revulsion rather than reassurance to her unfortunate patients.

All went well. The baby was a lusty boy, who throve from the time he entered the world. Job and Mary could hardly believe their good fortune and peered into his cot a hundred times a day to admire his fair beauty.

One early October day, when the child was a few months old, Mary was sitting at the table with a pile of mending before her. The boy lay asleep in his cradle beside her.

It was a wild windy day. The autumn equinox had stirred the weather to tempestuous conditions, and the trees in the little garden flailed their branches in the uproar. Leaves whirled by the cottage window and every now and again a spatter of hail hit the glass like scattered shot. The doors rattled, the thin curtains stirred in the draught, and the whole cottage shuddered in the force of the gale. Mary was nervous, and wondered how poor Job was faring outside in the full force of the unkind elements.

As the afternoon wore on, the gale increased. Mary had never known such violence. There was a roaring noise in the chimney which was terrifying and a banshee howling of wind round the house which woke the baby and made him cry. Mary lifted him from his cradle to comfort him, and walked back and forth with him against her shoulder.

There was a sudden increase in the noise outside – a curious drumming sound in the heart of the fury. To Mary's horror she saw through the window the small chicken house at the end of the garden swept upward and carried, twisting bizarrely, into the field beyond. At the same time a great mass of straw, clearly torn from a nearby rick, went whirling across the garden, and, as it passed, one of the apple trees, laden with golden fruit, snapped off at the base as though it were a flower stem.

Mary could scarcely believe her eyes. She stood

rooted to the spot, between the table and the fireplace, her baby clutched to her. The drumming sound grew louder until it was unendurable. Mary was about to scream with panic when a terrifying rumble came near at hand. The chimney stack crashed upon the cottage roof, cracking the rafters like matchwood, and sending ceilings, furniture, bricks and rubble cascading upon the two terror-stricken occupants of the little home.

When Job arrived at the scene of the disaster, soaked to the skin and wild with anxiety, he found the whole of one end of his house had collapsed. No one was there, for the neighbours were all coping with troubles of their own, and there had been no time to see how others were faring in the catastrophe that had befallen Fairacre in the matter of minutes.

He began tearing at the beams and sagging thatch with his bare hands, shouting hoarsely to his wife and son as he struggled. There was no answer to his cries. A ghastly silence seemed to pervade the ruined house, in contrast to the fiendish noises which raged about it.

An hour later, when neighbours arrived to help, they found him there, still screaming and struggling to reach his dead family. Sweat and tears poured down his ravaged face, his clothes were torn, his battered hands bleeding. When, finally, the broken bodies of his wife and child were recovered, Job had to be led away, and only the doctor's drugs brought him merciful oblivion at the end of that terrible day.

In the weeks that followed, while his house was being repaired, Job was offered hospitality throughout

Fairacre but he would have none of it. As soon as the pitiful funeral was over, he returned numbly to his work, coming back each night to his broken home and sleeping on a makeshift bed in the one remaining room.

Neighbours did their best for him, cooking him a meal, washing his linen, comforting him with friendly words and advice. He seemed scarcely to see or to hear them, and heads shook over Job's sad plight.

'There's naught can help him, but time,' said one.

''Tis best to let him get over his grief alone,' said another.

'Once he gets his house set to rights, he'll start to pick up,' said a third. Fairacre watched poor Job anxiously.

The men who had been sent to repair the cottage worked well and quickly. Their sympathy was stirred by the sight of the gaunt young man's lonely existence in the undamaged half of his tiny house.

At length the living room was done. The bricks which had crashed on that fateful afternoon had been built again into the chimney breast. The broken rafters had been replaced, the walls plastered and white-washed afresh.

Job met the men as he trudged home from work. They called to him with rough sympathy.

'It's ready for you now,' they shouted through the twilight.

'We've finished at last.'

A kindly neighbour had gone in to replace his furniture.

'There now,' she said, in a motherly burr, 'you can

settle in here tonight.' But Job shook his head, and turned into his old room.

Sad at heart, the good soul returned home, but could not forget the sight of Job's ravaged face.

'I'll go and take a look at him,' she said to her husband later that evening. 'If the lamp's alight in the room then I'll know he's settled in, and I'll go more comfortable to bed.'

But the window was dark. She was about to turn homeward again when she heard movements inside the cottage and saw the living-room door open. Job stood upon the threshold, a candle in his hand. Breathless, in the darkness of the garden, the watcher saw him make his way slowly across the room to the chimney breast. He put down the guttering candle, and rested his fair head against the brickwork. Before long, his great shoulders began to heave, and the sound of dreadful sobbing sent the onlooker stealthily homeward.

''Tis best by far to leave him be,' comforted the neighbour's husband, when she told him what she had witnessed. 'We'll go and see him in the morning. It will be all over by then.'

But there was little comfort for the woman that night, for the spectacle of Job's grief drove all hope of sleep away.

Next morning they went together to the house. Her heart was heavy with foreboding as they walked up the little brick path. Inside the silent house they found him, with a noose about his neck, hanging against the chimney breast which had crushed his wife, his child, and every hope of Job himself.

* * *

There was an uncanny silence in the sunny lane as Mr Annett finished speaking.

'And that,' he said soberly, 'is the tale of poor Job, as the vicar told it to me.'

Suddenly, a blackbird called from a hazel bush, breaking the spell. Despite the sunshine I shivered. We were alone, for Malcolm and his mother had gone ahead to pick primroses from the steep banks, and though we were surrounded by the sights and scents of spring I remained chilled by this strange winter's tale.

'You're sure it was a ghost?' I asked shakily.

'Other people have seen Job,' answered Mr Annett, 'and the vicar knew all about him. But I believe I am the only person that Job has spoken to.'

'I wonder why?' I mused aloud.

'Perhaps he felt we had much in common,' said Mr Annett quietly.

I remembered suddenly Mr Annett's own tragedy. He, too, had adored a young wife and had lost her in the face of overwhelming violence. He too had watched a broken body removed to an early grave. There was no misery, no depth of hopelessness which Job had known, which was not known too to young Mr Annett.

We were summoned abruptly from the shadowy past by the sound of young Malcolm's excited voice.

'There's a nest here,' he called, 'with eggs. Come and look!'

'Coming!' shouted Mr Annett, suddenly looking ten years younger. And he ran off, all grief forgotten, to join his wife and child.

CHRISTMAS AT CAXLEY 1913

Illustrated by J. S. Goodall

The market square of Caxley is the hub of that country town. It is here that its inhabitants meet in times of national rejoicing or disaster. On market day the local buses rumble in from the surrounding villages, from Fairacre and Beech Green in the north, and from Bent and its neighbours in the south. The people come to meet their friends, to do business, to seek bargains, and 'to see a bit of life'.

At the turn of the century, two families lived in Caxley market square in the premises above and behind their shops. One was the Howards, and Septimus Howard, the local baker, was its head. The other was the Norths, long-established ironmongers, and Bender North carried on a flourishing business.

The two men had been born and bred in Caxley, had attended the same school, played football together and married local girls. Hilda North was a pillar of the parish church, and much respected. Edna Howard was a flamboyant beauty, and local opinion held that

Septimus was a most unlikely candidate for her favours when he was pursuing her. But he had won her eventually, and the marriage had prospered.

The children of the two families grew up together, and helped when they could in the family businesses.

As King Edward VII's reign continued, Septimus's modest business grew apace. Bender's began to decline, for a large national firm of ironmongers opened a branch in Caxley High Street, and many of his old clients, particularly farmers, began to take their custom to Tenby's Ltd who were bringing a wide variety of new agricultural machinery to local notice.

By the winter of 1913 Bender North was a worried man, and another blow came when Bob, a trusted employee, absconded with a great deal of money.

In the meantime, Septimus Howard was cautiously assessing his good fortune, and continuing to work as zealously as ever.

There was plenty of work at the bakery as Christmas approached, for there were scores of large cakes to be iced, as well as extra supplies for family parties.

Although Septimus now employed several more workers, he still did as much himself in the bakery. The fragrance of the rich mixtures, the mingled aroma of spices, candied fruits and brown sugar cheered him afresh every year. It was his own personal offering to the spirit of Christmas, and he enjoyed the festive bustle in the warmly-scented bakery. It was a sheltered haven from the bleak winds which whistled across the market square beyond the doors.

The cold spell was lasting longer than expected, and the weather-wise old folk in Caxley prophesied a white Christmas. Sure enough, in the week before Christmas, a light fall whitened the ground, and powdered the rosy-tiled roofs of the town, while the lowering grey skies told of more to follow.

On Sunday afternoon, Sep took a nap on his bed. Edna had slipped out to visit friends and, unusually tired by the pre-Christmas work, Sep indulged himself.

When he awoke, he was conscious of a new lightness in the room. He made his way to the bedroom window. His hair was rumpled from his rare afternoon nap. He smoothed it as he watched the snow flakes fluttering against the window pane.

He judged that it was two or three inches deep already. The steps of St Peter's and the Town Hall were heavily carpeted. The snow had blown into the cracks and jambs of doors and windows, leaving long white sticks like newly-spilt milk. A mantle of snow draped Queen Victoria's shoulders and her bronze crown supported a little white cushion which looked like ermine. Snow lay along her sceptre and in the folds of her robes. The iron cups, in the fountain at her feet, were filled to the brim with snow flakes, and the embossed lions near by peered from snow-encrusted manes.

For a Sunday afternoon, there were very few people about. An old tramp, carrying his belongings in a red-spotted bundle on a stick, snuffled disconsolately past St Peter's, head bent, rheumy eyes fixed upon the snow at his feet. Two ragged urchins, no doubt from the marsh, giggled and barged each other behind him, scraping up the snow in red, wet hands to make snowballs.

Sep watched them heave them at the back of the unsuspecting old man. At the moment of impact, he swung round sharply, and raised his bundle threateningly. Sep could see his red, wet, toothless mouth protesting, but could hear no word through the tightly-shut bedroom window. One boy put his thumb to his nose impudently; the other put out his tongue. But they let the old man shuffle round the corner unmolested before throwing their arms round each other's skinny shoulders and running jubilantly down an alley-way.

Momentarily the market square was empty. Not

even a pigeon pattered across the snow. Only footprints of various sizes, and the yellow stain made by a horse's urine, gave any sign of life in that white world. Snow clothed the sloping roofs of Caxley. It covered the hanging signs and the painted nameboards above the shops, dousing the bright colours as a candle-snuffer douses a light.

What a grey and white world, thought Sep! As grey and white as an old gander, as grey and white as the swans and cygnets floating together on the Cax. The railings outside the bank stood starkly etched against the white background, each spear-top tipped with snow. There was something very soothing in this negation of colour and movement. It reminded Sep of creeping beneath the bedclothes as a child, and crouching there, in a soft, white haven, unseeing and unseen, all sounds muffled, as he relished the secrecy and security of it all.

There was a movement in St Peter's porch and a dozen or so choirboys came tumbling out into the snowy world, released from carol practice. The sight brought Sep, sighing, back into the world of Sunday afternoon.

He picked up a hair-brush and began to attack his tousled locks.

'Looks as though the weather prophets are right,' said Sep to his reflection. 'Caxley's in for a white Christmas this year.'

On that same Sunday afternoon Bender North set off to deliver two large saw blades for his old farmer friend Jesse Miller of Fairacre and Beech Green.

'He won't get much done in the fields,' commented Bender, wrapping the blades in brown paper. 'The ground's like iron. He'll be glad to set the men to sawing firewood tomorrow, and I promised him these as soon as they came.'

'Wrap up warmly,' said Hilda. 'Put your muffler on, and your thick gloves.'

'Never fear,' answered Bender robustly. 'I've known the downs long enough to know how to dress for them. I'll be back before dark.'

The horse trotted briskly through the town. There were very few people about and Bender was glad to be on his own in the clean fresh air. Now he could turn over his thoughts, undisturbed by family interruptions or customers' problems. He always felt at his best driving behind a good horse. He liked the rhythm of its flying feet, the gay rattle of the bowling wheels, and the clink of the well-polished harness.

The pace slackened as Bill, the horse, approached Beech Green. The long pull up the downs was taken gently and steadily. The reins lay loosely across the glossy back, and Bender reviewed his situation as they jogged along together through the grey and white countryside.

Things were serious, that was plain. Bob, the thief, had been picked up by the London police ten days earlier, and now awaited his trial at the next Assizes. He had been in possession of fourteen shillings and ninepence at the time of his arrest, and could not – or would not – give any idea of where the rest of the money had gone. Clearly, nothing would be restored to his employer.

What would he do, Bender asked himself? He could get a further loan from the bank, but would it be of any use? Had the time come to take a partner who would be willing to put money into the firm? Bender disliked the idea. He could approach both Sep Howard and Jesse Miller who had offered help, but he hated the thought of letting Sep Howard see his straits, and he doubted whether Jesse Miller could afford to give him the sum needed to give the business a fresh start. Jesse was in partnership with his brother Harry at the farm, and times were hard for them both at the moment.

The other course was a much more drastic one. Tenby's had approached him with a tentative offer. If he ever decided to part with the business, would he give them first offer? He would of course be offered a post with the firm who would be glad of his experience. They were thinking of housing their agricultural machinery department in separate premises. North's, in the market square, handy for all the farmers in the district, would suit them perfectly. They asked Bender to bear it in mind. Bender had thought of little else for two days, but had said nothing to Hilda. He knew that she would be all in favour of the action, and he wanted to be sure that it was right before making any final decisions.

He presumed that he would be offered the managership. In that case, there would be a steady income, with no worries attached. Bender, gazing unseeingly across the snowy fields, lulled almost into slumber by the rhythmic swaying of the trap, began to feel that selling North's might be the best way out of his many difficulties. But not yet, he told himself. He would hang on as long as he could, and who knows? Something might turn up. He'd been lucky often enough before. There was still hope! Bender North was always an optimist.

He put Billy into the shelter of a stable and tramped across the snowy yard to the Millers' back door.

He was greeted warmly by the family, and he was put by the fire to thaw out. The usual vast tea was offered him, but Bender ate sparingly, with one eye cocked on the grey threatening sky outside.

'I mustn't be too long,' said Bender, his mouth full of buttered toast. 'There's more snow to come before morning, or I'll eat my boots.'

They exchanged family news. Ethel's youngest was running a temperature, and was upstairs in bed, 'very fretful and scratchity', his mother said. Jesse's pigs were not doing as well as he had hoped, and he had an idea that one of his men was taking eggs. 'Times were bad enough for farmers,' said Jesse, 'without such set-backs.'

He accompanied Bender to the stable when he set off.

'And how are your affairs?' he asked when they were out of earshot of the house.

Bender gave a reassuring laugh, and clapped the other man's shoulders. 'Better than they have been, Jesse, I'm glad to say. I hope I shan't have to worry you at all.'

The look of relief that flooded Jesse's face did not escape Bender. It certainly looked as though Tenby's would be the only possible avenue of escape if the business grew worse.

Ah well, thought Bender, clattering across the cobbled yard, we must just live in hope of something turning up! He waved to Jesse, and set off at a spanking pace on the downhill drive home.

The snow began to fall as Bender turned out of Jesse's gate. It came down thickly and softly, large flakes flurrying across mile upon mile of open downland, like an undulating lacy curtain. It settled rapidly upon the iron-hard ground, already sheeted in the earlier fall, and by the time Billy had covered half a mile the sound of his trotting hoofs was muffled. He snorted fiercely at the onslaught of this strange element, his breath bursting from his flaring nostrils in clouds of vapour. His dark mane was starred with snow flakes, and as he tossed his head Bender caught a glimpse of his shining eyes grotesquely ringed with glistening snow caught in his eyelashes.

His own face was equally assaulted. The snow flakes fluttered against his lips and eyes like icy moths. It was difficult to breathe. He pulled down the brim of his hard hat, and hoisted up the muffler that Hilda had insisted on him wearing, so that he could breathe in the stuffy pocket of air made by his own warmth. Already the front of his coat was plastered, and he looked like a snowman.

A flock of sheep, in a field, huddled together looking like one vast fleece ribbed with snow. The bare hedges were fast becoming blanketed, and the banks undulated past the bowling trap smoothly white, but for the occasional pock-mark of a bird's claws. The tall dry grasses bore strange exotic white flowers in their dead heads, and the branches of trees collected snowy burdens in their arms.

And all the time there was a rustling and whispering, a sibilance of snow. The air was alive with movement, the dancing and whirling of a thousand individual flakes with a life as brief as the distance from leaden sky to frozen earth. At the end of their tempestuous short existence they lay together, dead and indivisible, forming a common shroud.

There was a grandeur and beauty about this snowy countryside which affected Bender deeply. Barns and houses, woods and fields were now only massive white shapes, their angles smoothed into gentle curves. He passed a cow-man returning from milking, his head and shoulders shrouded in a sack, shaped like a monk's cowl. He was white from head to foot, only his dark eyes, glancing momentarily at the passing horse, and his plodding gait distinguished him from the white shapes about him.

Bender turned to watch him vanishing into the veil of swirling flakes. Behind him, the wheels were spinning out two grey ribbons, along the snowy road.

He turned back and flicked the reins on Billy's snow-spattered satin back.

'Gee up boy!' roared Bender cheerfully. 'We both want to get home!'

JINGLE BELLS

Illustrated by J. S. Goodall

Mr Willet, the school caretaker, was brushing up coke in the yard as I went across to the school that morning. He was wielding the broom vigorously in his capable hands, his breath wreathing his head in silvery clouds.

'Nasty cold morning,' I called to him, scurrying towards shelter.

'This keeps me warm,' he replied, pausing for a moment to rest on his broom. 'But I s'pose I shan't be doing this much longer.'

'Only three days,' I agreed. 'And then it's the lovely Christmas holidays!'

'You should be ashamed!' said Mr Willet reproachfully. 'Young woman like you, wishing your life away.'

But it was too cold to argue, and I only had time to wave to him before whisking into the shelter of the lobby.

*

The last day of term, particularly the Christmas term, has splendour of its own. There is an air of excitement at the thought of pleasures and freedom to come, but there is also a feeling of relaxation from daily routine made much more acute by the deliciously empty desks. Books have been collected and stacked in neat piles in the cupboard. Papers and exercise books have been tidied away. All that remains to employ young hands in this last glorious day is a pencil and loose sheets of paper which have been saved for just such an occasion.

Of course, work will be done. There will be mental arithmetic, and some writing; perhaps some spelling lists and paper games, and stories told to each other. And today, the children knew, there would be Christmas carols, and a visit to the old grey church next door to see the crib recently set up by the vicar's wife and other ladies of the village. The very thought of it all created a glow which warmed the children despite the winter's cold.

They entered more exuberantly than ever, cherry-nosed, hair curling damply from the December air and wellingtons plastered with Fairacre mud. I began to shoo them back into the lobby before our virago of a cleaner discovered them, but I was too late.

Mrs Pringle, emerging from the infants' room where she had just deposited a scuttle of coke on an outspread sheet of *The Times Educational Supplement*, looked at them with marked dislike.

'Anyone 'ere seen fit to use the door-scraper?' she asked sourly. 'Don't look like it to me. What you kids wants is an hour or two scrubbing this 'ere floor like I 'ave to. That'd make you think twice about dirtying my clean floorboards.'

She cast a malevolent glance in my direction and stumped out to the lobby. The children retreated before her, observing her marked limp, a sure sign of trouble.

The clatter of the door-scraper and the bang of the heavy Gothic door announced Mrs Pringle's departure to her cottage, until midday, when she was due to return to wash up the school dinner things. The children's spirits rose again and they sang 'Away in a Manger' with rather more gusto than perhaps was necessary at prayer time.

The infants departed to their own side of the partition and my class prepared to give part of its mind to some light scholastic task. Multiplication tables are always in sore need of attention, as every teacher knows, so that a test on the scrap paper already provided seemed a useful way of passing the arithmetic lesson. It was small wonder that excitement throbbed throughout the classroom. The paper chains still rustled overhead in all their multicoloured glory and in the corner, on the now depleted nature table, the Christmas tree glittered with tinsel and bright baubles.

But this year it carried no parcels. Usually, Fairacre School has a party on the last afternoon of the Christmas term when mothers and fathers, and friends of the school, come and eat a hearty tea and watch the children receive their presents from the tree. But this year the party was to be held in the village hall after Christmas and a conjuror had been engaged to entertain us afterwards.

However, the children guessed that they would not go home empty-handed today, I felt sure, and this touching faith, which I had no intention of destroying, gave them added happiness throughout the morning.

The weather grew steadily worse. Sleet swept across the playground and a wicked draught from the skylight buffeted the paper chains. I put the milk saucepan on the tortoise stove and the children looked pleased. Although a few hardy youngsters gulp their milk down stone-cold, even on the iciest day, most of them prefer to be cosseted a little and to see their bottles being tipped into the battered saucepan. The slow heating of the milk affords them exquisite pleasure, and it usually gets more attention than I do on cold days.

'It's steaming, miss,' one calls anxiously.

'Shall I make sure the milk's all right?' queries another.

'Can I get the cups ready?' asks a third.

One never-to-be-forgotten day we left the milk on whilst we had a rousing session in the playground as aeroplanes, galloping horses, trains and other violently moving articles. On our return, breathless and much invigorated, we had discovered a sizzling seething mess on the top of the stove and sticky cascades down the sides. Mrs Pringle did not let any of us forget this mishap, and the children like to pretend that they only keep reminding me to save me from incurring the lady's wrath yet again.

In between sips of their steaming milk they kept up an excited chatter.

'What d'you want for Christmas?' asked Patrick of Ernest, his desk mate.

'Boxing gloves,' replied Ernest, lifting his head briefly and speaking through a white moustache.

'Well, I'm havin' a football, and a space helmet, and some new crayons, and a signal box for my train set,' announced Patrick proudly.

Linda Moffat, neat as a new pin from glossy hair to equally glossy patent leather slippers, informed me that she was hoping for a new work-box with a pink lining. I thought of the small embroidery scissors, shaped like a stork, which I had wrapped up for her the night before, and congratulated myself.

'What do you want?' I asked Joseph Coggs, staring monkey-like at me over the rim of his mug.

'Football,' croaked Joseph, in his hoarse gipsy voice. 'Might get it too.'

It occurred to me that this would make an excellent exercise in writing and spelling. Milk finished, I set them to work on long strips of paper.

'Ernest wants some boxing gloves for Christmas,' was the first entry.

'Patrick hopes to get--' began the second. The children joined in the list-making with great enthusiasm.

When Mrs Crossley, who brings the dinners, arrived, she was cross-questioned about her hopes.

'Well now, I don't really know,' she confessed, balancing the tins against her wet mackintosh and peering perplexedly over the top. 'A kitchen set, I think. You know, a potato masher and fish slice and all that, in a nice little rack.'

The children obviously thought this a pretty poor present but began to write down: 'Mrs Crossley wants a kitchen set,' below the last entry, looking faintly disbelieving as they did so.

'And what do you want?' asked Linda, when Mrs Crossley had vanished.

'Let me see,' I said slowly: 'Some extra nice soap, perhaps, and bath cubes; and a book or two, and a new rose bush to plant by my back door.'

'Is that all?'

'No sweets?'

'No, no sweets,' I said. 'But I should like a very pretty little ring I saw in Caxley last Saturday.'

'You'll have to get married for that,' said Ernest soberly. 'And you're too old now.' The others nodded in agreement.

'You're probably right,' I told them, keeping a straight face. 'Put your papers away and let's set the tables for dinner.'

The sleet was cruelly painful on our faces as we scuttled across the churchyard to St Patrick's. Inside it was cold and shadowy. The marble memorial tablets on the wall glimmered faintly in the gloom, and the air struck chill.

But the crib was aglow with rosy light, a spot of warmth and hope in the darkness. The children tiptoed towards it, awed by their surroundings.

They spent a long time gazing, whispering their admiration and pointing out particular details to each other. They were loth to leave it, and the shelter of the great church, which had defied worse weather than this for many centuries.

We pelted back to the school, for I had a secret plan

to put into action, and three o'clock was the time appointed for it. St Patrick's clock chimed a quarter to, above our heads, as we hurried across the churchyard.

I had arranged with the infants' teacher to go privately into the lobby promptly at three and there shake some bells abstracted earlier from the percussion band box. We hoped that the infants would believe that an invisible Father Christmas had driven on his sleigh and delivered the two sacks of parcels which would be found in the lobby. At the moment, these were in the hall of my house. I proposed to leave my class for a minute, shake the bells, hide them from inquisitive eyes and return again to the children.

This innocent deception could not hope to take in many of my own children, I felt sure, but the babies would enjoy it, and so too would the younger ones in my classroom. I was always surprised at the remarkable reticence which the older children showed when the subject of Father Christmas cropped up. Those that knew seemed more than willing to keep up the pretence for the sake of the younger ones, and perhaps because they feared that the presents would not be forthcoming if they let the cat out of the bag or boasted of their knowledge.

I settled the class with more paper. They could draw a picture of the crib or St Patrick's church, or a winter scene of any kind, I told them. Someone wanted to go on with his list of presents and was readily given permission. The main thing was to have a very quiet classroom at three o'clock. Our Gothic doors are of sturdy oak and the sleigh bells would have to be shaken to a frenzy in order to make themselves heard.

At two minutes to three by the wall clock Patrick looked up from drawing a church with all four sides showing at once, and surmounted by what looked like a mammoth ostrich.

'I've got muck on my hand,' he said. 'Can I go out the lobby and wash?'

Maddening child! What a moment to choose! 'Not now,' I said, as calmly as I could. 'Just wipe it on your hanky.'

He produced a dark grey rag from his pocket and rubbed the offending hand, sighing in a martyred way. He was one of the younger children and I wondered if he might possibly half-believe in sleigh bells.

'I'm just going across to the house,' I told them, squaring my conscience. 'Be very quiet while I'm away. The infants are listening to a story.'

All went according to plan. I struggled back through the sleet with the two sacks, deposited one outside the infants' door into the lobby, and the other outside our own.

The lobby was as quiet as the grave. I withdrew the bells from behind a stack of bars of yellow soap which Mrs Pringle stores on a lofty shelf, and crept to the outside door to begin shaking. Santa Claus in the distance, and fast approaching, I told myself. Would they be heard? I wondered, waggling frantically in the open doorway.

I closed the door gently against the driving sleet and now shook with all my might by the two inner doors. Heaven help me if one of my children burst out to see what was happening!

There was an uncanny silence from inside both rooms. I gave a last magnificent agitation and then crept along the lobby to the soap and tucked the bells securely out of sight. Then I returned briskly to the classroom. You could have heard a pin drop.

'There was bells outside,' said Joseph huskily.

'The clock just struck three,' I pointed out, busying myself at the blackboard.

'No. *Little* bells!' said someone.

At this point the dividing door between the infants' room and ours burst open to reveal a bright-eyed mob lugging a sack.

'Father Christmas has been!'

'We heard him!'

'We heard bells, didn't we?'

'That's right. Sleigh bells.'

Ernest, by this time, had opened our door into the lobby and was returning with the sack. A cheer went up and the whole class converged upon him.

'Into your desks,' I bellowed, 'and Ernest can give them out.'

Ernest upended the sack and spilt the contents into a glorious heap of pink and blue parcels, as the children scampered to their desks and hung over them squeaking with excitement.

The babies sat on the floor receiving their presents with awed delight. There was no doubt about it, for them Father Christmas was as real as ever.

I became conscious of Patrick's gaze upon me.

'Did you see him?' he asked.

'Not a sign,' I said truthfully.

Patrick's brow was furrowed with perplexity. 'If you'd a let me wash my hand I reckon I'd just about've seen him,' he said at length.

I made no reply. Patrick's gaze remained fixed on my face, and then a slow lovely smile curved his countenance. Together, amidst the hubbub of parcel-opening around us, we shared the unspoken, immortal secret of Christmas.

Later, with the presents unwrapped and the floor a sea of paper, Mrs Pringle arrived to start clearing up. Her face expressed considerable disapproval and her limp was very severe.

The children thronged around her showing her their toys.

'Ain't mine lovely?'

'Look, it's a dust cart!'

'This is a *magic* painting book! It says so!'

Mrs Pringle unbent a little among so much happiness, and gave a cramped smile.

Ernest raised his voice as she limped her way slowly across the room. 'Mrs Pringle, Mrs Pringle!'

The lady turned, a massive figure ankle deep in pink and blue wrappings.

'What do you want in your stocking, Mrs Pringle?' called Ernest. There was a sudden hush.

Mrs Pringle became herself again. 'In my stocking?' she asked tartly. 'A new leg! That's what I want!'

She moved majestically into the lobby, pretending to ignore the laughter of the children at this sally.

As usual, I thought wryly, Mrs Pringle had had the last word.

THE WHITE ROBIN

Illustrated by J. S. Goodall

To Macdonald Hastings
who gave me the idea

CHAPTER ONE

The Visitation

Village schools get rarer every year, but there are a small number, up and down the country, which still look much the same as they did some hundred years ago.

Fairacre School, where I am the headmistress, is one of them. It has, in common with many other country schools, the inestimable joy of a playground where the surrounding countryside invades the small patch of asphalt.

How lucky we are! The town child goes out to play at break-time on a vast, arid waste, criss-crossed with painted lines for various games, and rarely boasting even one desiccated plane tree. He would be hard put to it to find even a modest wood louse in this desert, whilst we in Fairacre enjoy the company of the birds and insects which share the trees, the meadows and the cornfields around us.

We are blessed with a fine clump of lofty trees which gives us shade at one side of the playground, a hedge of hawthorn and hazel which provides cover for the birds, and a dark corner where the playground touches the adjoining garden wall of the vicarage.

This secret haunt is the favourite place to play. Here grow, in wild confusion, all those rank plants and shrubs which flourish on neglect.

Elder trees, their bark criss-crossed and green, wave their ghostly flower heads in the shade, and fill the air with spicy scent.

On the vicar's side of the flint wall, mounds of rotting grass cuttings have accumulated over the years, providing a perfect habitat for outsize stinging nettles and majestic dock plants which raise their rusty spires above the wall. Little ferns grow from the crevices and, along the top, strips of moss like velvet ribbon flourish between the ancient coping bricks. Here and there great swags of ivy hang down on each side, the twisted ropey stems providing footholds for the inquisitive ones wanting to peer over the wall.

On our side of the wall, the same plants thrive, but we also have some blue periwinkles and some particularly hardy yellow aconites which some long-dead gardener must have introduced, and which seem to enjoy their murky surroundings.

Above all, spreading its arms in general blessing upon ecclesiastical and scholastic territory, is a superb oak tree, drawing nourishment, no doubt, from the vicar's grass cuttings and from the neighbouring churchyard with its mossy headstones.

Invariably, there are a few children enjoying this shady retreat. It is a fine place to rest after a spirited assault on the coke pile at the other side of the playground. There are always plenty of snails there, some small and elegant with pale yellow and brown shells, and many more of the common or garden variety, laboriously clambering up the wall and leaving their silver trails across the flints.

And in their wake come the birds. Blackbirds and

thrushes, wrens and robins, raucous starlings and ubiquitous sparrows all haunt the bushes for food, and also for places to nest in this delectable spot. It is no wonder that the children find it so attractive. Around them stretch open cornfields and meadows. The great bulk of the downs lies on their horizon some two or three miles distant. Under a vast sky, the open countryside shimmers in a heat haze in summer and endures the onslaught of bitter winds in winter. This enclosed and secret place, mysteriously quiet, the haven of shy wild things, is in complete contrast to the bracing downland in which they live, and is prized accordingly.

And it was here that one of the Coggs twins first saw what I brusquely dismissed as 'her vision'.

It was a day of July heat, with the end of the school year in sight. The schoolroom door was propped open with a piece of sarsen stone as big as child's head. We had already used the object as the theme for a useful lesson on the derivation of words, although I had the feeling that my explanation of 'Saracen', meaning a foreigner, turning into 'sarsen' had been only partially accepted. In this heat the children were more than usually lethargic, their minds running, no doubt, on the joys of the open air rather than the schoolroom.

From outside came the sounds of high summer. A posse of young blackbirds kept up a piping for food, following their hard-working parents, tattered now with weeks of child care, hither and thither across the playground. In the distance the metallic croak of a pheasant could be heard, and over all was the faint hum of a myriad flying insects.

The languorous hush was broken by Helen Coggs who raised a hand. It was the usual request, and I was swift to grant it. The Coggs children seem to need to visit the lavatory twice as frequently as the others, but they are poorly fed and poorly clothed, the product of two feckless and unhealthy parents, so that their little weakness is not surprising.

'You can take out your library books,' I told the class, as Helen vanished across the playground. It was pointless to try and compete with the heat. My efforts to enliven the derivation of 'sarsen' had met with so little response that I felt that their library books might offer more palatable food on a hot July afternoon.

While they turned the pages languidly, I busied myself with some marking at my desk. I had forgotten about Helen, and it must have been some ten minutes later when she appeared at my side looking unusually lively.

'Oi bin and sin a whoite bird,' she declared. The fact that she had seen a white bird did not excite me greatly. It was probably a seagull, I thought. They come inland when conditions are rough by the coast. Or maybe one of Mr Roberts's white Leghorn hens, or a goose, had strayed.

'You've been long enough,' I scolded. 'Go and get on with your reading.'

Somewhat dashed, the child returned to her desk and took out her book. Peace reigned again, and I continued to mark.

But some minutes later I put down my red pencil.

There was something odd about this white bird. Gulls would not be inland in this weather and, now I came to think of it, Mr Roberts, our local farmer, had given up keeping chickens over a month ago. He still had a few geese, I believed. Could one have strayed so far?

'This bird,' I said to Helen. The class looked up. 'How big was it?'

'It was a little 'un.'

'It wasn't one of Mr Roberts's geese?'

'No.'

'You're sure it was white?'

'Yes.'

'Well, come on! Tell me how big it was.'

The child put her hands three inches apart, but said nothing.

Like getting blood out of a stone, I thought despairingly. Most of the Fairacre children are barely articulate. The Coggs children are monosyllabic at best.

The rest of the class now began to take an interest in the proceedings.

'Could it have been a white blackbird?' I enquired. Some years earlier we had been visited by a partially albino blackbird. At this my class began to guffaw.

'A *white* blackbird!' repeated Patrick, pink with mirth. 'How can a *black* bird be a *white* bird?'

'You sometimes get a blackbird with a few white feathers,' I explained, but the children were far too busy enjoying the joke to take much interest.

The clock told us it was playtime, and I decided to shelve the problem. In any case, no fowl of Mr Roberts seemed to be involved, which was my first concern. Also I had a suspicion that the white bird might have been some other object, a piece of paper fluttered by the wind, or a white flower head. With some of the children I might have suspected that the bird was a figment of a lively imagination, but not with Helen Coggs. She was quite incapable of such a flight of fancy.

The children streamed out into the sunshine, their spirits brightened by the prospect of fresh air and exercise, and the enjoyment of Helen Coggs's disclosure.

'Some ol' magpie, I bet,' said Ernest derisively, as he passed her on his way out. She shook her head.

The classroom soon emptied, except for Helen.

'Run along,' I said.

'It were a *little* bird. On the vicar's wall. Up the back.'

This was one of the longest speeches I had ever known the child deliver. 'Up the back' was the term used affectionately to describe the bosky haunt I have described. The lavatories are nearby, and the child must have spent some time after visiting them in exploring this much favoured area. But a white bird? Much more likely to be a head of elder flowers, now in full bloom, caught by an eddy of air and visible briefly over the wall. I must get the school doctor to test the child's eyes on her next visit.

'Don't worry about it,' I said. 'Go and enjoy the sunshine. If there is a white bird about, you will probably see it again some time.'

What a hope, I thought privately, as Helen moved off. It was highly unlikely that the apparition would be seen again.

But it was.

This time the vicar saw the white bird, and hastened into the school to report the sighting. The Reverend Gerald Partridge visits our school regularly, not only because he is chairman of the managers, but because he is our parish priest and the friend of all Fairacre.

Having told me the news in some excitement, he turned to the class.

'I've just been telling Miss Read that there is a rare white bird about. No doubt some of you have seen it?'

The children looked at each other in silence. Then Ernest nudged Helen's shoulder.

'I sin 'un,' muttered the child.

'Where, my dear?'

'Up the back.'

The vicar turned to me for clarification.

'By your wall,' I explained. 'Where the elder trees grow.'

'Ah! And all the weeds! Yes, I suspected as much. The robins must have nested there again this spring.'

'Do they nest there every year?'

'I can't say with any certainty, but the vicarage garden always seems to have one or two pairs each year, and very little fighting over territory. I imagine there is enough room for all. One pair built in the ivy on the wall some years ago. We found the nest later.'

'And are they there again?'

'Somewhere there, I feel sure. There are so many ideal sites in that wilderness, and we have certainly seen three or four fledglings being fed recently.'

He turned again to the class.

'Now, this little white bird seems rather shy, and it may well be attacked by other birds as it looks so different. I want you to be very careful not to frighten it in any way, and to let Miss Read, or me, know if you catch sight of it again.'

'Is it a foreign bird then?' hazarded Patrick.

'No, my boy. I rather think it is a robin – an *albino* robin. Albino means that it has no colour.'

Here he paused.

'At least, albino birds are usually all white, but in the case of the robin or the bullfinch the *red* feathers still keep their colour, so you can see how very beautiful a white robin must look.'

There was a stir of excitement among the children. A white robin, with a red breast! Here indeed was something rich and strange!

'I intend to find out more from Mr Mawne,' he told my class. Henry Mawne is an ornithologist of some standing, and lives in Fairacre. He is a good friend of the vicar's, and the church accounts have benefited from his meticulous attention. Before his coming they were in sad disarray, as our lovable vicar has no head for figures, and since the advent of decimalisation has been more bewildered than ever. Henry Mawne has relieved him of his financial duties, and the village is grateful to him.

'Perhaps he will come and give you a talk about birds – particularly robins. I will ask him. I know he has some splendid slides of British birds.'

He said goodbye to the children, and I accompanied him into the lobby.

'And you think this really is an albino robin?' I asked.

'I'm almost sure. I've caught a glimpse of it twice now, and the second time I had my binoculars. Its breast is quite a pale golden colour at the moment as the bird is so young, but it was being fed by a true robin, I'm positive. Isn't it exciting?'

His face was radiant.

'Think how beautiful it will look by next Christmas! We must take great care of it. I'm sure you will impress upon the children how fortunate we are to have such a wonderful bird among us.'

I promised, and was about to return to my class when the vicar stopped me.

'But you knew already, I suppose, about this bird? I mean the child Coggs said she had seen it.'

'I'm afraid I didn't believe her,' I confessed.

'Didn't believe her?' echoed the vicar, looking shocked. 'But she is a truthful child, surely?'

'She's truthful enough,' I agreed. 'But it seemed such an odd thing to see,' I added lamely. 'And no one else had seen it.'

'And so you doubted the child's word?' He looked sorrowfully at me. If he had caught me robbing the church poor box I could not have felt more guilty.

'There are some things,' he continued gently, 'which are made manifest to children and to those of simple mind, and not to others. This may be one of those things, perhaps.'

He turned towards the door.

'I shall go straight to Henry's,' he said. 'He will know all about white robins, I've no doubt. What an excitement for the village, Miss Read! We are wonderfully blessed.'

His parting smile forgave me, and this particular Doubting Thomas returned to face an uproarious class.

By my desk stood Helen Coggs.

'I told you I sin 'un!' she said reproachfully.

CHAPTER TWO

The Odd Man Out

By the time the news of our rare visitor had gone round the village, Fairacre School had broken up, and I was as free as my pupils to enjoy all the pleasures of summer.

I had a week at home before setting off for a fortnight's holiday with a friend in Yorkshire, and naturally kept an eye open for the white robin during that time. But I was unlucky.

Birds in plenty visited the bird table, including robins. At this stage of the year most of them looked harassed and shabby. All the hours of daylight were spent in flying to and fro in a ceaseless search for food for their clamouring babies.

On one occasion only did I see a baby robin, paler than its agitated father certainly, but nowhere near being albino. It emerged from the box hedge in my garden, its mottled breast gleaming in the sunlight, its wings trembling with anxiety for food. Snatching some crumbs from the bird table, the adult robin bustled back to the bold child which had followed him, and appeared to hustle it away into the protection of the hedge. I saw it no more.

I ventured quietly several times into the weedy haunt where the albino robin had been seen, and scratched my legs on the vicious brambles abounding there as I strained to see over the mossy wall into the vicarage garden. But again, I was unlucky.

The day before I was due to go away, I walked along the village street to the Post Office. Just emerging into the sunshine were Henry Mawne and a small boy.

'This is my great-nephew, Simon,' said Henry, introducing us. 'Say "How do you do" to Miss Read.'

'Hello,' said Simon, looking acutely embarrassed.

He was a very fair child with silky, almost white, hair, and startingly blue eyes. I judged him to be about seven or eight, and definitely underweight.

'Are you staying here long?' I asked him.

He looked anxiously at Henry Mawne.

'Possibly for a fortnight,' Henry answered for him. He began to fish in his pocket and produced a crumpled pound note.

'Hop back and get me a packet of foolscap envelopes from Mr Lamb,' he said to the boy. 'I forgot them when we were in the Post Office.'

The child vanished, and Henry Mawne spoke rapidly.

'He's my nephew's boy, and my godson. Trouble at home at the moment. His poor mother's very highly strung, and has just had another attack. Under hospital treatment at the moment, and my nephew is beside himself. We thought it would be a good thing for everyone concerned to have the boy down here for a time. Difficult for us though. We're too old to have children round us, and he's not an easy child, I must admit. Precocious in some ways, and a baby in others.'

'If he's still with you when I get back,' I said, 'bring him to tea. And if you want some books for him, the schoolhouse shelves are bulging with them.'

'Most kind, most kind! Ah, here he is!'

The child handed over the envelopes and change solemnly.

'Well, enjoy your break, Miss Read. No sign of the robin, I suppose?'

'Not yet. I'm living in hope though.'

We made our farewells, and Simon gave me a dazzling smile on parting.

There was no doubt about it. Simon might be pale and skinny, but he was a very handsome little boy.

I arrived back from my Yorkshire holiday on a fine August afternoon.

Driving south I noticed the farmers busy in the harvest fields, and when I reached home Mr Roberts was already combining the great field which lies beyond my hawthorn hedge.

The air was filled with the clatter and throb of machinery as the monster skirted my boundary, and then faded to a constant thrumming as it chugged into the distance.

Mrs Pringle, the school cleaner, was in my kitchen. She 'puts me straight', as she terms it, once a week, and despite her glum disposition which at times infuriates me, I welcome her ministrations, if not her comments, on my abode.

'Had a good time?' she enquired.

'Perfect!'

'Some people are lucky! I could do with a break myself, but a chance'd be a fine thing.'

'I'll put on the kettle,' I said diplomatically, 'I'm sure you need a cup of tea, and I certainly do.'

'It wouldn't come amiss,' she agreed, wringing out a wet duster. She sounded somewhat mollified, and her next remark sounded positively enthusiastic.

'You missed something this afternoon.'

'What was that?'

It was obviously something pleasant from the clear satisfaction she showed in the fact that I had missed it.

'That funny robin! He come to the bird table not half an hour ago.'

'Really? How marvellous! You *were* lucky to see him. I haven't yet.'

Mrs Pringle tucked her chins against her throat with every appearance of pleasure.

'Well, I was always one for noticing things, and I'd put out the crumbs from your bread bin which you'd forgotten to scrub out before leaving. Seems he liked them, stale though they were.'

'What's he like?' I said, ignoring the slur on my slatternly ways. In any case, I am used to Mrs Pringle's comments on my housewifery.

Her normally dour countenance lit up.

'Oh, he's a pretty dear! He was perched on the table with the sun behind him, and he looked just like a fluffy snowball. Except for his red breast, of course. He's a real beauty, I can tell you!'

'Let's hope he comes back soon,' I said, making the tea. 'I believe robins like biscuit crumbs. And meal-worms. But I don't think I can face handling those.'

'I'll get old Mr Potts, as lives next door to me, to bring up some. He uses 'em for fishing. Come to that, I could bring up some in a jar when I come up to scrub the school out.'

'Don't you mind messing about with maggots?'

Mrs Pringle stirred her tea briskly.

'I'd do *anything* for that robin,' she declared stoutly.

If Mrs Pringle felt such devotion, I thought, what must be the rest of Fairacre's reaction to our rare bird?

'Who else has seen it while I've been away?'

'Ah now, let me think!' Mrs Pringle put her cup down upon the saucer with much deliberation. Her mouth was pursed in concentration.

'There was Mrs Partridge,' she said at last. 'And Mr Willet who was hoeing the vicar's rosebed last week. He was dumbstruck, he told me. Said he'd seen a white blackbird over at Springbourne when he was a lad, but never a white robin! Of course, he didn't see it real *close*. Not like I did just now.'

Mrs Pringle looked smug.

'Anyone else? Any of the children? I hope they won't scare it.'

'Not as I've heard. But Mr Mawne has built a funny little house in the vicar's garden, all covered in branches and that, with a few spy holes to look out of. Got his camera in there, so they say.'

'A hide,' I said.

'No, his *camera*,' repeated Mrs Pringle.

I let it pass.

'He's going to write a bit for the *Caxley Chronicle* and wants a picture to go with it. He's a clever one, that Mr Mawne.'

'He is indeed. I hope he manages to get a photograph.'

'Well, if he does, I reckon we'll get plenty more wanting to take snaps of our robin. Bring plenty of visitors to Fairacre, that bird will, I shouldn't wonder.'

'I hope not,' I said. 'I'm beginning to think that the less said about it the better. We don't want strangers frightening it away.'

Mrs Pringle's neck began to flush and her four chins to wobble. I know the signs well. Mrs Pringle had taken umbrage.

'You asked me yourself to tell you about the bird,' she began. 'We can't expect to keep a thing like that secret, so it's no good getting hoity-toity about it.'

'Sorry, sorry!' I cried. 'You misunderstood me. Have another cup of tea.'

Mrs Pringle buttoned up her mouth and pushed her cup towards me. The gesture was conciliatory, but I could see that I was not forgiven.

Certainly the advent of this little albino robin was causing a surprising stir in Fairacre.

For instance, the village fête, usually held in the vicarage grounds on a Saturday in August, was shifted this year to the garden of Henry Mawne at the other end of Fairacre.

There was considerable discussion about this locally.

'It's Mr Mawne's doing,' said one inhabitant accusingly. 'Just because he's bird-barmy us has to keep out of the vicar's garden. All for a *bird*!'

Others defended the plan.

'It's the right thing to do!'

'This white bird's *special*. No point in frightening it off. Why, it might go to Beech Green! And who'd want that?'

'Anyway, it'll make a nice change to go to the Mawnes, and Mrs Mawne's doing the teas herself.'

'Bribery,' muttered the first speaker, but it was plain that she was in the minority. Ninety per cent of Fair-acre's population were devotedly in favour of giving the white robin every chance of survival.

Henry Mawne called one morning to return a book he had borrowed. We sat on the garden seat and I begged to be told the latest news.

'As far as I can tell there are four young robins. The other three are of normal colouring.'

'And where is the nest?'

'Oh, without doubt, in the ivy on the wall! This brood will be the last this season, I'm sure. It really is most exciting! I have seen the albino about half a dozen times now, and have taken several snaps which I'm about to develop.'

I told him that Mrs Pringle had seen it, and also that I rather feared that the bird was too popular for its own safety.

He nodded thoughtfully.

'Firstly, it's the children who might frighten it,' he said at last, 'but I'm sure you will do all in your power to protect it when they return to school. It faces danger too from other birds, as well as from any madman with a gun.'

I reassured him.

'And how is Simon?' I asked, now that the question of children had cropped up. 'Is he still with you?'

'No, he's returned home. I was going to say, "thank goodness", but that sounds heartless.'

'Children can be exhausting. Even angelic ones.'

'Oh, Simon's no angel, I can assure you! But he's plenty of reason to be difficult.'

He paused for a moment, as if trying to decide whether to confide in me or not. The cat wandered up and began to weave about my legs. I scratched the tabby back near the tail, a ploy most cats enjoy, while the silence lengthened.

'The fact is,' exploded Henry at last, 'the boy is odd man out in his family! There are three much older than he is – all sturdy, dark-haired extroverts like their father, my nephew. Not a nerve in their bodies! Strong as horses, never ill, good at games, and work as well. All out in the world and thriving.'

'Much older than Simon then?'

'Yes, he was one of these little afterthoughts, and I don't know that he was particularly welcome. Teresa thought her family was off her hands, you see, and then Simon came along.'

'Is she fair like the little boy? I thought he was a very handsome child.'

'So's his mother. Yes, a very pretty girl with a mop of fair hair. You could quite see why David fell for her.'

He sighed.

'*Very* pretty,' he repeated, 'but quite unsuitable.'

'Why?'

'A bundle of nerves. Always imagining she has something the matter with her. The complete hypochondriac! You should see their medicine cabinet. Twice the size of normal, and crammed with dozens of patent medicines. It's a marvel to me that the children are as healthy as they are. Even Simon, who is so like her, is comparatively cheerful, though no doubt he'll get more morbid as he grows older.'

Henry sounded gloomy.

'There's no reason to suppose that,' I said comfortingly. 'Apart from being rather thin and pale, he looked pretty healthy to me.'

'He's very attached to his mother, and I don't think it is altogether a good thing. Especially at the moment.'

'Is she too possessive?'

'Far from it. If anything she tends to reject the child. To be honest, I think she resents any attention which is not aimed at herself. My poor nephew is having a hell of a time.'

'Has she seen her doctor?'

'Too often, to my way of thinking, and all he says is something about her age, and being patient, and adjusting to situations, and similar codswallop. Sometimes I wonder if she needs a job of work, something to take her mind off herself. Though I pity anyone who employs her.'

'She certainly sounds most unhappy.'

'So's my poor David! He has to shoulder all the burdens while she sulks in this nursing home.'

'So she is getting treatment?'

'Yes, and at vast expense. They say it's a nervous complaint that should respond to whatever they're doing to her. I only hope it does. David and Simon are having a pretty thin time of it. They have a girl there who keeps house in a sketchy sort of way, but it's all very unsatisfactory.'

He sighed again, and stood up.

'Well, I mustn't burden you with my troubles.

Simon took to you, incidentally. You should feel honoured. He doesn't like many people, poor child, and I'm afraid many people don't like him. He has a pretty quick temper, unlike the other three. As I said, he's the odd bird out in that family.'

'Like the albino,' I said to turn his mind to happier things.

At once his face cleared, and he smiled.

'Like the albino,' he agreed. 'What a comfort nature is! Always something there for consolation.'

A sentiment with which I heartily concurred.

The holiday weeks sped by far too rapidly, and I enjoyed myself picking and bottling fruit, making jam, taking geranium cuttings and tidying the garden. I also decorated the kitchen, and although the standard of workmanship was far below that of Mr Willet, our local handyman-sexton-school-caretaker – and general factotum to Fairacre, I was pleased with the result. Even Mrs Pringle commented grudgingly that 'it must be cleaner'.

When people ask me, as they frequently do, what I find to do in the long holidays which form one of the more attractive aspects of my job, I answer with some asperity. I do as they do. I clean my house, attend to the garden, prepare for the winter, go shopping, visit the dentist, put my meagre financial affairs in order, and so on. Why people imagine that teachers fall immediately into a state of suspended animation the minute term ends, I cannot think, but it is an attitude of mind which one often encounters.

As well as my own personal activities during

August, I tried to pull my weight socially, helping at the fête in Henry Mawne's garden, supplying a local fund-raiser with a mammoth tray of gingerbread, and dispensing hospitality to a number of friends who had been kind enough to invite me to their homes during the past term. My old friend Amy, who lives at the village of Bent some miles distant, was one of these, and I was surprised to hear that she already knew about our white robin.

'But there's no secret about it, is there?' she enquired. 'You can't keep such a phenomenon to yourselves, you know.'

'I suppose not. It's just that I tremble for the bird. Too much publicity could put it in peril.'

'Rubbish!' said Amy stoutly. 'A sturdy albino robin can stand up to any amount of publicity, I'm sure. Robins are tough birds. I can't see any robin – white or coloured – being pushed around.'

I only hoped she was right, for certainly the subject of our rarity was cropping up quite often in the course of conversation with friends and neighbours.

What struck me was the affection, one might almost say reverence, with which they spoke of it. Country people are not given to sentimentality over animals. At times I think they go the other way, but I realize that I am a soft-hearted woman, incapable of passing a poor flattened hare or a squashed hedgehog on the road, without a pang of pity.

Very few of us had yet had a glimpse of the albino bird, but we eagerly questioned those who had, and a number of people remembered other white birds of the past.

On the whole, the blackbirds were those chiefly recalled, and as Henry Mawne told us that this particular variety of bird made up almost thirty per cent of albinos, it was not surprising. Miss Clare, who used to teach the infants at Fairacre School, remembered one white blackbird who had become very tame and had enchanted the children of an earlier generation in the village, and Mrs Willet, who had been one of those children, also remembered it vividly.

'There's nothing prettier than a pure white bird,' she declared. 'That one was white as a lily. Made you think of churches and altar cloths and that,' she added, waxing poetical.

Was this, I wondered, the reason for the awe which our white robin was inspiring? Did we unconsciously connect its albinism with holiness and purity? Whatever were the reasons for our interest, there was no doubt that we were all eager to see it, and to cherish it.

I was lucky. I did not have to wait long.

On the very last day of the holidays the early sunshine woke me. I sat up in bed, and looked into the branches of an ancient apple tree outside the bedroom window.

There, its tiny talons gripping a lichen-covered twig, sat the white robin. Its eyes were dark and shining against the white satin of its head. The breast was still more orange than red, and glowed against its snowy plumage.

It was a breathtaking sight, and I did not dare to move. For a full half minute it sat there motionless, and then with a flash of white wings, it had gone.

Full of elation, I rose and dressed.

Now I was one of the élite who had actually seen the white robin!

CHAPTER THREE

Snowboy

Term began, and in the usual flurry of settling the new babies in the infant class, and the young juniors in my own, there was little time to give to bird-watching.

Nevertheless, one or two of the children saw the robin, and we all learned a great deal from the long account of albinism in birds generally which Henry Mawne contributed to the *Caxley Chronicle*, complete with photographs taken from his hide in the vicar's garden.

To be honest, the photographs meant more to most of the *Caxley Chronicle*'s readers than Henry's somewhat erudite account of white birds. The early part of Henry's essay was devoted to genetic inheritance which successfully bogged down a number of readers anxious to assimilate the news of the robin rapidly, before passing on to the local football results.

For those still pursuing the subject of albinism there was a tricky passage involving the term NN, standing for the normal robin, and WW standing for the white variety. The offspring, wrote Henry, become NW, and as the albino gene is recessive further complicated combinations and permutations occur. As Mrs Pringle said: 'I didn't take in all that double-north and north-west stuff, but that Mr Mawne must have a good headpiece on him, that's for sure!'

She spoke for most of Fairacre.

As always when something unusual crops up, the subject of white birds occurred in various forms. There was a letter in *The Times* from a north country reader about a white blackbird which frequented his garden. To this Henry Mawne wrote a reply, and all Fairacre basked in the reflected glory when the letter was printed.

At much the same time, whilst I was reading that delightful book *The Country Diary of An Edwardian Lady*, I discovered that one of the January entries mentions 'a very curious Robin' which the author describes as light silvery grey and looking like a white bird with a scarlet breast when in flight. She comments truly, that 'it is a wonder it has not fallen a victim to somebody's gun'.

This fear, of course, was always with us, but we comforted ourselves with the thought that in such a small community as Fairacre we were united in wishing to protect our treasure. Certainly, if anyone were so wicked, or so foolhardy, as to raise a gun against our robin he would bring down the wrath of all upon his head. It would not take long to trace the culprit, that was sure.

That particular September the weather was warm. The low golden rays of the sun glinted upon the bales of straw waiting to be picked up and stacked in the barns. The streams of golden grain which had poured into the waiting wagons were now safely stored.

All the world seemed bathed in golden light. Yellow sunflowers and golden rod in the cottage gardens added to this mellow warmth, and the first few falling leaves gleamed from the ground, awaiting the showers of bronze and gold which would join them later.

The dew was heavy each morning, and the children found mushrooms and early blackberries. In the gardens of Fairacre a bumper crop of plums weighed down the trees: round yellow gage plums dripping with sweetness, the old-fashioned golden drop plums so much prized by the jam-makers and, best of all, the enormous Victorias still awaiting a few days more in the sunshine to reach perfection.

There were plums everywhere. Baskets of plums were carried to neighbours. Bowls of plums stood on kitchen dressers. Bottles of plums gleamed like jewels from kitchen shelves. Jars of plum jam, plum jelly, plum chutney and plum preserves of all kinds jostled each other in kitchen cupboards.

Plums dominated the side desk in the schoolroom where the children left their elevenses. Usually, a few packets of biscuits or crisps, perhaps an apple or a banana, were to be seen but during the plum season the appearance of the ancient long desk was transformed by the local crop, now forming the main item of the dozen or so 'stay-bits', as the old people termed the snacks.

It was a lovely time when Fairacre enjoyed the fruits of its labours. Runner beans were being stuffed into freezers. Great bronze onions hung in ropes from outhouse beams, and bunches of drying herbs from kitchen ceilings.

Marrows swayed in nets, like drunken sailors in hammocks. Potatoes rumbled into sacks, and apples were carefully wrapped in quarter sheets of the *Caxley Chronicle* and put to bed in rows in slatted boxes.

Housewives were red-eyed from peeling and pickling shallots, and their fingers appallingly stained by the constant handling of crops.

But who cared? This, for us country dwellers, was the crown of the year. We rejoiced in this plenty, and faced the coming winter with serenity, secure in the knowledge of our squirrels' hoards.

Harvest festival, as usual, found our parish church more crowded than at any other service in the year.

Perhaps country people are more conscious of the need for thanksgiving than their town cousins when the crops have been safely gathered in. Certainly the old familiar hymns from *Hymns Ancient and Modern* were sung lustily and sincerely, as our eyes roved over the bounties of the earth displayed in St Patrick's.

The children had contributed to this handiwork, as they had each year for generations. Each pew end bore a bunch of ears of corn, looped by a length of green knitting wool from the needlework cupboard. The base of the font was beautified by a garland of scrubbed carrots alternating with well polished apples. Giant marrows, dark green, pale green, and striped like tigers, were propped up in the porch for all to admire as the worshippers wiped their Sunday shoes on the mat.

The pulpit, the altar, and the steps to the chancel were left to the ladies of the parish to decorate, and a splendid job they made of it. Some said that their efforts were almost too artistic, and that feelings ran high when they were asked to incorporate six large loaves, contributed by the local baker, into their floral scheme.

Mr Partridge, with his usual pastoral tact, managed to calm the ladies' outraged feelings, and the loaves were removed from the delicate arrangements of wild bryony and sprays of bramble to a more suitable setting against the oak of the rood screen where they stood in a sturdy row and were much admired by those in the front pews.

'I very near broke a piece off one of they,' said our oldest shepherd. 'With a bit of tasty cheese that'd have passed the time lovely during parson's sermon.'

But temptation was resisted, and as always, the good things were gathered up after Harvest Festival Sunday and taken to Caxley Cottage Hospital for the patients' delectation.

'When I was there one Michaelmas,' recalled the same old shepherd, 'we had marrer and marrer till it come out of our ears. We was right glad to get back to tinned peas again, I can tell you.'

Mrs Pringle, true to her word, had prevailed upon her neighbour, Mr Potts the fisherman, to provide her with some mealworms for the robin.

She brought them on the first occasion in a round plastic box which had once held margarine.

'There!' she said, whipping off the lid and displaying the revolting wriggling mass under my nose. 'Lovely, ain't they? They should bring the little old boy along.'

She put the open box on the asphalt part of the playground, in full view of the children in the classroom. As the weather was so warm, the door was propped open and there was every chance of someone seeing the robin if it appeared.

Frankly, I was doubtful. It was some weeks since I had enjoyed that breathtaking glimpse, although other robins had come to collect crumbs from my bird table as usual. Nevertheless, the mealworms were duly left in the strategic position selected, and we all waited for results.

We did not have long to wait. A gust of wind tipped over the light container and whipped it towards the school, spreading a trail of squirming maggots in its path.

'It's blown away!'

'It's gorn!'

'Them worms is runnin' away!'

'We've lost 'em!'

'Get 'em quick!'

'You get 'em! I can't touch 'em!'

There was instant pandemonium, and a concerted rush to rescue the mealworms.

'One of you hold the box,' I ordered, 'while the rest of you collect the worms. I'll go and fetch a heavier box for them.'

I hurried across to my kitchen, secretly thankful to be absent from maggot-collecting, and unearthed an ancient china pot which had once held Gentleman's Relish. It had a fine heavy base and was just deep enough to hold the robins' treat.

The children greeted it with rapture. The maggots

were tipped in whilst I averted my gaze, and peace was restored.

There must have been one or two robins watching these proceedings from hiding places in the hedges for within a few minutes a pair came to snatch our largesse. But, to our disappointment, the white one did not appear.

'He'll come one day soon, you'll see,' Mrs Pringle assured the children when they told her of that morning's adventure. 'If I brings them worms regular, you won't have to wait long. You mark my words.'

The Gentleman's Relish jar was approved by the lady, and after that was in daily use.

'If I was you,' said Mrs Pringle, 'I'd have some of these nice maggots on your bird table. After all, that's where I saw him once, and maybe he's too timid to come into the open, seeing he's so conspicuous. You try it, Miss Read.'

Averse though I was to handling the things, I could see the sense of Mrs Pringle's argument, and I was also so eager to woo the robin to our territory that I braced myself to shake a few mealworms on to the bird table each day, shuddering the while.

There was no doubt about it, robins adored them. I only saw one robin at a time actually on the table, although I felt fairly sure that the pair which frequented the jar in the playground both came separately to my garden. I became convinced that they had nested somewhere in one of my hedges and that some of the young robins, now to be seen about, were their offspring.

I had no means of telling if other robins from the

vicarage garden also came to get the mealworms from my table, but I suspected that they did. They must have watched very sharply for there were no fights. Any outsiders were careful to come when the coast was clear, so that there were no squabbles over territory, as often happens.

As the weather grew colder, more and more birds sought out the scraps provided, both on my garden bird table, and in the playground. They seemed to come in groups. A blue tit would appear, followed by half a dozen more. Then the chaffinches would sense that here was food to be had, and the blackbirds and always, of course, the ubiquitous sparrows and starlings.

They would make a concerted rush upon the food available, and then something would startle them and the bird table would be empty in a flash of wings. It was after just such a sudden exodus when I was turning away from the window that the white robin came again.

With his matchstick legs askew, and his liquid dark eyes cocked upon the bounty, he was poised there for a full minute pecking at the scraps which he now enjoyed alone. His orange breast glowed like embers against the snowy feathers. He was even more handsome than on his first appearance.

And he was bolder. He must have glimpsed a movement of mine, for he hopped about to face me, head still cocked, but picked up a maggot without undue hurry and flew off with it in the direction of the vicar's garden.

Later, that same day, the children saw him come to

the mealworms in the playground, select a fine specimen, and depart.

It certainly looked as though Mrs Pringle's prognostications were correct.

By the time term ended, the white robin had become a frequent visitor to both my bird table and the playground, although he always chose to come when there were no other birds about.

He was now affectionately termed Snowboy, Snowball, Snowflake, Whitey, or Robbie by the children, and I had no fears that they would frighten the bird.

They treated it with devotion and deference. For them, and for the majority of Fairacre folk, the coming of this beautiful bird was a little miracle, and when school broke up for the Christmas holidays, I had to promise to cherish 'our Snowboy' on their behalf.

The congregation in St Patrick's Church on Christmas morning was not as large as that which gathered for Harvest Festival, but was certainly bigger than usual.

Many of the housewives were at home supervising the Christmas dinner, but there was a fair sprinkling of visitors to engage our attention, and plenty of new gloves and scarves to admire which had obviously been acquired that morning.

The flowers and evergreens caught our eye. Christmas roses, late chrysanthemums, trails of shiny ivy leaves, holly and mistletoe wreathed the font and pulpit, and two splendid poinsettias flanked the altar.

What with all this excitement, and the thought of presents at home and the feasting to come, it was hardly surprising that the choirboys went a trifle flat. Mr Annett, as organist, thumped out the Christmas hymns in as staccato a manner as was humanly possible, in an effort to quicken the pace, but he might just as well have spared himself.

Fairacre boys, as I know to my cost, 'will not be druv', and they lagged half a bar behind and were blissfully unaware of their choirmaster's rising blood pressure.

I was interested to see my young friend Simon again, standing in the Mawnes' pew and flanked by his dark-haired father, whom I knew slightly, and a pretty fair-haired woman who was obviously Teresa, his mother.

She was tall and slim, wrapped in a short chinchilla coat. She did not join in the singing, but stared straight ahead, ignoring the sidelong glances which both Henry Mawne and her husband David occasionally cast in her direction.

The party came out of church fairly quickly, so that I was able to observe Simon's mother as she came up the aisle.

She was exceptionally pretty, but her face was pale and expressionless. It was the brilliance of her eyes which struck me. They were large and of that intense pale blue which is sometimes seen in fanatics. Garibaldi, they say, had just such eyes, and so too have several unbalanced criminals.

I felt a quiver of fear as my gaze met hers for one fleeting moment. Here, I was sure, was someone desperately unhappy, and potentially dangerous too.

Poor woman! Poor David! But most of all, poor young Simon, I thought, watching his fair head, level with the beautiful grey fur coat, as he followed his mother into the winter sunshine.

CHAPTER FOUR

Bitter Weather

The worst of the winter weather came, as usual, after Christmas. Heavy snow towards the end of January kept a few of the children at home for a day or two, and those that did arrive frequently had coughs or head colds.

So many of the mothers were out at work that I sometimes wondered if a few of the children were sent off to school when they would have been better off at home in the early stages of a cold. In former times, there would probably have been a granny sitting by the fire, or a single aunt who would have been free, and more than willing to care for a sickly child, until its mother came home, but grannies and single aunts also went to work these days, and children had to learn to stand on their own feet rather earlier than my own generation did.

All that I could do was to ensure that the stoves were kept banked up, although there was considerable opposition to this, of course, from Mrs Pringle. I heated the children's milk too, for those who could not face a bottle with flakes of ice at the top, and stirred in a spoonful of drinking chocolate from my store cupboard, if they liked it.

At least most of them were warmly clad these days. Even the Coggs children had wellington boots, and some shabby slippers to change into when they arrived. And, while the weather was at its most bitter, I relaxed my stern rule about everyone playing outside for the full quarter of an hour at break time, and let them cluster round the tortoise stove for half the appointed time.

Snow always brings out the worst in Mrs Pringle. She looks upon it as a personal enemy, a despoiler of clean floors, a hazard to life and limb, and the unnecessary salt rubbed into the wounds of everyday living.

'It isn't as though I was getting any younger,' she grumbled to me after the children had been buttoned up, gloved and scarved, and sent on their way.

'It's this weather as makes my leg flare up,' she continued. 'I don't say nothing about it in the ordinary way, as well you know, Miss Read.'

This was news to me, but I forebore to comment. Experience has taught me to let Mrs Pringle have her head when she is indulging in personal martyrdom.

'But all this extra work Takes Its Toll, as they say. That lobby needs a good scrub out every evening, and I can't do it. As for sacks, I'm down to my last two. I did ask Mr Roberts if he'd got any to spare, but they're all these useless plastic things these days that don't sop up nothing.'

'We could wipe them,' I suggested.

'*Wipe them*?' boomed Mrs Pringle, turning red in the face. 'What good would that do? Might just as well wipe the floor itself while I was at it!'

'Of course, of course!' I said hastily.

'No, I sometimes wonder if the folk who live abroad aren't best off. Take my cousin's boy. He's in South

Africa, and she had a letter last week to say he was sunbathing. *Sunbathing*, mark you! In January!'

'Lucky chap,' I said.

'Well,' said the lady, heaving herself to her feet from the desk top where she had been seated. 'This won't buy the baby a new frock. One thing I know, if I win the pools one day I'll spend the winter in South Africa.'

One good thing about the cold spell was that the birds, including Snowboy, came much more boldly for the food we put out.

Even the rooks came down into the playground for our largesse, and one, bolder than the rest, took to balancing precariously on the bird table, much to the annoyance of the smaller birds.

There was no doubt that the coming of Snowboy-Snowball-Snowflake-etc had created much more interest in birds generally in the village, and when we heard that Henry Mawne had been invited to appear on local television and to show some of his pictures of the albino robin, we were heady with pride.

'Henry will be on soon after six o'clock on Thursday,' the vicar told me, 'and if you would care to come and see him on our set, my wife and I would be delighted.'

As the vicar has a colour television I accepted gratefully.

'Watch out for Thursday soon after six!' shouted Mr Lamb from the Post Office, when he caught sight of me at the post-box on the wall of his abode.

'Don't forget Mr Mawne's on Thursday,' warned Mrs Pringle.

We all reminded each other when we met. It was quite apparent that everyone in Fairacre would be watching on the great day.

The *Caxley Chronicle* carried a reminder to its readers on the front page, and was careful to point out that Henry Mawne was one of its distinguished contributors. Side by side with this pleasurable announcement, was the unwelcome news that the price of this valuable journal would be going up by one penny at the next issue. I felt that the editor and staff could not have chosen a better time to make the announcement. Henry Mawne's fame sugared the pill very nicely.

On Thursday evening, I presented myself at the vicarage, and found several other friends there. With glasses of sherry in our hands, we stared at the screen awaiting Fairacre's great moment.

I must say that Henry looked extremely elegant and unusually tidy in the studio. The make-up department seemed to have smoothed over most of his wrinkles, and given him a healthy flush, although the heat from the lights or general excitement might have accounted for his robust look. He was wearing his best hacking jacket and his National Trust tie, and we all agreed that he was a worthy representative of the village.

But naturally enough, the white robin eclipsed him in splendour. About a dozen slides were shown, for the first time, and we sat entranced at the bird's beauty. Henry had certainly managed to get some superb pictures, and when the allotted ten minutes were over, and the screen filled with an appalling picture of a head-on crash, police cars, and ambulances with doors yawning as stretchers were being inserted, we watched the vicar switch off, with relief, and lived once again our splendid distinction on television.

It was the next evening when my old friend Amy drove over from Bent.

Amy and I were at college together many years ago, and although she is married, much travelled, always exquisitely dressed and wealthy, in complete contrast to me, we have a great deal in common, and the bond of friendship grows stronger with the years.

She has a tiresome habit of trying to reform me, and another, equally annoying, of trying to find me a husband. Luckily, as the years go by, the chances of this being accomplished grow slighter, and Amy's efforts are less wholehearted, much to my relief.

'My dear Amy,' I have said to her on many occasions, 'you must know, surely, that some people are the marrying sort and some are not. I'm one of the latter, so do stop beating your head against a brick wall. I am perfectly happy as I am.'

I am not sure that Amy really believes me, but she is gradually coming round to the idea that I do not sob myself to sleep each night because I am unwed.

Of course we discussed the programme. In contrast to all Fairacre's enthusiasm, Amy was somewhat cool.

'Personally, I question that bird being an albino,' she said. 'I always understood that a *pure* albino bird had pink eyes and no colour in its legs and so on.'

'Well, it's albino enough for most of us,' I said stoutly. 'And come to think of it, I believe Henry did say something on that point.'

'Not enough. In a brief programme like that he should have been *much* more precise. I've no doubt that he will get plenty of criticism from true ornithologists.'

'But Henry *is* a true ornithologist!' I cried. 'You really are a carping old horror, Amy!'

She began to laugh.

'And you and the rest of the Fairacre folk are absolutely besotted with that blighted bird! But I readily admit that it's a beauty, and I can't say fairer than that, can I?'

'Have a glass of sherry,' I said, forgiving her. 'And tell me all the latest news.'

'You haven't, by any chance, a drier sherry than that, have you?' enquired Amy, watching me pour out a fine tawny glassful.

'Sorry, no! I won this at the summer fête.'

Amy shuddered.

'It's jolly good. Rather like that raisin wine we used to buy in Cambridge at three and six a bottle in the old days. But if you don't like it you can have Robinson's lemon barley water instead.'

'I'm sure this will be delicious,' said Amy, lying bravely, as she accepted the glass.

'What news of Vanessa?' Amy's attractive niece is a great favourite of mine. Now that she is married and lives in a castle in Scotland, I do not see much of her, but we keep in touch.

'Thriving, I'm glad to say. Both children doing well, and I believe she is already planning for a third.'

'Good heavens! Does she really want *three*?'

'She wants *six*, so she says. Personally, I consider it

rather selfish, but of course there's much more room in Scotland, and you could lose six children in that barn of a castle without missing them for a fortnight.'

'Well, all I can say is, I admire her pluck. Of course, young things can plan families so much more easily these days, can't they?'

'You shouldn't know anything about it,' said Amy severely, 'as a respectable spinster.'

'You and Lady Bracknell,' I replied, 'would make a good pair. She didn't believe in tampering with natural ignorance either.'

Amy put down her glass.

'Talking of marriage, would you like to meet our new organist at Bent?'

'I don't mind meeting the new organist, but I warn you that I shan't have marriage in mind.'

'I'm having a little dinner party next week. Do come. The poor fellow knows no one locally, and is in rather wretched digs. I don't think he gets enough to eat. James said he'd be home, and said you must come, as he is so fond of you.'

'Don't flatter me, Amy dear. Of course, I'll come, and I shall look forward to seeing your attractive husband, and the new organist. What's his name?'

'Unfortunately, it's Horace Umbleditch. Quite tricky to say when one is making introductions. But he's quite a charmer, and has a most elegant figure. James said: "Fatten him up, but don't marry him off!" At times, James is a trifle coarse.'

'James is a sensible man,' I told her. 'More sherry?'

'Do you know, I think I will. It's rather like a blend

of good quality cough linctus and elderberry wine. It's growing on me.'

'Well, keep yourself in hand. It's no use becoming addicted to the stuff. This is all I've got.'

I filled her glass again, while Amy enlarged on the guests whom I should meet at the proposed party, and I looked forward even more eagerly to my evening out.

The weather continued to be cold and miserable. Although most of the snow had cleared, there were still white patches under the hedges and on the northerly slopes which the sun did not reach.

'It's waiting for more to come,' said Mr Willet gloomily, surveying the dark corner by the vicar's wall. Here, in the cold shade, slivers of snow lay under the bushes, undisturbed by the children. In this weather they rushed to the nearby lavatories, and back again, at record speed, thankful to regain the shelter of the schoolroom and the comfort of the ancient tortoise stoves.

As usual, Mr Willet was right. I would back his judgement about our weather against any professional weatherman in the country. In the last week of term, the skies grew ominously overcast, and one night the snow fell from ten o'clock until six in the morning. Once again the lanes of Fairacre were white. The fields glistened beneath their blanket of snow, dazzling against the dark clouds above them.

The bare black trees and hedges made the whole scene look like a stark charcoal drawing. It hurt one's eyes to look for long. One craved for a splash of colour to warm the bleak outlook.

'You'd think by March,' said Mr Willet, 'that we'd see a bit of sun. Dear knows what's gone amiss with spring these days! Why, when I was a boy we reckoned to pick primroses and violets in March. Not much chance of that this year.'

He watched me scattering crumbs for the birds.

'Poor things! No weather for the young 'uns. Seen anything of our robin?'

'He comes most days. He's looking marvellous, and I believe he's made a nest in my garden somewhere.'

'Has he now? You watch out that cat of yours don't get the young 'uns. Be a bit of all right if they turned out white, wouldn't it?'

Ernest and Patrick had wandered up and were listening to our conversation. They took up the theme with enthusiasm.

'How many eggs do robins lay?'

I offered them what scanty knowledge I had gleaned from the bird book on my shelf.

'About half a dozen, I think,' I hazarded.

'Then we might get six new white ones!' cried Patrick. He grabbed at a passing infant who had just arrived. 'Hear that, fatty? We might get lots more Snowballs this spring.'

'Run inside,' I said to the children. 'I'm just coming, and it's far too cold to stay outdoors.'

'Well, I hope the boy's right,' said Mr Willet, preparing to set off to his home. 'Be a fine thing if we had a few more white 'uns.'

'I've a feeling it doesn't work that way,' I replied. 'Didn't Mr Mawne's article say something about missing a generation? I must look it up.'

'If it was that bit about the Ns and Ws, I was fair flummoxed,' admitted Mr Willet. 'I was out of my depth after two lines of that, but I do remember there was a bit of doubt about it.'

'I'll ask Mr Mawne when I see him,' I promised.

'That'll be some time. He's off on one of these cruises. Gone to Crete, I believe, on a boat with a lot of other bird people. He's lecturing them, so Mrs Mawne told me.'

'Has she gone too?'

'No, she said she had quite enough of birds in Fairacre without going overseas to see a lot more.'

'She would have missed this beastly cold spring,' I said.

'Ah well! Maybe it'll all be over before you break up. Think of that! You'll have your deck chair up before the month's out!'

'That'll be the day,' I said, folding my coat more tightly about me.

And picking my way through the slushy playground, I went into the school to face my duties.

CHAPTER FIVE

A Nest of Robins

I spent a considerable time getting ready for Amy's dinner party, and wished I had asked her the usual question, 'Long or short skirt?', when I had been invited. As it was, I had left this vital question too late to bother her, and weighed up the pros and cons for the umpteenth time.

In this bitter weather a long skirt could be a great comfort. On the other hand, it was the devil to drive in, and in Amy's well-heated house it might well prove too warm. It must be admitted though, that if one wished to honour one's hostess, a long skirt looked as though one had really made some effort.

But then again, one did not want to appear over-dressed, and it seemed that short skirts were in again for evening occasions. Also I had recently bought a stunning silk shirt-waister which Amy had not yet seen, and I was strongly inclined to put it on. After a good deal of shilly-shallying I decided to wear the latter, and if every other woman was sweeping around in floor length kaftans and black velvet skirts, good luck to them!

One of the comforts of middle age, I find, is the comparative peace of mind which engulfs one when one has finally decided what to put on. When young, one's evening can be ruined by the thought that one's shoes are the wrong colour, or one's hair needs shampooing. Advancing age has its modest compensations.

The night was clear and frosty. Some snow still lay along the edges of the road and covered the sloping banks which faced north. The car's headlights made dark tunnels of the trees ahead on my way to Bent, and there were few wayfarers about in the winter cold.

Amy's house was as warm and welcoming as her greeting. Great mop-headed chrysanthemums graced the hall table, and two bowls of shell-pink Lady Derby hyacinths scented her drawing-room. Mine, needless to say, had hardly put their noses through the fibre.

Horace Umbleditch proved to be an elegant man with dark hair and a gold-rimmed monocle swinging on a black silk cord about his neck. From Amy's description I had expected a somewhat pathetic figure, undernourished and shy, but the new organist, although enviably slim, was obviously fit and distinctly voluble. I could see that he would more than hold his own in the assembled company.

James, Amy's husband, enveloped me in a bear's hug, kissed me on both cheeks, and held me at arm's length to admire my new silk frock. One can quite see why James is so attractive to the opposite sex. I am not very susceptible, but even my elderly spinster's heart melts when I meet James. He looks at you very closely, as though you were the only woman he was waiting to see. I think it is because he is short-sighted, and he is far too vain to wear spectacles, but the result is the same, and very pleasurable it is. Knowing James, I forgive all – and there is plenty to forgive – but I adore him.

There were ten of us at dinner, mostly Bent friends, some of whom I had met before. I was interested to see that short skirts outnumbered long by three to two. The vicar's wife sported a long black one, made of such heavy ribbed silk that I longed to stroke it, and the youngest wife present wore a dashing spotted affair with frills reaching to the ground.

As always, Amy's food was delicious. A creamy fish dish, sizzling in our ten ramekins, was followed by pheasant, then lemon sorbet or apple and blackberry tart, and a superb dessert of black and white grapes, pears and peaches.

'Coffee in the drawing-room,' Amy called to me as I went upstairs. I always relish Amy's bathroom. It is a symphony of primrose yellow and deep gold. Even the soap echoes the colour scheme, and best of all, the towels intended for visitors' use are clearly labelled GUEST. How often, in less elegantly appointed bathrooms, I have wondered whether to wipe my wet hands on a corner of my hostess's – or possibly host's – towel, or use the foot mat. It is plain sailing if there is one of those little huckaback items, embroidered with a lady in a crinoline standing by some knot-stitch hollyhocks, but distinctly daunting if one is confronted by six equally sized towels shoulder-to-shoulder on the towel rail.

Horace Umbleditch brought my coffee and sat beside me.

'Amy has been telling me about your famous Fairacre robin. I'm particularly interested as I know Henry Mawne's nephew slightly.'

'David?'

'That's right. My sister is a neighbour of theirs, and occasionally sits in for young Simon if they are going out. She had heard about the robin from them, of course.'

'It's a terrific thrill for us. So far the robin has thrived. We're hoping there will be more one day.'

'Simon's much impressed, I gather from my sister. She sees quite a bit of the boy. She trained as a Norland nurse and has a very soft spot for young Simon. His mother has been ill, as no doubt you know.'

I said that I did.

'There's some talk of the boy going to boarding school next September. A good thing, I should think. Teresa gets no better, and it's affecting Simon badly. I know my sister worries a lot about the family.'

'They are lucky to have such an understanding neighbour.'

'Well, it works both ways. They have always been good to Irene on the rare occasions when she has been ill. Thank God we're a hardy family, and don't ail much.'

Amy bore down upon us at this juncture and carried Horace off to talk to the young wife in the spotted skirt. As James took his place, I was well content, but I pondered on this comment on Teresa Mawne as I drove home under a starlit sky, and was considerably disturbed. The memory of that blank, blue, fanatical stare was fresh in my mind, and I trembled for those who lived with it.

It was during the last few days of term that I caught a glimpse of the white robin in my garden. To my joy, he was feeding a normal coloured robin, presumably a female, who was quivering her wings and obviously begging for food.

Was this his mate? Would we soon see some young robins? I put these questions to Henry Mawne as soon as he returned from his tour of Crete.

He was looking remarkably hale, with a splendid suntan which contrasted noticeably with the pinched blue complexions of the rest of us Fairacre folk.

'Almost certainly his mate,' he said. 'And I've no doubt you'll soon hear the young birds somewhere in that hedge of yours. But don't expect any white ones. I told you all about that.'

I hardly liked to say that I had not quite taken in this important fact, but Henry guessed.

'I suppose you, and all those silly children, and everyone else in the village for that matter, expects half a dozen snow-white robins this spring.'

'Well—' I began diffidently.

'I don't know why I bother to explain these simple facts, I really don't. Did you read my article?'

'Yes, I did.'

'I made it quite plain, I thought, that the *children* of an albino would be normal in colouring. It is *just possible* that an albino might occur in the grand-children. And then probably only one in four.'

'Thank you for explaining,' I said humbly.

'So do spread the word, Miss Read, that we shall not see any more white robins this spring.'

'I will. But we might see one, say, next year?'

Henry Mawne looked severe.

'That's looking rather far ahead. Anything might

happen to this year's brood. I shouldn't like to say that we should see a white one *next* year even. Too many hazards. Your cat for one.'

This wholly unjustified attack on poor Tibby, not even present to defend himself, quite took my breath away.

Seeing his advantage, Henry walked away briskly before I had time to answer.

Easter fell early in April, and although the weather over that weekend remained overcast and chilly, the wind changed towards the end of the week, and welcome sunshine flooded the countryside.

It was wonderful, after such a long bleak spell, to wake to warmth and gentle breezes. The crocuses burst into bloom. The daffodil buds seemed to shoot an inch higher overnight, and in all the cottage gardens hoeing, raking and digging began with renewed hope.

Joseph Coggs appeared on my doorstep and offered his services as assistant gardener. I gladly accepted.

Mrs Coggs was out at work, I knew. The twins were looked after, somewhat sketchily, by a neighbour who had children of the same age. The youngest pair were taken with Mrs Coggs to work at the various establishments in the village where she was employed as a daily help.

Joseph was the odd man out, and I was glad to have him safely with me, and to enjoy his company at my lunchtime. He seemed happy to come and make himself useful, and certainly appreciated my cooking. He was observant, and unusually knowledgeable about natural life.

I watched him staring at a worm which was wriggling purposefully towards a damp garden bed. He accepted a mug of coffee without shifting his gaze.

'Them 'as got eight hearts,' he informed me.

'Really?'

'And you chop 'em in half and they makes two worms.'

'I hope you're not going to try it.'

'Course not!' He sounded affronted.

'What are you going to do when you grow up, Joe?'

I thought of his drunken father. Not much of an example there for a young boy.

'I be goin' to be a gamekeeper. Like my grandpa was.'

'I think you would be good at that.'

'And you gets a new suit every two years. And real leather boots. Proper tweed the suit is. My grandpa told me.'

'And where did he work?'

Joseph looked nonplussed.

'A good way off. For some Lord Somebody. Might have been Aylesbury or round there. My grandpa liked him, and this Lord Whoever give him a watch when he was an old man.'

Joseph is not usually so forthcoming, and I was interested to learn something of his background.

'Snowboy's been in and out the box hedge,' he said, handing over the empty mug. 'Shall us go and look?'

'No, no,' I said hastily. 'We mustn't disturb him. Do you think there's a nest there?'

'I bet she's sitting,' said Joseph, 'and Snowboy's taking in some grub for her. What we got today, miss?'

'Cottage pie, and apple fluff.'

'Smashing!' said my gardener, setting off to hoe with renewed energy.

Apart from a couple of days when I was out visiting, Joseph spent most of the hours of daylight with me. It seemed to suit Mrs Coggs, young Joe and me as well. He was no bother, happy and obedient, and opened my eyes to a number of things in the garden I had missed.

A blackbird had built in the crook of two branches in the hawthorn bush. Joseph spotted the nest in a trice, but was careful, I noticed, not to visit it too often.

'Four eggs,' he told me proudly. 'And down the field bank there's a wren nesting, but she's been too durned clever for me. Can't find it nohow, but I'll lay she've got more'n four.'

I quoted the old verse to him.

The dove said: 'Coo,
What shall I do?
For I have two!'
'Pooh!' said the wren,
'I have ten
And bring them up
Like gentlemen!'

It appealed to the boy, and I had to repeat it several times until he had it by heart, I made a note to teach it to my class next term.

One morning of bright sunshine, I carried his mug out into the garden, but could not see him anywhere. Then I became aware of a grubby hand beckoning me silently towards the box hedge at the farthest corner of the garden.

I approached warily, and with some feeling of annoyance. The boy had been told explicitly to keep well away from the white robin's possible nest. It would be infuriating if the parent birds were disturbed and deserted the nest.

'She'm off for a minute,' breathed Joseph. He was holding aside a sturdy branch. The boy's face was alight with wonder, and I had not the heart to chide him.

There, on the ground, in a mossy cup, lay five

robin's eggs, white as pearls, and freckled with tiny pink spots. It was a sight to catch the breath.

'Cover it again,' I whispered, 'and come away.'

We crept quickly back to the garden seat near the house, and almost immediately a flash of white wings showed that Snowboy was returning to see if all was well with his wife and potential family.

'I wonder how many white 'uns among them five,' said Joseph, clutching his mug.

'None this year,' I said.

'Might be two or three,' continued Joseph, still bemused.

'Mr Mawne said we couldn't expect any white birds this year,' I said patiently.

Joseph took a long drink, wiped his mouth on the back of his hand, and settled back with a sigh.

'Wouldn't it be fine if us got *five*?' he cried, eyes shining.

Against such touching faith I was powerless, and gave up.

CHAPTER SIX

Our New Pupil

Term had begun when Henry Mawne rang me one evening.

He sounded unusually agitated, and so was I when he asked if he could call immediately about a pressing matter.

'Of course,' I said. 'Bring Elizabeth and I'll get some coffee ready. What's it about?'

'Oh, I couldn't possibly tell you on the telephone, and I won't bring my wife, though many thanks for inviting her. And please don't bother with coffee. I find it keeps me awake these nights. I'll be with you in half an hour or less.'

If there is anything I dislike it is suspense. Why on earth couldn't Henry have given me some clue? To say, in a somewhat shocked voice, that the subject was unsuitable for relaying over the telephone system, was to bring to mind the worst excesses known to man. What had Henry discovered in our midst? Murder, mayhem, illegitimacy, fraud, bigamy? My mind ranged over all as I tidied away piles of marking, and took out the dead flowers, which I had intended to remove throughout the evening.

It was too bad of Henry to keep me dangling like this, I thought, even if it were for only half an hour. I recalled the poor young wives in war time who were only told that their husbands were missing, and no further word was given to them, often for months or years. One in particular I remembered, who wailed tragically, saying: 'I'd sooner know Bob was *dead*, than not know *anything*!'

There had been looks of horror and disgust at this *cri de coeur*, but she had my entire sympathy.

By the time I had faced a raving lunatic at large in the village, various fatal accidents, unspecified incurable diseases with which the Mawnes had been afflicted and which involved asking me for advice, a court case against me for maltreating a child – a clear case here of guilty conscience, as I had administered a sharp slap to Patrick's leg when he had attempted to kick one of the infants – and a number of other unpleasant contingencies, the doorbell rang, and I hastened to admit my tormentor.

To my chagrin, he looked remarkably calm and happy, the maddening fellow.

'Do sit down,' I said, trying to appear equally at ease. 'Now how can I help?'

'It's about Simon,' he said, coming with admirable brevity to the nub of the matter. 'Trouble at home again.'

'I'm sorry to hear it.'

'Teresa's had a pretty frightening attack. David came home to find her tearing up everything she could lay hands on. Flowers, Simon's toys, David's books! Ghastly! The worst of it was that poor Simon couldn't get out of the room, and had to watch it all. David feels sure that she might have attacked the boy if he hadn't arrived in time.'

'So what has happened to her?'

'She's back in the nursing home. I honestly don't know if it's the right place for her, but at least she's safe for the moment, and so are David and Simon. The thing is, we've offered to have the child again, and I wondered if you could possibly admit him to the school for an unspecified period?'

'No bother at all,' I assured him. 'We'd like to have him, and he knows some of the other children. He'll soon settle, I'm sure.'

Henry sighed gustily.

'Well, that's a relief. I promised David that I would speak to you and ring him tonight. How soon can he be admitted?'

'As soon as you like.'

Henry rose, and shook my hand warmly.

'I'm so very grateful. It will be a weight off David's mind. He's due to go to Holland on a business trip of some importance to the firm, and I hope he can still make it. This will help enormously.'

I accompanied him to the door. He was still profuse in his thanks.

I returned exhausted to the sitting-room, and collapsed upon the newly plumped cushions.

'Tibby,' I said to the cat, 'there's a lot to be said for casting your burdens, as long as you are not on the receiving end.'

Mrs Pringle's temper improved with the weather, I was thankful to note. She was even heard to sing, in a deep lowing contralto, as she washed up the dinner plates.

'Glad to see the back of that cold weather,' she admitted. 'I'm thinking we could just about do without the stoves. Wicked to burn fuel when there's no need.'

'I think we'll see how we go until next week,' I said hastily. 'The wind is still quite sharp.'

'Well, we'll wait and see then,' said Mrs Pringle, with unusual docility. 'But the Office won't like it if we wants more coke this term.'

At that moment, the white robin flew down to the tin of mealworms, snatched up a beakful and flew off to my garden.

'The babies are hatched,' said Mrs Pringle.

'How d'you know?'

'I heard them.'

'Heard them? When?'

Mrs Pringle looked slightly abashed.

'Last evening. I come up with some fresh tea towels, and you was on the phone, otherwise I'd have knocked. I felt I must have a peep.'

'Oh, Mrs Pringle! And you know how we've threatened the children about frightening them!'

Mrs Pringle drew herself up huffily, and her face resumed its normal expression of dudgeon.

'Well, I never *looked*. Wasn't no need. Just as I was creeping up to the nest, old Snowboy flew in, and I could hear them youngsters twittering. Sweetly pretty it sounded, I can tell you.'

'That's marvellous news,' I cried, relief flooding me. 'I must let Mr Mawne know.'

'You needn't bother. I told him myself as I went

back home,' said Mrs Pringle, sweeping out majestically.

How is it that that woman always has the last word?

Henry brought Simon to school on the following Monday morning.

The child looked peaky, with dark smudges under his eyes, but he seemed glad to be with us, and I put him to sit next to Ernest, who is a kindly child and enjoys looking after people and animals.

Henry was profuse in his thanks as I accompanied him into the lobby.

'I'm glad to have him,' I assured him. 'How is his mother?'

'Much the same. Elizabeth is visiting her today, and intends to give her news of Simon, but I doubt if she'll be interested. It's a difficult case. Even the doctors admit that, and heaven alone knows where it will all end.'

'Well, you can do no more than you are doing, and at least you have the comfort of knowing she's in safe hands.'

'That's true, as far as it goes. But is *safety* enough? We all want to see her restored to normal mental health, with the usual maternal feelings, and pleasure in family life. But can this nursing home do that? That's what worries me. Are we any nearer curing mental illnesses than we were when the poor things were carted off to the local Bedlam?'

'Of course we are,' I said stoutly, trying to rally the unhappy man. 'I should think more advances have been made in that field than in any other. I'm sure you'll see progress in a week or two's time.'

Henry Mawne shook his head sadly, and made no reply, but clanked across the door scraper and set off towards home. Watching his departing figure, it occurred to me that my old friend had aged suddenly in the past few months, and I could only hope that Simon's mother would improve rapidly before the strain disrupted her family still further.

CHAPTER SEVEN

A Tragedy

May arrived, serene and sunny. There were no 'rough winds to shake the darling buds', and the late narcissi and tulips stood up straight as soldiers in the sunshine.

The children came to school in summer frocks and tee-shirts. The stoves were empty, and polished to jet black for the summer season. Woe betide anyone dropping pencil parings or toffee papers behind the glossy bars of the fire guard! Mrs Pringle intended her handiwork to remain unsullied for several months. An occasional dusting, or a little light attention with dustpan and soft brush was all that should be needed now that her arch-enemy, the coke, was not in evidence.

There was plenty of activity in my box hedge. Snowboy and his mate flew in and out a hundred times a day, and the twittering grew stronger. We all resisted the temptation to peep, but Henry Mawne had a quick look, pronounced that there were definitely four babies, and that they would be out of the nest within the week.

He did not have time to dally on this occasion as he was expecting a telephone call, but I went with him to the gate, and watched him enter the car.

'Any white ones?' I called.

'Of course not,' said Henry, quite snappily, and it dawned on me that probably everyone in Fairacre asked him the same question, despite his reiteration of the fact that we could not expect any albinos in this year's broods.

At the end of May we had our first view of the babies. They were fluttering after Snowboy in the empty playground, clamouring to be fed. I saw them from the schoolroom window, and debated whether I should let the children know the good news. I decided that I would risk opening the door very gently, so that the class could see the family at a distance.

They were so breathlessly quiet you could have heard the proverbial pin drop. One or two stood up at the back of the room to get a better view, but I was touched by their intent silence and look of wonder on their faces.

After a minute or two, the white robin fluttered away towards my garden, followed by his four vociferous youngsters. His anxious mate met him halfway, and together they shepherded their family towards their home.

Very gently I closed the door.

'Ain't that *nice*!' said Patrick with immense satisfaction.

There was a chorus of agreement, and then Eileen spoke.

'But no white ones.'

There was a general sigh.

'You'd think there'd be *one*!' said Ernest sadly.

'Well, you know what Mr Mawne told us,' I reminded them. 'We might get some next year.'

'My Uncle Henry,' said Simon, in his high polite voice which contrasted so noticeably with his companions' country burr, 'says he's bloody tired of trying to explain just that.'

We were all so taken aback at his casual use of a swear word that he went unreprimanded.

'Very understandable,' I said at last. 'Now take out your atlases, and turn to map eighteen.'

*

As the summer term progressed, I observed Simon with considerable interest.

He was certainly gaining strength, and seemed much more at ease, although he remained pale and did not seem to put on weight.

He seemed attached to Ernest, his desk mate, and Ernest obviously looked upon our visitor as his special charge, but the rest of the children did not seem to accept the boy completely. I put it down to inbred country suspicion of anything foreign, and realised that I could do little about it except to see that no antagonism was shown towards him.

In some ways Simon was admired. For one thing, he was always immaculately dressed, and his fair hair beautifully trimmed. Also he was quiet – almost laconic – in his conversations with his fellows. Only once did I see the flash of temper about which Henry Mawne had spoken. Someone knocked over his paint water, by accident, ruining his picture. Simon flew at the child, his eyes blazing, but luckily his victim had retreated rapidly and in good order, and nothing worse ensued.

He was also in some demand when it came to team games, for he had an unerring aim, and as a fielder could knock down a wicket at a considerable distance when we played our rudimentary cricket or rounders in Mr Roberts' field. The vicar had presented the school with a set of deck quoits some years earlier and at Simon's plea these were dug out of the cupboard and used at playtime. The base was set up some distance from the birds' mealworm tin, a chalk line drawn for the competitors, and this game, which had been unused for a long time, now found fresh favour in the summer sunshine.

I was particularly pleased about this, as it kept the children from the alternative attraction of scaling the coke pile, and also from the dark overgrown corner where a number of young birds were making their first forays.

As for Simon, it gave him an extra chance to shine, and I felt sure that this was an excellent thing to help him back to a normal life. The news from home, I gathered from the Mawnes, was dispiriting. Teresa remained in the nursing home, David struggled along on his own, his wife's treatment was hideously expensive and very little progress towards recovery seemed to have been made.

I felt extremely sorry for all of them. The Mawnes looked exhausted. They were not used to children in the house, and of course they were over anxious about young Simon. It could not have been easy for the child either. The Mawnes' house was full of exquisite furniture and expensive carpets, and a boy, even one as comparatively docile as young Simon, must have been a hazard among their treasures.

He had no other child to play with during the long light evenings. The Mawnes did not seem to think of inviting others as companions, or perhaps they felt that they could not face the responsibility. I wished that some of the parents would ask the child to play with their own, but the fact that Simon was staying at 'the big house' may have made them shy of offering an invitation.

The result was that the boy was definitely lonely. I noticed an odd streak in his character, as the time passed. He was easily made jealous.

If I praised someone's drawing, Simon would thrust his own before me. If I singled out one child to be a monitor, Simon would cast a look of bitter loathing in my direction. It was a difficult situation, and ignoring it was not enough, I felt.

Here was a damaged child who had watched his mad mother destroy his treasures before his eyes. He had been the object of her resentment and hatred. Was it any wonder that he too resented anything which drew praise and attention away from himself?

On the other hand, I could not afford to show favouritism, and justice must be done to my permanent pupils. I was particularly anxious that no resentment towards the newcomer should build up. They were a friendly and tolerant collection of children, but one could not expect them to put up with flashes of bad temper.

One instance had put me on my guard. Patrick had drawn a splendid map of Fairacre, a perfect riot of colour, and his industry had earned it pride of place on the wall. Inexplicably, it was found torn in half on the floor. No one would own up to its damage, and as Patrick seemed quite happy when we had mended it with adhesive tape, the matter was dropped, but I felt pretty sure that this was Simon's doing. I sensed too, that the children suspected him. Although this particular cloud blew over, I could not see many such incidents occurring without some retaliation. I could only hope for calm weather ahead.

We continued to see the robin family about, sometimes in the playground, but more often in my garden at the school house.

One unforgettable moment for me came one summer evening when I was washing up at the kitchen sink, and watching through the window the coming and going of blackbirds, thrushes, greenfinches, and a host of tits. The garden seemed full of activity, when suddenly the white robin appeared and perched on a branch of an old plum tree some yards from the window.

The ancient gnarled bark had exuded a sizeable drop of golden resin, over the last few months, and this was illuminated by the rays of the sunset, glowing like some precious bead of amber.

It exactly matched the colour of the robin's red breast, fiery against the purity of its white feathers. The two spots of warm ambience were a joy to see, one enhancing the other, until the bird flew off again with a whirring of snowy wings, and only the glowing gum remained to remind me of it.

By July the weather was really hot, and we were all beginning to long for some rain for our parched gardens. The children found the heat trying at midday, and I had to shift my desk from under the direct rays of sunshine through the skylight.

The shady corner abutting on to the vicar's wall became a popular spot to play, and the deck quoits were shifted into the shady part of the playground.

Quite a number of the children elected to take a book under the trees which border the field next to the school during their dinner hour, for the unusual heat did not encourage them to race about in their normal fashion.

Simon, with his fair colouring, seemed to feel the heat more than most of his companions, and moved restlessly about in his desk, sighing at intervals.

One brilliant morning of exceptional heat, he was more fidgety than usual. The schoolroom door was propped open to get any air available, and the children had a clear view of the mealworm tin.

Now that the young birds appeared to be capable of looking for their own food, there were fewer visitors to the tin, but the white robin still made occasional trips, and this morning I realised from the sudden cessation of my class's activities and the rapt attention on their faces that he had arrived several times.

When Simon asked to be excused I was glad to let him go. A walk across the playground might make him settle to his work more readily when he returned.

He was gone for some time. In his absence, the robin must have come once more to the tin, for the children's pens remained poised, and their eyes were fixed on the playground.

Suddenly, there was a sharp cry from Ernest and a horrified gasp from the class at large. To my astonishment, the children rose as one man and surged towards the door, with Ernest in the lead. I leapt forward to see what was going on.

There, at the side of the tin, lay the white robin, a

deck quoit hard by. In the shade, near the lavatories, stood Simon, another quoit like a bracelet on his arm. He stood absolutely still, white and shaken, but there was a gleam in his blue eyes which, to my mind, showed triumph.

It was Ernest who picked up the robin. He passed it to me, but continued to stroke the beautiful feathers. It was plain that the bird's neck was broken. Its tiny body lay warm and pathetic in the palm of my hand,

and the children stood close to me, their faces anguished and their eyes fixed upon their dead friend.

It was Ernest who broke the silence with a most appalling howling noise. The tears burst from his eyes and sobs racked his body.

The sight of Ernest, the biggest, the calmest, the most reliable boy in the school, reduced to such a state seemed to galvanise the rest of them into action. They turned towards Simon and surrounded him before I had time to reach the child.

When I saw their faces, contorted with fury, I realised how a mob bent upon lynching must look.

For one moment, I feared that I had lost control of my children, but pushing between them, still holding the dead bird, I ordered them to go into school.

They hardly heard me at first, so intent were they upon wreaking vengeance, but gradually one or two began to make their way to the schoolroom door. There were tears on most cheeks now, and I looked at Simon.

He was dry eyed, but obviously terror stricken. As I watched him, he took a deep shuddering breath, and slipped to the ground in a dead faint.

At that moment, the infants' teacher appeared, alerted by the fracas.

'Settle them inside,' I begged her, 'and then come and help me with the boy.'

Five minutes later, Simon was lying on my couch in the school house. The white robin lay motionless on the window sill, its dead red breast aflame in the sunshine.

My assistant had returned to her double duty, and I went to the telephone.

'Henry,' I said when Mr Mawne answered, 'we are in terrible trouble here. Can you come at once?'

CHAPTER EIGHT

Fairacre Mourns

I was extremely sorry to have to add to the Mawnes' worries, and waited for Henry's arrival with considerable agitation.

I had explained briefly on the telephone about the sad event. It was going to hit Henry doubly hard, I was afraid, both on Simon's account and the rare albino robin's.

The boy still lay listlessly on the couch, his small hands folded on his chest. They looked too fragile to have dealt that deadly blow which would soon shatter the joy of Fairacre.

The crunch of tyres on gravel announced Henry's arrival. I went to meet him, lifting the pathetic corpse from the window sill, and putting it into the patch pocket of my cotton frock.

Henry looked even more shaken than young Simon. I took him to the boy's couch. Henry touched the pale hair gently.

'Feeling better?'

The boy shook his head, and his mouth began to quiver. It might be a good thing, I thought, if the tears of remorse came now. But the child remained dry eyed and silent.

'Come and have a look at the garden,' I said to Henry, 'while Simon's resting.'

I took him out of earshot. We sat on the garden seat, out of Simon's sight, and I withdrew the little corpse from my pocket.

Henry took it in his hands very tenderly. He seemed considerably closer to weeping than the boy we had left indoors.

'I wouldn't have had this happen for all the tea in China,' he muttered. 'And to think Simon did it! It makes it so much more horrible. Tell me what happened.'

I explained, while Henry nodded thoughtfully.

'He's an uncanny shot,' he said, 'and that allied to his unpredictable temper makes him a dangerous child, I fear.'

He sighed heavily.

'Sometimes I think he's abnormal. Like his poor mother.'

'He's only abnormal in that he's badly hurt just now. He'll grow out of these tantrums. At the moment he craves attention. That accounts for these violent flashes of jealousy – envy of any child who gets more than he does, and envy of any other object, even an innocent robin, if it is admired.'

'You're kind,' said Henry, 'but I'm past comfort at the moment.'

He held out the robin to me.

'I'll put it in the garden shed, and bury it later on,' I said. 'I've no doubt the children will want to know what's happened to it, but I'm sure none of us can face a harrowing bird funeral, which one or two might favour.'

We walked together through the sunlit garden.

'But what's to be done?' asked Henry. 'The boy can't stay at school, obviously. When does term end?'

'In less than two weeks. And I must say, I think you're right about keeping Simon out of the way of the other children. They are an easy-going lot normally, but this has upset them dreadfully, and I wouldn't like to answer for the consequences. Besides, the child needs rest – nursing, one might almost say. If you and Elizabeth can manage it, I should think he would soon recover with you. I take it David can't have him?'

'Impossible at the moment, and Teresa is no better. She gets these destructive moods, I gather, and they are having to treat her with some sort of tranquillisers. She's done a lot of damage to her room.'

He sighed again, and I felt helpless to comfort him.

Truth to tell, I was in a state of shock myself, and was doing my best to control involuntary trembling.

'What an unhappy family!' cried Henry. 'Well, we must do what we can. Thank God, the child goes to prep school in September. He needs an entirely fresh start.'

'He can rest here for another hour or two, if you like,' I offered.

'No, no. You have been more than kind, but you have all the other children to see to. It's a sad day for them all. I'll take Simon back in the car, and we'll get him to bed, and call the doctor. I must get in touch with David tonight when he gets home. Poor boy! He has nothing but trouble.'

Simon was still prone on the couch when we entered, but sat up when Henry said they would be going home.

He was still pale, and seemed shaky as he accompanied his uncle to the door.

He said no word until he reached the car. Then he turned and proffered a small hand – the same hand that had killed our dear robin. I took it in mine.

'Thank you for looking after me,' he said politely, and then clambered in beside Henry.

I watched them drive away. Was that the last I should see of poor young Simon, I wondered?

Well, he was in safe hands, I told myself, and there were others to try and comfort now.

I returned to school with a heavy heart.

The news of the robin's death upset the inhabitants of Fairacre far more severely than I had imagined.

Country people are attuned to violent ends among animals, and can meet these tragedies with stoical calm. But somehow, the white robin had meant more to them than just another garden bird.

I think that the fact that it had created so much interest in the wider world, after Henry's article and the television programme, made the Fairacre folk intensely proud of their rare visitor. Of course they were genuinely fond of the albino – their doting looks and eager enquiries were proof of that – but without Henry's enthusiasm their interest would have been less keen.

How much he meant was brought home to me sharply by seeing, for the first time, tears in Mrs Pringle's normally stony eyes. I felt profoundly shocked. She had ministered to the bird right from the start, zealously bringing the mealworms he so enjoyed, but I had not realised how devoted she had been to him.

The children were inconsolable, and surprisingly mild in their remarks about Simon's part in the tragedy. Had he been present it might have been a different story, and I was glad that he was safely at the Mawnes'. I had not forgotten the ugly scene immediately after the bird's death.

I was relieved too that they did not demand a funeral for the bird, and accepted the fact that I had buried the corpse near the box hedge. But when Ernest arrived one morning with a somewhat rickety wooden cross bearing the words:

OUR SNOWBOY

and pleaded for it to be erected on the grave, I had not the heart to refuse. If it gave the children some comfort, then why not?

About a week after the sad event, Amy rang up. She too had heard about the albino bird. News travels fast in the country, I know, but I was surprised that it had travelled so far and so quickly.

'I don't know why you should be,' said Amy, when I remarked on it. 'My window cleaner has connections with Fairacre, and he keeps me up to date with the news. What a horrible shock for you all. What happened?'

I told her, my tongue loosened by her unexpected sympathy. Amy had treated our absorbed interest in the bird with some amusement. I think she felt we were somewhat ridiculous, but now that disaster had come she could not have been kinder.

'Heavens! That makes the whole affair much worse. May I tell Irene Umbleditch?'

'Who?' I said, bewildered.

'You know,' said Amy impatiently. 'You met her brother Horace here.'

'Sorry, sorry! The organist, of course. I remember he mentioned a sister who knew Simon.'

'Well, she's staying with her brother at the moment, and he is standing in for your organist next Sunday, and I said I'd drive him over this evening to try the organ. He's picking up the key from Mr Annett at Beech Green as we come through. It's such a lovely evening, I thought Irene might enjoy the drive too. Can we call to see you?'

'Please do. And certainly tell her if you want to. It's

no secret, I'm afraid, but the child is being kept well away from everyone until his father can collect him.'

'Best thing to do,' said Amy heartily. 'He'd probably be torn limb from limb if he encountered any of your pupils in the village.'

I was about to protest indignantly at this slight on my children, but Amy cut me short.

'See you later then,' she said, and rang off.

I took to Irene Umbleditch as soon as we met. She was small and plump with soft dark hair. No one could call her pretty, but she had a sweetness of expression, and a low musical voice which made her instantly attractive.

We women were left together when Horace departed towards the church, and we wandered round the garden enjoying the warm evening air.

Irene stopped by Ernest's lop-sided cross, and looked enquiringly at me.

'Are they still upset?'

'I'm afraid so. Nothing quite so tearful as when it first happened, but they often mention the robin, and I know they have great hopes of another white one some day.'

'And Simon?'

'They hardly mention him.'

'I meant do you see anything of him? I know he's still with his Uncle Henry.'

'Oh, now and again. He doesn't look very happy, but one could never call the child robust.'

She nodded.

'I should very much like to see him. We always got

on well when I did a little baby-minding for Teresa and David. Perhaps Horace would let me call while I'm staying with him.'

'Why not see if they are free this evening?' suggested Amy.

'Let's ring up,' I said. 'I expect Simon's still up on a lovely evening like this, and if not you can arrange another meeting.'

Irene looked a little hesitant, but finally agreed, and we went indoors.

'Shall I get the number?' I asked. Since the tragedy, I had become only too familiar with it.

'Please,' said Irene.

Henry answered. He sounded somewhat bewildered.

'Sorry, I can't hear properly. This line's poor. Just a minute while I put on my spectacles. I always hear better when I'm wearing them.'

I waited patiently, listening to various clicks and mutters as the search went on. At last he spoke again.

'Right! Who did you say?'

'Miss Umbleditch wants to speak to you. She's here with me.'

'Miss Umbleditch? Oh, *Irene*! Good, put her on, please.'

I handed over the instrument with some relief, and rejoined Amy in the garden.

'She's a nice woman,' I remarked.

'Very. Must have been much appreciated when she was a nanny.'

'Why? Isn't she one now?'

'I know she's looking for a permanency in the near

future, but I gather she gave up when old Mrs Umble-ditch became senile, and stayed with her. She died last month, I'm told, so now Irene's free to find another job.'

We sat on the garden seat in companionable silence. The rooks were flying homeward, and far away some sheep bleated. It was all very peaceful. A heavenly smell of roses and pinks wafted around us, and some-where, far above, a late lark carolled away before going to bed. How lovely to live in Fairacre, I thought, for the umpteenth time! I never wanted to leave it, and with any luck I could be transported the few yards from the school house to the nearby graveyard with the minimum of fuss.

I was indulging myself with pleasantly melancholy thoughts of a few sorrowing pupils following my coffin, and trying to decide if it should be a spring or autumn occasion (I was jolly well not going to peg out in high summer!), and had already settled for *Ye Holy Angels Bright* as a good rousing hymn, when Irene returned from the telephone.

'I've said I'll walk down immediately,' she said, her eyes were bright. 'I had a word with Simon too. It was lovely to hear him.'

'I'll run you down,' said Amy, overcoming polite protests. 'You don't know where they live.'

'Well, I'll walk back. Horace should be finished within the hour.'

It was settled that we would all meet again for a drink at my house, and I went to get a tray ready while Amy and Irene departed. On the way, I picked up the heavy china Gentleman's Relish jar which had held the mealworms for Snowboy and his friends. I had put it on the window ledge on the day of the tragedy, but it was in a precarious position there, and would be safer put away in the garden cupboard.

Would it ever be used again, I wondered, as I rinsed it under the tap? I did not intend to leave it in the playground. The school bird table, and my own, would provide adequate feeding space, and the white china pot was too poignant a reminder of our lost robin.

A wave of indignation assailed me as the tap ran. That damned boy! Why should we all have been robbed of our lovely bird? And why should the bird itself have been robed of its joy in flight, in exploring the hedges and gardens of Fairacre, and its growing pleasure in its human friends? Really, it struck at the very roots of justice, I told myself crossly.

Ah well, I sighed, replacing the pot on its allotted shelf, it's an unfair world!

The sound of Amy's car returning brought me back to my immediate duties, and I fetched the tray.

There was a beautiful sunset as we sipped our drinks.

Horace was enthusiastic about the organ at Fairacre church, but doubtful about the organ blower in the vestry.

'If it was Ernest,' I told him, 'he will be absolutely reliable.'

'No, this one was called Patrick,' said Horace. 'Ernest was having his hair cut, but will be there on Sunday.'

'Then you have nothing to fear,' I assured him.

'And how did you find Simon?' enquired Horace of his sister.

She turned from admiring the sunset, still dazzled by the blaze across the sky.

'Very sweet, but not well at all. As a matter of fact, I may as well tell you now, I've offered to look after him until he starts school in September.'

Her brother looked startled.

'But what about the jobs you were applying for?'

'They can wait,' said his sister calmly.

'I'm sure the Mawnes would be much relieved,' I ventured.

'Oh, nothing's definite yet. David will have to make the decision, of course. I think Mr Mawne will be in touch with him this evening, but that child wants looking after.'

'You're right about that,' I said.

And no one, I thought privately, is better able to do it than Irene Umbleditch.

CHAPTER NINE

A Second Shock

Term ended a day or two after the visit of the Umbleditch pair, and I went away almost immediately.

A favourite aunt of mine lives in Dorset, and I was with her for three weeks, relishing her astringent views on life in general, and trying to keep up with her outstanding physical energy. Although she is in her seventies she gardens, walks and cycles, chattering the while, and is game for a brisk hand of whist or bridge until midnight. My own life at Fairacre seemed a rest cure in contrast.

Things seemed remarkably quiet when I returned and, of course, I knew nothing of the result of Irene Umbleditch's offer to the Mawnes. I did not have to wait long.

One of my first jobs was to go to the post office and the village shop. The morning was young and dewy. Later it would be really hot, I noted with satisfaction, but the freshness of the morning air brought out goose pimples on my bare arms, as I made my way through the village.

Outside the post office Henry Mawne's car was standing, and inside sat Elizabeth. She looked very smart in navy blue with a moiré silk turban to match.

'We're just off to catch the 9.45,' she said, glancing

at her watch, 'but I wish Henry would hurry. As usual, we discovered at the last minute that we had about ten pence in the house, so he has just gone to ask Mr Lamb to cash a cheque.'

'You've chosen a nice day for a spree,' I said.

'No spree unfortunately. Far from it, in fact. David rang last night. His wife died suddenly.'

'No! How dreadful!'

'Luckily, Irene is looking after Simon, so that should help.'

At this point, Henry emerged, stuffing notes into his wallet and looking agitated.

'Don't dare stop,' he called, struggling with his seat belt. 'Got to catch the train.'

With a roar they were off to Caxley, and I went into the post office to buy stamps.

Mr Lamb was alone, and looking unusually grave.

'Heard the news, I suppose?'

'Mrs Mawne told me that Teresa Mawne had died.'

'Did she tell you how?'

'Well, no.'

'Threw herself off the roof of that nursing home evidently.'

'Threw herself?' I echoed aghast.

'Mr Mawne said she's been very violent of late. Seems she broke away from her nurse, rushed up to this roof garden place, nipped over the railings and dropped.'

We gazed at each other in shocked silence.

'Best thing really,' said Mr Lamb at last.

'But ghastly for the family.'

'It is now. But won't be in the long run. There was

no future for that poor soul anyway. She was bound to come to some violent end. Had it written in her face.'

This was so close to my own private feelings that I could find nothing to say.

'And what can I do for you?' enquired Mr Lamb, resuming his usual brisk manner.

I told him, and watched him tearing out the stamps with his deft careful fingers. How comforting everyday jobs were in times of shock!

We wished each other goodbye, and I continued on my way to the grocer's in more sober mood.

I was careful to say nothing about the Mawnes' loss. As far as I knew, only they, Mr Lamb and I had heard about Teresa's death. If suicide were the cause, then the family might well wish the matter to be kept quiet. No doubt young Simon would be kept in the dark about this aspect of the tragedy. He would be hard enough hit, in any case, by the loss of his mother, little though she had contributed to the child's happiness.

But, versed in the ways of village communication, I was not surprised to hear from Mr Willet that Teresa's end was common knowledge in the community. Well, I thought, at least the news wasn't leaked by me.

Mr Willet had offered to take some geranium cuttings for me and 'to bring 'em on at home', for which I was sincerely grateful. He visited me, sharp knife in hand, one afternoon towards the end of the holidays.

'She was a poor tool, that one,' remarked Mr Willet, referring to David's late wife. 'He got caught in a tangle of fair hair when he was young. Not the first neither. Blondes has a way with 'em. Still, it's sad to see her end this way.'

I agreed, watching Mr Willet's horny hand holding the geraniums aside with great delicacy as he searched for suitable cuttings.

'Can't wonder that boy turned out such a varmint,' he went on conversationally. 'If I'd have been there when our robin was killed I'd have given that boy the biggest larruping of his borns.'

'He fainted as it was,' I protested.

'Ah! And he'd have fainted a damn sight quicker with me around! What about the other kids? They were upset enough, in all conscience! I bet they'd have set about him proper if you hadn't been there. We hear 'em, my missus and me, still talking about their Snowboy. It was a cruel wicked thing to do, and they don't forget it. Come to that, neither do us old 'uns.'

'We all miss him,' I said, 'but there was no point in letting the school run riot once the deed was done.'

'All I can say is, I hope that blessed boy don't show his face in Fairacre no more. We've seen enough of that one. I'm sorry about his ma, of course, but that don't alter what he done. I can't bring meself to forgive him, that I can't.'

'I thought you were a Christian,' I said.

'Well, I may be. But I'm what they call a militant one,' replied Mr Willet, snipping energetically.

'Do militant Christians drink tea?' I asked.

Mr Willet smiled.

'Try 'em,' he said.

*

A few evenings later, Amy called in to tell me about an organ recital being given by Horace Umbleditch to raise funds for Bent church.

'It's the roof fund again,' said Amy, accepting a glass of sherry. 'We hover between the roof and the organ at Bent. If it's not one cracking up, it's the other.'

She surveyed her sherry with approval.

'You didn't win this at a fête,' she commented. 'What happened to the cough linctus?'

'You hogged most of that,' I told her. 'I was driven to spending my hard-earned cash on a bottle of Harvey's.'

'Well, you couldn't have done better,' said Amy kindly. 'Have I told you the latest about Horace?'

I hoped she was not going to tell me more about Teresa Mawne. It was time the poor soul was left in peace, I felt.

'What about him?' I said cautiously. Amy had that speculative look in her eye, which I know from experience goes with her match-making efforts.

'He's moving into a house at the school.'

'What school?'

Amy tut-tutted testily.

'The school he works at! Surely you knew he was the music master at Maytrees?'

'The first I've heard of it.'

'Rubbish! I'm sure I told you *all* about him when he first came to Bent.'

'Honestly, I had no idea he taught. I just thought he was the organist at your church.'

'And very fat he'd get on *that* salary,' said Amy. 'Of course he had to have a job somewhere, and I'm sure I told you all about it. You don't listen half the time.'

'Well, I will now,' I said magnanimously. 'Fire away! So he teaches at Maytrees Prep School, and is going to live there.'

'That's right. There wasn't a house available in the grounds when he was appointed, which is why he had to go into those wretched digs. But now the classics man has retired and there's a nice little house free.'

'Good. More sherry?'

'You'd like it there,' said Amy.

'I'm not likely to be asked to visit very often, I imagine.'

Amy sighed.

'I wish you weren't so *prickly*. Here's a very nice young man – well, perhaps not *young*, but quite spry – and I really think he would like to be married—'

'Amy,' I broke in, 'you are nothing but a meddlesome busybody! How do you know he wants to get married? Like me, he's probably perfectly happy as he is. And in any case, there are lots of more suitable candidates for the honour if he is intending matrimony.'

'Hoity-toity!' cried Amy. 'Very well, I promise never to mention marriage again!'

'Thank God!' I replied.

'But you will come and have a drink before the recital?' said Amy, picking up her bag. 'Horace will be there, of course, and our new doctor who is quite devastatingly good looking, and needs *friends*.'

'Thank you, Amy,' I said resignedly.

During the summer, the bird tables had been less used, but at the beginning of September an unusually chilly spell of weather brought some of our friends back, including several young robins.

The children showed their usual interest, and not surprisingly the name of Snowboy cropped up frequently.

They mourned the beautiful bird with genuine sorrow. He had been a rare and exciting visitor. The mere fact that he had been with us for a comparatively short spell made the memory of him doubly dear. The violence of his end made that memory doubly poignant.

As well as remarks about the dead robin, both verbal and written, there were innumerable pictures made, and even one or two poems. I had tried not to encourage too much harping on our lost albino, hoping that the children's natural exuberance would lessen their grief as the weeks went by, but on the other hand, it seemed to give them some comfort to remember him in various ways, and I thought it best to let the subject wear itself out naturally.

The weather helped. September developed into a warm golden period. With the harvest in, the farmers were busy ploughing, with a retinue of gulls and rooks following the lengthening chocolate-brown furrows.

The children played outside day after day, and our nature walks became more frequent. Before long, the winds of autumn and blizzards of winter would keep us confined within the ancient walls of the little school. We might as well get all the fresh air and exercise while we could, I felt.

This halcyon spell pleased Mrs Pringle too. The floors kept cleaner than usual, and the lighting of the tortoise stoves could be postponed, saving work in bringing in coke from the playground to feed the monsters. She became positively mellow, and I wondered privately if she were sickening for something.

She even offered to come and clean the windows of the school house one evening, and told me the Fairacre news as I rewarded her efforts with a cup of strong tea.

After a brief survey of the vicar's recent bout of indigestion ('Too much lardy cake for his age'), her niece Minnie's indisposition ('Another baby on the way') and the aggravating habits of her immediate neighbour ('Dragged up in the slums of London, so what could you expect?'), she turned to the young slayer of our lamented robin.

'Never could take to that boy,' said Mrs Pringle. 'Sly! Couldn't trust him, I always said. Looked as though butter wouldn't melt in his mouth, and then he done a wicked thing like that.'

'He'd had a pretty raw deal one way and another,' I pointed out.

'So what? I gets tired of people making excuses for other folks' wicked ways. When I was a girl there was Right and Wrong, and you got a good hiding if you Done Wrong, and not much praise if you Done Right! You should've Done Right anyway, was how my ma and pa looked at it!'

'But things aren't quite as simple as that,' I began, but Mrs Pringle ignored me. You might just as well try to dam the River Thames with a matchstick as to stop Mrs Pringle's flow when she is in full spate.

'But nowadays no one Does Wrong, as far as I can make out. Look at that Mrs Coggs as was had up for stealing. What happened to her? "More to be pitied than blamed," everyone said. "Her with her blackguard of a husband and all them kids, and not very bright up top to begin with." Excuses, excuses! It ends up with no one reckoning to pay the price for Doing Wrong. We've got free will, ain't we? What's to stop us choosing Right? I gets proper fed up with all this namby-pamby way of going on.'

I must admit that a great deal of Mrs Pringle's

forthright arguments appealed to me, but I did not intend to say so.

'In Simon's case, his poor mother's illness definitely had an effect on him.'

'Maybe. But he's got a good dad, and a grown-up sister and two brothers. They could've helped, I should've thought.'

'I don't think they were at home then,' I said.

'No, they weren't. I taxed Mr Mawne with it one morning when I met him in the street.'

Trust our Mrs Pringle, I thought.

'Them Mawnes are too old to cope with a young boy. I told him so, and he said there wasn't no one else really free. The sister's married and lives in New Zealand, and one boy's in the army and pushed from pillar to post, as you might say, while I forget now where the younger one is. Cambridge, perhaps, or Oxford, or one of those college places where they idle away their time till they're too old to learn anything.'

I let this trenchant criticism of our revered universities pass without comment. I was still admiring Mrs Pringle's successful attempts to elicit information from her victims.

'Anyway,' continued my informant, struggling to her feet, 'it's a good thing that Miss Umblethingummy's taken on the child. Them Mawnes were at the end of their tether, and she looks capable of giving that young man a walloping when it's called for. Though no doubt she lets him get away with murder, like the rest of these folk who should know better!'

She gave me a dark look, summing up, without

speech this time, her opinion of those in authority, particularly headmistresses, who let sinners go unpunished.

The organ recital took place at the end of September, and I drove to Amy's along lanes already beginning to take on the beauty of early autumn.

Sprays of glossy blackberries arched from the hedges, and the hazel nuts were plumping up. The lime trees were beginning to shed a few lemon-coloured leaves, and the apples were turning from green to rosy ripeness. It was a time of year when nature showed its kindly side, and the knowledge of winter to come could be comfortably shelved.

Amy's garden blazed with dahlias, and the house was beautifully decorated with bowls full of the velvety blossoms. About two dozen people stood about admiring them, drinks in hand, when I arrived, and among them was Irene Umbleditch.

I made my way towards her. Her brother, elegant as ever, was surrounded by a number of friends. It was quite apparent that Horace had soon found his feet, despite Amy's early solicitude on his behalf.

Of course I enquired about Simon.

'He's settled in fairly well at school,' said Irene. 'We took him down about ten days ago, and the matron has been very kind and kept us in the know. She was told about Teresa. It seemed only right, and I must say, she's a wonderfully motherly person, and Simon seems to have taken to her.'

'He's bright enough,' I said. 'Now that he's settled, he should do very well academically.'

I did not intend to mention the robin incident. It was over and done with, as far as I was concerned, but Irene herself brought up the subject.

'It was an appalling thing to happen,' she said, her face very grave. 'The other children must have suffered dreadfully. Do they still talk about it?'

'About the robin, yes. But they don't speak of Simon.'

'I wonder if they still hold it against him?'

I was torn between the truth and sparing this nice woman's feelings.

'Well,' I began, 'I know they bitterly resent what happened, and they hear their parents and other grown ups discussing the affair, of course. But they are pretty good tempered, and I don't think they bear much of a grudge against Simon now, although they did at the time.'

She nodded.

'He won't speak about it. Whether he'd be willing to come and visit Fairacre again, I don't know, but it certainly wouldn't be wise to try it yet.'

I agreed, and asked her what her plans were now that the boy was at school. Her face lit up.

'I'm taking new babies by the month,' she said. 'You know, from birth on for a few weeks. It's just temporary nursing, my favourite age, and I can fit in Simon's Christmas holidays then, and perhaps his Easter one, if he still needs me.'

'I'm sure his father is very grateful,' I hazarded.

'He can do with all the help he can get,' said Irene soberly. 'I don't think many men could have coped with such misery as bravely as he has.'

'Now, you must come and meet Doctor Manning,' said Amy, bustling up. 'In another half an hour we must make our way to the church. I really believe every seat will be taken. It augurs well for the roof fund, doesn't it?'

CHAPTER TEN

The Long Wait Over

Term rolled on. The usual autumn activities enlivened our school progress – harvest festival, the doctor's medical inspection and preparations for Christmas.

The glowing spell of weather broke at last to give several weeks of rough wind and driving rain. The bird tables were well patronised by chaffinches, greenfinches, blue tits, coal tits, marsh tits, and the ubiquitous sparrows and starlings.

The young robins now sported breasts almost as red as their older relatives, and were bold in coming to the table and looking out for any crumbs scattered by the children at playtime.

Since the advent and death of the albino bird the children took more notice of the robins, I thought. The hope of another white one in the spring was kindled anew as the time passed, and explained, in part, the extra cherishing that came the robins' way.

I mentioned this to Henry Mawne one cold January day when we met at a managers' meeting at the school.

'Well, don't raise their hopes too much,' he advised me. 'The chances are slight, you know. And I wonder if albino robins aren't better forgotten perhaps. A second tragedy would hurt them badly, and as you know, these albinos can get set upon pretty viciously by the normal birds.'

'Snowboy didn't,' I pointed out.

Henry sighed.

'No, I'm afraid he was set upon by the most vicious predator of all. Man has a lot to answer for.'

He looked so sad that I hastened to drop the subject, but bore his warning in mind.

He came back to the school house with me after the meeting, to collect some bird books I had borrowed.

'Simon all right?' I asked.

'Looking fine. We saw them over Christmas, you know. Seems to like his school, and had a cautiously optimistic report. The head's a kindly sort of chap, and knows about the boy's background. In fact, I told him about the robin. Perhaps I shouldn't have done, but he was such a sympathetic listener, I'm afraid I let it out.'

And probably did you a world of good to do so, I thought.

Aloud I said, 'What did he say?'

'Nothing. But he's going to put the boy in charge of the frogspawn, and I bet those tadpoles will be guarded against all comers.'

'He'll enjoy this term then. He's back, I suppose?'

'Yes, David and Irene took him down last week. That girl is an angel. She came in every day to look after things during the holiday, and it's made all the difference to the child. And to David,' he added, as though he had just realised it.

'I liked her enormously,' I said, 'and hope I shall see her again some time.'

'Won't be for a bit,' said Henry. 'She's off to a case at the end of the month, and thoroughly looking forward to it. Seems strange to me. New babies are so *unfinished*, aren't they?'

'No worse than newly hatched birds,' I said. 'They're positively *grisly* without feathers.'

A look which can only be described as maudlin spread over Henry's features.

'They're *perfect*,' he told me, and I did not contradict him.

Excitement began to mount towards the end of term as the nesting season began. I did my best to warn the children against over optimism, with Henry's words in mind, but I was up against fierce hope, and who could be too daunting after all that they had suffered?

We watched the robins in particular, of course. On two occasions we saw a female fluttering her wings and begging for food, while the male bird fed her attentively. We could not be sure if it was the same pair, but rather hoped that there were two couples. It doubled our chances.

The children were not alone in their hopes. Mrs Pringle had no doubt at all that we should have another albino this time.

'Very possibly two or more,' she pronounced, in the hearing of the children, which alarmed me slightly.

'You'd best get out that mealworm dish again,' she told me. 'Might as well do it now. Get 'em used to bringing their babies along.'

Mr Willet was equally positive.

'If it's happened once it'll happen again. Didn't Mr Mawne say so?'

I responded that Henry had warned us not to hope, but my fears were dismissed disdainfully.

Mr Lamb, Mr Partridge, the Misses Waters, the Hales, Miss Quinn, and in fact everyone in Fairacre, it seemed, awaited the arrival of another albino robin with supreme confidence. I trembled for them.

As far as I could make out, the robins were not nesting in my garden this spring. Henry Mawne had *carte blanche* to roam about it whenever he so wished, in his researches, but he agreed that there seemed to be no sign of a robin's nest, though he had discovered two blackbirds', a tit's and two thrushes' abodes.

The vicar's garden, he told me, seemed more promising, and the bosky corner near the lavatories was under his particular surveillance. I told the children about this, and they obligingly hurried from the lavatories and tried to resist the temptation of lingering in their favourite hiding place. Any embryo albino robin in our vicinity was getting every consideration.

In the end, Henry discovered two robins' nests. One was just over the dividing wall among the vicar's neglected weeds. The other at the far end of the vicar's garden towards the churchyard. We waited avidly for further developments.

Obediently I had put the Gentleman's Relish jar back in the playground, in full view of the class. Mrs Pringle kept it supplied with mealworms, and we had a generous number of bird visitors, including robins. Some days I refused to have the door propped open because of the draught, and the children eyed me resentfully on these occasions.

Their anxiety was summed up, I felt, by one brief incident. They were busy painting one afternoon and the room was blissfully quiet.

Patrick looked up from his work.

'What if we don't?' he enquired.

'Don't what?' I replied, connecting his remark with his artistic efforts.

'Get a white 'un,' he enlarged, ignoring his paint brush dripping wet paint.

As one man, the class rounded on this Doubting Thomas within their midst.

' 'Course we'll get one!'

'Maybe two. Mrs Pringle said so!'

'Shut up, you old misery!'

'Us had one before, didn't us? Well then!'

Patrick quailed before the onslaught, and I had to calm the rabble.

Peace was soon restored, but it was a startling display of undaunted hope. Would it be justified?

It was at the beginning of the summer term that the excitement became intense. Three young robins were seen by the mealworm dish being fed by their parents. Handsome though they were, they were welcomed with modified rapture by the children.

Could there be an albino among this brood which had not yet been seen? Had the second clutch hatched yet? Was there a white robin among it? How soon should we know the worst? Or best?

It was Mrs Partridge, the vicar's wife, who raised

our hopes to even more exalted heights. The vicar passed on the news to me in the lobby, shutting the classroom door with some care.

'I should be sorry to raise their hopes falsely,' he assured me, 'but my wife certainly had a glimpse of something white among those deplorable nettles by my compost heap. Of course, we're keeping a sharp watch from the hide. If only Henry were here!'

We all echoed the vicar's heartfelt cry. Everyone in Fairacre had been bitterly disappointed when Henry had been asked, at short notice, to take over another birdwatching expedition, this time to Turkey. Mrs Pringle, in particular, looked upon his departure as downright treachery.

'Should have thought his place was here with our robins,' she said, 'not gadding off to some foreign place where the birds can't understand the Queen's English.'

Her feelings were shared by all in Fairacre, but not so roundly expressed.

I returned to my children, surprised to find that I was trembling with excitement at the vicar's disclosure. Could it be? Could Mrs Partridge really have seen an albino robin? Or was it, as I had first thought on hearing of Helen Coggs's sighting of Snowboy, just a flutter of white paper or a nodding blossom?

The day was fine, and I propped open the door. The mealworms writhed in their unlovely way in the depths of the china pot. A robin came, dived in his beak, and flew off to feed his family.

The children were copying a notice from the blackboard. It was to be taken home, announcing the times of our school Open Days, and they were doing their best to write legibly, so that their parents would have no cause for complaint.

It was Ernest who saw it first, and how right and proper it was that he should be the one whose eye first lighted upon our little miracle.

Quite alone, the white robin stood, legs askew, and dark eyes cocked upon the mealworms. His snowy feathers gleamed in the sunshine, his speckled breast glowing against the shining white satin of his young plumage.

'He's come,' whispered Ernest, standing up. Behind

him the rest of the children rose too, the better to see their long-awaited visitor. Their faces were rapt, their eyes as bright as the white robin's.

Without hurry, fearless in his beauty, the white robin selected a mealworm, spread his dazzling wings into two perfect fans, and made off towards the vicar's wall.

Joyous pandemonium broke out in the class room. Children thumped their neighbours. Children hugged each other. Children crowded round my desk, and made enough noise to raise the roof. We might have been at a football match for all the emotional fervour shown.

In the midst of it, Mrs Pringle entered, black oil cloth bag on arm.

'He's come!' they yelled, surging towards her. 'Another white robin! He's come again!'

Solid as the Rock of Gibraltar amidst the waves of children tumbling around her, Mrs Pringle stood unmoved.

Above the hubbub her voice boomed triumphantly.

'Well, what did I tell you?'

TALES FROM A VILLAGE SCHOOL

Illustrated by Kate Dicker

CHRISTMAS CARDS FOR FORTY

Now this afternoon we're all going to make a lovely present to take home. People who fidget, Michael, will be standing outside the door and naturally there will be *no* lovely present for them.

Let me see if I can see two nice children to give out the paper. Don't hold your breath, dears, and don't push out your stomachs like that, Anna and Elizabeth.

Don't touch the paper till I tell you. We don't want dirty marks on our Christmas cards, do we?

Yes, Harold, they're going to be Christmas cards.

Don't touch!

There now! If you hadn't touched it, it wouldn't have fallen down and been trodden on! All put your hands behind your backs, and stop talking!

The fuss!

Everyone ready? Then listen carefully.

Fold your paper over like this and smooth it gently down the crease.

Richard, your hands! Look at that horrid black smear down your card. All show hands!

What on earth have you boys been doing?

Clearing out what drain?

Miss Judd told you to? I'm sure she told you to wash afterwards as well.

Well, anyway, you should have the sense to do so. Don't quibble! Great children of *five*, *six* some of you, and not enough common sense to wash before Art.

Very quickly run and wash.

The rest of you can sing a little song while we wait.

What shall it be? No, John, not that one your daddy taught you. Perhaps some other time. Let's have 'Bingo'.

Very nice. Here come the others. How wet you boys are!

Who threw water over who? Whom? Who?

Well, never mind. Let's get on or these cards won't be ready till *next* Christmas!

That'll do! That'll do! It wasn't as funny as all that.

All quiet!

Now let me see if the fold is by your left hand. *Left* hand, children. The side by the windows, then.

Good! Now don't turn them over or they'll open backwards.

On the front we're going to draw a big fat robin. You can copy mine from the blackboard.

Watch carefully. See how I use up all my space. His head nearly touches the top and his feet nearly touch the bottom.

Who can do a really beautiful robin? Use your brown crayon and begin.

Run along, Reggie.

All hold up robins. Some are very small. They look more like gnats.

Of course, Michael, yours would be different.

Where are you going to put his legs? A fat lot of good it will be to have them on the next page!

Right. Now shade a nice red patch on his breast like this.

Now inside in the middle we are going to write 'Happy Christmas' and underneath 'from' and then your own name.

I shall put 'from Mary' on the board but you will put 'from John', or 'Pat', or 'Michael', won't you, just *your own name*. Do you all understand? Hands up those who don't understand?

Carry on, then. Beautiful printing. While you are doing that I shall bring you each a piece of red wool to tie round your card in a lovely bow.

Richard, why have you put 'from Mary'? Is your name Mary?

Yes, I know it's on the board, but I explained all that.

Who else has been silly enough to put 'Mary'?

Nearly all of you! Now we shall just have to do them all over again! Another afternoon wasted, and we've got carols to learn, and the school concert tomorrow, and our class party to get ready, and Parents' Afternoon and all the reports to do before the end of the week!

Ah, well! Is that the bell? Lead out to play.

Richard and Joan, collect the Christmas cards and put them all in the wastepaper basket.

THE CRAFTSMAN

'Seems a pity, really,' said Ernest reflectively, paint-brush poised above his Christmas card, 'All this work, just for one day.'

'You should've chosen a quick way to make 'em,' advised Patrick, beside him. He was experimenting with his first cut-out Christmas tree, a dashing affair, contrived from folded green paper. Ernest watched his neighbour's scissors making dramatic slashes in the paper, little triangles falling like confetti on to the desk, and he sighed enviously as Patrick opened out his successful tree.

'Done!' said Patrick smugly, and he applied a pink tongue to the gummed back of his tree. Ernest watched him place it carefully in the centre of his Christmas card. He thumped it with a grubby fist and leant back to admire the finished article.

'I shall cut out a bird, and stick him on just there!' He placed a dreadfully bitten fingernail in the corner. 'Then that's finished! Ten I wants altogether, counting my aunties.'

'Reckon I'll be lucky to get this one done today,' replied Ernest gloomily, bending to his task. 'Have to make some at home, I suppose, that's all. Threepence they wants at Mobbs's for cards! Think of that . . . *threepence*!'

'Ah! But they've got sparkle-stuff on 'em,' argued Patrick reasonably. 'That always makes 'em a bit pricey, sparkle-stuff do!' He counted nine pieces of green paper, stacked them neatly on top of each other, and started to fold them over. 'See, Ern? This way I'll get the lot cut out all at once. Bet I gets my ten done before your one! Old-fashioned, all that slow ol' painting,' he added scornfully.

Around them, the rest of the class drew and painted, folded and snipped. They had chosen their own means of making their Christmas cards, and it was interesting to see how their choice had varied. Most of the younger ones had chosen to decorate theirs with cutouts of bright paper. Bulky, scarlet Father Christmases leant at alarming angles, awaiting white trimmings and black boots to their ensembles. Stocky reindeer tended to overflow the available space, leaving room for only midget sledges; and robins, balancing on the pin-point of their claws, like top-heavy ballerinas, were everywhere to be seen.

Most of the girls had preferred to use coloured crayons, and had taken infinite pains in drawing babies asleep, in cots that were so rickety that one would have thought them incapable of supporting the mammoth sacks that hung at their ends. Golliwogs, teddy bears, dolls, ships, trains and striped trumpets balanced at the mouths of the sacks, defying the laws of gravity in a remarkable manner.

Ernest's choice of pencil and paint brush was consistent with his habitual caution and patience. He had chosen to draw a church, set against an evening sky. Its windows were carefully criss-crossed into diamond panes. The door was grooved, and studded at equal distances with heavy pencil dots. The cross of St George floated from its crenellated tower . . . rather stiffly, to be sure, as if it had been well starched and was now aloft in a half-gale of unvarying velocity. All this minute work was largely covered when Ernest applied his paint, and had to be picked out afresh with the finest brush that he could find in the cupboard. Had he been alone his work would have given him unadulterated joy, but the sight of Patrick at his mass-production cast a shadow over his own slow-growing effort.

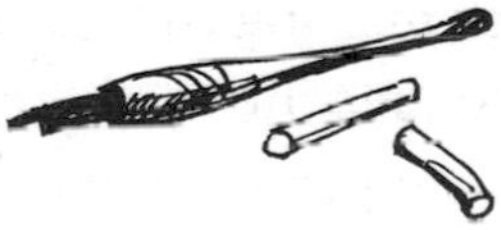

'When you thinks,' he repeated dejectedly, as he waited for his windows to dry, 'that it's all for one day!' It reminded me of Eeyore's sage remarks on the follies and fusses of birthdays . . . 'Here today, and gone tomorrow!'

'Never mind, Ernest,' I said, trying to cheer him, 'most preparations are just for one day. Getting ready is all part of the fun.' But such sententious nonsense clearly gave Ernest small comfort, and his mouth turned down glumly as he tested the church windows with a delicate fingertip. They had dried to such a fierce orange that one might be forgiven for imagining the entire contents of the building on fire, with pews, cassocks and congregation being done to a turn inside.

Doggedly, Ernest dipped his finest paint brush into the black puddle in his box, and, with his mouth puckered, began the slow, detailed work of picking out the submerged diamond panes. Beside him Patrick gave a sudden yelp of dismay. He gazed, in horror, from one hand to the other. In each he held the fringed fragments of half-Christmas trees.

'Blow!' said the mass-producer, scarlet in the face. 'I've been and cut through the blessed fold!'

With a smile of infinite satisfaction the craftsman beside him bent to his handiwork again.

CAROLS FOR FORTY

I shall take you myself for singing this afternoon, children, as Miss Twigg is at home with a sore throat.

Can I go and open the piano?

Can I give out the carol books?

Can we sing the new carol Miss Twigg is learning us?

She's learning Miss Green's too, and we're trying to win 'em.

Remind me, all of you, to take yet another lesson on 'Learning-Winning' and 'Teaching-Beating' tomorrow morning. And I don't want bedlam either here or in the

hall. I am looking for two conscientious and light-footed children who can lead this class at a rational pace from here to the hall door. John Todd, we'll see if you can take a little responsibility today. And Anna.

Miss Twigg always lets someone go first and open the piano.

Very well then. Pat, run ahead. Lead on, the rest of you. Don't gallop, John Todd! I might have guessed! Nor crawl, maddening boy! Just step it out briskly. Straight in, children, and stand in your usual places. For pity's sake, Pat, stop crashing the piano lid. You children seem to think that baby grands come down in every other shower.

Are we going to have carols?

Breathing exercises first, dear. All breathe in! Hold it! Out! *Much too much* noise on the 'Out'!

Miss Twigg says that's old-fashioned. She lets us do paper bags. We blow and blow at pretend bags, and then we *do* them, with a bang.

Very well. Blow! And again! Bigger still! Now pop! *One pop*, children, is more than sufficient. Miss Twigg's nerves must be in better shape than mine, I can see. All on the floor, sit. There is no need, Michael Jones, to roll about all over everyone else. Some of you boys make mayhem with a single movement.

Can we have our carols now?

Miss Twigg always lets us boys give out the books.

All hush! What is this squeaking that is going on?

It's our crêpe soles, Miss. Sideways on, Miss, to the floor, Miss.

Then sit still. I shall give the books out from here.

Pass them along to the end, child. Brian Bates, don't hold us all up by peering inside each book.

I left a bit of silver paper in mine last week.

We seem to be six books short. Some of you must share. And that doesn't mean a wrenching match, John Todd. You will be left with the nether half of that book if that's the way you handle it. We'll start with 'Good King Wenceslas' if it's in C. All listen quietly.

Miss Twigg don't play it like that. She always uses two hands.

That will do. Off you go, and anyone scooping 'Fu-oo-el', like a siren, stands by me. Stop a minute. Is someone singing bass?

It's Eric, Miss. He always honks like that.

Well, Eric dear, it isn't that you aren't *trying*, but your voice is rather strong, so sing rather more softly, will you?

Do let's have our new carol, Miss. Number ten.

One of those mid-European ones, I see; and unfortunately in five flats. I think it might be better to practise that a little longer with Miss Twigg.

Miss, there's someone hollering outside.

It's Miss Judd, Miss.

Open the door for her then. Perhaps Miss Judd would like to hear us sing a carol? There is just time for one more.

Please can it be our new one?

Would you like to hear it, Miss Judd? I think it would sound better unaccompanied. When I can see faces and not backs of heads, John Todd, and Michael Jones has stopped that silly giggling, and Brian Bates has pulled his carol book down from the front of his jersey, and Richard Robinson has quite finished looking at his tongue – I will give you the note.

That was lovely. While you were singing, Miss Judd gave me some good news for you. Miss Twigg is much better and will take your next singing lesson. Isn't that wonderful? For all of us.

SNOW ON THEIR BOOTS

A shrivelling east wind had blown for a week, flattening the winter grass and withering the young wallflower plants. It had whipped cruelly under the school door, where the step had been worn away, hollowed by the scraping of children's boots for eighty years.

During the morning, cold rain had lashed the latticed windows. Later sleet had appeared, and now, by half-past two, the snow came racing down, whirling blackly and madly as one looked up at it against the pallid sky, but drifting dreamily, like feathers, as it settled into the puddles in the playground. I decided to send the children home early. This announcement caused such pleasurable stir, such unbridled joy, that one might have thought that confinement in school was on a par with incarceration in the darkest dungeon, with periods of refined torture thrown in.

'Can you all get indoors?' I inquired, when the ecstasy had died down sufficiently for me to make myself heard. 'Is there anyone whose mother is out?'

'Mine's up the farm on Mondays . . . scrubbing out,' said Patrick, 'but us keeps our key in a secret hiding-place, under a flower-pot by the back door, so I can get in all right.'

'Secret hiding-place!' scoffed his neighbour. ' 'Tisn't no secret if you tells us, is it, Miss?'

Patrick flushed at this taunting. 'It don't matter if us

all knows . . . not here in the village. It's for strangers like . . . those men as sells notepaper and that, and those old men walking to the workhouse.'

By this time Ernest's hand had gone up. His mother worked in the nearest town.

'I can go to my gran's, with my sister,' he said, his eyes brightening. I knew the cottage well, and could imagine what a snug haven it would be to children on a bleak afternoon like this. The range would be shining like jet, and giving off a delicious smell of hot blacklead, its roaring fire reflected in the plates and covers on the dresser opposite; while, best of all, on the high mantelpiece would be standing the sweet tin, a souvenir of the coronation of King George V and Queen Mary, rattling with 'Winter Mixture', red and white striped clove balls, square paregoric lozenges and lovely, glutinous mint lumps.

They all trooped into the lobby, and there was a bustle of scarf-tying and glove-finding, and much grunting as wellington boots were tugged on. Away they all straggled, heads bent against the storm; all but one solitary figure, who was rooting about in the corner. It was Patrick.

'Can't find my boots,' he explained.

'See if they are by the stove,' I told him, pulling the pail out from under the sink. The most peculiar things got found here, but today there was nothing but a mammoth spider, which advanced in a menacing manner. I retreated to the schoolroom.

Patrick was running one finger in an aimless way up and down the piano keys. There were no wellingtons by the fireguard, and his feet were still shod in sandals

from which his grey socks protruded, the toes of his sandals having been prudently cut off to allow for growth.

'Are they under your desk?' I persisted. He ambled off and hung upside-down surveying his habitual place and its environs, while I opened cupboards, peered behind the piano and under my own desk. At last we sat down to review the situation. We looked at each other, frowning.

'You can't have come to school in those sandals?'

'Can't've!' agreed Patrick.

'Someone must have gone home in yours by mistake.'

'Must've!' agreed Patrick.

A heavy silence fell. The wall clock ticked and a cinder tinkled into the ash pan. Outside, a flurry of snow hissed against the window.

'Well, Patrick,' I said, at length. 'You can't go home like that, and you can't walk in mine, so what's to be done?'

Patrick's eyes had assumed an intent look. I know it well. Thus does he look during multiplication-table practice, when, having had 'seven eights?' fired at him, he stands, with one leg curled round the other, awaiting inspiration. This time it came.

'In that old play-box,' he began slowly, 'there's a pair of boots what we used for the *Tin Soldier*. I can get into them.'

We hurried into the infants' room and threw up the heavy lid. Velvet capes, moulting feather boas, wooden swords, paper crowns, beads and fans jostled together; and there, beneath them all, were the boots . . . an incredibly dandified pair of Russian boots with Louis heels. Very dashing they must have been a quarter of a century ago, but they presented a pathetic sight as they stood, side by side, with their tops drooping dejectedly.

Patrick sat on the floor and, with much deliberation, forced his feet in. I hauled him up and we surveyed the effect.

Patrick winced. 'Got my socks rucked up,' he said, and sat down again abruptly. Very slowly he began to edge them off. Outside, the snow fell faster.

'For pity's sake, Patrick,' I urged, 'hurry up. You'll never be home at this rate!'

I straightened a torn lining, while he smoothed his socks. He put his feet in gingerly and stood up. Then

he stamped happily, in the ridiculous things, to get his coat. I gazed anxiously out of the lobby window as he dressed.

'Tell your mother about losing your wellingtons,' I began, when I became conscious of a certain tension in the air. Patrick was now fully muffled, and stood in the porch. His face wore its earlier look of concentration, mingled with some sheepishness.

'Come to think of it,' he said, in a still, small voice, 'I left 'em under the dresser at home, for my dad to put a puncture patch on.'

'*Patrick!*' I began forcefully but, after one look at my face, he had prudently withdrawn, and was already battling his way across the playground, in his pantomime boots; preferring, no doubt, the storm that raged outside, to that which was so surely brewing up within.

FORTY IN THE WINGS

Miss Judd says we are on in ten minutes, and are we quite ready?

I hope so, dear. Stand still everyone! If you get so excited you will forget your words. Holly Elves, stop sliding up and down in your stockinged feet. This is no time to get splinters in them. Any wobbly-winged fairies line up by my desk and I will put a final pin in you.

Miss, please Miss, you—

For the nineteenth time, Christmas Sprite, *go away*! You've done nothing but haunt me.

But, Miss, you've never done nothing about them bells what you said about.

What bells I said about? Stand still, fairy, or I shall never get these wings straight. Oh, the *bells*! Good heavens, boy, they should have been sewn on long ago. Fetch them quickly from the plasticine cupboard.

Do you know, Miss, I can't remember what I have to say.

Nor can I.

It's funny really, isn't it?

John Todd says he can't remember *nothing at all*. Not even the song part.

Don't panic so, children, it will all come back when you are on the stage. Simply remember to throw your voices right out to 'The Boyhood of Raleigh', and you will do very well.

John Todd says that stage ain't safe and we could easy go through.

'Isn't', not 'ain't', and if John Todd spreads such alarmist rumours I shall have to speak to him.

But, Miss, it does sort of squeak.

Simply the wood moving. You really are the most easily depressed set of fairies I've ever met. No more fuss now. All find a seat before I count three. Fairies, don't keep crashing into each other with those wings. I'm not made of safety pins.

Now when you are quite quiet – *quite quiet* I said, John Todd, fuss-fuss-fuss – I will open the door so that you can hear Miss Twigg's children singing carols.

For mercy's sake, that idiotic fairy in the front, take off those wellingtons! Nobody wants to see fairies galumphing about like a lot of Russians stamping the snow off their boots. Ready now?

Don't they sing lovely!

Very lovely. Lovelily. Beautifully, I mean. They've only two more carols to sing and then it's our play. Just make sure you've all the things you're supposed to have with you. Mother, where's your wooden spoon for mixing the pudding?

Them babies had it first for Miss Muffet.

Then rush like mad – *creep*, rather – to the babies' room and ask for it back. Hurry now, you are on first.

John Todd says he don't feel very well.

I'm not surprised at all. If I had been making the hideous faces he has behind my back I shouldn't feel very well. All actors feel like this before the play starts. It's nothing to worry about.

I feel funny too.

My legs wobble.

It's my inside that feels the worst. It goes up and then down.

So does mine.

Never mind, never mind, no more complaints now. Let me look at you all and see if you are ready. Father Christmas, where's your beard?

I dunno.

What do you mean, 'You don't know'? You had it just now, didn't you? Where is it? Whatever made you take it off?

Too hot.

Too hot indeed, in the depths of winter too! Here's a pretty kettle of fish! Everyone search quickly. You as well, Father Christmas, lolling back there sucking your thumb while we slave all round you! The very idea! You are a thoroughly naughty little boy, Brian Bates, and this is the last time you are chosen to act, whether your aunt takes elocution classes or not.

Here it is, Miss, behind the radiator.

Pot black, of course, but you must lump it. Put it on at once and don't dare to take it off again.

Can't breathe.

Brian, understand this. Either you choose to wear that beard cheerfully, or Michael Jones puts on your costume this minute and is Father Christmas instead. Well?

Beard.

I should think so. Now we are all ready. I will open the door just a little. Not a sound!

I can see my mum.

So can I.

Here come Miss Twigg's children. Lead up on to the stage.

It won't really give way, will it, Miss?

Miss, I don't feel well.

Nor me.

Miss, them babies said they never had no wooden spoon off of us, so what had I better do instead of?

Brian Bates says he don't want to be Father Christmas, and he's not going to say his words.

Do we *have* to do this old play?

It's too late to turn back now, children. Fairies, point your toes, all smile! Right, boys, up with the curtain, and hand me the prompt book.

COPYRIGHT INFORMATION

No Holly for Miss Quinn first published in 1976 by Michael Joseph

Christmas at Fairacre School from *Village Diary* first published in 1957 by Michael Joseph

The Christmas Mouse first published in 1973 by Michael Joseph

Village Christmas first published by Michael Joseph 1966

The Fairacre Ghost and *Jingle Bells* from *Over the Gate* first published by Michael Joseph 1964

Christmas at Caxley 1913 from *The Market Square* first published by Michael Joseph 1966

The White Robin first published by Michael Joseph 1979

The following stories are taken from *Tales from a Village School*, first published by Michael Joseph 1994

CHRISTMAS AT THRUSH GREEN

If you have enjoyed *Christmas with Miss Read*
don't miss

CHRISTMAS AT THRUSH GREEN

⁂

by Miss Read

with Jenny Dereham

The villagers of Thrush Green celebrate Christmas in a way that has hardly changed over the generations. Children eagerly hang up their stockings, families go to church together – and when the snow arrives, it seems as if Christmas will be perfect this year. But not everything is as peaceful as it seems.

Phyllida and Frank have their work cut out when an outbreak of chicken pox disrupts preparations for the Nativity play. The indomitable Ella Bembridge has been behaving strangely, much to the concern of her friends. Then there are the Burwells, newcomers to Thrush Green, who cause a stir with their meddling and their tasteless Christmas decorations. And Nelly Piggott, owner of The Fuchsia Bush tea shop, receives an unexpected letter that sends her into a spin . . .

ISBN: 978 1 4091 0254 0
UK £7.99

EARLY DAYS
A Childhood Memoir

* * *

Miss Read

From the author of the bestselling
FAIRACRE *and* THRUSH GREEN *series*

'The larks were in joyous frenzy above. The sky was blue, the now distant wood misty with early buds, and the air was heady to a London child. A great surge of happiness engulfed me. This is where I was going to live. I should learn all about birds and trees and flowers. This is where I belonged . . . This was the country, and I was at home there.'

Early Days is alive with vibrant childhood memories of an extended family of grandmas, uncles, aunts and cousins, and their houses – full of mystery and adventure – where Miss Read lived in the shadow of the First World War.

At the age of seven, Miss Read moved to a small village in Kent, into a magical new world where her love of the English countryside grew – a passion that would be found in her much-loved novels. Her evocative descriptions of the village school, the joys of exploring the woods and lanes, toffee-making and riding on the corn-chandler's cart, vividly convey this time as one of the happiest of her life.

Full of unforgettable characters, tender memories and the colourful intrigues of everyday life, *Early Days* is a charming and affectionate insight into the childhood of a bestselling author, and a bygone era.

ISBN: 978 0 7528 8220 8
UK £7.99